*Jove titles by Christi Caldwell*

ALONG CAME A LADY
DESPERATELY SEEKING A DUCHESS

# Desperately Seeking a Duchess

## CHRISTI CALDWELL

JOVE
New York

A JOVE BOOK
Published by Berkley
An imprint of Penguin Random House LLC
penguinrandomhouse.com

Copyright © 2022 by Christi Caldwell
Penguin Random House supports copyright. Copyright fuels creativity, encourages
diverse voices, promotes free speech, and creates a vibrant culture. Thank you for buying
an authorized edition of this book and for complying with copyright laws by not
reproducing, scanning, or distributing any part of it in any form without permission.
You are supporting writers and allowing Penguin Random House to continue to
publish books for every reader.

A JOVE BOOK, BERKLEY, and the BERKLEY & B colophon
are registered trademarks of Penguin Random House LLC.

ISBN: 9780593334935

First Edition: May 2022

Printed in the United States of America
1  3  5  7  9  10  8  6  4  2

Book design by George Towne

# Chapter 1

Courtland Balfour, the seventh Duke of St. James, had long appreciated the irony of the word "saint" being affixed to his name.

A notorious rogue, with a reputation for being able to charm any woman from age eighteen to eighty-eight, no one would dare dispute Courtland belonged firmly in the column of sinner rather than saint.

And yet, on this particularly warm spring day, visiting the far-flung corners of Staffordshire, Courtland thought, for the first time, perhaps he might be deserving of that title.

After all, it wasn't just any brother who'd take on the unenviable task of passing himself off as his twin and playing at man of affairs to the Duke of Bentley.

His twin's arrangement had shocked all of Polite Society. For even the *second* son of a duke didn't take on employment. And he certainly didn't take on work for his late father's friend. But Keir, Courtland's twin, had craved a sense of purpose, and was denied that ability while their father lived.

Only when that miserable, heartless scoundrel had

kicked off—in the bed of a courtesan, no less—had Keir pursued that opportunity. His bluntly spoken, socially awkward brother, who'd landed a role as man of affairs to the Duke of Bentley, was paid *handsomely*.

The part his brother did not fully know, however, was that Courtland's visit this day wasn't *entirely* altruistic.

Neither Courtland's twin nor their three sisters nor any other member of Polite Society was aware of the full truth: that the previous Duke of St. James had left Courtland staring down a sea of debt collectors and a nearly bankrupt title.

Given the state of their family's finances, the Balfours weren't in a position to lose the monies that funded their sister's Season . . . or that important connection.

As such, whereas Courtland and Keir had swapped identities quite often as young boys, today's deception was no child's play. This time Courtland had volunteered to be the one to convince Bentley's by-blows to journey to London so they might assume their rightful place among Polite Society.

It was curious, that. Most any other—nearly every other—illegitimate child of a duke would have surely leaped at the prospect of trading life in a mining village for a comfortable existence in London. And, to boot, a father who wished to have something to do with them. Certainly, as the son of a late duke himself, Courtland had never known a thing about paternal affection.

Apparently, however, Bentley had sired three curious and *contrary* children.

Courtland guided his black mount down the dusty path, armed with directions he'd managed to ply from the mouths of stonily stubborn patrons at the tavern, who'd proven more amenable when Courtland had urged the innkeeper to let the ale flow freely that day.

There'd been several ribald songs he'd joined in on.

And then, at last . . . directions.

Nudging his horse, Ace, up over a slight rise, Courtland

drew on the reins, and halting his mount, he scanned the green countryside below.

So much greenery; more in fact than he'd ever believed possible in any part of England. Even his estates were peppered with ponds and stone structures; lands that had been tamed long ago. Courtland squinted, the sun's glare blinding, and he lifted a palm to his brow to blot out the brightness.

There it was.

A speck upon the horizon.

Clucking his tongue, he squeezed his knees slightly and urged Ace on to the small, narrow drive.

Dismounting, Courtland looked about, and locating a block, he looped his horse's reins to it, then turned all his attention to the house ahead, and the task at hand.

Upon close inspection, the distance and light hadn't been playing tricks with his vision. The cottage truly was as small as he'd taken it for in the distance, dwarfed all the more by grounds and gardens long overdue in terms of tending.

Courtland patted Ace one more time, and then, collecting his satchel from his saddle, he headed down the overgrown pathway, filled with so many blooms; the neglect had all but created a veritable buffet that invited insects.

Bees buzzed. Butterflies danced around them. Beetles. Ladybugs. Each insect vied for a place, all the while their brains too tiny to register that there was enough food and space contained within this ill-tended area to keep them for several summers.

Courtland gave his head a wistful shake, as for the first time since he'd arrived, he felt a frisson of . . . guilt, about asking anyone to give up the comfort of obscurity here for the garish opulence that was the Town.

Ace whinnied noisily, and Courtland absently stroked the loyal creature between the eyes. His nostrils flaring, Ace arched his head back into that favorite-of-his touch.

From the corner of his eye, Courtland caught a faint flutter, and he swung his attention to find a person watching him.

The less-than-furtive figure in the cottage pressed her forehead against the glass.

"It appears we have company," he murmured, patting Ace once more. "Which isn't terrible, as it means the sooner I finish, the sooner we're free to return to London."

Ace gave a toss of his head in clear equine disapproval.

"It appears we are of like opinions then, on that score," Courtland said, winking at his horse.

Once again, those curtains parted slightly, and a young woman peeked through the crack in the fabric.

Enormous, saucer-sized blue eyes, filled with mistrust, met Courtland's gaze.

The sister, then.

He grinned. "Good afternoon," he called, and sketched a bow. "I'm here to speak with Mr. Audley."

Judging by the stretch of silence to follow, the young woman was anything but impressed. Alas, while he was on the other side of a doorway, without a line of sight to his quarry, she was afforded an unhindered view that put Courtland at a distinct disadvantage.

Giving Ace another pat, Courtland started down the walkway.

"Stop there!" she shouted, a healthy dose of anger and suspicion freezing him halfway down the path.

Anger and suspicion, both of which, as a duke, he was unaccustomed to being greeted with.

"What do you want?" she called, her voice muffled by the oak panel.

What did he want? Or what did he *need*?

A fortune.

Security.

His siblings settled.

All of which indirectly accounted for his being here.

Bringing himself back to the matter at hand, Courtland offered another smile and held his empty palms up. "I want nothing more than to speak with your brothers . . . or you," he cajoled, using soothing tones meant to bring her outside.

At last, the wood panel swung wide, affording him his first full, unobstructed view. And Courtland went absolutely motionless.

*Oh, hell.*

The young woman, with her full, ivory-hued cheeks and golden blond hair, had the height of a child, but the hardened stare of a woman some three decades her elder. Unfortunately for Courtland, that flinty stare was leveled at him.

Along with her ancient-looking firearm.

Reflexively, Courtland's palms went flying up in surrender.

The late summer sun glinted off the end of the barrel. That enormous weapon looked all the more enormous when held as it was by one of her spritely size.

He swallowed hard and cursed long and harder inside his head.

The young woman flicked a derisive glance over Courtland's person, before settling it upon his face, her gaze bored; and his ears went hot, as for the first time in his life he knew what it was to have a woman find him lacking.

"Why does it not surprise me at all that a fancy London fellow like you would come here issuing orders to me?" she drawled, the lyrical, lilting quality of her voice in almost farcical juxtaposition to the threat hanging on her words, and the very real threat of murder she directed his way.

Courtland kept his smile firmly affixed, and when he spoke, did so in the careful, placating tones he used with his easily riled younger sisters. "Perhaps had you taken a moment to hear me out and discuss the business that brought me here, then I wouldn't have had to issue them, Miss Audley."

Her flaxen eyebrows went shooting up. "Are you . . . *challenging* me?" The rifle wavered on her arm.

Oh, bloody hell. He was usually better at speaking to the fairer sex. Much better. It should so happen that the one time he failed to charm would likely land him a bullet in the chest—and a swift end to his miserable existence.

*"Well?"* she demanded, dipping slightly and adjusting the weapon on her arm.

He winced. "I believe you've already determined that I was challenging you, and as such, it hardly seems necessary to confirm with a verbal statement, Miss Audley." He bit out each syllable, giving up on the gentle warmth he'd previously attempted.

She lowered the rifle slowly, and he took heart. "Now," he said, taking a step forward. "If you would be so good as to lower your weapon all the—"

A loud report thundered in the afternoon quiet, cutting off the remainder of his words, and he flew back, hitting the ground so hard the air was sucked from his lungs.

Bloody hell. This was how he would end his short reign as duke—by taking a bullet straight to the chest.

# Chapter 2

Cailin Audley, bastard daughter of the Duke of Bentley, had grown accustomed to the men sent to Staffordshire to try and retrieve her and her brothers from their cozy mining village.

Never before, however, had he sent a tall, well-built messenger with loose golden curls, a cleft in his chin, and a dimple in his right cheek.

Cailin's heart thundered against her ribcage.

And she'd gone and killed him.

Absolutely motionless, Cailin stood frozen on the stoop; unblinking, afraid to move.

*Oh, God.*

Sprawled on his back, with one strong arm bent slightly above his head and the other stretched out sideways, he may as well have been a man casually slumbering and not prone on her walkway.

With every fiber of her being she despised the duke and the men he sent 'round to try and manipulate her and her siblings . . . but still, she'd not wish any of them dead. And certainly not by her own hand.

Cailin remained stock-still; her pulse pounded away in her ears, mingling with the report of that gunshot. *Her* gunshot.

Then she heard it.

Her ears pricked up.

Low and faint at first.

A groan.

". . . I'm dead . . ."

There'd never been a sweeter sound than those two words.

Letting the rifle fall, Cailin went sprinting down the drive, kicking up gravel and dust and rocks as she went.

She skidded to a quick stop before the felled gentleman; the speed with which she stopped sent gravel flying into the latest messenger's face.

Sputtering, he lifted a glove-encased hand and swiped at his eyes and mouth, brushing the remnants of tiny stones from his face. "Good God, it isn't worth it," he moaned.

A wave of guilt swept through her, but also another healthy swell of relief. "What isn't worth it?"

"Any of it," he muttered, his response vague enough to leave her with questions.

Making quick work of the small ivory buttons of his fine wool jacket, Cailin loosened the garment and slipped her fingers inside.

Hard.

He was all sculpted muscle, rock-hard and solid. Each contour of his belly and chest chiseled of stone, more suited to the miners who often went bare-chested during their shifts at the mines and whom Cailin had always had to steal surreptitious glances of, lest any of her brothers catch her gawking. Except there was nothing soft about this London gent. In fact, but for a change of garments, he may as well have been any man who worked for her brother.

Her mouth went dry and her search slowed, and Cailin drifted her fingers higher as she looked for the shot, praying it had gone clean through. She should be properly ashamed for appreciating his male form as she now did.

*Stop it. He is just a man. You've seen any number of men.* Certainly just as broad and tall and powerful, and . . . why, she'd had a sweetheart. One who'd broken it off altogether too easily with her, but also one whose form she'd seen when she visited the Cheadle mines.

No, she was decidedly not one to lose her head.

Refocusing on the task at hand, Cailin purposefully shoved the gentleman's jacket off, past a broad pair of shoulders, and she continued her quest. As she ran her hands, seeking the sticky warm heat of his blood, she scanned her gaze over him, searching out the injury. The crisp white lawn of his garments revealed not a hint of crimson staining, and she focused on that far more important detail rather than the fact that he was chiseled in all the places a man should be.

This time, her heart knocked a beat faster and her mouth went dry, for altogether different reasons.

Lord help her for being wicked and shameless, she was—

"Perhaps I was wrong," he said in silkily amused tones, slightly roughened with a note of pain threading through them. "Perhaps it was worth it, after all."

It took a moment for his words to penetrate . . . and Cailin glanced up.

Her gaze collided with his, a smoky gray stare that fairly spilled over with a heavy dose of amusement, some pain . . . and also . . . desire.

With a gasp, Cailin yanked her stare away from his and focused it on his prone form. "Well, you're the first scoundrel sent by the duke," she mumbled, keeping her head bent on her task in a bid to hide the guilty blush on her cheeks. Driving one knee into the earth and the other against his hip, she used all her weight to propel him over.

Or she tried to.

She was slightly out of breath from her efforts, and several curls escaped her plait and fell over her brow.

She blew them back and this time slipped one hand onto his narrow waist and anchored her other on his shoulder.

"What are you—?"

Leaning forward, she put all her energy into it, and turned him over, face forward.

A muffled groan filtered from his lips, the ground muting but not blotting out his complete misery.

"You're a strong thing, aren't you," he spoke facedown in a patch of grass, his words buried in that bit of earth.

"I'm not a 'thing,' Lord Fancy," she said, this time making herself focus completely on searching for the area she'd hit.

*Except* . . .

Narrowing her eyes, Cailin sank back on her haunches and dusted the sweat from her brow. "I *didn't* shoot you."

The gentleman rolled himself over onto his back and flung a broad forearm across his brow. "You sound entirely too disappointed, love."

*Love.*

It was a flippant endearment that slipped from his roguish lips when there was nothing casual about that sentiment. Why, her first—and last—sweetheart hadn't even addressed her so. "Of course not," she said gruffly. He possessed a rogue's charm that would devastate a weaker woman. As it was, even she—Cailin Audley, who'd every reason to doubt and mistrust everything and anything romantic—found her belly fluttering at that huskily spoken sweet word. "Given your refusal to leave, it would have served you right if I *had* put a bullet in your chest."

He scoffed. "I'd say the crime certainly doesn't fit that punishment." He promptly winced. A little groan slipped from his lips, one that he quickly tamped down.

Cailin frowned. "You *are* hurt."

"You sound accusatory," he said, and it didn't escape her notice that he'd not denied her statement.

"Where are you injured?" she demanded, her heart picking up its rhythm once again.

"It is nothing. I merely fell back when you shot at me."

"I didn't shoot *at* you . . . I shot," she clarified weakly. "And it was an accidental firing at that."

"Knowing that you had a rifle trained at my chest, and had no idea how to aim or shoot, leaves me with a new-found appreciation for the Lord, love."

"I do have an idea how to fire it, Lord Fancy Pants." Thinning her eyes, Cailin leaned forward and looked him square in the eyes. "If you'd care to see me reload and shoot again?" Her words were intended as a bold challenge, and yet before she'd uttered them Cailin really wished she'd considered her positioning to Lord Fancy Pants. Or recalled the mesmerizing quality of his dark irises, which conjured turbulent skies as a summer storm rolled along the horizon.

His gaze slid over her face, lingering a moment on her mouth before moving up a fraction to meet her eyes. A devil-may-care grin formed on his lips. "I am going to have to pass on that invitation, love."

There it was again: *love*.

She straightened. "I've got no invitations for you, Lord Fancy Pants," she said stiffly.

"They aren't that fancy, and my name is Co . . . *Keir*." He stumbled over his words, and Cailin sharpened her eyes on him. What was the reason for that hesitancy? Or had she merely imagined it? "Balfour." He muttered that last part of his name under his breath, and raising a hand, he touched the back of his head . . . and winced.

Her earlier annoyance forgotten, Cailin scrambled around the other side of him.

"It is nothing," he said. Cailin slipped her fingers into the most luxuriant silken golden curls she'd ever felt, and her stomach fell. "Just a bump on the—"

"You hit your head," she said, nausea churning her gut, as she remembered a young miner whom she'd helped look after following a blow to his head. How swiftly that once-strapping man had been forever altered, proving how fragile the mind really was, and how easily an injury to it could leave a person changed.

"Whoa, there's no need to look so green," the gentleman said in a soothing tone. "Why, you appear a good deal more bothered about the prospect of me knocking my head than shooting me straight through the chest." The teasing quality was ruined slightly by the pitch of pain contained within his husky baritone, and her worry deepened.

Steeling her jaw, Cailin shoved determinedly to her feet. "Can you stand?"

His smile slipped, and he glanced about.

She frowned. Oh, dear. Mayhap he was already addled in the brain. "Yes, you, Lord Fancy Pants," she said gently but firmly. "Who else would I be speaking to?"

He retrieved his hat, now caked with dust. "No one?"

"Exactly." She sent a prayer skyward. He'd gotten that answer quickly.

"Come along, then," she urged, motioning him to stand, and then offering him a hand.

He stared at her fingers a moment, bringing Cailin's eyes to them, and she looked at them in a new light: her nails cracked, her palms callused, the tops of her hands dry and coarse.

Reflexively, Cailin curled them up into fists and drew them to her side. "Well?" She paused only long enough to be sure the latest summoner was able to stand, and that when he took to his feet, he followed, before she started back down the pathway to her cottage.

While they walked, Cailin kept her gaze fixed ahead on the modest cottage. She felt him moving closely behind.

Though *modest* was a generous descriptor of her home.

There was nothing grand or even great about the residence. It bespoke Cailin's common roots, and also struggle. It represented that, too. It was the same cottage she and her brothers had occupied since she'd entered the world, bastard daughter to a duke and his courtesan . . . a secret she'd only managed to learn from Wesley, the youngest of her brothers, before he'd left to fight Boney. He'd gone to the duke, asking that he secure him a commission, and with that request had opened up the rest of the Audleys' world to the influence of an all-powerful duke.

She'd never been embarrassed of her lot. There wasn't a reason to be. Not when almost all in these parts lived exactly the same as Cailin and her family.

Until now.

In the same way she'd noted her brittle hands against those long, tanned, unmarked digits, now she saw the state of the cottage she brought a gentleman to.

Something about this man, however, was . . . different.

Perhaps because of the finer quality of his garments and speech.

Or mayhap it was for the simple reason that, unlike the others who'd come, he bore the title "lord" before his name.

Whatever it was, Cailin, always unflappable and certainly not one to be moved in any way by a man, found herself oddly at sea and uncomfortable around this stranger.

Reaching the entrance, she grabbed the handle and let herself inside.

Lord Keir waited on the step behind her.

It wasn't until she reached the middle of the living room that she realized he remained outside, and had no intention of entering without her express permission. Cailin wheeled back. "For someone who made a pest of himself outside, you're really now going to stand there all day," she drawled, and the gentleman sprang into motion, joining her inside.

Like Rafe and her brothers, too tall to ever fit comfortably in this place, Lord Keir had to duck slightly as he walked through the doorway. The moment he was inside, he doffed his hat with one hand . . . like the gentleman he was, and with the other he closed the door behind him.

He stood there, this latest emissary of the duke, passing an assessing gaze over the cottage. He lingered his focus on the fading, threadbare upholstery of the sofa and seating, most of which was covered by blankets she'd stitched to add a spot of brightness inside. His eyes landed on a hole along the arm of the chair. Hastily draping Lord Keir's jacket over the side, she hid that mark. And yet, unlike the men who'd come before him, his lip didn't peel back in a sneer. There was no pity in his eyes. In fact, there was nothing she could make out of that opaque gaze, those dark gray irises concealed by lashes so long and so thick men and women alike would envy him.

She curled her toes sharply in her serviceable boots.

"Come with me," she said brusquely, heading straight for the kitchen, not knowing why she should care that he saw precisely how she and her family lived here.

It was just . . . it had been vastly easier to turn out the other fellows who'd been openly condescending and not charming.

She started forward once more, with the gentleman following suit.

When he swayed slightly.

Gasping, Cailin immediately corrected course and raced over. She took him by the arm and steered him to that same sofa she'd been so very determined to keep him from seeing.

"I'm quite fine," he said thickly, clutching at the back of his head and casting only doubt upon the veracity of his assurances.

It didn't escape her notice that he didn't resist her efforts to get him seated. "You're a liar, Lord Keir. And a poor one at that," she added for herself as much as him. After all, it was important to remember that a man who smiled like this one, and from whom mistruths slipped so easily, was one to be wary of. "Now, sit," she said, adding a firm layer of emphasis onto that last part of her command, and she shoved him gently down.

As he went tumbling into the seat, he flashed another of those rogue's grins that she hated her heart for noticing. "Well, I'm not *really* lying. I'm standing." He paused. "Or I was before you pushed me . . . and I'm also alive, so there is that."

She wrinkled her nose. "I didn't push you. I—" She caught the good-natured glimmer in his eyes. "You're teasing."

"I'm trying to set you at ease," he corrected.

"I don't need to be set at ease, Lord Keir. I'm perfectly at ease. In fact, I've never felt such ease." *Stop talking. You are the opposite of breezy with this gentleman.* "Ever," she couldn't stop herself from adding.

He inclined his head. "I see."

It was on the tip of her tongue to ask him precisely what

it was he thought he saw. And yet, the longer she stood here jabbering with him and at him, the longer he remained. Returning to the sole reason she'd brought him inside her household, she pointed to the sofa. "Lie down."

"That won't be—"

"Lie. Down. Lord. Keir."

He promptly complied, resting his head at one end and stretching his impossibly long legs out; they dangled far beyond the end of the opposite arm, once again drawing her attention to that form.

Her injured guest at last settled, Cailin marched to the kitchen, and the moment she closed the door between her and Lord Fancy Pants, some of the tension in her body slipped out.

He was an odd sort, which certainly accounted for this flustered state she found herself in around the duke's man. The men in these parts, they were blunt and direct and certainly didn't bother with charm. Even her former sweetheart had been all gruff, rough miner, without a smooth tongue. As such, she didn't know what to do with an oddity like him.

That wasn't altogether true.

She needed to get rid of him. Because she didn't like how he flustered her, or that he was charming and not condescending as the men who'd come before.

Fueled by those truths, Cailin hurried about the kitchen to gather up materials to tend the duke's injured servant so she could send him on his way.

# Chapter 3

❦

The lady was . . . *not* what he'd expected.
  In any way.

Everything from her voluptuous pixie-like form to the rifle she'd brandished, and then her palpable worry after she'd taken him down.

With the young woman now gone, busy at work in the kitchen, Courtland popped up, and his head immediately protested that abrupt movement.

Resisting the urge to groan at that splitting pain, he stood and did a little sweep of the young woman's household. The mismatched furniture, revealing its age and wear, spoke of the threadbare existence the lady and her family knew. It wasn't squalor, but neither was their existence here in Staffordshire a comfortable one. And yet, even with that, they'd still fight the duke against returning to London and laying claim to a fortune and future.

It didn't make sense with anything he knew of people and human nature.

Having inherited a bankrupt dukedom, with his country estates crumbling and the veneer on his London properties losing its shine and revealing how lenders had kept his family afloat all these years, it was a foreign concept. To be granted unlimited funds with which to help both himself and his siblings and simply . . . refuse it?

The Audleys possessed a pride and obstinance most people—himself included—were not in possession of. For Courtland, his siblings' comforts came first and foremost. It was why he was here. It was why he'd ultimately have to do the right thing by the title . . . and his brothers and sisters.

Still, it didn't stop either his intrigue or—yes, to some extent—appreciation for the lady and her family.

Courtland's gaze landed on a thick leather book on the oak table. Stealing a glance at the kitchens, and confirming the lady remained occupied, Courtland ignored the pain in his head and headed for that enormous leatherbound volume.

*Recherches sur les ossements fossiles de quadrupèdes*

He furrowed his brow in puzzlement. "Research on quadruped fossil bones," he mouthed.

A cabinet slammed, and he looked up swiftly.

Miss Audley, however, remained busy in the kitchens, speaking to herself as she worked, her faint murmurings indistinct and muted by the doorway. Returning his attention to the book, Courtland picked up the musty volume and proceeded to flip through. A blend of sketches and exposition, the dog-eared pages contained annotations written in tiny ink, lettering almost too small for the human hand to make, and even harder for the human eye to make out. Courtland brought the book close to his face.

". . . mammoths were different than elephants . . ."

Underneath that annotation, the reader of the book had made a little arrow that pointed down to the word *l'éléphant*. Beside it remained a little question mark.

"What do you think you're doing?" she snapped.

The book tumbled from his fingers and clattered to the floor.

Bloody hell.

Both he and Miss Audley looked to where the volume lay, forlorn and indignant upon its spine.

"My apologies," he murmured, already bending to retrieve the book.

Even with arms filled as they were, the lady moved with the speed of a sprite. Setting her things down hard on the table, she grabbed up her book and drew it protectively close. Fury brimmed in those cornflower-blue eyes, eyes so big that every emotion spilling out proved bigger.

And whatever headway he'd made appeared now squandered. Mistrust from the fairer sex, guns being turned on him, and people speaking to him with an acerbic edge were all . . . foreign.

He braced for the sting of her outrage. Instead, she stretched an arm behind her and deposited the book onto the table. "Sit," she ordered, in a tone better suited to one of those generals off fighting Boney, and Courtland instantly sat.

And yet, for all the lady's ire at finding him snooping through her things, the hands that came up and brushed aside his hair possessed a tenderness. Gently parting the strands, Miss Audley brushed them back, and Courtland's eyes slid closed, not out of pain but from the beguiling caress.

"Mmm," she murmured distractedly to herself.

"That bad?"

"Worse," she said, and even as she probed at a knob that had formed on his skull, she did so with her delicate touch. Then, dropping her hands, the lady reached for a wet cloth. She wrung it out, twisting the material back and forth in her fingers several times and draining the excess liquid before applying it to Courtland's wound.

"You've experience tending injuries," he remarked.

"I have three brothers who were coal miners, one of whom is a foreman responsible for any number of men who also work in those mines; what do you think?"

He thought she was more capable than any woman of his acquaintance, and he wondered what exactly that meant in terms of what she'd done . . . and seen. When he'd reviewed the file with his brother, going over the details of his assignment, Courtland had largely focused on the elder brother, who'd be the one making the decision. Now, he tried to recall what he'd read or learned about Miss Audley. Was she eighteen? Or nineteen? Either way, the lady was near in age to all three of his sisters, and, even in those tender years, she'd certainly seen more and struggled more than them. And the reminder of Lottie, Elsie, and Hattie, and the uncertain fate they faced, proved sobering and focused him on the current task at hand: ensuring his brother, Keir, retained his post and his earnings.

"One of your brothers' books, I take it?" Courtland spoke into the silence as Miss Audley dunked the white linen cloth.

She paused mid-wring, giving him a questioning look.

Courtland gestured to the leather volume she'd set aside, and she followed his stare.

"Tell me, why do you expect the book should belong to one of my brothers?" Unlike the more common thread of annoyance that lined her responses to him, this one contained a heavy shade of amusement. "Because it is so hard to believe that a woman should have an interest in fossils and lizards and minerals?" Her nostrils flared, and she didn't permit him a word edgewise. "Furthermore, you really are going to press me about my reading?" she asked, incredulity filling her voice. "After I allowed you an out from me blistering your ears for that insolence?"

"I'm not pressing you . . . I merely sought to discuss it with you."

Miss Audley faltered, wavering, and her thin, perfectly formed golden eyebrows dipped. "Why?"

Why, indeed?

"Consider me curious," he murmured, and interestingly . . . he was. For reasons that had nothing to do with his mission to bring her and her equally stubborn brothers back to London, and everything to do with this odd creature who aimed rifles at visitors and read books about fossils.

"You find it odd that I, a woman, should be interested in scholarly topics?"

"Actually . . . it is a foreign concept. To me, anyway," he was quick to clarify when she fixed a dangerous glint on him. "I've three sisters." And he'd had a score of mistresses since his Oxford days. "They all read gothic tales or stories about happily-ever-afters." Tales with romantic moments upon those pages. And the mistresses he kept were ladies more engrossed in new fashions and gossip than in books. "None of them are much interested in . . ." He consulted the title once more. "Research on quadruped fossil bones."

The lady's eyes lit, and she leaned down, collecting the front of his shirt, and drew him close. "That is what it says?" Her eyes glimmered like a thousand stars in the skies, and he found himself entranced by the sight, lost in those cornflower pools lit by her excitement. Courtland's breath stuck oddly in his chest, a foreign response for him, a jaded rogue, unfazed by much where beautiful women were concerned. As such, it took a moment to recall her words, and when he did, the realization hit him.

"You cannot read, then," he remarked, before he thought better of it, before he could call the words back.

A blush burned the lady's cheeks, painting them a fiery shade of red that chased away the smattering of freckles upon that canvas of her skin.

Miss Audley released him so quickly he fell back into the sofa, and he tamped down a curse as that jolt sent another shooting pain through his head.

"I can read," she said sharply. That adorable button nose of the lady wrinkled up. "Just not French." The gruff quality to her bell-like voice marking that admission as one she struggled to make.

He moved his gaze over her face, to that lone spiral curl that kissed her cheek, and before he could stop himself, he collected that lone strand, as stubborn as the lady herself. Not that he would have called for restraint in this moment. Even as he should have. "Vous pouviez voir le monde," he murmured. *You could see the world.* "Visitez vos musées." *Visit your museums.* "Découvrez la splendeur d'un monde entièrement nouveau." *Discover the splendor of an entirely new world.*

Her eyes darkened. With desire. With curiosity. He'd wager his soul the answer was a blend of both. "What are you . . . saying?" she whispered.

His experience as a rogue and his previous relationships with the fairer sex had taught him the subtleties of a woman's response . . . and body. The slight hitch in her chest as her breathing increased in tempo. It was the first time in his life that he'd found a value and use for the endless hours of French tutoring he'd suffered through.

"There are bookshops the likes of which will satiate your thirst for unconventional knowledge," he said, and some of that perpetual flair for the fight that lived within the lady ebbed as he properly read what this particular lady longed for.

"Bookshops?"

"There is the Temple of the Muses. Some say there are greater than five hundred thousand volumes upon their shelves."

Her breath hitched and her gaze softened, and for the first time in his life, he discovered himself in the presence of a woman ardently in love with the possibility of exploring new words and worlds. And here he'd not believed it possible to resent an inanimate object, and at that a rival that existed from nothing more than his telling.

"Tu es si belle," he murmured, drinking in the sight of her lush golden curls. *You are so very beautiful.* And then the urge proved too great. He slid one of those tresses between his thumb and forefinger. "So very soft," he marveled, imagining those strands fanned upon his pillow as he—

The lady slapped his fingers, hard.

He drew back his smarting hand. "First my head, now my hand, it will be a wonder if I make it out in one piece, Miss Audley," he drawled.

"You should have thought of that before you came here trying to force me and my brothers to do something we don't want *and* touching me and . . . and speaking French."

"I was merely brushing the loose bit of hair back," he said easily, and lying even more easily.

"And speaking French."

"Yes, given the state of our affairs with those frogs, I certainly see—"

"I was referring to how you were using your French language," she said tersely.

"Oh."

She eyed him warily. "I don't trust you."

*Clever woman.*

Glaring, and even more than a foot shorter than Courtland, she managed to give him an impressive look down the length of her nose. "Has the duke sent you snooping to report back with information about me, Lord Fancy Pants?"

Ah, he was back to Lord Fancy Pants, then.

"May I suggest we call one another by our Christian names," he offered, wanting to hear his name upon her lips, before recalling too late that he'd never do so. That to her he was Keir. "And the duke hasn't sent me snooping." He paused. Perhaps it was better to get right to the heart of it. "His Grace asked I retrieve you and your brothers." Or he'd tasked Keir. There was a momentary spot of guilt at deceiving her as he did.

A sharp laugh escaped her. "Are you a man or a spaniel? Sit," she ordered. Before he could comply on his own, she gripped his forearms and gave another light but firm push.

As he took that seat, and she hurried over to fetch the bowl and pitcher she'd previously abandoned, he looked between her and the book she'd left just out of sight and out of reach.

Miss Audley moved 'round the back of the sofa and took his head between her hands.

For her gruffness and clear annoyance, the lady handled him with a gentleness that briefly distracted from the dull throbbing at the back of his skull. Hers was a siren's touch; as she brushed back his hair, she lightly probed the area he'd hit.

He winced.

"My apologies," she murmured softly, distractedly, as she continued to search.

"Never say you fear for my demise."

Except this time his teasing wasn't met with her familiar annoyance. Instead, her features twisted, contorting into a blend of shock and sadness.

"Here," he murmured, angling himself better on the sofa so that he might see her more clearly. He cupped her cheek. "I was teasing."

She dampened her mouth, and his gaze slipped to her lips as he took in that slight, distracted, and yet highly erotic sweep of her tongue over generously formed flesh.

He swallowed hard.

Oh, damn it all.

"I do believe I'd like to kiss you." And that was bad. Because she was the duke's daughter, and his brother's assignment, and there was the matter that Courtland was here on a lie.

"Is that a request?" she whispered, her voice slightly breathless, hinting at a shared desire.

And because hers wasn't a rejection . . . because she angled her neck back a smidge and tilted her head back a smidge more, he was lost.

Cupping her nape, he drew her close and kissed her, claiming those lips with his as he'd longed to do, worshiping the pillowy contours.

She gripped his shirtfront, drawing him closer, and then it was she who deepened the kiss.

Desire swelled, and his shaft lifted.

And suddenly, he felt no pain.

He felt only her full breasts pressed against his chest, and the softness of her.

And—

Then it ended.

Deliciously breathless, the lady drew back, her expression stricken and her eyes filled with horror, both altogether foreign sentiments to meet Courtland after an embrace.

"Sit down," she commanded in a furious whisper.

"I . . . am seated?"

As one, they looked at the sofa he decidedly still occupied. For now. Courtland had a sinking feeling he was on the cusp of ending his tenure here in Staffordshire.

With a gasp the lady released him. "I meant turn your head." This time, she gripped him at the temples and guided him so he faced away from her.

He flinched. "Are you *trying* to hurt me?"

"I should . . . you know. The audacity of you, Lord Keir." The lady dropped her voice several decibels. "Kissing me like that." The moment the whispered words left her, she stole a frantic glance about as though she feared someone might be around to overhear that scandalous admission.

He flattened his lips into a hard line to keep from pointing out that, one: he'd decidedly asked the lady and given her ample room to reject him. And two: she'd returned that embrace with an impressive and very real zeal . . . before she hadn't.

"Now, will you just let me tend you so that I can be assured you aren't dying and then send you on your way?"

He allowed her to work in silence. He'd made her skittish. With that unwise embrace he'd gone and complicated his efforts here exponentially. As it was, he'd limited time here with her. For as soon as she bandaged him up, she'd do precisely as she said, send him on his way, and then he'd have failed his twin.

"Have you ever been to London, Miss Audley?" Courtland asked, keeping his voice deliberately conversational.

The lady hesitated, then shook her head.

"I expect a woman with your interests would be served by visiting such a place."

She dampened her mouth. "Such a place?"

He recalled his mother tugging along a passel of him and his siblings and leading the way through museums, because she'd known the duke wouldn't take them. Until the duke eventually barred her from taking them, filling their heads with—

"Lord Keir?"

He started, coming to the moment. "Museums. I was speaking of museums." It had been so long since he'd thought of his mother. Not because he'd not loved her, but because he had, and it had been easier to not think of her and the better life she'd deserved and been denied. "If you appreciate natural curiosities, you'll be entranced by the Leverian."

She hesitated, indecision in her eyes.

She was a proud creature. One who clung tight to her passions. And that restraint, the challenge she posed, made her dangerously tempting.

Alas, her natural interest proved stronger.

She took up the tiniest spot left on the sofa beside him. "All right, Lord Keir." Folding her arms mutinously, she nudged her chin up, and urged him on. "Tell me about your Leverian."

"Well, everyone believes the Royal Museum is the premier one."

"And they're wrong?" she asked wryly. "Everyone, that is, except you?"

He leaned close and tilted his mouth in a teasing smile. "Oh, undoubtedly so."

Her lips twitched, and his gaze slipped to that enticingly lush flesh.

As if feeling his study, the young lady quickly compressed them into a hard line.

Courtland cleared his throat. "That isn't to say the Royal Museum isn't wondrous in its own right," he said swiftly, lest he lose her any more than he already had. "It is. It is just that . . . the Leverian . . . has the manner of collection that defies expectations." Or it had. It had been years since he'd gone. He'd been a boy. Surely not much had changed? "There are displays of rare birds, shells . . ." He paused, letting the moment stretch on for effect. "Fossils."

The lady froze, and then it was as though she came to life in an instant. She gripped him hard by the shirtfront and dragged him up slightly. "Fossils?" she asked, her eyes sparkling with wonder and excitement. "There is a room dedicated to fossils."

Wincing at the jolt of pain that went to his recent head

injury, he managed a nod. "Oh, yes. The museum has it all. There are some"—he searched his mind for the number his mother had mentioned, when she'd been tugging him and his siblings along—"thirty or forty thousand artifacts. The first hall comprises weapons."

She wrinkled her nose. "Weapons?"

Where his youngest sister, Ellie, with her love of war and battlefields, had been endlessly fascinated by weaponry and warfare, Cailin appeared anything but. "There is also a Mineral Room." Or that was what his mother had referred to it as, anyway. "Which features minerals and vegetables." In response to Cailin's visibly waning interest, he recalled that which had sparked her enthusiasm. "And then, the South Room houses fossils."

That light returned to her eyes. She sighed; it was the breathy little exhalation that generally came from the lips of desirous ladies. Never had he seen a woman sigh so at the mention of a . . . fossil, and he found himself . . . charmed. "They are fascinating, are they not? The world tends to see rocks, but I always see them as a frozen glimpse of the past."

Her lips went slack, and she nodded. "Yes," she whispered. "And it raises all manner of questions about how life was, and how it changed, and . . . even how it could be?"

How it could be?

Stilted. Uninspired. Constrained. Or, at least, that was the world of Polite Society. He glanced about her household: small, the furniture mismatched. It was cozy, but also in its sparsity spoke to a life absent of ease.

Only . . . was that such a hardship if one was granted a pardon from being pressed under the repressive thumb of Polite Society?

She caught his stare and narrowed her eyes. "I take it you find my existence here wanting."

"No!" She released him with a gasp, and Courtland went collapsing back, with another slight groan. "Not at all." Quite the contrary.

Cailin Audley moved swiftly: in a quick, noisy rustle of

skirts, she stormed to her feet, and with her hands planted akimbo, she towered over him. "Do you think I don't know what you are doing?" She glared. "Do you think I can't recognize a devil come a-tempting with an apple, trying to seduce me into leaving Staffordshire, so I might go and fulfill the duke's wishes?"

And in that moment, Courtland found himself acknowledging a new, sudden realization: perhaps he wasn't the charming rogue the world had taken him for. Because the lady before him spoke of temptation and seduction . . . not as a result of the embrace they'd shared, or any desire on her part toward him, but because of those museums she longed to see.

She frowned. "Why are you looking at me like that?" she asked, suspicion making her voice thick and husky and further weaving a spell over Courtland because of it.

"I believe you see a whole new world awaiting you, Cailin," he said, laying dominion to her Christian name and how easily it rolled from his lips. "And I believe you want it." Her jaw slackened, drawing his focus to that lush mouth, and he reached out to run the tip of his index finger along that plump flesh. "Don't you, love?" he murmured, and somewhere along the way he'd become confused as to what specifically he spoke of in this instant—a second kiss that hovered on the air, or that journey to London she so resisted making.

"I'm not your love." The breathy quality of that disavowal shattered all hint of outrage he'd wager she strove for.

No. He wasn't a man who believed in love. Given his parents' dismal marriage, and the number of unhappy wives and gleeful widows who'd graced his bed, there were plenty of reasons to doubt any sentiments involving the heart.

Still, he who found himself transfixed by none found himself bespelled by her.

Hooding his lashes, he lifted his head, just as she lowered hers.

The door flew open, exploding with such force the panel

cracked against the back of the wall, jolting him and Cailin apart.

The young lady gasped. "Rafe!" she exclaimed, and then jumped several paces away from Courtland.

As in Rafe Audley.

As in the duke's eldest son.

As in the man whom Courtland was to convince.

A beast of a man stared back. Some thirteen and a half stone and an inch past six feet, none would ever consider Courtland a small man by any stretch of the imagination. And yet at several inches taller, and at least a stone heavier, there could be no doubting the other man had Courtland's death on his mind.

Courtland swallowed hard.

Bloody hell.

"Who the hell are you?" Mr. Audley growled.

"He is here at the behest of the duke," Cailin Audley said on a rush, and the furious fellow's attention whipped briefly over to his sister.

Belatedly, Courtland stood. "Mr. Audley," he greeted, and bent in a low bow. "It is a pleasure."

"What is? Your coming here and putting your hands on my sister?"

Another gasp escaped Miss Audley. "Rafe!"

Oh, bloody, bloody hell. A guilty—and worse, damning—flush climbed up Courtland's cheeks.

The man who stood with his nostrils flared and his face red—looking very much like the ornery bull his closest friend, Lord Seagrave, had hired for a house party with a matador waving a crimson flag and daring it forward—was going to be a tough one to convince . . . of anything.

"Perhaps if we might focus on the matter of my—"

With a savage roar, Audley charged.

"Oh, hell," Courtland muttered. His reflexes dulled from the fall he'd already taken, Courtland darted right and knocked into the arm of the chair.

He lost his balance.

The other man was already upon him.

More specifically his fist.

Courtland grunted as Rafe Audley clipped him hard in the jaw, knocking him down to his knees.

"Rafe!" Cailin cried out. "Will you stop?"

"No," the lady's eldest brother uttered conversationally, as though he were speaking with his sister about tea and biscuits. "Do you know, I don't think I shall." Then, with a gleeful smile, the other man drew back. This time, his fist connected with Courtland's chin, propelling his head back.

Stars danced before his vision.

He'd been properly schooled by Gentleman Jackson himself.

He'd also been known for taking down the famed instructor, along with most every other gentleman he'd faced in the boxing ring.

And yet, never before had he squared off against a man who punched and fought like this one who'd felled him, and certainly not with a crushing megrim from the fall he'd taken.

"If you do not stop, I shall never forgive you." That furious charge came as if from a distance, like when he'd hidden under the lake on his family's Leeds estate while his brothers and sisters had all searched him out, their voices emerging muffled by those waters.

He gave his head a hard shake in a bid to clear the cobwebs clogging his mind.

It proved the wrong motion.

Groaning, Courtland clutched a hand at the back of his skull.

A soft whisper of air wafted over his face, and, dazed, he looked over to the young woman who'd joined him on the floor. "Are you all right?" she asked, and he followed her lips as they moved. That mouth he'd just been kissing moments ago. That same mouth that had led him down a path to trouble this day and resulted in the vicious beating he'd been dealt.

He managed a slight nod, offering a silent lie. Bloody hell, he'd bungled this one badly.

And now, if Audley took the time to write Bentley what had happened here—

Courtland's mind recoiled from the implications of Keir and Keir's beloved—and also much needed—post.

The lady flew to her feet, and like some warrior princess, she positioned herself between Courtland and Audley.

"What do you think you are doing?" she stormed. "Acting like some brute, Rafe?"

"I'm the brute? Someone came to the mines reporting they'd heard gunfire at our cottage, and I come here to find this man kissing you."

"We were not kissing, Rafe." The young woman's voice was rich with such exasperation Courtland, who'd both kissed her and been about to kiss her a second time before the interruption, could almost believe her himself. She'd challenge her eldest sibling? For him? It was a staggering discovery, unexplainable given her earlier annoyance with him. "We were speaking about the duke and—"

"Then there is even more reason to beat him." The planks of the flooring groaned as the other man surged forward, and, towering over his spritely sister, Audley glared at Courtland. "You can tell Bentley he can go straight to hell. He could send God himself, and I wouldn't answer his summons. Now, get the hell out and don't come back. That is, unless you want me to rip out your entrails and choke you with them."

"Well, that is . . . certainly a strong opinion." With all the dignity he could muster, Courtland stood. Or he *tried* to. His legs wavered.

Cailin gasped, then rushed to help.

From over the top of Cailin's radiant golden curls, Courtland's gaze locked on Audley.

The other man pounded one fist against an open palm, all the while his death glare dared Courtland to accept the lady's assistance.

Alas, it was Courtland's intention to escape this day with his life, and his person, fully intact.

At last getting himself to his feet, Courtland collected

his belongings and offered a bow to Rafe Audley. He made one more vain attempt. "Are you certain I might not have a moment of your time in which to try and persuade—"

"Get the hell out," Audley hollered.

Hastily backing away, Courtland adjusted the strap of his satchel. "If you *do* change your mind—"

"I won't."

Courtland fetched one of the duke's cards from his bag, and laying it on the table, he slid it closer to Cailin's fingertips.

The young lady stared at the card a long moment.

Across the top of it, his gaze met hers. And Courtland knew. He knew even now she thought of the stories he'd told of London, and that she yearned to come and feed her hungering for knowledge.

Just as Cailin was about to pick up the duke's calling card, her irascible brother grabbed it. "Give me that."

And this time, Courtland was wise enough to take his leave, lest he risk earning any more of the miner's wrath. As he went, however, having failed Keir and the duke on an assignment Courtland had anticipated would be an easy one, it did not escape his notice that Cailin Audley hadn't rejected journeying to London.

For all her insistence to the contrary, the lady had wanted to go, and he could not help thinking how much more interesting London would be with a woman such as Cailin Audley there.

# Chapter 4

When she'd been a girl, Cailin had dreamed of leaving her village in Staffordshire. She'd not dreamed so very big as to imagine going away forever, because the only forever a person born to a working station knew was the promise of more work.

In her imaginings, her travels had always taken her to a nearby town. A different village. Never London. London had been a dream too fantastical, too grand, and too far.

It hadn't been until the whisperings of a gentleman who hailed from that grand city that she'd allowed such an aspiration to take root and grow.

Alas, she should have known better.

Cailin stood at the floor-to-ceiling-length crystal windows and stared wistfully down at the streets below. Behind her, for the fourteenth straight day, Cailin's sister-in-law, Edwina, continued on with the lessons meant to prepare Cailin for the upcoming soiree hosted by the duke and his wife.

". . . we needn't go very much beyond what we've already covered in terms of introductions and greetings, and you've already demonstrated the steps of several dancing sets quite nicely," her sister-in-law was saying.

*This* was what London, her grand adventure, had become.

Lessons on how to curtsy.

Who to curtsy to.

When to curtsy.

When *not* to curtsy.

How to dance.

How *not* to dance.

Which fork to eat with, and when.

Which fork not to eat with.

So. Many. Forks.

Why would anyone need more than one fork? The question screamed around her mind, begging to be set free from her lungs, expelled into the torrid air of London's High Society life.

But this was what she had asked for.

Wasn't it?

Her wishes and dreams for her time here, and her life in general, had become all mixed up in her mind, like threads impossibly twisted upon an embroidering frame that could not be undone or sorted through.

"Cailin?"

"When going in to dinner, the gentleman of the house must escort the highest-ranking lady present. The remaining dinner guests will also be so paired and enter the dining room in order of rank," she repeated by rote, not missing a beat.

Edwina gave a happy little clap. "Splendid! As I said, you're doing splendidly . . ."

Yes, splendid.

Only there was nothing splendid about *any* of this. In the beginning there'd been a trip to the museum with Edwina and Rafe, but then Cailin's life here had gone through some kind of shift. As though her family had all forgotten that exploring life in London was what she'd craved, and her yearnings had instead been absorbed into the sweltering cloud of propriety and decorum that hung over this glittering world.

Now, all that remained for her was a loneliness, an absence of friends. Her brothers. There was Rafe, but he was newly married and deserved not to have a lonely sister shadowing his steps.

And Wesley, who—across the channel in France, fighting Boney as he was—wrote less and less.

And Hunter, consumed with his new role of foreman at the Cheadle mines, which the duke had purchased from the previous owner and gifted to his sons. Well, with those newfound responsibilities, Hunter's letters came not at all.

Her brothers had their own lives.

Cailin understood that better than anyone.

But how she missed them . . . and also envied them.

The whispered words of another person's voice silenced the latest lecture Edwina doled out.

*". . . I believe you see a whole new world awaiting you, Cailin . . . And I believe you want it . . ."*

The memory of Lord Keir's murmurings rolled through the chambers of her mind, sweeping in like the ocean's tide and then gently ebbing. Over and over his unerringly accurate words replayed. A prediction made by a man who'd been a stranger but knew implicitly more than her own brothers that which she longed for deep inside.

Her gaze alighted on a slow-moving carriage, and touching a fingertip to the impeccable glass, Cailin allowed that digit to make the journey the garish pink barouche now did, following it, following it—until it was gone. Her lonely finger collided with the place where the window met the ivory satin wallpaper.

She let her arm fall.

After Lord Keir had been run off by Cailin's brother, she thought often about him . . . and that day.

Not that she was a woman given to thinking about men. She wasn't. She'd had her heart broken once by love, and she'd little wish to walk that path again.

But she'd thought of him. And their discussions about

London museums, and his fascination with the fact that she read.

He'd shown a real interest in that book, and he'd spoken French. Both of which had been foreign. Why, even her former sweetheart had been more indulgent than anything in Cailin's interests.

No doubt Lord Keir had been encouraging merely because it served his interests. He'd likely been tempting her with the possibilities that awaited in the hopes that he'd manage to tempt her into going.

And God help her, with his talk of the culture she might find in Town, he had enticed Cailin with the possibilities that existed there.

Long after he'd gone, and the duke had sent new men and eventually a governess, Edwina—now Cailin's sister-in-law—Cailin had gone throughout her day thinking of those museums and what the gentlemen had spoken of.

That desire to visit London had felt like a betrayal of her brothers, and guilt became a constant companion.

And then, of course, there had been guilt because of how her meeting with the gentleman had ended: with Rafe beating the other man senseless. At no point had Lord Keir fought back or attempted to defend himself.

A rider approached, and she distractedly followed this latest lucky person free to come and go as he pleased, until he stopped.

Outside.

Cailin froze as her gaze locked on the impressively tall figure below, now awaiting entry into the duke's residence.

She'd always thought she would see him again.

Since her recent arrival in London, she'd even looked for him.

As her father's man of affairs, Lord Keir would undoubtedly be a fixture in the duke's household.

Surely, however, with her silent remembrances, she'd conjured him.

The bright morning sun played off those golden curls, toying with the many blends of blonds, those lush strands stunningly bright and even more closely cropped than when she'd last seen him; they were locks a woman would recognize anywhere.

Pressing her palms and forehead against the window, she peered down.

It was *him*.

Lord Keir.

And something in seeing him, even as he was still basically a stranger, the familiar face of a man who'd come out to Staffordshire, left her light inside, which was certainly an undeserved feeling considering the beating he'd taken on account of her.

Guilt, the same emotion that had dogged her following his being run out of Staffordshire, immediately chased away that brief joy as she recalled the reason she'd hoped to see him again—so that she might apologize for how their exchange had ended.

Behind her, Cailin's sister-in-law, Edwina, esteemed for her work training ladies—and Rafe—in the ways of Polite Society, and fitting in, went over the day's agenda.

". . . It might be daunting . . . however, you'll see, Cailin, the evening will be lovely . . ." Edwina was saying.

"Lovely," Cailin murmured.

As if he felt her eyes upon him, the gentleman looked up; his gray gaze locked briefly with hers, and her heart froze. This time there was no flutter, but rather a chill brought on by the deadness of that stare.

There was no flare of recognition. There was no hint of the teasing, charming rogue who'd set out to convince Cailin to journey to London and see the museums so she might feed her thirst for knowledge.

Only a flat, emotionless coldness met her stare . . .

*What did you expect after how he was treated at your brother's hand, and because of you?* a voice jeered.

Lord Keir yanked that frigid stare forward, dismissing her outright, and she drew back a fraction as that knot in her chest grew tighter and harder.

"Perhaps we should review the transition between dinner and the dancing?" her sister-in-law pondered aloud. "Though we did seem to discuss that in depth. What. Next." There came the rhythmic *tip-tap-tip-tap* of a pencil as Edwina contemplated where Cailin would go with the day's tedious lessons on Polite Society and decorum and topics Cailin absolutely needed to learn for her entry into High Society, but also the items she cared least about.

Below, the door was opened by the duke's butler, and Lord Keir disappeared inside.

"I have it!" Edwina exclaimed, her tone triumphant, and Cailin jerked her gaze over to her sister-in-law. "Why don't we enlist Rafe for more dance l—"

"If you'll excuse me?" Cailin said quickly, and Edwina immediately stopped mid-sentence. "I . . . there is a matter I must see to," she said, and with her sister-in-law staring in wide-eyed surprise, Cailin gathered up her hems and took flight.

She raced past the footmen standing at attention at various points of the corridor, calling her usual greeting and waving as she went. She made a path for the duke's offices, knowing invariably that was where she'd meet him.

She turned the corridor and collided with Rafe. All the air left her, knocking her off-balance.

"Whoa!" Her eldest brother caught her by the shoulders, steadying her before she could go flying back on her buttocks. "What is the ru—"

"Excuse me," she said, breathless from their collision and the pace she'd set for herself. "I've . . . matters to see to."

His brow dipped. "Matters?"

Without another word, she took off racing once more.

Her dogged, blasted obstinate, and overprotective brother put himself in her path, catching her this time by the forearms when she would have fallen.

"I asked, what matters?" Rafe demanded, and had she not been racing against time to get to Lord Keir before he disappeared for his meeting with her father, she would have taken her brother to task for those insolent tones.

Keeping her features expressionless, Cailin handed him

the one phrase that would make any man regret having pressed a woman for answers: "Womanly ones."

"Uh—of course!" In his haste to move out of her path, Rafe stumbled. "As you—"

Her brother forgotten, Cailin was already dashing off.

She'd worried that "almost-kiss" in Staffordshire had cost Lord Keir his post. But it hadn't. He was here!

She took the turn to the duke's offices quickly, catching the edge of the wall to keep herself from propelling forward on her face. And then she spied him.

Just outside the rooms, his fist lifted to knock on that mahogany panel.

Breathless from her exertions, she called out. "Stop!"

Lord Keir glanced around, his steely gray eyes ultimately landing on Cailin.

Those hard lips that had covered hers so masterfully and curved up so tenderly in a charming rogue's smile remained flat. As emotionless and unfeeling as his frosty stare.

What accounted, then, for his . . . indifference?

She resisted the urge to rub at her arms in a bid to chase away the prickling upon her arms. "I . . . have been hoping to see you." Perhaps his charm in Staffordshire had been nothing more than a facade, a perfectly crafted act to gain her trust and get her to return with him. Or mayhap it was just that mingling among High Society inevitably stole the light and soul and joy of all who dwelled here, converting each person into a placid replica of one another.

"You wanted to see me?"

Cailin may as well have sprung a second head and a tail to go along with it for the way he looked at her.

"I don't even know you."

Cailin winced. "I deserve that." Yes, he may have kept his employment, but he'd suffered a vicious beating that day at her brother's hand.

She'd had all this time to apologize. She'd had countless days and hours to think about what she'd say when they met again, but every single word flew out of her head. Because when she'd imagined this exchange, he'd been the charming rogue of that day in Staffordshire. And with that clear show of antipathy, she found herself with an urge to cry.

Turning his attention back to the duke's door, the gentleman lifted his hand once more. She should let him get on with his business. She *should* leave him alone.

"I wanted to speak with you," she said, interrupting him before his fist fell.

Again, he stopped. He glanced down the length of that aquiline nose, a bold slash of flesh that bespoke his aristocratic roots. "What could we possibly have to talk—?"

Cailin caught him by his wrist.

"Hey now!" he exclaimed. "What do you—"

Cailin was already steering him to the open doorway behind them, pulling him into the sun-filled parlor, and closing the door.

More than half-fearing he'd escape if she didn't, Cailin leaned against the panel.

His gray eyes bulged. "What do you think you are doing?"

"I already told you . . . I wanted to speak with you."

That managed to cut across his icy coldness. "What could we possibly have to discuss?" He cocked his head in an endearing way that sent curls tumbling over his brow, and they softened him, reminded her of who he'd been that day. They also gave him a boyish look that made him more approachable than the furious gentleman whom she'd pulled inside.

"About . . . what happened." Her cheeks went warm. "Not . . . that part." *The kiss.* She couldn't bring herself to mention it. She'd been embraced before, almost twice by him, and even before that . . . by Ian. Granted, those embraces had been so very different. Something about Lord Keir this time, however, made him more of a stranger than he'd been even that day. Perhaps had he borne any resemblance to the roguish gentleman who'd visited her that day, and for whom it had been so very easy to talk to him.

His eyebrows dipped. "What part are you referring to, Miss—?"

"Cailin," she said tightly; for the first time since she'd managed to corner him, annoyance took root. "I believe you were the one who suggested we refer to one another by our given names?"

"By our . . . ?" More confusion filled his eyes. "I did?"

She frowned. Such a wealth of confusion couldn't be feigned.

And then came a flash of understanding. "I did!" Or was it remembrance? Before he hooded those stormy gray pools, his long, thick lashes concealing every emotion contained within those irises.

At last, however, it appeared she'd gotten through that wall of icy indifference. Cailin linked her fingers and clasped those interlocked digits before her. "I've been wanting to say how sorry I was for how my brother responded that day."

He continued to eye her with that opaque expression.

Unnerved, she fiddled with the lace overlay of her white dress. "I would have never wanted him to beat you as he did."

"Beat me," he said dumbly.

She bit the inside of her cheek. Of course. Men and their fragile egos. "Not that he *beat* you," she said in the soothing way she spoke to their cottage mouser when he landed himself in a tree after chasing birds. "Two punches, which you handled well."

His face whitened.

Oh, blast. She was making a mess of this. "That is, considering how groggy you were from when you hit your head on the walkway."

He stared unblinking at her. "I hit my head."

She paused. Perhaps he'd suffered damage to his brain that day after all? "Have you had difficulty remembering your visit?" He continued to stare blankly at her. "When I shot at you. It was, however, as you know, accidental." Except . . . what if he didn't recall? "I didn't intend to fire."

Lord Keir strangled on a swallow; his face went red, and

fearing he'd choke to death on his own spit, she rushed over and thumped him hard on the back, square between the shoulder blades.

He instantly recoiled, bolting away from her. "D-Do not!" he barked, jabbing a finger at Cailin, and ordering her away.

She rocked on her heels, allowing him that space he desired. "Forgive me," she said, issuing a second apology of the day. "It was not my intention to offend you . . . just to . . . apologize," she said weakly. She should have never brought up all the infractions she and her brother were guilty of that day. Cailin took in a deep breath. "I also wished to thank you for encouraging me to come to London. I . . . have had the opportunity to visit—"

The door burst open, and she went flying forward, landing hard against Lord Keir.

He cursed, folding his arms about her, catching her, steadying her.

"What is the goddamned meaning of this?" Rafe thundered.

Cailin briefly closed her eyes. "Not again."

"Again?" Lord Keir dittoed her own sentiments.

With an ear-splitting roar, her brother charged.

"I have no idea what you are talking about," the other man cried.

Rafe snarled. "Oh, I think you do."

The gentleman's lips formed a stiff line. "The lady steered *me* inside here to speak."

Silence met that outraged pronouncement.

Cailin slapped a hand over her face.

It was the wrong thing to say.

The truthful and the right one on Keir's part, but the wrong one, too.

With another shout, Rafe barreled at the gentleman.

Unlike last time, Lord Keir was prepared for it. He bolted, positioning himself behind the pink upholstered sofa, keeping that length of furniture between him and Rafe. "Hold on there," he commanded.

Rafe's nostrils flared. "You'd order me about?"

"If by order you mean I'd demand that you speak about this like a civilized gentleman? Then ye—"

Cailin raced around, positioning herself in front of Lord Keir before her brother reached him. "Just *stop*, Rafe. You are making something out of nothing. Again."

"I do believe you've done enough," Lord Keir said to Cailin, and she winced.

Yes, he was correct on that score.

Still, she owed it to him to try and smooth this situation with her blockheaded brother. "I requested that he meet with me so that I might apologize."

"Apologize for what?"

As one, she and the other two men present looked to the front of the room to where the duke stood, frowning.

He shut the door swiftly behind him.

Oh, bloody hell.

This was not good.

# Chapter 5

≈≈≈≈≈

Absolute silence was the key to winning a battle.
     And an ability to remain stealthily out of sight and
hidden.

All of which were skills Courtland possessed in spades.

Alas, unfortunately, his younger sister possessed far
more.

"Freeze there, you dastardly cur!"

From the side of the Louis XVI walnut commode he
knelt beside, Courtland kept as still as possible for so long
the muscles in his legs screamed in protest.

He'd learned long ago his sister's every trick on the pretend battlefield.

Too many times when she'd called out, he'd revealed
himself, inadvertently giving himself away.

Courtland brought his toy weapon slowly up.

The click of a toy bayonet filled the quiet parlor.

"Do not move. Not one bit." His youngest sibling issued
that gleefully menacing order, her voice coming close
enough to confirm he'd been found out.

*Caught.*

Courtland sighed. "This really isn't an honorable way to fight, you know," he felt inclined to point out, and he let his toy weapon drop.

"How convenient that you only should mention that when you've been cornered," his sister drawled. "It works for the Americans. In fact, that is how they defeated the British army, you know."

"A man should know who his opponent is."

"A *woman* knows it doesn't matter if one sees one's opponent, only that one knows who that person is, and that they are defeated."

He shuddered. "Egad, you are ruthless." And she was. Utterly terrifying. Of course, he'd have her no other way, but she terrified him out of his everlasting mind.

She waved her weapon. "On your feet, Courtland."

Coming up and out slowly with his hands up, he faced Ellie, the fourteen-year-old dervish.

She released the trigger, and it made another little click.

Courtland let his weapon slip from his fingers, and with an exaggerated groan, he staggered back several steps until he collided with the wall.

He sagged, making himself go limp, then absolutely still.

"Your dying is much improved," she praised, and he took that as leave to open his eyes and climb to his feet.

"I've had a good deal of practice at it," he said, coming over. He ruffled the top of her cropped curls. When she'd been a girl of five—to their father's horror and fury—she'd hacked them off herself, and she'd continued chopping them short.

"I am good at what I do, aren't I?" Ellie puffed her small chest out.

"Committing fratricide? The absolute best."

His sister shoved her bayonet against his side, and he grunted. "What was that for?"

"Because you're making light, and it's nothing to make light of, Courtland," she said. Exasperation filled her voice, and her eyes glimmered with that sentiment. Ellie flopped down onto her back and sprawled her arms wide, letting her bayonet rest within finger-reach. "The world is an unfair, cruel one to women."

Courtland took up a place beside her, lying on his back, so that they were shoulder to shoulder. "Well, in fairness, you're still a girl."

She gave him a sideways kick, and he grunted.

"It really isn't amusing, you know. You are a duke. You are a man. You get to make your own decisions. The same goes for Keir. And I?" She flung an arm across her forehead. "I shall never serve in the military. I shall never have the opportunity to take down Boney."

He smiled wryly. "Yes, well, let us hope that by the time you're of an age to make the march to war the French frog isn't wreaking terror on the Continent." As soon as the words left him, he edged his leg back, sparing himself from a second kick. He sighed. "Forgive me, Captain," he said, reading the moment and employing the proper degree of gravity the situation called for. "The world, it isn't fair."

"Certainly not for women," she muttered. Clasping her hands, Ellie folded them at her belly and stared at the chipping mural overhead.

"No. You are right there." The world certainly wasn't fair for women or to them. Though, in truth, Courtland didn't have the freedoms his sister thought he did. A man was only as free and stable as his finances allowed him to be. There was a responsibility to her, and their two other sisters, and his twin brother. Obligations that were hard to see to with the financial straits their father had left them, and their properties. Of course, he couldn't say all of that to her. He couldn't say any of it. Instead, he donned his usual smile and playful attitude and kept the depth of their circumstances from her.

Suddenly, Ellie rolled onto her side, and propping her head on her hand, she spoke excitedly, her youthful enthusiasm restored. "There's still a way for me to fight, you know."

"Oh, absolutely," he concurred. "We can—"

"No," she interrupted with an eye roll. "I mean, *really* fight. Why, there was Epipole."

She stared at Courtland as though he should know this, and given his sister was constantly handing down battle-field details and military facts, he probably should have. With an exasperated sigh, Ellie took mercy and clarified. "She took part in the Trojan War against Troy." Her little features pulled. "Of course, Palamedes punished her and she was stoned to death."

He smiled drolly. "Well, if *that* isn't a moral lesson, I don't know what—" The dark glower she turned his way killed the remainder of those words. He cleared his throat. "I would be remiss, however, if I didn't point out, Ellie, that the Trojan War is a myth. It's not real," he said gently.

Ellie shot a finger out, catching him in the chest, and he grunted. "Oomph. What—"

"Hua Mulan. In the fourth century, China required all families to have a male relative in the household join the army. But her father was frail." As most fathers were . . . just in different ways. "The legend of Mulan is based on a real person."

As he warmed to her telling, his sister scooted closer. "Also, Deborah Sampson. She disguised herself as a man and enlisted in the Continental Army."

Oh, hell. "Yes, but I don't think *that* is a good—"

"And then, there is—"

"*Courtlaaaand!*"

That thunderous shout came from somewhere in the house; a booming voice, shaking with fury.

What now?

A moment later, footfalls pounded from within, some-where dangerously close, drawing closer . . . and closer. Door after door slammed, with such force walls shook.

"He sounds angry," Ellie whispered.

"He" as in their brother, Courtland's twin. "Nonsense," he scoffed. "Keir doesn't get angry."

*Boom.*

"*Courtland!*"

Her eyes flaring, Ellie jumped as another door in the same hall as their current hiding spot slammed.

"I think this time he is," she said in nearly inaudible tones.

Yes, his sister was indeed correct. It appeared Keir was capable of shows of temper. Which was saying something. Courtland's twin rarely gave in to displays of emotion. He was a master of self-control.

The door exploded open, and he and Ellie popped up.

Keir did a sweep of the room, and when his gaze landed on Courtland, the fury within those matching eyes threatened to burn.

"Brother!" Courtland called out cheerfully in a bid to defuse whatever it was he'd done to upset his younger brother.

"What have you done?" Ellie whispered out of the side of her mouth.

He gave his head a nearly indecipherable shake. "You know me. It could be . . . anything."

"You!" Keir hissed, and stalked forward. "What have you done?"

Courtland found his feet. "That seems to be the question of the day," he drawled. "What brings you here in the middle of the day, little brother?" Wholly devoted to his work as the Duke of Bentley's man of affairs, nothing short of a sacking would see Courtland here in the middle of the—

Courtland went motionless. Oh, hell. No. Let it not be that.

"Excuse us, Ellie." It wasn't a request. And while Keir spoke that command to their youngest sibling, his furious stare remained locked on Courtland.

Courtland's unease grew. What had he done to account for this degree of rage?

"I'd rather stay," Ellie chirped as she collected her bayonet and hopped up.

At last, Keir shifted his attention over to the girl. "Not. Now. Leave us."

"Ellie," Courtland said warningly, and with a sigh Ellie collected her provision of pretend weaponry and headed for the door. "We aren't done here, Courtland." She drew the door shut hard behind her.

The moment she'd gone, Keir exploded: "What the hell have you done, Courtland?" Keir hissed through his teeth.

"I'm afraid—"

"You suggested you refer to one another by your given names?"

He knew. "'Christian names,' I believe is the phrase I used?" He offered a sheepish smile. Oh, hell. Courtland tugged at his suddenly tight cravat. "Either way, it seemed . . . best at the time."

"You suggested an intimacy with the duke's daughter?" his brother snapped. "How can that ever be best?"

"Well, it's a good deal easier to try and converse with someone and convince them to come to London if one is speaking less formally."

"You were supposed to be 'me,' Courtland. A damned servant would never be so forward. Not that I expect you, a bloody duke, would know anything at all about that."

No, Courtland didn't. The expectations the world had for most tended to not apply to dukes and ducal heirs in quite the same way. His brother spoke of that privilege and lambasted him for it. The truth was, however, that Courtland had always abhorred that special treatment. Until this moment, with his brother's rage directed at him, he'd not realized the boldness he'd ridden into at that Staffordshire cottage. "I may have failed to properly consider the reversal in our roles."

"Damned straight you did," Keir barked. "You offered to go in my stead. You weren't to go as a damned charming duke. You were supposed to go as a servant with a glib tongue and persuade the Audleys to return."

There'd always been a certainty that Courtland's visit that day and the scandal surrounding his departure from the Audleys' cottage would come to light. He'd simply grown complacent and convinced himself that time wasn't coming.

His twin, however, wasn't done with him. "I said charm the damned family, not seduce the duke's bloody daughter."

"Oh, that."

Keir's eyes bulged. "'Oh, that'?"

"If it is any consolation, I did not seduce the lady," he said hopefully. He frowned. "Is that what she said?"

She'd not seemed the manner of person to lie about such matters.

"No, she didn't say it. The lady's hulk of a brother, however, informed me and the duke of how he came upon you kissing his sister."

"I wasn't kissing her at that moment."

"At that moment?" his brother snapped.

Courtland closed his mouth quickly. His brother had always possessed an uncanny way of filtering out a person's secrets. As his twin, there was nothing Keir missed.

Keir briefly closed his eyes, and his mouth moved in a long, nearly inaudible curse. "You *did* kiss her, then."

Courtland opened his mouth, but God help him for being more honorable than he cared to be in this instant. "I . . . am not of an inclination to say." Which of course said absolutely everything his brother needed to know. "You may rest assured, however, that we were not discovered doing anything improper."

"That reassures me not at all," Keir muttered. "For it does not escape my notice that you did not deny *something* happened between you and the lady."

Such disappointment and fury reflected in eyes a perfect mirror of Courtland's own, the like of which had never been turned Courtland's way . . . not by this man, his best friend and brother. It hit like the blow Rafe Audley had delivered that day, now at the heart of this discussion.

It was on the tip of his tongue to point out that the kiss and embrace had been almost simultaneous in their initiation. The lady had very much responded and encouraged him. Of course, he could not say as much. He would never say as much. Not even to the brother whom he'd been closer with than anyone. Theirs was a bond that ran deep, which was what made the tangible disappointment so unbearable.

The fight seemed to go out of Keir, and he collapsed into the folds of an enormous silk damask Louis XVI chair.

Hesitantly, Courtland took the seat across from him. "You . . . saw her, then."

"And her brother." Keir's nostrils flared. "Her very big, very powerful brother, who attempted to kill me."

"That seems to be his way," Courtland muttered.

They sat there in silence for several long moments. Unlike Courtland, who as a child had always been happy to talk to anyone and everyone, Keir had never been much for words. Even so, there'd always been something comforting and soothing in their silence. Identical twins, who'd shared a bond even before they'd entered the physical world.

Not this time, however.

This time, Courtland sat there with the sting of shame and his own regrets. He shouldn't have kissed her. Granted, when he'd gotten his arse beat by Rafe Audley, it had only been on the assumption of a kiss.

"I was sacked," Keir whispered, and all of Keir's muscles seized. "The duke dismissed me." A pained laugh escaped Courtland's brother. "With two months' wages, of course, because of his generosity." Keir's entire body slumped in his seat.

They needed Keir's work. He didn't know as much. Or at least not the full extent of how vital his income was.

A man of affairs made £20 at most if his employer was generous. The duke had paid Keir an actual fortune. Three thousand pounds, to be exact. Funds that furnished Hattie's London Season.

Courtland had simply withheld that some of those monies *also* went to help with their leaking roof and the fraying curtains.

The loss of those desperately needed funds should be the focus . . . and yes, there would be time enough later to panic about their situation.

Courtland took up a place beside his brother on the sofa, and it wasn't their finances he considered, but rather the very real loss that this was. Keir's life was his work. There wasn't much the other man enjoyed, at least not that even Courtland, as his twin, could name on a hand, let alone three fingers. This loss of his employment, a role he'd taken pride in, would be the greatest, most devastating of blows.

*And it is because of me. I did this . . .*

Courtland touched his brother's shoulder and gave it a slight squeeze.

Always at odds with a physical touch, Keir stiffened, but he did not pull away from that show of support.

"I can talk to the duke," Courtland said quietly. "I've an invitation to his soiree this evening. I will find time to speak with him there and explain—"

"You'll explain what? That it wasn't me who kissed his daughter, but rather my identical brother whom I sent in my stead to deceive both the duke and his daughter and sons?"

Courtland managed a sheepish grin. "Yes, well, when you put it in those terms, I certainly see that might not be the way to reclaim your post."

His brother didn't return that smile. He just further slouched in his seat and buried his forehead in his right palm.

Courtland's chest constricted. He would have preferred Keir's earlier show of fury to this defeated side of his always-imperturbable brother.

"Regardless, I will talk with him tonight," Courtland reiterated. "You have my word." He paused. "And . . . I am *so* sorry, Keir." Sorrier than his brother could ever know.

His twin stiffened, and then he came to his feet. "Yes, me, too," Keir spoke in tight, clipped tones. "About so much."

*Him.*

Enlisting Courtland's help.

Courtland winced. He deserved that. He'd blundered this badly.

Without another word, without so much as a glance at Courtland, Keir stalked off, and this time as he exited the parlor, Keir drew the door shut quietly behind him.

The solitude lasted no longer than a fraction of a heartbeat.

The door opened an instant later, and Ellie saw herself back inside.

Folding her arms in an exaggerated manner that fluffed the enormous yellow bow sewn along the top of her white dress, she stared at Courtland in a shrewd way.

"I take it you heard some of that?" he asked, praying she'd not—

"I heard *all* of that." She waggled her blond eyebrows. *Splendid.*

A blush heated his neck and ears, and he gave another restless tug of his already rumpled cravat. Good God, blushing? *What in hell was happening to him?* "You shouldn't be listening at doors, Ellie."

"And you shouldn't be kissing Keir's employer's daughter, but"—Ellie threw her arms wide, gesturing in his direction—"here we are."

Here they were, indeed.

Courtland let himself fall back into his seat and shot his legs out in front of him.

Skipping over, Ellie dropped onto the sofa beside Courtland and let her little limbs splay in a perfect match of his position.

They sat there for several moments.

At the same time, they dropped their heads along the back edge of the sofa. "You shouldn't have done that, Courtland."

"I know. I know," he said, before she'd even finished with her insightful pronouncement.

God help him. He was the only duke in the history of dukedoms to be the frequent recipient of dressing-downs from his younger siblings, little people some fifteen years his junior.

"This is not good. Not. Good. At. All," Ellie spoke quietly to herself.

Leaning over, he tweaked one of her short curls. "Aren't you supposed to possess a child's innocence and bright-eyed optimism?"

"Because I'm fourteen?" His youngest sister slapped his hand away. "Please, I study military strategies and the number of battlefield casualties. Do you really take me as the happily-ever-after, fairy-tale dreamer my sisters are?"

"You have a point there," he mumbled.

They fell silent and remained with their gazes on the ceiling overhead.

"Let me think," she said to herself. "Let me think," she repeated, carefully enunciating each syllable of each word. "Keir's employment was important to him . . . and us."

He jerked so quick his legs left the table. She knew that.

Ellie rolled her eyes. "You think I don't know our family is in dire straits?"

Keir didn't even know the half of it. Courtland had sought to protect all four of his siblings from the true state their father had left them in.

Ellie patted his knee and leaned close to whisper, "Worry not. Hattie and Lottie are blissfully unaware."

"I . . . would keep it that way," he said tentatively.

"Of course." He'd have preferred all his sisters had been unaware of their plight. Hattie and Lottie were dreamers, believers in love: a marvel, considering the fact that both young women had witnessed the same misery of their parents' unhappy union; their father's philandering; their mother's moroseness and constant state of being with child. "But we do need funds . . ."

Steepling her fingertips together, Ellie pressed and flexed them, over and over, in that way she always did when she was deep in thought. Which for Courtland was almost never a good thing. "What to do? What to do?"

And with his youngest sibling sitting there as stumped as Courtland himself, that remained the question to which he was singularly unable to find an answer.

What was he going to do?

# Chapter 6

S ince her arrival in London, Cailin had been unhappy.
Never, however, had Cailin been more miserable
than she was now, on display for the duke and duchess's
esteemed guests.

It was worth it. Enduring the glittering affairs at which
she'd never belong was a small price to pay.

It was worth being here.

From the sidelines of the Duke and Duchess of Bentley's
crowded ballroom, presently filled with waltzing couples
whirring past in vibrant satin skirts, Cailin reminded herself of that over and over again.

Perhaps one of these instances, she just might believe it.

She swept her gaze around the room, and her eyes
snagged upon a young lady seated among the other wall-
flowers. Whereas the other young women surrounding her
looked deuced glum in their partnerless state, she sat, ankles crossed, reading.

Admiration for the unconventional lady filled Cailin, as
she identified a woman who didn't shrink or hide, but rather
enjoyed the time here on her terms.

"You're having a good time, my dear?"

Cailin started and spun to greet the owner of that voice.

Her father's wife: recently married, and very much in love, the duchess had been only gracious to Cailin and her brothers. In fact, she'd welcomed Cailin into the folds of the family with far greater beneficence than most any other wives would their husband's by-blows.

Unlike Cailin's father, who, but for a handful of brief, if warm, interactions, tended to stay away.

The duchess arched an eyebrow.

"Yes," she blurted out, lying for the other woman's benefit. "I'm having a splendid time."

Taking up a place at Cailin's shoulder, Her Grace looked out over the crowded parlor, brimming with guests. "Yes, there is nothing more enjoyable than a too-crowded, too-hot ballroom filled with staid guests," the older woman said.

Furrowing her brow, Cailin glanced over.

The duchess flashed a smile and winked. Then, looping her arm through Cailin's, she leaned in.

"When I was your age," she whispered against Cailin's ear. "I made it a habit of sneaking off whenever the chance presented itself. I'm not saying you should do that." Her Grace paused. "Just that I'd understand if you felt like you wished to."

They shared a smile and together looked straight out.

Cailin froze, and whatever response she'd intended to speak, whatever matter she and the duchess had been discussing, flew right out of her head. Her eyes, however, deceived her, played the oddest of tricks on her, until she wondered if she'd hit her head.

Which only recalled another time, when another person had in fact suffered a blow to the skull.

Which also, surely, accounted for her seeing him.

She blinked several times, but the sight remained.

Lord Keir, with a champagne flute dangling between his fingers, speaking with one of the duke's many guests.

His garments had been fine in Staffordshire, and by their quality, there'd have been no disputing that the man

who'd come to her family's cottage and attempted to convince them to return had been a gentleman.

But, also, that man hadn't looked like . . . this man.

A snowy white cravat, artfully arranged, with a sapphire
pin stuck in the center. A velvet collar to his peaked black
jacket only emphasized the crisp silkiness of those adorn-
ments at his throat.

Given the ugliness of their latest meeting, the last person
whom she'd expected to see at her father's ball was him.
"What is he doing here?" she blurted.

The duchess's eyebrows came together. "Who?"

Cailin discreetly motioned to the dashing gentleman
with those golden curls; he very much had the look of a
fallen Lucifer.

"Him," Cailin said.

From the corner of her eye, she caught the frown as it
formed on Her Grace's lips. "Your father will not hold the
crimes of one man against the other."

*"Your father will not hold the crimes of one man against
the other."*

Thoroughly befuddled, she looked to the duchess.

Confusion, followed by a dawning understanding, lit the
duchess's pretty blue eyes. "Of course. You do not know."

"Know what?"

"Lord Keir, your father's former man of affairs, is an
identical twin."

Cailin's gaze went flying from that impressive figure.
An identical twin?

She fixed her gaze upon the golden-haired gentleman,
his focus on the guest with whom he spoke, and she used
the opportunity to study him. Peering. Searching.

Because surely, even with an identical twin, one couldn't
truly be . . . identical, carrying oneself with the same art-
less charm and grace as this man across the ballroom.

At every turn, the gentleman was approached by guest
after guest.

In all those instances mamas and papas thrust their
daughters closer to him.

Through it all, the gentleman remained gracious, bowing over each hand, making each young lady feel as though she were somehow special.

Annoyance settled in her stomach, because Cailin knew what it was to be made to feel special by that gentleman.

Her fingers reflexively formed balls at her sides, and even through the fabric of her gloves, she felt the bite of her nails.

For there could be no doubting or disputing that this dashing gentleman, capable of charming a wax candle out of its flame, was in fact the same man who'd come to her cottage and sought to coax her into going to London.

The duchess settled in at Cailin's side, and together they followed the gentleman's slow turn about the room. "That is Lord Courtland, His Grace, the Duke of St. James. He recently received the title after his father passed. The duke's father was one of *your* father's . . . reprobate friends, something of a rogue. More than a rogue, really. A rake."

Cailin whipped her focus back over to the gentleman, currently bowing over the hand of some other lady. Whatever he said in that moment made the young woman blush and smile, and the mama at her side clasped her hands happily as though she'd secured a future bridegroom for her daughter. "I don't . . . understand," she said carefully.

"I know. It is uncanny, is it not? The resemblance between them," the duchess said. "Your father always had a soft spot for the late duke's children, and he knew Lord Keir's desire to work . . . a desire the previous duke would have never countenanced. Lord Keir couldn't be more different from his father." With a beguiling, crooked grin, Her Grace lingered her attention on the charming figure. "St. James's reputation, however, precedes him . . ." Lydia paused, clearly weighing her words. "Something of a rake in his . . . pursuits, he's more similar to his late father than Lord Keir."

"So he's a scoundrel?" Cailin asked bluntly. As in the manner of man capable of feeding a woman lies and charming her . . . not unlike the stranger who'd visited her in Staffordshire.

She balled her hands hard enough that her fingers ripped through the fabric of her gloves.

"Many would say so. Not that *your* father would pass judgment too much, given his own history," Lydia added wryly. "Geoffrey wouldn't entertain a match between you and the young rascal, per se, but he has always supported the boys."

The boys? There was nothing boyish about the stranger across the room, tall and dashing and wearing a dangerously wicked smile. "My father has no worries on that score," Cailin said under her breath. "I've no wish to marry the duke." Or anyone else for that matter.

Lydia either failed to hear or deliberately ignored Cailin's sentiments on the wedded state, continuing on with her story about the Balfour family.

"It wasn't until their father's passing that your father employed Lord Keir."

As the duchess proceeded on a lengthy list of all the ways in which the gentlemen were antitheses of one another, Cailin narrowed her eyes, focusing them upon the powerful lord.

No, Lord Keir couldn't be any more different. Completely different. As in a completely different gent altogether.

". . . one was always precocious and the other more serious . . ."

"Oh, I'd wager I know the precocious one," Cailin muttered.

The duchess paused briefly in her telling. "What was that?"

"I was just saying . . ." Cailin tripped over her explanation. "I'd wager it was difficult knowing one from the other."

"Indeed," Lydia agreed. "Near impossible. Why the duke . . ."

As Her Grace went on, Cailin gnashed her teeth. Near impossible, her left foot.

Why, the bounder had lied to her.

About his name.

About his identity.

For the frosty fellow whom she'd steered into one of her father's empty rooms yesterday bore no actual resemblance, in the ways that mattered, to . . . to . . . this *duke*.

"Would you care for an introduction with the duke?" the duchess ventured, and Cailin started.

She looked blankly at her father's wife.

The other woman lowered her voice. "Your father might not approve of a match." Lydia flashed a sly smile and leaned in. "But you know what they say . . . reformed rogues do make the best husbands. Should you like a formal intro—"

"No!" Cailin exclaimed, loud enough to attract glances.

It was a reminder, and an unnecessary one at that, that her father and his wife would eventually expect Cailin to wed. Even as they'd both been gracious and generous and warm toward her, the duchess's comment was a reminder: ultimately, Cailin was a burden. Because she couldn't stay underfoot here forever. "I . . ." She should accept that introduction, just as if she was a proper, dutiful daughter; she should consider marrying. But God help her, she couldn't bring herself to think of that future for herself.

And certainly not the stifling existence that would come with her being *a duchess*.

"No," she murmured. "That will not be necessary."

The duchess hesitated.

She wanted to insist. Undoubtedly, she regretted even asking and not simply coordinating that introduction.

"Please, you needn't keep me company all night," she assured her step-mother. The last thing she cared to be was what she'd always been—to her brothers, to the mother who'd lost her life birthing her, and now the duke and duchess—a burden. Not when Lydia—as she insisted Cailin refer to her—had been so very kind.

"Would you like to accompany me—"

"No!" As much as she appreciated Lydia's willingness to take Cailin under her wing and squire her about, she didn't wish to be on display any more than she already was. "That is, thank you, but I find myself preferring . . . my own company."

Her Grace leaned down and kissed Cailin on the cheek, an open and touching display of affection, and that support sent a wave of emotion through her. "You are much like me, my dear. I shall be close," she promised, and then hastened over to converse with several of the distinguished noble guests.

Cailin brought her attention once more to the Duke of St. James.

*Not* Lord Keir.

As he spoke, Cailin's gaze continued to return to the duke. Not because he was a duke, and certainly not because he was a gentleman whom she had any romantic feelings for. Rather, she remained unable to shake the niggling feeling of doubt about the man who was an identical image of Lord Keir.

And for the first time that night, she found herself intrigued.

It had been inevitable.

Following the beating he'd been dealt in Staffordshire, Courtland had known the time would come when he'd be formally introduced to Bentley's daughter.

It looked increasingly like this would be the night.

From where he stood with Lord and Lady Chatterley as they extolled the virtues of their pleasingly full-figured daughter, he made every show of attending that never-ending enumeration. All the while, he attempted to hide behind the taller-than-most Lord Chatterley, so as to avoid the intent stares fixed on him by Cailin Audley and the Duchess of Bentley.

At various times in his life, Courtland had been discovered in any number of uncomfortable situations: there'd been the time he'd stolen into the empty offices of one of his instructors at Oxford and got caught sneaking the scholarly fellows' scientific periodicals.

Or then, years later, there'd been the time he was found in the bed of his latest mistress—by the lady's husband.

None of those discoveries, however, had been as dangerous or disastrous as this looming one now: Miss Cailin Audley was watching him.

And closely.

Not in the way he was accustomed to, by ladies who stared on with seductive eyes and covetous interest—for his title, of course. It was always about his title.

Even the length between him and the lady studying him did little to conceal that all-too-familiar suspicion in Miss Cailin Audley's expression.

She knew.

On the heel of that came a swift rejection of the very thought.

Why, it was impossible.

She could not know.

It was merely fear and horror at even the prospect of bringing further shame to Keir.

He was quite fine with whatever gossips had to say about him and his reputation. They'd spoken freely about him over the years. All those other instances, however, had involved Courtland and his reputation; one that could always be salvaged. After all, even facing down a mountain of debt and an uncertain financial future and fate, there was always salvation awaiting a duke.

The world was a good deal less tolerant and forgiving of a duke's younger brother; a self-made man, once employed as a nobleman's man of affairs and now in need of new work . . . as Courtland had been wholly unsuccessful speaking to the benevolent duke.

Suddenly, he had an overwhelming urge to leave. In fact, he wished to avoid the whole damned affair. The sole reason he'd come had been that talk with Bentley. A meeting he'd promised Keir he'd make happen. Alas, the duke had been disinterested in both discussing the situation and leaving the festivities. Having failed in that endeavor, the wisest course was to return home.

Particularly with Cailin Audley eyeing him the way she did now.

". . . Given all that," Lady Chatterley preened, "I trust you will see our Beatrix is—"

"If you will excuse me," he said, bowing hastily and making his excuses before the indiscreet pair could attempt to maneuver him into a damned marriage. Courtland made a beeline across the room, skirting other dogged mamas and papas with their daughters between them, angling for a meeting.

Courtland made his way to his sister Hattie. He'd become somewhat adept at evading marriage-minded families seeking the title "duchess" for their daughters.

Eventually he'd have to see to the matter of making a match and saving his family and their finances, but this night, with that entirely too-clever lady watching him, would not be the one.

Courtland reached his sister. Buried behind a gothic novel as she invariably was, oblivious to his arrival, it didn't appear she would object much to their leaving.

The women in the row behind her and at the end of the row beside her all leaned toward him hopefully.

"Ahem."

When Hattie merely turned the page and continued her reading, Courtland slid onto the seat beside her. "Let's go."

That managed to get her attention. Hattie looked up, for the first time that night, with curiosity brimming from behind her spectacles. "Who have you offended?" The word "now" hovered unspoken, and yet clear, on the end of his sister's question.

He felt his ears go hot. "No one." Not yet.

At her dubious look, he shifted on the entirely too-small, miserable, green-upholstered side chair. "I haven't."

Hattie snorted and went back to reading. With her eyes moving quickly over the page and her silence extended, it became apparent she'd no intention of budging.

"You don't even want to be here," he insisted.

"On the contrary, big brother. I'm enjoying myself immensely."

She was?

He searched for some hint of sarcasm from his notoriously droll sister, but ironically this time found . . . none. Only truth.

"You are enjoying yourself here?" Either way . . . "There is no reason you can't continue your reading at home. Now, if you would . . ." He stood.

And remained standing there, with his sister firmly in her seat. All the while, every nearby stare, and not-so-nearby stare, went to Courtland.

Oh, bloody hell.

He resisted the urge to tug at his cravat.

Courtland promptly fell back into the chair he'd previously vacated. "Why?"

And that question really contained so many within it: why was she so contrary? Why would she not let him quit this affair? Why could she not just continue reading at home, in their family's run-down gardens—anywhere that wasn't here?

"Because you want to leave, and I find that interesting, Courtland."

Presented with that honesty, Courtland closed his eyes briefly. "God, you are insufferable."

She smiled, dimpling her right cheek. "Yes, and you oft told me you preferred that to subservient and obedient."

"Did I say that?" he asked. "I don't recall."

"You know you did."

Yes, he did. Back when he'd found her weeping in the stables because their cur of a father had lambasted her for being a free spirit who wouldn't shut her mouth and keep her opinions and thoughts to herself. She'd been just seven.

And any other time, he'd have welcomed her shows of rebellion.

Courtland stole another glance across the room and found Miss Suspicious-Audley staring baldly back.

This, however, was decidedly not one of those times.

"You won't"—*help me*—"leave?" he tried once more.

"I absolutely will not." Hattie glanced up from her reading once more, and a mischievous glimmer sparked in her eyes. "Why, the evening has just gotten enjoyable."

So there'd be no salvation from his sister that day. She'd make him stay and suffer through the attention being paid his way by the mistrustful Miss Audley. "Traitor." Courtland yanked at one of Hattie's ringlets.

Laughing, the eldest of his sisters swatted at his hand. "Now, shoo. You have women to woo, do you not?"

Of course, she meant because he was a notorious rogue in London. When, in actuality, she wasn't so far from the mark. He needed a bride.

His sister glanced up, and gone was her earlier sisterly teasing, replaced by a stricken expression. "I wasn't suggesting you are like Father," she said in hushed tones. Hattie snapped her book closed. "That wasn't my intention at all."

It was a testament to her devotion as a sister that she was upset enough at the prospect of having hurt him that she would quit reading her romance novel.

"You must know that I'd only accept you having the grand love of Emily and Valancourt, brother."

"I take it this is someone I am supposed to know."

Hattie rolled her eyes. "You would be the only one who does not. Emily and Valancourt from *The Mysteries of Udolpho*. Theirs was the greatest of loves that triumphed over all." It never ceased to amaze him that any of his sisters had maintained the dream of love and romance. "You must have that, or nothing at all."

With their finances what they were, it appeared increasingly as though it was to be "nothing at all." "I will take your concerns under advisement," he drawled.

Hattie stuck her tongue out.

"What was that for?"

"As though I cannot detect droll sarcasm, Courtland. You forget I am the master of droll sarcasm." Hattie gave a dismissive little flutter of her fingers. "Now, really this time: off you go." With that dismissal, she again opened her book, raised it before her eyes, and promptly left Courtland to his own devices.

Muttering a curse, Courtland took off. Careful to stay on the fringes of the ballroom, he avoided those seeking an audience. Born the son of a duke, with the whole world knowing that illustrious fate that one day awaited him, evading people had been one of the skills he'd acquired through the years. He put those efforts to work now, slipping and weaving about until he'd put the ballroom behind him, and found his way along the quieter corridors.

Reaching the duke's notorious billiards room, Courtland let himself in. Doused largely in darkness but for a handful of sconces, the empty quiet beckoned.

He'd come here often, when Courtland and his family had been invited guests of the Duke of Bentley. The last time he'd entered this room was when his father had died and he came to request help with employment for Keir.

It had been a request Courtland's own father should have made on his younger son's behalf, and never would have. But with Keir's social awkwardness and order of birth as spare, their father had held about the same regard for Keir as he had for his daughters—none.

Now, Courtland headed across the same room in which he'd secured Keir's beloved post and availed himself of a bottle of brandy, a snifter, and a stick mounted on the wall. Carrying his provisions over to the side of the table, Courtland set the items down. After he'd poured himself a drink and taken a long swallow, a much-welcome swallow, he exchanged the glass for the triangle frame and arranged the balls.

Aside from the skills he'd acquired as a master evader, he'd perfected the ability of hiding. Similar skills, but also altogether different.

After he'd arranged the balls, Courtland grabbed the cue, and bringing the stick into position, he let it fly.

*Crack.*

That satisfying *thunk* of ball striking ball filled the otherwise quiet of the duke's billiards room, the sound of it a welcome and calming one.

The matter of his family's finances increasingly required

his attention, and given the dire straits their disgraceful father had left the Balfours in, there were few options that would get them out of their situation. To date, Courtland had catalogued personal artifacts that mattered to his siblings, sorting through what items he could part with. He'd studded out his best mount. Unlike his father before him, he'd even scheduled regular meetings with his tenants, advising them on the cost of their crops so that they might together maximize the profits coming from the land. But Courtland could meet with every last one of those hardworking men until the cows came home, and it wouldn't be nearly enough to drain the new fields or see to the repairs required of those same tenants' homes.

Courtland *did* know that the lifeblood of an estate for both him and his family rested in the ones working those lands. Where his father—God rot his soul—may have neglected both, Courtland hadn't been so self-absorbed. The problem was, righting years of neglect and converting any of those properties into a profit remained nigh impossible tasks.

He didn't have the head his brother did for numbers, and being a duke, he could not dabble in trade and business . . . not when it would reflect upon his sisters and impact the respectable matches they might make. Or to be more precise, respectable matches they *wouldn't* make were the world to discover a duke had dared to work.

The *ton*, believing work to be beneath a peer, would only ever shun a lord who dared sully his hands. It was snobbish and foolish, and yet he was bound by those strictures. At least for his sisters. Why, even Keir's post for Bentley had first been met with shock and whispers . . . which eventually receded. That was a luxury, however, afforded his younger brother, as the spare. Such leniency would never be shown a duke.

Courtland assessed his shot and drew his stick back.

The Balfours' greatest hope, the most obvious opportunity to save them from their situation was—*marriage*.

His shot went wide.

He paused to rub a hand along the back of his head.

Except it was the wrong distracted gesture, only conjuring up thoughts of a not-so-long-ago time, when his own desire had got the better of him, and in embracing the duke's daughter, he'd cost Keir his employment.

Perhaps he'd merely imagined that keen way in which she'd studied him?

Perhaps it had been nothing more than his own guilt, and the fear of discovery . . .

Shrugging out of his jacket, Courtland tossed the garment along the back of a nearby leather button sofa.

Rolling his shoulders to rid them of the tension, he collected the cue once more and devoted himself to his next shot.

Leaning over the velvet table, he closed an eye and focused his attention on the white ball positioned dead center.

*Click.*

Courtland went stock-still.

"Tell me," that bell-like voice drawled from behind him. "As I'm new to the ways of your world, you must enlighten me as to which is a greater offense? Stealing about one's host's home and availing oneself of that same host's brandy and billiards table? Or lying about one's identity . . . *Lord Keir?*"

Courtland's heart dropped, making a swift descent to his boots.

"Or should I say, Your Grace?"

*Oh, bloody hell.*

She'd found him.

And worse, she'd found him *out*.

# Chapter 7

Cailin had been the recipient of enough stares and had been met with enough less-than-discreet gossip this night to know Polite Society had been scandalized by the presence of the Duke of Bentley's by-blow.

But this . . . tracking down a powerful duke at her father's ball and challenging him outright was surely the manner of boldness that would have left both Polite and Impolite society horrified.

The gentleman straightened slowly, not unlike the way he had when she'd greeted him with a rifle outside her cottage.

"I don't know what you are—"

"Do not." She jabbed a finger into his chest, cutting off that effortless lie slipping from his tongue. After watching him as she had that night, having been as near to him as she had in Staffordshire, she knew this was in fact the man who'd come to fetch her, and who'd filled her ears and head with all the wonders awaiting her here in London; and after the misery of these past weeks, that was enough to make her wish for a rifle to train on him all over again. "Just . . .

do not lie. Again," she added. Furthermore, after her very short meeting with his identical twin, there could be no doubting the pair were . . . anything but identical.

"I've not lied to you." The gentleman bristled with such indignation she momentarily wavered.

Cailin peered more closely at him, taking in his tousled, loose flaxen curls, cropped at his nape. Those lips. Lips that had—*Do not think of that kiss*. She shifted her attention over the harsh, angular planes of his face, the bold slash of his aquiline nose. The slightest cleft in his chin. What if she were wrong?

"I can certainly see the reason for your confusion," he allowed, while she continued searching for the truth of his identity. The tones he adopted were soothing, almost placating, and decidedly nothing like the ones belonging to the brusque gentleman whom she'd tugged into a parlor at her father's earlier that day. "As an identical twin, this is not the first time I've been mistaken for my brother."

And then . . . the gentleman before her smiled.

That was it. His roguish, charming, and easy grin that her father's former man of affairs couldn't have mustered that day to save his career, let alone his life.

"It is *you*," she said, wagging a finger under his nose.

His smile wobbled a bit at the corners, and it was as though, as a man of perpetually good cheer, he resisted with everything the loss of that ease and amusement. "I'm afraid I do not understand, Miss Audley."

Cailin widened her eyes. "Ah-hah! I *knew* it. We have never even been introduced, and yet you should identify me by name."

"You *are* the duke's daughter," he said dryly, without so much as missing a beat. "And as a guest of His and Her Grace, it was not so very difficult to deduce the presence of the young lady beside them."

She wrinkled her nose. *Drat*.

No doubt, he and his brother had extensive years of experience at playing whatever game of pretend they had, duping the unsuspecting . . . which she'd been.

Rankled by that reminder, she scowled at him. "I met my father's man of affairs this week," she said. "He was decidedly not the same gentleman to come and try and collect me in Staffordshire, and you"—she jabbed another gloved index finger—"are decidedly *him*."

Shifting on his makeshift seat on the edge of the billiards table, the young duke folded his arms at his chest.

All the while he elegantly reclined there, he eyed Cailin. Suspiciously? Warily? Concernedly?

If the nob had even a smidge of a brain in his head, the sentiment was decidedly the latter.

"Nothing to say, Your Grace?" she jeered.

"Miss Audley." This time, when the powerful nobleman spoke, he did so with a chilliness and reserve that more matched the frosty fellow she'd maneuvered into one of her father's many parlors, the brusque tones belonging to a peer below a prince. "I don't know how to account for the certainty of your opinion; however, it is an erroneous one."

For the first time since she'd caught sight of him that evening, her confidence flagged.

"Though I expect," he continued in that cool, clipped way, "that it is humbling to find yourself both in the wrong and incorrect about your opinion."

Humbling?

In the wrong *and* incorrect about her opinion?

Her *opinion*?

Oh, this was really quite enough.

Shooting a hand out and up, she pushed the curls away from his noble brow, revealing a narrow, raised, thin, puckered scar just at his hairline. A thrill of triumph went through her. "Tell me, do both you and your identical twin brother also have matching scars, Your Grace?"

A dull flush—a guilty one—marred his harsh cheekbones.

"I *knew* it," she exclaimed, as on the heel of her victory came a host of other sentiments. Humiliation. Embarrassment. Hurt.

She'd been . . . lied to.

He'd duped her in the most spectacularly awful fashion.

It wasn't the first time she'd found herself lied to by a blasted man. A memory of her former sweetheart slipped in, dark where the duke was light. Brooding where His Grace was a model of charm. One a workaday man, while the other possessed the most elevated of titles. Both, however, had proven alike in one regard—each had deceived her.

She sank back on her heels. "I knew it," she repeated.

Only she'd not really known. She'd not known for certain until this very instant that the man who'd visited her in Staffordshire, who'd kissed her so passionately, had been lying about his identity.

Lord Keir—except that wasn't correct. *His Grace* brought his hands up in a slow, exaggerated, and . . . *mocking* clap! "Brava, you've figured it all out. How *proud* you must be."

"*You* are upset?" Cailin choked out.

"Do you think I should not be?" he retorted. "I'm the one who took a beating and whose brother got sacked, so if either of us is put out with the other, Miss Audley, then I would say I am decidedly the wronged party." With that, he stepped around her, grabbed his half-empty drink, and lifted his glass in salute.

As he drank, she studied him, and then it hit her with the weight of a thousand bricks falling on her. He wasn't just perturbed . . . "*You* are annoyed with *me*."

"Correction"—his littlest finger came off the snifter, and he pointed it at her—"I'm annoyed with the situation I now find myself in because of my dealings with you."

She bristled. "Need I point out that had you not gone and passed yourself off as your brother, and he'd seen to his own business, then neither of us would be in this situation."

"No, you needn't," he said tightly. "I'm well aware of my family's circumstances." He dropped a hip on the table once more. "I've got a brother sans employment. Tell me, Miss Audley, what are your changed circumstances, hmm?"

Cailin paused, and she faltered. As a sister with three brothers to whom she was devoted, and for whom she'd do anything, she could commiserate with this man who was upset on his brother's behalf. She knew what it was to wish to spare one's sibling pain, and yet—

*What are you doing?*

He was, after all, the one who'd been playing a child's game with their identical appearances.

Why, she'd not feel bad. Cailin found her footing. "Well, then perhaps you shouldn't have gone about lying to me. About your identity." She took a furious step forward. "And furthermore, mayhap your brother would have best been served coming to speak with me himself."

"He wouldn't have." He grimaced. "Though, in fairness, he couldn't have bungled it more." His high brow wrinkled, leaving several contemplative creases. "Or he could have . . . just in a different way."

Cailin cocked her head, staring at him as he appeared to . . . argue with himself. It was peculiar, and . . . even strangely endearing.

Strangely endearing?

What in tarnation was she thinking? Even so, that question was compelled by curiosity. "How would it have been different?"

This time, he tipped his head, matching her movements in the opposite way.

"It is just you said, 'He could have bungled it even more, just in a different way.'"

"My brother is blunt. He wouldn't have . . ." A bold flush suffused his cheeks.

"Attempted to seduce me?"

His Grace tossed his arms up and cursed both blackly and impressively. "I did *not* attempt to seduce you. Is that what you said?" he demanded.

She choked. "*Of course* not."

"Because I didn't. I even asked permission, and you kissed me—"

"I know I did," she said in a furious whisper, glancing about.

"Which I obviously should not have done," he added.

The rich wealth of regret in that pronouncement shouldn't have needled . . . and yet, it did.

"Well, that makes two of us," she said, wishing she'd a greater verbal retort than *that*. "Good evening, Your Grace." Yanking her skirts aside, she marched angrily toward the exit. The moment she reached the front of the room, she grabbed the handle—

And then . . . stopped.

She did have bruised pride and hurt feelings. She did feel betrayed.

But she was not so very self-centered that she could simply dismiss the gentleman's concern for . . . his brother. His brother, who'd proven a surly, curt fellow.

Cailin slowly turned back, even as she *knew* she'd regret doing so. Even as she recognized she should leave immediately and cut all dealings with a man who'd lied to her once. After all, once a deceiver, *always* a deceiver.

And those perfidious sorts could only ever bring hurt.

From over where he still lounged at the billiards table, he eyed her circumspectly.

It was a peculiar concept . . . that he, an all-powerful duke, should be nervous around her. Certainly it should have been the other way around. And perhaps it would have been, had they not spoken about museums and her interests and passions. Even if those discussions had been born of lies and a need to lure her to London on his brother's behalf.

She paused. "And it . . . matters very much to you about your brother's work?"

His hard lips, those same lips that had taken hers in a kiss that had curled her toes and that she dreamed about still, tipped up in a wry grin. "Do you think there's a reason I should not care about my brother, Miss Audley?"

She was Miss Audley.

"Was I only Cailin because you were attempting to ingratiate yourself to me, and sought to break down my defenses that day?"

"You were."

She gripped her toes into the soles of her slippers so

hard her arches ached. Cailin asked a different question.
"Why did you come?" she ventured hesitantly. What duke
would voluntarily take on the chore of journeying into the
far-flung corners of Staffordshire, to the Cheadle mining
town, to meet . . . with her.

The duke's jaw clenched, and a muscle rippled along
that prominent bone. He didn't answer for a moment, and
she suspected he didn't intend to.

"My brother is . . . a different fellow," he finally spoke,
grudgingly, hesitancy there in his tone. "Keir is loyal and
hardworking and great with numbers, and yet he's . . . not
great or even very good or even slightly good at his interactions with people."

Ah. And now it made sense.

Unwittingly, Cailin started to drift over, compelled closer.
Until she registered the path she'd made back to him.

She stopped, several paces away. "You thought you might
succeed in convincing my brother and me to journey to London where Lord Keir would fail?"

"I thought I'd have greater success at it." He flashed a
wry grin. "That is, certainly greater than I did." His smile
dissolved, and she silently lamented the loss of it, preferring him grinning.

The men in Cheadle, the men in her family, even her
former sweetheart, had all been brooders. Dark, heavy fellows whose smiles were rarer than sunshine in England.

"My brother loves his work. He takes pride in it, and it is
not brotherly pride when I say he was deuced good at what
he did for your father . . . though there is, of course, pride,
too." The Duke tensed his mouth. "And now he's without the
one thing that brings him a sense of accomplishment, and
that he enjoys far more than he enjoys people."

Oh, hell.

Cailin didn't want that answer to matter. She didn't want
to care about the reason the duke had done . . . what he'd
done. And she certainly didn't want to have found the one
nobleman who didn't turn his nose up at working men.
Why, even her own duke of a father had desperately wished

for Rafe to return and have nothing to do with the Cheadle mines. Her fingers caught the sides of her dress, and she crumpled the satin. "I . . . would you like me to speak to . . . the duke?" Cailin still couldn't bring herself to call the duke her father. It was still too new.

"No."

That response came immediately and without hesitation.

"No?" she asked. "For someone who speaks so of the importance of his brother's employment and love of it, I'd expect you'd not turn down such an offer." Mayhap he was a good deal less supportive of his brother's history of working after all.

"If I thought it would make a difference, I would have asked Satan himself to meet with your father." He rolled his drink back and forth between his large, tan hands. They didn't look like the soft hands of a duke, but rather those of a man of power, unafraid to shuck his gloves—even in the middle of another duke's ball—and use them. "But I know your father will not relent, because I attempted to speak with him this evening." She jerked her focus back to his face and forced herself to attend a matter of vastly more import than the sheer size of his hands. "Despite my promise to my brother to speak with the duke, even as I knew my own efforts were in vain . . ." He held her eyes squarely. "Because I know your father, and I know noblemen, Miss Audley," he said impatiently. "Not a single one of them would dare employ a servant who'd been linked to one's daughter . . . even if just out of a misunderstanding. Bentley believes Keir attempted to seduce you, and even if he didn't believe that, the possibility of that rumor getting out is something he will not risk."

How confident he was. "Ah, but I have not spoken with him." That is, not about Lord Keir and his work. "I will remind him that it was a misunderstanding and ask that he reinstate your brother to his previous post."

"It won't matter."

Why, he didn't believe she was capable of changing her father's mind. "You are wrong, Your Grace."

The young duke lifted his snifter, toasting her. "Then, I would never be happier to be proven so."

"You shall see."

"*We* shall, won't we?"

Cailin should leave and return to the festivities. It was her debut, a *small* affair held in her honor. As such, the crowd would notice she'd gone missing, and worse . . . Rafe and Edwina would know it as well . . . and the last thing Cailin needed was for Rafe to go hunting for her and find her shut away with the duke.

Still, she lingered.

The duke watched her from under hooded eyes.

"What is *your* given name?" she asked.

"Courtland."

*Courtland*, she repeated it in her mind, silently testing those syllables. It suited him. Far more than Keir. "I'll have you know, Courtland, I'm not doing this because of you. I remain furious with you still for deceiving me. But I do appreciate that your brother required help with his assignment, and I would like to help see he is restored to his post."

He eyed her for a long moment. "You really intend to help me?"

And it occurred to her, he didn't fully trust her pledge to speak to the Duke of Bentley. Oddly, she found herself more curious than outraged. "Should I not?"

"Given the nature of our meeting, I'd trust you'd happily tell me to go hang."

"Oh, I'll *still* happily tell you that, but that doesn't mean I won't help where I can."

Courtland slid his gaze over her face, his brow furrowed like one fixed on solving an impossible riddle. "Why?"

Why, indeed? And the truth of it was, she couldn't quite say how much had to do with her, as a woman from a working family, understanding and appreciating how important his brother's assignment was to him. And how much was because . . . of him, Courtland. A loyal brother, who despite his lofty status still supported his working-class brother's role as servant. "Are you unaccustomed to people helping for no reason than because they wish to?"

"I am. That is not the way of Polite Society."

How sadly matter-of-fact he was. "Well, that is the way of *mining* towns, Your Grace." In fact, she'd failed to properly appreciate those displays of support that came for no other reason than because the men and women there inherently believed people helped others.

"I find I prefer the way of the mining towns," he murmured.

She wrinkled her brow, certain she'd misheard. "Your Grace?" For what nobleman would speak to preferring any aspect of the world she'd left behind to his own lofty lifestyle?

"Courtland," he supplied, ignoring her query. "If we are partnering to help my brother secure his previous post, I believe we might use one another's given names."

"Do you mean our real given names, Courtland?" she asked dryly, and wonder of wonders, an adorable color filled his cheeks. A blush from an all-powerful duke. Unwilling to end the uneasy truce between them, Cailin stuck her palm out.

Courtland stared at her gloved fingers so long she released an exasperated sigh and grabbed his right hand, vigorously pumping it up and down. "This is another way of mining towns. Men and women who strike a partnership shake on it."

"Partners?"

"Partners," she vowed. "Just until we secure Lord Keir's post."

And the moment they'd sealed their arrangement, Cailin took her leave, happy to prove him wrong.

# Chapter 8

B y my estimation, barring no change to your circumstances, Your Grace, you find yourself facing debt collectors stripping your rooms bare and then, depending on their generosity . . . a debtor's prison."

Courtland's stomach muscles seized, and his fingers curled reflexively onto the edge of his desk, biting into the mahogany and leaving little crescent marks there. His own fate was secondary, though if he were being truthful, the idea of being sent away—especially for debts that were largely his late father's—left him equally nauseated and enraged. He forced a smile and responded with a dose of sarcasm to Higgans's enumeration of his fate: "Ah, why don't you tell me like it really is, Higgans."

The tall, bearded fellow lifted his head from his notebook and looked up. "I . . . just did, Your Grace." There was a question there in the young man's voice. "I mentioned debtor's prison and—"

"Yes. Yes. I was being sarcastic. Making a jest," he said when his man of affairs continued to stare back confusedly. With a sigh, Courtland shook his head. "My father's creditors," he said, bringing them back to the details of his financial affairs.

"Two of them have agreed to an extension. Three of them have not. However, I've managed to secure the end of the Season, at which point you will be expected to pay . . ." Humming to himself, Higgans directed his focus at the page and skimmed his fingertip across his books. "Ten thousand pounds."

His stomach sank. Oh, bloody hell.

"And then the others," Higgans went on in between his off-key hum, "they'll allow through the summer." Higgans glanced up with a wide smile, as though he expected some manner of praise for that reprieve that wasn't really a reprieve.

Pressing his fingertips together, Courtland stared across the top of them at the man of affairs whose hire Keir had arranged upon their father's passing and the sacking of the late duke's thieving, drunkard servant. "At which point?" he brought himself to ask.

"At which point, you're looking at"—Higgans lifted his right palm—"debtor's prison." His left hand came up, so he sat there with his hands outstretched like the scales of justice. "Or paying off your debts and not."

At present, Courtland was firmly in the "or not" column.

How casually he spoke about the fact that Courtland was two feet in dun territory with the shite climbing quick—and threatening to drown him.

Failure to resolve their finances would see them ruined, all in different ways; his dowerless sisters wouldn't make a match. In fact, as it was, if any respectable fellow was to court Hattie or Ellie or any of them, they'd ultimately discover the late duke had pissed away his own daughters' dowries on whores and mistresses.

"And the other properties?" Courtland brought himself to ask, even as he knew.

"They are . . . not profitable, Your Grace. They are, as you are aware, in a state of disrepair. The most hopeful one being on the fringe of Staffordshire."

He sat upright. "Staffordshire, you say?" he asked quickly.

Higgans stared perplexedly at him. "Er . . . yes. I do believe I mentioned as much." The servant rustled through his papers and pages, speaking to himself as he did. ". . . Where is it . . . I know it is here somewhere . . . where are—ah." The young man brightened. "Here it is. Yes, we spoke about it briefly. Very briefly. You were not interested, however, as the properties include a mining property that is currently unstaffed and would require a full team of workers; and then even at which point, who is to say how profitable the quarry is."

Who, indeed?

And given the deuced bad luck he'd had with everything that had been left him, one could be certain that there was nothing more than mud and rock, and not the valuable kind, at the bottom of that quarry.

"What say you, Higgans?"

His man of affairs scratched at his black beard. "What say I about what?"

As Higgans was second only to Keir in his inability to read social moments, Courtland explained. "What say you about solving this situation?"

"Ah." The servant's eyes widened, his dark eyebrows lifting slightly above the wire rims of his spectacles. Higgans grimaced. "I regret to say all further appointments to the modiste for Lady Hattie must be suspended," and there was more than a heavy wealth of regret underlying that admission, indicating the other man did care for this family he now served. "Of course," Higgans went on, matter-of-fact business once more; "that will merely ebb the flow of further funds you do not have; it will not provide you with the monies you need to address your existing debt."

"My father's," he gritted out.

Let there be no mistake that that old cur was the one behind the sorry state the Balfours found themselves.

Higgans doffed his spectacles, and tugging a kerchief free from his pocket, he dusted off the frames and returned them to his face. "Which you inherited," Higgans reminded him.

As if Courtland needed a reminder.

"No. No. I'm aware." Courtland motioned with his hand. "Please, continue."

"I am a master with numbers, alas not a magician with them. I . . . could inventory the remaining articles available to you." As in, available to sell.

"Thank you," Courtland said. "I would . . . appreciate it." Even as he'd hate it. Not because he had an affinity for anything in this godforsaken household, which his father had favored above all his other properties. Rather, because it represented Courtland's failure to fix . . . any of this.

Slowly, carefully, Higgans removed his spectacles again. "If I might make . . . another suggestion."

Warning bells went off. He knew what was coming. Even before he nodded and the other man spoke.

"It would . . . behoove you to find a—"

"That will be all!" he said quickly, interrupting that unwanted suggestion; the same one his father had no doubt been given years ago when he'd made the decision to wed Courtland's mother.

Collapsing into the folds of his seat, Courtland sighed and rubbed a hand back and forth across his eyes.

The servants who remained on, whom they'd been able to keep on, were endlessly loyal. But the minute items were marched out, the world would take note, and questions would be raised, and the gossip would stir, and—

"As much discretion as you are able to manage in . . . handling this, I would be grateful."

"Absolutely, Your Grace," Higgans said solemnly. "My fealty is to your family. Is there anything else you require, Your Grace?" he asked, the shuffling of papers and the snapping of his ledgers indicating that was the end of today's latest bad news.

Was there anything else Courtland required? A fortune. A miracle. "No, that is all, Higgans." Courtland stood.

Taking that as his cue, the wiry-thin fellow hopped up. "I am, of course, happy to serve, Your Grace."

Higgans's employment was a kindness Courtland hadn't deserved. A generosity extended by a young man who could certainly command a far greater salary, but who offered his services at a reduced rate because of his friendship with Keir.

Sketching a bow, Higgans let himself out.

The moment the panel had shut, Courtland sank into his seat and let loose a stream of black expletives. This was bloody—

His sister popped out from behind the curtains, and he startled.

"Bloody hell, Ellie!"

"I have it."

Courtland was already shaking his head. He didn't want to know. He—

"We shall find you a wife!"

He strangled on his spit, coughing violently. And he'd been proven correct once more. Ellie's thinking invariably portended disaster.

His sister immediately hopped up, and, joining him, she pounded Courtland hard between the shoulder blades.

"You need a wife, and we need a fortune."

"Are you suggesting . . . are you thinking to . . . make me a *fortune hunter*?" His voice came out garbled from his fit, caused by the horrifying, and also ruthless, proposal put forward by his youngest, most innocent sister.

Innocent.

She pointed her eyes skyward once more. "Not one of the ruthless sorts. Why, you'll fall in love first, of course. Make some lady love you. You are a duke and a rogue, so it shouldn't be all that hard."

His sister's was a mercenary proposal, and yet she spoke of love, which . . . well, which wasn't something that truly existed in marriages. At least, none that he'd witnessed in Polite Society. Husbands were unfaithful. Wives, too. The cycle of unhappy, unhealthy unions went on, as constant and steady as rain in England or afternoon tea.

Ellie settled a hand on his shoulder, and he glanced over.

She stared back with eyes wide and wise beyond her years. "This situation isn't going to fix itself, Courtland."

"No. It isn't."

And atop the empty coffers, there was now an unemployed Keir to worry about. Nothing short of Courtland . . . *marrying*—his mind twisted around even the thought of that word—wouldn't fix the situation they now found themselves in.

Marriage . . . he'd resisted it for years, first because he'd been content to live his rakish existence. And then . . . later, because of a fear he'd bungle the dukedom as badly as his father had and leave a wife as miserable as his own mother had been. After all, what other result could there be when there wasn't a single lady whom he could imagine spending the rest of his days with?

"*. . . Tell me, why do you expect the book should belong to one of my brothers? . . . Because it is so hard to believe that a woman should have an interest in fossils and lizards and minerals?*"

As that memory of his first meeting with Cailin flitted forward, he felt the stirrings of a smile.

A woman such as her was enough to make even the most committed bachelor forget his fear of that wedded state.

Given Courtland's state—a man with little to offer outside a title, Cailin Audley was certainly better off without.

"You're worrying about having to get married, aren't you?"

God, Ellie missed not a thing. The king's army didn't know what they were costing themselves by not allowing these ruthless little ladies within their ranks. "I'm trying to sort through Keir's situation," he said.

"So that you won't have to marry," Ellie shot back.

"No." In fairness, he'd not been worrying about it as much as lamenting his own many failings. Ones that put a lady like Cailin Audley beyond his reach.

Beyond his reach? He grimaced. Egads, what nonsense *was* this? He didn't want marriage to *any* woman. Entrancing Cailin Audley or not.

His sister gave him a look. "Do you really expect me to believe this doesn't have to do with you fearing marriage?"

"Just a small part, then," he allowed, because it was decidedly a good deal safer to leave it at that than so much as hint at his real musings. "But mostly I am focused on helping Keir."

"Hmph." Ellie elevated her chin a begrudging smidge. "I'll allow that, and *only* because I know you are a devoted brother. I will leave you to your thinking." With that, she hopped off and took herself out, leaving Courtland with the hell of this day and his sister's avowal—one that he decidedly did not deserve—reverberating in his mind.

# Chapter 9

The following morning, Cailin, eager to prove one duke wrong by exerting herself over a different duke, wasted no time in seeking an audience with her father.

And hers was an early morning meeting at that.

For after she'd left Courtland's side last evening, all hope of sleep had eluded her.

Even as she shouldn't have felt remorse or worry about the duke's brother, the fact had remained: she didn't want to be behind the reason a man had lost his employment. Work mattered, and it undoubtedly mattered more to the duke's younger brother, who had the privilege of being a duke's brother . . . without the very same lofty privileges that came with being a duke.

As such, after a brief night of restless sleep, she'd risen eager to resolve this entire situation, so that she could be done with the duke and his family—and this sense of guilt for his brother's changed circumstances.

Alas, it appeared putting the whole matter to rest wasn't going to be as easy as she'd anticipated. Or, if she wished to be more accurate, *bragged*. In fairness, she'd not believed she was bragging. She'd simply never doubted how this exchange could or would go.

"No," the duke said from behind his desk. "I am afraid not, Cailin."

Cailin frowned at her father. And it was more than a little annoying that Courtland, who'd been arrogantly confident in his opinion, should be proven correct on this.

"No?" she repeated when the duke continued to smile serenely back, as if he'd not just flat-out rejected what had been more a demand than a request on Cailin's part.

"I'm sorry," he said, and she didn't care that her father truly sounded sorry about the rejection.

That was it.

It was a moment before Cailin properly processed that her father, the duke, who'd so quickly declined the favor she'd put to him, had no intention of elaborating.

She gritted her teeth.

This bloody world, where women had so little say—no say—over decision-making and business and life on the whole.

The duke's smile slipped.

Good, he'd at last noted her annoyance.

"Come, my girl. Sit," he said gently. "It occurs to me that I was a bit blunt."

"And wrong," she added, coming the remainder of the way and sliding into one of those chairs he'd motioned to.

Her father sat back in the throne-like seat he occupied and steepled his fingers together. "Yes, well, I wouldn't go so far as to say all that."

She returned his smile. "Perhaps you wouldn't. I, however, would."

A blush splotched his cheeks.

Yes, she'd trusted he possessed the same confidence and arrogance of another certain duke, and being questioned in any way was a wholly foreign concept. Using his discomfiture to her advantage, Cailin pressed ahead.

"Was Lord Keir a good man of affairs to you?"

The duke opened his mouth, and then closed it. He did so a second time. "Why . . . yes."

With that capitulation, Cailin edged forward in her seat, her muslin skirts crunching noisily, and she pressed her advantage.

"I don't"—her father adjusted his skewed cravat slightly—"see that we need to speak about this, Cailin. You don't need to involve yourself in . . . this," he finished weakly.

"Why?" She winged a single eyebrow up. "Because I'm your daughter, or because I'm a woman."

His expression grew pained, and he glanced past her to the door, wishing for rescue? Or escape?

"Because . . . the matter is settled," he said when he'd returned his focus forward. He spoke with a finality that alluded to the end of this discussion. "I don't allow my servants the manner of misstep of which your brother accused him."

She pounced. "That is it exactly. Rafe accused him."

"Did anything . . . improper happen between the two of you?"

She paused, remembering a different man and a different kiss.

That brief hesitation cost her all the headway she'd been making.

"That is my point precisely."

"Nothing did happen between me and Lord Keir," she spoke with a vehemence that came altogether easy for the truth behind them. Cailin pressed her palms to the edge of his desk. "You have my word on that. If Lord Keir was the manner of servant you say that he was, then his firing is unfair to the both of you."

He wiped a hand over his furrowed brow. "Cailin," he said, his tone pained. "I appreciate that you are concerned about the gentleman's welfare; however, this is for the best."

"For whom?" She scoffed. "You? Because you needn't worry about gossips catching word of a story that isn't a story, and what of him?" A young gentleman who, by his brother's account, had struggled with social interactions in a way that had proven an impediment to him and his ability to gainfully secure employment.

"I am not saying it's fair, Cailin," he spoke mollifyingly, in a way that all of her brothers did, and it grated. "I am saying . . . it's settled . . . and it's . . . unfortunately, the way of the world."

This time, an air of finality upon that little speech.

It was decided.

He'd not change his mind.

"Thank you for your time." Cailin came to her feet stiffly. "That is really . . . all I came here seeking." She made to go.

Her father flinched. "Cailin," he said, and, hopeful she'd broken through this wall of propriety he was bound by, she faced him. "I do worry about your reputation, Cailin . . . I worry about your happiness. I want you to feel comfortable in this new world."

Unnerved, she sat back. Her mother had died giving birth to her, and as such, she'd never known a parent's concern or regard. She'd been so accustomed to only her brothers caring for her over the years. Having this . . . paternal figure worry after her was foreign, and perhaps five, ten, or even fifteen years ago she would have welcomed those sentiments. Being a grown woman now, she'd come to resent and regret all the male influences in her life attempting to coddle and protect her and keep her from making decisions. "I don't need you to worry about my reputation," she finally said. She'd no intention of marrying and certainly not a lord of the peerage. If she'd had her heart broken by a miner from Cheadle, what havoc might a charming lord in London wreak?

Once more, the rogue who'd brought about so much of this trouble came sliding back into her musings.

"I think you should have the full experience of a London Season," he began.

"I have no interest in a London Season," she cut him off. The hell she'd have this conversation. She'd allowed the ball introducing her to his world, not hers, but there'd be nothing beyond that. That was all she and Rafe had allowed. That's all she would agree to. "Now, if you'll excuse me?"

This time, as she left, he didn't try to stop her. And he certainly didn't change his mind and relent to what Cailin had asked. Because why should he? Why should he take into consideration what she was asking for, and what she knew to be best and just and right? Fury and frustration propelled her steps, and she walked briskly.

As she sailed through the door, a servant shut it behind his powerful employer.

"Calvin," she murmured, a hello and good morning for the servant. It was, after all, decidedly not his fault that the world was what it was here for her. In fact, his experience in Town was one that resonated far more with her.

"Miss Audley," the strapping fellow returned with a bow.

That was it: Miss Audley.

There were no casual conversations between her and him, or for that matter *any* servant. Unlike Staffordshire, where the villagers saw her as a social equal, because that was what she in fact was. She was a lady only by her birthright to the Duke of Bentley, and even so, she wasn't a true lady. Not really. Not to Polite Society.

*But neither will the servants speak to you as though you are the same as them . . .*

"May I fetch you anything, miss?" the footman asked haltingly, offering his assistance, when she didn't want to be served.

"No. I don't require anything, Calvin," she said softly.

Nothing but friendship and a sense of belongingness in this place where she could not find either.

The young man sketched a second ridiculously deep bow, low at the waist.

Suddenly stifled, feeling a great sense of pressure weighting her chest and suffocating her, she clawed at the bodice of her high-neck gown before she caught herself. And she took off, rushing through the halls, continuing on down long corridor after even longer corridor of plush, carpeted flooring.

Until she reached her rooms.

The moment she was inside, Cailin shoved the panel shut and leaned against it. Resting the back of her head, she set the door a-rattle.

Women had no place in society. Not really. That had been something she'd always been well aware of. Their responsibilities were different from those of the men who ruled the world.

And yet, as powerless as she'd known a woman's lot to be in Staffordshire, her existence there had been nothing like . . . this.

As a village woman, she'd run her own household and was involved in affairs at the mines, and tended hurt men, and had a voice.

Here . . . she was . . . invisible.

It was why the duke had been so confident that her offer to interfere on his brother's behalf would in fact go nowhere. Because he knew this world. This world Cailin did not.

And it chafed for so many reasons . . . the greatest being this new, grotesque understanding of life for ladies in the peerage. And not the least being the fact that she had to go to the other duke and explain what he'd known all along would happen—she'd failed. She'd failed in an endeavor that should not have even been a minor undertaking.

*But you don't really have to have that discussion with him to explain you were wrong and he was right.* And that his brother was still as unemployed this morn as he'd been yesterday and the day before, because of a misunderstanding caused by a well-meaning sibling.

Cailin chewed at her bottom lip, worrying that flesh.

Why, for that matter, her path needn't even cross with Courtland's again. He was a duke, and she one of Bentley's many bastards. There was no London Season for her, so it was not as though she'd run into him at *ton* events.

Cailin warred with herself. She closed her eyes and cursed into the quiet. "Damn it all."

That, however, was the coward's way. To never see the duke and tell him how spectacularly she'd failed. And explain to him the brother he worried after remained unemployed.

And she was many things . . . but she was decidedly not a coward.

Crossing over to the armoire, Cailin fetched a cloak from within, a deep sapphire muslin finer than any garment she'd ever donned, and prepared for her second meeting that day.

W ell?" that frantic, curt question cut across the most delicious dream Courtland had been enjoying; one that had included him and a delectable if tart-mouthed minx of a woman with full cheeks and even fuller lips. Lips he'd taken under his, in a kiss that had also brought down the ruin of his brother's livelihood and the loss of monies funding his sister's Season.

Just like that, the dream dissipated and the reality intruded.

"Can we perhaps speak about this at a godlier time?" Courtland mumbled.

"It's seventeen minutes past ten o'clock," his brother announced. Stalking across the room, Keir yanked the curtains wide, letting in a blinding flash of sunlight. "Certainly not early by any standards. I've been up for five and a half hours."

"That is barbaric." Wincing, Courtland groaned and put a hand over his eyes to blot the glare.

It didn't help.

Collecting a pillow, he buried it over his face. "Both the ungodly hour at which you insist on arising each day and your opening those damned curtains." The article muffled the steady footfalls of his approaching twin. "Need I point out that I was attending Bentley's ball and only just returned at thirty minutes past four?"

Keir yanked the pillow from Courtland's face. "If dancing and conversing are fatiguing you, then you need new pastimes, brother," Keir said with his usual bluntness. "Well?"

Courtland opened his mouth to continue their previous disagreement over the hours he kept, but then stopped himself. Rather, the unexpected glimmer of hope in his always-stoic brother's eyes stayed whatever Courtland had been about to say. With a sigh, he sat up and swung his legs over the side of the bed.

"I'm afraid . . . I did not have an opportunity to speak with the duke."

His brother's face fell, and in an instant Courtland's twin was transformed into the boy whose father had kicked his toy soldiers out of the neat, meticulous line he'd always loved assembling anything in.

"But hope is not lost."

Perhaps if he'd not just been dragged out of a deep slumber, he'd have been more careful than that.

As it was—

"You . . . spoke to the lady?" he whispered, stalking over.

He squirmed. "I didn't say that."

"You didn't need to," Keir seethed. "I know you."

"Yes, well, we spoke freely about . . . what happened."

"You mean, you told her we had deceived her."

"Yes, well, she didn't take that particular part of it altogether well."

Keir's eyes slid shut, and he pressed his palms over his face, then suddenly let his arms drop to his sides. "Only *you*, with all your ability to charm, a goddamned darling of society, would think nothing of mentioning to the woman that you'd deceived her and her family."

He paused. "Yes, and I suppose, when you present it in those terms, I can see your point. The lady, however, offered to talk to His Grace." Gathering up his timepiece from the side of his bed, he consulted the numbers there. "Now, if you'll excuse me, I have a meeting shortly with Mr. McKendrick." The obscenely wealthy wine merchant, with his discretion and uncharacteristic kindness, had proven the ideal person for Courtland to sell his family's belongings to. Still, the fact remained there was something . . . hard about being so humbled. "And I really need to—"

"You sent the young woman to speak on my behalf?" Keir thundered.

Alas, it was too much to hope his brother would let the matter of Cailin Audley rest, that Courtland doing his part to keep their family afloat would be enough.

Swinging his naked legs over the side of the bed so his feet hit the floor, Courtland rubbed at his suddenly aching temples. "I didn't ask her." Some of the tension left his brother. "It was more that she . . . volunteered," he finished.

By the crimson flush on his brother's cheeks and the bulge of his eyes, Keir had the look of their father right before he'd suffered his apoplexy. "She volunteered?" he shouted.

"For what it is worth, I told her that it was futile and pointed out she was wasting her time," Courtland said hopefully, as he shoved to his feet and headed across the room to the washstand.

From where he stood at the mirror, he caught his brother's furious visage reflected back.

"Nothing. It is worth absolutely nothing, Courtland. Did you decline that *offer*?"

Courtland lowered his face and splashed cold water upon it.

"Courtland?" Keir spoke warningly, in tones better suited to a big brother than the younger one he was.

Burying his face into the bowl, he welcomed the sting of the waters and the way they muffled his brother's lecturing from behind him.

Alas, a man couldn't stay buried under water forever. He came up fast, gasping for air, and gave his head several shakes, dislodging droplets and spraying the residual water about the hardwood floor. "I thought if she was willing and might bring Bentley around," he said.

A knock sounded at the door, and a moment later, the panel opened and his butler stepped inside. "You have a visitor, Your Grace," his butler announced over Keir's tirade.

"Yes, yes. Thank you, Grassley." Courtland returned his

focus to his brother. "Now, as I mentioned, I have a meeting with Mr. McKendrick. If you will—"

"Do you really believe I'm going to simply let you rush off and let the matter rest?" Keir barked.

"Hoped?" Courtland said with a sheepish grin.

Levity and attempts at humor, however, had always been wasted upon his brother. Keir resumed his diatribe.

"Ahem," Grassley called into the noise of arguing brothers. "It is not Mr. McKendrick, but rather a . . . lady. I've shown her to your office."

That managed to silence both Courtland and Keir, mid-argument.

They both looked to the loyal servant. More loyal than the late duke had ever deserved, and certainly capable of finding greater wages were he to quit Courtland's struggling household. Grassley stared back.

A lady? Given the rules of propriety and the risk to her reputation, what lady could or would possibly pay a visit to Courtland's family household? Why, it would have to be a person who'd absolutely no idea the way of Polite . . .

He froze.

Impossible.

Except . . .

For once, Keir, for whom words were a chore, found his voice. "A lady is here." A sound of disgust escaped him. "So you've now reached the point of disreputable women paying visits to your family's household."

He frowned. "I resent that. I have never entertained women here. You know that."

"I thought I knew a lot of things about you, big brother." Keir gave him an up-and-down look that hurt as only a twin's contempt could.

"Gentlemen!" Grassley called out in the paternal, stern tones he had adopted when they'd argued as young boys—more a fatherly figure to them than their own had been.

"I will be down shortly," Courtland said, and Grassley nodded, then rushed off with the same rapidity to his steps that had been there in the man's thirtieth year.

When he'd gone, and the door had been closed behind him, Courtland turned his focus back to his fuming brother and the matter at the heart of their argument. "I understand you are proud and would chafe at a lady intervening on your behalf," he said quietly to Keir, "but I would do anything for you." He spoke with a firm insistence, attempting to break through whatever emotional wall had always existed in his younger brother. "Anything to see you happy in life and with your work." He gave Keir's shoulder another light squeeze.

"But it really wasn't about me when you went and kissed the duke's daughter, was it?" Keir said, cocking his head. "It is always about you. As the heir, you haven't had to worry about what your future would be. You have always known your place."

Courtland's fingers curled reflexively on his brother's arm. "Is that what this is about? My title?"

Keir's nostrils flared. "If you think I give a *damn* about the title, or the fact it belongs to you, you don't know me . . . at all, big brother." With that, Keir shrugged off Courtland's touch and stormed out.

The instant he'd gone, Courtland sank into the side of the mattress, the feather-stuffed article bouncing under the addition of his weight. He ran his hands through his hair, mussing the still-damp strands.

Damn it all. Damn the situation. And most of all . . . damn the late duke. "Though, those two really go hand in hand," he muttered under his breath.

*Rap-Rap-Rap.*

"Your Grace?" Grassley's urging on the other side of that doorway came muffled.

"I'll be down shortly," he called back in response to the question there. For it may as well have been the days of old when the servant had rushed to collect Courtland for his daily lessons.

With a sigh, Courtland strode over to his armoire, tugged out a pair of clean trousers, and stepped into them. Next, he pulled on a fresh lawn shirt and stuffed it inside the waist of his pants.

Heading downstairs, he found his way to his office. A servant stationed outside went to reach for the handle, but Courtland quickly waved him off with a word of thanks, then dismissed him.

After the young footman had gone, Courtland waited several more moments, staring at the carved oak panel . . . and then he let himself inside.

Across the room, perched on one of the chairs before his desk, sat Cailin Audley.

Of course it was her.

Still, all the breath in his lungs froze. Along with the earth. It ceased spinning on its axis, and then resumed its turn backward at a dizzying rate.

Courtland scanned his gaze over her plump, petite form. A vision in yellow silk that hugged her curves, the sight of her sucked the breath from his lungs. She was—

The lady jumped up. "Did you just arise for the morning, Your Grace?" she asked without preamble, bringing him crashing back from his desirous musings.

He shoved the door shut behind him. "Of course not." He'd *almost* just awakened for the day. That was altogether different.

As Courtland crossed over, joining the lady behind his desk, he felt Cailin's eyes upon him. "And may I say it is a pleasure, as always, Cailin." Nor was he being facetious. He enjoyed the unpredictability and realness that came in their every exchange.

Cailin ignored that flattery. She wrinkled her nose. "It *appears* as though you've just tumbled out of bed."

"I . . ." He was wholly unfamiliar with women so blunt as to speak conversationally about his . . . bedtime habits. And the women who did speak about them were eager widows and unhappy wives who only spoke on the matter of wicked acts they'd performed in his bed. "Don't tumble out of bed," he said, flashing a half-grin. "It is undignified."

"You've scruff on your cheeks," she pointed out.

God, she was tenacious.

"Is this really what you've come to discuss, Miss Audley?" He clipped out his words. "About my morning habits?"

Another lady would have blushed and felt properly chastised. He should have expected different from this spirited chit.

"Of course not," she scoffed, and he narrowed his eyes, willing to wager what remained of his estates that she had deliberately echoed his words from before. "I'm here on the matter we discussed last evening . . . regarding the duke. That is, my . . . father the duke. Not you."

His entire body became alert, and he motioned for her to reclaim her chair.

He needn't have bothered. She was already settling herself into folds that looked enormous with her diminutive frame within them.

Scarcely daring to hope, and yet unable to fight the pull of that emotion, he waited until she sat. "Yes?" he prodded.

"You . . . may have been right."

He stared blankly at her.

Cailin Audley glanced down at her lap before raising her gaze boldly back to his; regret tinged those expressive blue pools. "That is, regarding how the duke would respond to my request."

Just like that, all hope shriveled up and died.

Courtland sat.

Or rather, he dropped himself into his seat.

"The duke proved a good deal less reasonable than I'd anticipated."

Courtland rubbed his aching neck muscles once more. "I . . . see."

And he did.

He saw that Keir remained unemployed.

He saw they no longer had the monies to fund Hattie's already cripplingly expensive Season.

He saw they were increasingly without options.

It was, as she said, what he'd predicted. And yet, he'd allowed himself to feel hope.

Now he saw his own hopelessness.

The leather groaned as the lady shifted forward in her seat. "Do you have anything to say?"

Courtland blinked slowly. "I . . . thank you?" he ventured, because what else did she expect him to say.

The lady frowned, indicating he'd been off the mark on what the lady expected of him. "I'm not looking for gratitude." She wrinkled her pert, freckled nose. "Particularly for a job I was unable to successfully complete. No, I just . . . thought you might wish to speak about it."

"Speak about what?" he blurted, *really* trying to follow along.

The little lines at the corners of her mouth drew down all the more. "I thought, given what you revealed about your concerns regarding your brother, you would benefit from a friendly ear."

It was a wholly foreign concept. People didn't invite other people to share their thoughts or opinions on matters pertaining to how they felt.

But then, nor did a lady pay a visit to a gentleman's household unescorted.

Courtland glanced to the closed doorway, as an increasing sense of alarm at Cailin's presence began to set in. They'd both be ruined if she were discovered here.

"Courtland?" she ventured, startling him back into the moment.

"Speaking about it with you or anyone else isn't going to change my brother's"—*our*—"circumstances," he said tiredly. "Now, if you would." He came to his feet as he gestured to the door.

Frowning, the lady looked up at him but made no attempt to vacate her seat. "Are you attempting to throw me out?"

"Escorting you to the door."

The tenacious minx gripped the arms of the chair in a clear statement that she'd no intention of going anywhere. "But we've not discussed—"

"Ladies do not visit gentlemen's households," he said painfully. What the hell upside-down world had Courtland landed in, that he found himself doling out lectures on propriety to innocent young ladies?

"I beg your pardon?"

"There are strict rules of decorum that make your being here . . . perilous for the both of us."

Cailin blushed. "Oh," she said, weakly.

Wanting to save her from that embarrassment, preferring her as she always was, bold and unapologetic, he added: "And you were not wrong. The fault rested with me and my brother." He paused. "Though the entire plan was mine, and I was the one who . . . failed in the endeavor."

Why must he go and do that?

Why mustn't he be a self-centered, pompous nobleman who laid blame at the feet of others and didn't accept responsibility for his actions and decisions?

Because once again, Cailin found herself presented with evidence of a good man, one who'd acted out of concern for his family. It made him relatable.

In fact, it made him the first person she could relate to.

And the irony wasn't lost on her that the one person whom she could find herself forging a bond with should be a lord in possession of a title just shy of royalty.

He eyed her warily. "What?"

"Are you saying that to get rid of me?" At his confused look, she elaborated. "The part about being to blame for your brother's firing?"

"No." He paused. "In some part, yes. In larger part, no. I do appreciate now the full extent of folly in . . . all of our efforts. Now." He looked behind her, and she puzzledly followed his stare, expecting to find someone else had arrived. Only to see a still-empty doorway.

"I'm confused."

His eyes slid closed yet again, and his mouth moved

with Cailin making out several clearly enunciated "Lord"s.
When he opened them, he spoke to her like she were a
slow-to-learn child. "There is the matter of your being
here . . . in the middle of the day."

*"And?"*

She may as well have sprouted wings for the way he
looked at her.

"And your reputation," he said, tossing his arms up.

That was what he was worried after? Her . . . reputation.
"Well, that is silly." Of course, she'd already had a maid
assigned her by the duke and duchess to squire her about
for company when she visited London, and given the way
they'd attempted to suffocate her, she shouldn't be surprised that they'd frown at something as innocuous as her
paying a visit to a household. "Young women pay visits to
cottages where men are. We bring food to their families
when they are ill and gifts at holiday times and—" At the
dawning look of horror expanding on his face, she went
silent.

"I'm a bachelor," he said bluntly. "And a rogue at that."

His was more a matter-of-fact statement than that of a
gent preening over his reputation.

"A gentleman who is living with siblings, are you not?
So it's not *really* as though you are alone." She smiled . . .
a smile that he absolutely did not return. "In fact, I'd venture society would not even say anything."

"Society *will* say."

She stared at him.

"It is what society *will* say. There is absolutely no way
your presence here was not noted and will not be a matter
of discussion." Courtland rubbed at his temples. "Your father and brothers will also be included among those who
have something to say about your being here."

"I will just explain . . ." At his pointed glance, she let her
words trail off. Yes, he was right on that score. She'd proven
her word didn't hold much water where the men in her family were concerned.

And for the first time, her confidence flagged, as she was

reminded all over again just how very foreign this world of the Town, in fact, was to her. Of course she should have realized her appearance would be met with questions and gossip. The people in these parts were nothing if not busybodies by nature. Though, in fairness, gossips weren't reserved for London. They existed aplenty in Stafford-shire, too.

"Miss Audley?" he asked, and Cailin jumped.

"I had my hood up," she said defensively. Granted, that had been because of the glare of the sun.

"And your carriage?" There was a thread of hope contained within that uptilted query.

"It *did* deposit me outside your household."

The duke's hands came up to cover his face. "You were visiting with my sister Hattie."

She drew her eyebrows together. What was he on about? "No. I did not even know you had a sister. Though I take it she is lovely and I wouldn't be opposed to meeting her, she was not who I—"

"You will pretend you were visiting my sister to put to rest any possible questions about your presence here," he interrupted. "I'll speak with her shortly and explain . . . her role."

As in the cover. Splendid. "Ahh." She brightened. "Then, you needn't go rushing me off now?" She smiled.

"But there is nothing for us . . ." He gestured between them. "To speak about."

There *was* nothing for them to talk about. And yet, in the English countryside, there had been discussions about fossils and museums and—

*And was this visit really about informing him of your father's refusal to intervene, or is it about seeing him?*

Sadly, pitiably, she feared it was in fact the latter.

And what was even more pathetic, everything that day in her cottage with him had all been feigned on his part. He had all but said as much. All his efforts had been part of a campaign to charm her and convince her to come to this very place she now found herself.

"You are correct," she said stiffly, coming to her feet. Her cloak rustled about her legs. "I could have certainly sent 'round a note informing you of the outcome of my discussions with the duke."

He stepped into her path. "I've offended you."

It wasn't a question, and as such, she compressed her lips and gave him her silence.

"That was not my intention," he murmured, dusting a fingertip along the curve of her cheek in a tantalizing back-and-forth caress.

Her stomach did a somersault. "I'm not offended," she said belatedly, that tardy response a product of that danger-ous touch.

"You're a terrible liar."

Which only served to throw cold water upon the heat that ran through her in waves. Hastily, Cailin took a step back, dislodging his touch. "And you are too good at it, Your Grace, which I'll also have you know," she said, lift-ing a fingertip and wagging it his way, "is precisely why we are in the situation we are . . . because of your lying."

"You are the first and only to ever tell us apart, you know."

That took her aback. "Impossible," she said, dismissing him outright.

"It is true. The servants. Our tutors." He grinned. "Which obviously came in handy."

"Obviously," Cailin parroted.

He had the good grace to flush, and his smile fell. "Uh, yes."

Courtland coughed into a fist. "As I was saying, you've been the first. Even my sisters have struggled to discern the two of us apart."

Cailin's brows crept up a notch. "Why, you're *nothing* alike. Your demeanors are completely different, as is the way you carry yourselves and conduct yourselves; and that tiniest of scars aside, your hair curls, here." She stretched a hand up and brushed a lone flaxen tress that hung endear-ingly over his right brow. "While your brother has a cow-lick, one that flips up ever-so-slightly. And—"

Courtland stared at her wide-eyed, and she caught herself. *Stop. Just stop talking.*

Alas . . . "What of your parents?" she asked. "Surely they were able to tell you both apart."

He immediately went tight-lipped; his features grew serious, and his expression shuttered. "No."

Cailin opened her mouth, but then . . . took in the tension in his frame, the harsh set of his jaw. And she stopped herself.

He didn't wish to speak about his parents. His physical response to the mention of them was one she recognized all too well. It was another unlikely bond between them. One that was too intimate, too personal for her to press or discuss with him. As such, she let the matter rest.

"And your curls are slightly longer," she couldn't keep herself from adding.

It proved the right response. His crooked grin was instantly back in place. "I am . . . impressed, Miss Audley."

"Miss Audley, am I?" she couldn't resist teasing him with his own words.

Once again, however, hers proved the wrong course. Courtland drifted closer. "Yes," he murmured, coming even nearer, and she really should make herself move again. To back away. And yet, as he stopped before her, she could not. Her feet remained fixed to his hardwood floor. He moved his hooded gaze over her face. "I expect, given the intimate nature of our exchanges thus far and your presence here this day, that we should do away with all formalities."

"H-Have they truly been intimate?" Her voice came breathy.

His lips quirked. "I would say one kiss, and one almost-kiss, and two private meetings certainly places us in that column."

She dampened her mouth, and his gaze slipped, and his smile fell, and her belly wobbled again. "Yes, you might be right on that score," she said, attempting at breeziness and failing splendidly.

His plain-speaking proved fresh and welcome, and his

words also conjured that shared embrace. Desire stirred. Despite the fact she'd been courted, and almost wed, she'd never felt . . . like this. And perhaps she had shades of her mother's wickedness within her soul, for Cailin tipped her head back and leaned up to know the duke's kiss once more.

He stiffened, and then his hands went to her trim waist, and he drew her close.

Her hands came up reflexively, and she gripped the fabric of his fine wool jacket, clutching him. Against her palms, the contoured muscles of his chest rippled and spasmed.

He parted her mouth, and she let him in; he swept, and they danced with their tongues, an erotic waltz, and fire flared to life within.

Her legs went weak, and she sank onto the edge of his desk, the hard mahogany surface forming a perch behind her.

She let her thighs part slightly, allowing him to step between her legs, wanting him to, and he obliged. Sliding closer, he pressed his palms on the desk, on either side of Cailin, framing her, trapping her, and shamefully, it was a place she found herself hungering to be.

She angled her neck, arching back, encouraging his attentions.

She'd only ever known the embraces of her sweetheart; the same man who'd broken her heart and betrayed her. After his accident, when he revealed he'd only pursued a relationship with her for the connection she represented to the foreman of the Cheadle mines, she'd gone over in her mind every kiss, tepid and hesitant; they'd always been pleasant, but there had never been the spark of passion. There'd been an absence of fire.

Unlike with Courtland's kiss.

His was the manner of embrace that consumed: a spark that kindled into a fire until a woman was set ablaze in the happiest of conflagrations, which left one feeling born anew of the ashes of past heartbreaks and regrets.

He moved his hands searching over her hips, and her

breath hitched, her chest quickening from the force of her breathing.

And then, abruptly, he stopped.

Dazed, Cailin fluttered her lashes and forced her eyes open.

Horror filled Courtland's gaze.

The duke stumbled out of her arms, tripping over himself in his haste to back away from Cailin, and there was no greater killer of a young woman's ardor than Courtland's response. He held his palms up as if warding her off. "You . . . that is . . . also should not have happened. I thank you for offering to speak with me regarding your meeting with your father. However, I have . . . other business I must see to."

Cailin stared after him as he hurried across the room.

The gentleman, by the brief bits the duchess had unwittingly divulged about the real man who'd come to collect her and Rafe, was a known rogue. Which no doubt accounted for the speed with which he wished to be free of her . . . a need that also clearly far exceeded any roguish propensities he felt for her.

Taking her cues from his need to conceal her presence here as much as she was able—and also attempting to hide the flush of embarrassment on her cheeks—she brought her hood up.

Courtland drew the door open and said something to a servant in the hallway.

Leaning around, she caught sight of the butler nodding before rushing off. Courtland remained near the doorway . . . staring intently out the slight opening, and it did not escape Cailin's notice that the duke went out of his way to avoid so much as looking at her.

It was . . . a foreign way for her.

The villagers in Staffordshire had always treated her with respect because of her relationship as sister to the foreman. But none of them had taken great pains to avoid her. There wasn't this formality between people, and in Cheadle, where all the men and women alike were employed in some capacity by the mines, there was also not this . . . great divide between the genders. Women might be powerless in ways, but they contributed and had a voice.

Unlike . . . this. The foreign world of Polite Society, where ladies and gentlemen must go to lengths to avoid being seen with one another, unless there was a romantic connection or prospect of marriage. Her toes curled sharply in the soles of her slippers as it suddenly hit her just how very out of place she was in this world—this duke's world. Committing gaffes. Worrying about her reputation.

Within moments, the butler returned . . . with a young lady in tow. One entirely familiar. Recognition set in as Cailin identified her as the young woman seated, reading, in the middle of the ball last evening. Now, the young woman—the duke's sister?—spoke at length to the gentleman. While they spoke, the duke closed the door. Cailin twisted her fingers in the fabric of her cloak.

She had been singularly fascinated by the bespectacled lady who'd been so disengaged in the evening's festivities. She'd also . . . both envied her for the lack of attention trained on her and admired her for thumbing her nose at society by reading that book through the tedious affair.

Just then, the pair looked her way, and she stopped fiddling with the fine muslin article she wore.

"Miss Audley, may I present my sister Hattie. Hattie. Miss Audley."

The young woman swept over.

"How do you do?" The young lady spoke in a high, singsong voice, bell-like in quality and infused with warmth.

"Hattie will escort you to your carriage."

Curtsy. Cailin did know she was supposed to do that. She sank into the steps her sister-in-law had instructed, the movements still rusty and uncomfortable. "My lady."

"Oh, please, none of that. Hattie shall suffice."

"All curiosity or questions at your being here will be explained away by your friendship with my sister," Courtland explained.

Her friendship . . . Cailin looked to the kindly young

woman smiling back. What the duke suggested was a ruse that might prevent gossips from remarking upon the fact that Cailin had paid him a visit. "I . . . thank you for your time. Both of you," she added.

Her smile widening, Hattie linked her arm with Cailin's. "No need to thank me." With that, Courtland's sister steered Cailin from the room. As they passed, Cailin stole one more last glance at Courtland, his veiled expression inscrutable, impossible to read.

"I think it is silly, too, you know," the young woman said as they quit the room and continued their walk. Courtland's sister dropped her voice several shades. "The whole idea that men and women cannot speak about matters of business, or anything for that matter, without it being assumed and expected that those matters pertain to romance and marriage."

"It is not like that everywhere," Cailin murmured in response as they reached the end of the hall and continued down the left corridor.

"Well, that sounds a good deal more preferable to Polite Society, which is so very stilted," the girl said under her breath.

Yes, stilted was a good way to describe . . . all of this. Suffocating.

It was all precisely as Cailin's brother had predicted when he attempted to dissuade her from wishing to venture into London months and months earlier. She'd imagined museums and culture and expanding her mind, while all along she failed to consider there were balls and rules and society's scrutiny. And also, mistakes. So very many mistakes because she didn't understand the way this other half lived.

"Here we are," Hattie announced, bringing them to a stop.

They reached the foyer, and the duke's fastidious butler drew the panels open, allowing the afternoon sun to come pouring in. Cailin squinted; those rays gleaming off the marble white floors were blinding in their brightness.

The young woman, near in height to Cailin, leaned close

and whispered: "Though my brother advised that we should be seen together outside."

To perpetuate the ruse and explain away her being here. "Thank—"

Hattie patted her fingers. "Remember, none of that," she said, for a second time silencing Cailin's attempt at expressing gratitude. "Come." She tugged Cailin along outside and ushered her down the many stone steps until they reached the carriage.

Courtland's sister lingered. "I . . . we could truly be friends, you know," the young woman said softly, her words whisper-soft for Cailin's ears alone. "It doesn't have to just be because . . . because . . ." Hattie's gaze slipped off toward her family's home, more palatial manor than London townhouse.

In Staffordshire, there'd been no shortage of young women or even young men to speak to. Mining communities were tight-knit, with villagers like family members. There'd always been people ready with a kindly word or jest. Hattie's, however, was the first offer of friendship she'd come across in her time in London. A lump formed in her throat.

The young woman faltered. "Unless you'd rather n—"

"No! I should like that very much," she said, tears in her throat. Cailin accepted the footman's gloved palm and allowed the servant to help her into the carriage.

The moment he closed the door behind her, she edged the curtains back and stared wistfully at the household she'd just departed. Between Courtland and his kindly sister, for the first time since Staffordshire, she felt not so very alone.

# Chapter 10

"Who was that?"

Releasing the curtain quickly, Courtland spun about and nearly tripped over the sister whose approach he'd failed to hear. Lost as he'd been, staring after the intriguing Miss Audley.

He looked back at his middle sister, and relief swept through him. "Lottie," he greeted. If any sister would come upon him staring out after his unexpected afternoon visitor, this was decidedly the one.

Their father had mocked his middle daughter, insisting that, small and invisible as she was, her name suited her.

Courtland, however, had always appreciated the quiet calm she possessed. For that matter, she hadn't ever been pushy or pressed him for—

Lottie crossed her arms at her chest. "Well?" she urged; as she uttered that query, she reached past him to brush the brocade curtain aside. She angled her head left and right. "Who is she?"

Oh, hell. Could there be no secrets where any of his siblings were concerned? There was little hope for him if even Lottie, content to stay out of other people's business and focus only on her own, was now pressing him for information. "A . . . visitor." He fought the need to wrestle with his suddenly constrictive cravat.

The moment the carriage disappeared from sight, Lottie let the curtain fall, and the heavy fabric fluttered noisily back into place. "A female visitor," she said contemplatively, tapping a finger against her lower lip. "Very interesting. *Very* interesting."

Yes, it would be a matter of interest to all the world. And now to his suddenly more-aware-than-she'd-ever-been sister.

"Well, she is gone now," he said, heading back to his desk so he could get back to the latest round of notes and debts that had been called in. "So 'interesting' moment over, as I really do need to attend business."

Alas—

Lottie hopped up onto the chair Cailin had previously occupied; the one she'd abandoned for the edge of his desk instead, when she kissed him and let her legs part ever so slightly and—

"She doesn't *seem* your usual sort."

Heat exploded in his cheeks. "Do I have a usual sort?" he hedged, desperately eyeing the doorway, the windows—hell, the underside of his desk. And also immediately wishing he hadn't voiced that rhetorical question aloud.

"Of course you do. Women with daring gowns." As if that merited clarification, she tugged at her bodice.

Blanching, he slapped a hand over his eyes. "Do stop with that, will you?"

"And then there are the women with scandalous intentions and wicked reputations—"

"That is enough," he croaked. At what point had Lottie, of all people, become aware of *those* particular details about his life? Ellie, he would expect such a line of questioning from. Lottie? Never.

Flinging her legs over the arm of her chair, his middle sister pumped her knees back and forth the way she had when he'd pushed her on a swing. How much simpler absolutely everything had been then.

"Women do read, you know, Courtland."

"I am well aware of the fact." He infused a droll edge into his reply. Unbidden, a thought slipped in of another woman, one who was fascinated with books on fossils and nature and—

Lottie gave him a queer look. "Are you all right?"

"Fine," he said swiftly. "I'm merely surprised to learn you've been reading the gossip pages." Ellie and Hattie, yes. Lottie, never.

Her legs came to an abrupt stop. "I read what is being said about members of my family," she countered.

For a moment his heart stopped, and he froze, besieged by a fear she'd already gathered what Ellie had about their family's circumstances. Or worse, that she knew and had informed Hattie, and they all knew. Attempting to keep his features even, and fighting for a calm he didn't feel, Courtland searched for a hint or sign of how much she had—or had not—gleaned.

His sister gave him another odd stare. "Why are you looking at me like that?"

"Like what?"

"Like you swallowed a spoonful of gudgeon."

In fairness, he felt like he'd swallowed a spoonful of that slimy fish. Rancid ones at that.

The door burst open, and a breathless Hattie exploded into the room, saving Courtland from further probing from his inquisitive sister. "I like her," she panted.

"Would you close the door?" he pleaded.

Yes, the servants whom they'd been able to retain had been with the Balfours for years and certainly weren't ones to gossip, but neither did he need to risk the possibility of any other scandals this day.

"Oh, yes. Of course." Hattie shoved it closed and rushed over, availing herself of the vacant seat alongside her sister. "I must be her friend. I am ever so glad you coordinated our friendship."

"I didn't coor—"

"What did I miss?" Hattie turned a dismissive shoulder, putting her question to their younger sister.

". . . coordinate any friendship," he said, finishing that sentence for himself.

"Oh, it is as you'd expect." Lottie gave an exasperated flick of her hand. "He is hedging and hemming, destroying his cravat and choking funnily when he speaks."

Hattie's eyes went wide. "Oohh . . . is it romantic?" Batting her eyes, she leaned in. "Your newest lady."

Courtland scrubbed his hands up and down his face. "It is *not* romantic," he said, his words coming muffled through his hands. "And I do not have a lady." He had debt and a title and a number of bothersome siblings, and that was all.

Nor, for that matter, would it have made a difference had he shouted his assurance: his sisters were firmly engrossed in their discussion with one another about his relationship with Cailin Audley, and apparently required no further input on his part.

Lottie gave her hands a decisive clap. "Hush. Hush. As Courtland said," she announced to the room at large, "Courtland doesn't *have* a lady."

Well, apparently someone did listen to him, after all. "Thank—"

"Not any respectable ones, anyway," Lottie continued over his expression of gratitude.

"You," he muttered.

"In fact," Lottie said, sitting upright. "That is what makes it very peculiar that any respectable lady *should* arrive here."

As one, his sisters' attention swung his way, eyes narrowed, gazes suspicious and probing, and the urge to flee hit him all over again.

The door burst open for a second time. Their youngest sister scowled at the three of them.

"Now what?" Courtland asked in pained tones.

"'Now what?' you ask?" Glaring, she headed over with her fingers dangerously close to the pretend pistol she'd settled into a holster at her hip. She reached their sisters and positioned herself directly between the two leather winged chairs her older sisters occupied. "Surely you don't think I'd be the last to know."

As she stopped positioning herself, Courtland kept his features deadpan. "I would never be so much of a fool to think that," he said, speaking God's truth. For Lord help Lady Jersey when Ellie at last made her come out. With Ellie's ability to ferret out people's secrets, those leading patronesses of Polite Society had no hope for attaining their power role as lead gossips.

"Hmph," Ellie muttered and gave a flick of her hand.

Lottie immediately popped up, relinquishing her seat to their taskmaster sister, who plopped herself down. "I'll certainly not be left out of any discussions on ladies you are inviting over."

Dropping his head onto the desk, he rested his forehead upon the open ledger he'd been attempting—and failing—to attend this day. Not that looking was going to change a damned thing. Frustrated with their circumstances and the grilling he found himself suffering through, he growled. "I did not invite any lady over." He directed that vow facedown to his pages.

"So she just . . . arrived here," Ellie ventured. There was a brief pause. "On her own?"

The wealth of fascination and admiration on their part sent unease coursing through him. The last thing he needed was for any of his sisters to begin paying visits to the households of rogues and rakes like Courtland.

When he didn't answer, Hattie elucidated. "Miss Audley arrived with no appointment and no companion to see Courtland."

The leather groaned, indicating his youngest sister had sat back in her chair. "That is interesting. *Verrrry* interesting."

The way she managed to squeeze three extra syllables into that overemphasized word inspired holy terror in him. She wasn't going to let this go, which meant none of his sisters would.

In the end, salvation did come.

The door opened for a fourth time, this time more measured and reserved, and Keir stepped in. With a groan, Courtland lightly knocked his head against his ledger. "Anyone else?" Cursing silently, he forced his head up to greet his latest visitor. "Should we invite Lady Jersey? Perhaps Lady Cowper and Lady Sefton? For tea and biscuits while we talk?"

Crossing over, Keir took up a place at the head of Hattie's seat.

He gave his twin a perplexed glance. "Why ever would you wish to have gossips present for this discussion?"

Ellie sniggered, burying a little giggle behind her palm.

Hattie gave her a sharp look, then turned her focus on her other elder brother. "Courtland was making an attempt at being funny."

Keir's frown deepened. "I don't see how potential scandal is a matter to find amusement in."

"It was the sarcastic sense of humor," Ellie said, exasperated. Younger in years, she'd still failed to gather—the way the rest of her siblings had—the struggle Keir had in reading people and matters of humor.

Turning a dismissive shoulder to the young girl, Keir honed his gaze on Courtland. "Did she bring news regarding my post?"

Courtland gave his head a slight shake.

Even as it was too late.

Hattie scrambled upright in her chair, her entire body stiffening as she glanced between her brothers. "Keir lost his employment?"

Oh, hell.

Keir went tight-lipped.

All eyes went to Courtland.

Yes, because each sibling knew how much that post meant—or had meant—to Keir.

"Yes," Keir said bluntly when Courtland only offered more silence. "I was . . . removed from my post."

Courtland found himself and spoke quickly in a bid to

spare his brother—to spare either of them, for that matter—from further probing. "It was a misunderstanding, is all."

Alas, Keir once again failed to take that respective lifeline and cue. "A misunderstanding that I was only indirectly involved in cost me my work for the duke," Keir said, running a hand down the side of his dejected face.

Yes, because *Courtland* had been directly involved. It had been Courtland and Cailin's embrace and the almost-embrace her brother happened to walk in on that accounted for Keir's change in circumstances.

Ellie inched closer to the edge of her seat. "What *kind* of misunderstanding?"

Keir at last seemed to catch that he'd said too much. He cast a hopeful glance at Courtland.

"Whatever took place is between Keir and the duke." *And Cailin and me.* Just as long as it was not the remainder of his siblings or any member of Polite Society.

He layered such a level of finality into his statement that Courtland managed what he'd previously believed impossible: silence among his three loquacious and most stubborn sisters.

Such silence sadly proved short-lived.

"Wait a moment!" Hattie shot a finger up. "I have it."

All eyes swung her way.

She sat upright, preening under all the attention she'd managed to command.

"What?" Keir barked impatiently.

"Oh, hush, let her have her moment," Lottie chided.

Clearing her throat, Hattie gave a little toss of her head. "It is just that Keir was sacked by the duke, and the lady who visited was in fact the duke's daughter and . . ." She stared pointedly at each occupant of the room.

Perplexed at where she was going, Courtland found himself shaking his head along with his siblings.

"Oh, will you just say it already?" Ellie said, exasperated.

"Keir fell in love with the duke's daughter."

Courtland strangled on a cough. That was the conclusion that his sister had arrived at? Given her romantic nature, that supposition shouldn't come as any manner of surprise, and yet—

"Keir . . . in love?" Ellie's freckled face pulled. "Disgusting."

"I am not in love." Keir spat his words, and then gave a little shudder.

Her earlier confidence melted away. "*Courtland* is in love, then?" Hattie asked hesitantly.

"Absolutely not," he said. And for that matter, unlike his romantic sisters, he wasn't entirely convinced such sentiments *could* exist between people. His parents' failed union had been proof enough of that.

Suddenly, Lottie froze. "I have it!"

Courtland was already shaking his head. For nothing about to come out of her mouth could be good.

"Courtland seduced the lady," his middle sister finished.

And there it was. Nothing good could come out of it, indeed.

Oh, for the love of God in heaven. He dropped his head atop the desk. "I did *not* seduce the lady," he said, not bothering to conceal his exasperation. He'd kissed Cailin. Embraced her and wanted to do a whole lot more . . . but seduce her? Absolutely not. "I am not a seducer of innocents." In fact, one might argue the point that the first embrace had been initiated on both their parts simultaneously, and the second had been initiated by the lady herself.

Keir finally showed Courtland some mercy. "Courtland was attempting to use the lady as an emissary to speak to her father."

Courtland swiftly picked his head up. "And I wasn't using the lady, either, for that matter." He turned his attention to his undoubtedly sympathetic sisters. Strong-willed ladies in possession of their own minds and opinions, they could certainly relate. "Miss Audley volunteered to speak to her father on Keir's behalf, and though I did not ask her to do so, neither did I refuse. She was merely visiting today to tell me the outcome of that meeting."

Keir took a frenzied step closer. "And?"

Their sisters asked in time with their older brother: "And?"

"And it proved . . . unsuccessful."

Just like that, the gathered members of his family deflated. Systematically, they all went silent and glum. And in that instant, the room was transformed, recalling a different moment in time, their mood so similar to when he'd come upon them in the nursery, sad-eyed and silent after one of the rare visits from their impossible-to-please father. Except . . . this time he found himself unable to muster the energy or ability to erase their frowns and restore their joy.

One by one, his siblings filed out.

Until he was left alone . . . with just one.

The scariest of the lot.

Her little arms folded at her chest, Ellie stared back. "You should run—"

"Keir is without employment."

He sighed, then steepled his fingers together. Courtland held her stare. "I am aware," he said solemnly.

"And the duke paid him a fortune. Certainly more than he was worth, certainly more than any man of affairs."

He frowned. "How do you know how much Keir earned?"

"I know everything, Courtland." Ellie thinned her eyes into terrifying little slits. "*Everything.*"

Resisting the urge to squirm in his seat, he cleared his throat. "Uh . . . yes. Well, you needn't worry about . . . any of this."

Worrying hadn't helped a damned thing where caring for his brother and sisters was concerned. He'd been doing it since he was in the nursery and their father bullied Keir around.

It was a mantle he'd accepted willingly and gladly for the simple reason that he loved his siblings.

"With you left to fix it?" his sister scoffed. "Of course I need to worry."

Most of the time. He loved his siblings most of the time.

"Thank you for your faith," he said dryly.

"Oh, it isn't that I don't have faith in you on the whole. I think you're entirely capable of . . . most things. But I think you hating marriage the way you do, and going all uncomfortable when Lottie and Hattie are speaking about their romance books, it's going to take you a bit to come 'round to the way to fix our problems."

"Ah, this again." Courtland sat back in his chair. "Making me a fortune hunter."

Ellie shot a single digit up. "A *marriage* hunter."

It was hard to say which of those terms was worse, or which inspired the greater horror. Suddenly, Courtland was even more eager to have her gone.

Her face fell. "Alas, despite our sister's optimism that a rogue can be reformed, I have my doubts. After all, Father . . ." Ellie added that last part softly, as though speaking to herself.

Only . . . she'd uttered those words aloud.

*After all . . . Father.*

The miserable cur who'd constantly kept his wife, Courtland's mother, with child, all the while continuing to take his pleasures with mistresses and prostitutes and married women.

His sister had hit the nail on the head. He was his father's son. That reprobate's blood rolled along through his veins. He'd no doubt make any lady he wed as miserable a wife as his mother had been. Sad-eyed and morose and perpetually heartbroken . . . Courtland didn't look forward to being the criminal responsible for some unknown-to-him-for-now woman's misery.

But he also knew what was expected of him. Had there been no siblings, he'd have been content to live his life and let the title pass to some distant cousin after him. But there *were* siblings: three sisters and a brother, all of whom relied upon him to make right everything their father had made wrong.

A wealthy wife represented the surest way to bring security to his family.

As soon as the thought slipped in, his gut churned and bile slicked his throat.

For there was no escaping that truth. If Courtland wed a

lady for her fortune, he was no different from his father. A man who'd married Courtland's mother for her impressive dowry, only to then squander those fortunes, wasting it on wagers and women.

"You're considering it, I see," Ellie said, misunderstanding the reason for his silence.

He gave his head a slight shake, dislodging those uncomfortable comparisons one could not help but draw between him and his miserable sire. "I'm thinking you need to run along."

She flashed a gap-toothed smile and hopped up. "Very well. I'll leave you to it." Suddenly, she shot her pretend pistol out, pointing it at Courtland's heart. "Think about what I've said."

Courtland brought his palms up, surrendering. "You have my promise, Captain."

And God help him . . . she did.

He stared after her retreating frame as she skipped off, and then he slammed the door in her wake.

For his hadn't been a false assurance.

He was increasingly without options. Even Keir's employment, which Courtland had helped to secure, had never been a long-term solution to the state the late duke had left their family in. It had been a temporary patch, but also one that put the onus of supporting their sisters upon Keir. And yet, that had never been Keir's responsibility. As heir and eldest brother, Courtland was the one who needed to take care of his brother and sisters.

And he would.

No matter what.

Even if, as Ellie pointed out, Courtland must marry a young lady with a sizable dowry—

He let his head drop, for a third time that day, and groaned.

As if on cue, a knock sounded at the door.

Grassley appeared. "Mr. McKendrick has arrived, Your Grace. Per your request, I've shown him to the White Parlor."

Splendid. That was precisely what would improve his mood, and this damned day: sorting out the artifacts and articles to sell to save his family and himself from debtor's prison.

With a sigh, he set aside thoughts of the delectable Cailin Audley and went to meet the fat-in-the-pockets merchant here to purchase his family's valuables.


Cailin wanted to escape.

To her powder-blue bedchambers.

To another parlor. In fact, any parlor would do.

Back to Staffordshire.

Why, she would have even seen gladly to that kitchen work she so hated if it meant she was not here.

At least, in this instant.

For in this moment, having returned from Courtland's and met with a summons from her father, Lydia, Rafe, and Edwina, Cailin wanted to be anywhere else.

Seated on the Louis XVI gilt-frame settee, her hands clasped upon her lap, Cailin stared mutinously ahead at the four people lined directly across from her. All the while, she bit at the inner flesh of her right cheek.

God, how she missed having her other brothers close.

Always optimistic and armed with a smile and wink, Wesley would have ruffled the top of her head the way he'd done since she was a girl and promised all would be fine, because nothing could take down the Audleys.

And Hunter—she felt tears prick behind her lashes and glanced down at her lap—she and Hunter would have shared a private look and rolled their eyes, commiserating about the ridiculousness of the way the other side lived. And then they would have snuck off and shared jests regarding the fact that Rafe had suddenly become so very keen about following the strictures of the *ton*.

Alas, the only brother here with her in London was . . . Rafe.

Cailin crept her stare up, bypassing the duke, his wife,

and Edwina, all of whom wore matching worried expressions, and focused on her oldest sibling.

*Devastated.*

His sharp features were as twisted and tortured as when he'd found Wesley gone, only a note remaining that stated his intentions to seek out a commission from their father so that he could fight Boney's forces.

She silently raged. Wesley's nighttime flight, when they'd not even had a goodbye from their brother, had left a gaping hole in their tight-knit unit. How? How could Rafe wear a like expression to her morning visit with the duke?

No. She'd be damned if she'd be made to feel badly. This tight-laced, suffocating world of High Society, with all their rules about everything and propriety and a lady's place, was utter rubbish.

Determined to take control of the impending exchange, Cailin broke the impasse of tense silence. "You are making more out of this than there is."

Her father tensed, and then, deferring to his son, looked to Rafe.

And it chafed that Courtland had been correct. That she need worry about the appearances of her merely paying a call . . . to her family, even.

"I was visiting the duke's sister," she said belatedly, hating herself even as the fabrication slipped out for becoming a woman who felt the need to prevaricate. "H-Hattie." It was a slight stumble; one her brother would notice. She'd not, however, anticipated being challenged on the matter by her father and brother, of all people. And she'd also not expected how awful it would feel lying about something that she shouldn't have to lie about.

Rafe gave her a searching look, the gentle one he'd employed since she was a girl. "You went to visit Lord Keir, didn't you?"

And that was what came from a familial closeness. She wouldn't have traded that love and devotion for anything. But it left one vulnerable, with one's brother able to decipher a fib from a truth.

Torn, the silence thick and impenetrable, Cailin battled herself.

*Lie. Rafe will not press you.*

She saw it there in the desperate glimmer in his eyes. The sideways, almost imperceptible glance he cast their father's way. Rafe was not only offering Cailin an out but showing a willingness to let the matter rest. It was the greatest restraint she'd ever witnessed of her hotheaded brother.

*". . . we've got honor, Cailin Audley. Never forget that. The fancy sort might have their wealth and grand estates, but what we have has a value far greater than a monetary one . . ."*

Hunter's stern lesson from long ago, spoken to her when she'd been just a girl of five, played around her mind.

Yes, she could lie. Cailin, however, was no liar. It had been one thing letting the ruse Courtland had concocted circulate among Polite Society. But this was different. This was her brother, and she'd be damned if she adhered to those rules of propriety with her kin.

"Cailin?" her father gently prodded.

She looked squarely at her brother. "Yes, I believe we've already established that particular detail. I was paying a visit to . . . the gentleman." As soon as the truth left her, she cursed her pride.

Rafe briefly closed his eyes. "Oh, Cailin."

All her muscles recoiled.

That was it.

Just: *Oh, Cailin.*

Edwina rested a palm on her husband's sleeve. "Rafe," she said softly.

Never in all of Cailin's years had her brother yelled at her. He'd bellyached and groused, but never had he raised his voice. In this moment, she found herself preferring a thunderous response to . . . *this*. This restraint and quiet.

Edwina spoke hushed words to her husband.

Nodding at his wife, Rafe took a breath, and when he looked once more at Cailin, some of the angry color had faded from his cheeks. "Cailin—"

"Nothing happened, Rafe," she rushed to promise him. "Nothing improper or untoward, then or now." Those proved minor, though essential, lies. "I promised to speak to Father on his behalf, and I owed him an explanation as to the outcome of that discussion."

"No, you didn't," he said, a trace of desperation in his voice. "You didn't, Cailin."

The duke held up a staying hand, silencing Rafe, and miraculously her brother ceded the talk to their father.

"All of that may be true, Cailin," he began.

She cut him off. "It *is* true." Dismissing him, she glanced over at her brother and attempted to reason with him, because they were two people from the same village; two people born outside all of this stuffiness and pomposity. Because of that shared existence, she could reason with him. Remind him of their roots and who they were. "I'm a grown woman. In the course of my life, I have visited any number of men. I've brought baskets for new widowers in the village. I've conversed with men at the May Day festivals. Why, I've even tended half-naked men who were hurt at the mines."

Edwina and the duchess wore matching blushes, and the duke coughed noisily into his fist.

Not her brother.

It was that reminder of where they came from she'd been counting on. Separated as she was from her other brothers— Hunter, who was overseeing the Cheadle mines, and Wesley, off fighting Boney—this link to the only sibling before her seemed all the more vital.

For a moment, she believed she'd reached him.

But then . . .

Abandoning his place at the duke's shoulder, Rafe joined Cailin. He dropped to a knee, bringing their gazes to the same eye level. "Cailin, this is *not* Staffordshire," he spoke with his usual bluntness. He'd always been hopeless when it came to soothing tones. He was a protector, but he was rough around the proverbial edges. "These people here in London? They aren't the miners of Cheadle, Cailin. They conduct themselves differently here. I told you all this when you first expressed an interest in coming."

And there it was: that inevitable pronouncement falling from her brother's lips.

She fisted her hands. "I trust it must bring you some satisfaction in being proven right." *Mayhap he'd not wished to visit London because he knew you'd fail*, a voice at the back of her mind taunted.

His features stricken, Rafe sank back on his haunches. "That isn't true," her eldest brother said; hurt laced his denial.

And the regret in his eyes gleamed with his sincerity.

A sincerity that didn't make her feel any better.

Nor did hurling petty words. Rather, she felt all the worse.

"It is a foreign world," Edwina said softly, gently inserting herself back into the discussion. It was. An entirely different one. "It is even harder to be part of it if you are not schooled on the ways of Polite Society."

"Edwina is correct," the duchess said in support.

"I've already had lessons," Cailin said calmly, even as she silently screamed those same words inside her head.

"Obviously not enough," Rafe said with more of that protective-brother warmth, despite that harsh fact.

Cailin winced.

The duchess gasped, and Edwina threw an elbow into Rafe's side.

"*Ooomph*," he grunted. His features whitened. "I didn't mean it as an insult," he said quickly, whipping his gaze from Edwina and the duchess to Cailin. "That *wasn't* what I was saying, Cailin. I was—"

"You were speaking the truth," Cailin said softly. She was hopeless in the ways of Polite Society.

"You are doing just fine," the duchess interjected. "Why, the ways of the *ton* are complicated for even those of us who spent our entire existence here."

Cailin offered a grateful smile.

Her father's wife was even worse of a liar than Cailin . . . but she appreciated that kindness.

Ever a ball of sunshine and optimism, a smiling Edwina stepped forward. "Your brother had the advantage of a mother who schooled him. He had access to books that she insisted he read about Polite Society and the rules of decorum and propriety. Knowing your brother, he didn't."

A sheepish blush burnished Rafe's cheeks.

Cailin avoided his eyes, neither wanting nor needing an admission of guilt. Mothering her had never been his responsibility. Nor had his role been to act as a father to her. And yet, that was precisely the role he'd stepped into: de facto parent for her and Wesley and Hunter. He'd done the best he was able in a job that shouldn't have been his.

Abandoning her seat, Edwina came over to take up one beside Cailin. It was a show of support from her sister-in-law, and Cailin was grateful for it. "You have done splendidly."

Splendidly.

Cailin swallowed a miserable giggle.

Her sister-in-law angled herself so she was close to Cailin. "If you would like more lessons"—*No!*—"and do as Rafe has done and join Polite Society—" Behind her, Rafe made a sound of protest, but his wife gave him a sharp look that silenced him once more, before turning back to Cailin. "And even if you do not wish to take part in the *ton* events, and only wish to remain and continue exploring the culture and museums, I can teach you still, too . . . so you needn't worry about . . . what happened today."

What happened today.

Cailin's patience snapped. Shoving back her chair, she stood, the legs of her seat scraping the hardwood flooring. "Nothing happened," she repeated yet again for the room at large. "Furthermore, the duke . . . that is, the Duke of St. James"—was every man in her life now a blasted duke?—"agreed my visit this morn can be neatly explained as though I was paying a visit to his sister. As such, there really is no reason to worry about my visit to the Balfours today." Before her family could object, she quickly added, "And I don't wish to receive further lessons, and I have absolutely no interest in joining Polite Society. Now, if you'll excuse me." And before one of the four present could get another word in edgewise, she left, never having felt more alone than she did that moment.

# Chapter 11

It was somewhere around the time a team of maids rushed into her chambers, and when Cailin arrived downstairs to find an even larger army of servants rushing about, that she gathered one important detail: they were leaving London.

Hugging the wall as she walked, book in hand, Cailin took in the young maids and footmen with their arms filled, heading in the direction of the foyer. All the while, she made her way to the breakfast room, taking in the flurry of activity.

She entered the breakfast room and came to an abrupt stop.

As did the conversation that had been taking place—between her brother, her father, his wife, and Cailin's sister-in-law. Clustered close around the circular mahogany table, the quartet had the look of military persons plotting their plans into their next battle.

Her stomach sank.

The silence stretched on; a long, awkward pall.

A damning one.

Ever graceful in every situation, Edwina was the first to

break the impasse. "Cailin," she greeted her warmly. When Rafe remained motionless, guilt stamped across his features, his wife gave him a look.

Cailin's brother immediately came to his feet, setting the rest of the quartet into motion.

"I daresay we needn't stand on formality with one another," she said dryly with a levity she didn't feel. Her heart knocking uncomfortably against her ribcage, Cailin headed for the buffet, making every attempt at seeming casual. With her back to them as it was, she made a show of serving herself, waving off the servant's offer of help. She welcomed the slight reprieve . . . from a discussion that she'd so clearly been cut out of.

A discussion about her.

The slight scraping of wood upon the floors indicated her family had reclaimed their seats . . . but they continued to watch her.

Cailin felt their stares.

Heaping her plate with eggs and sausage, an amount greater than she'd ever eaten to break her fast, and ever would, she would have continued piling it high if it meant she didn't have to join the gathering behind her.

Alas . . .

Tamping down a sigh, she headed for the empty seat beside Edwina.

Edwina, who immediately snapped her lesson-planning book shut.

But not before Cailin caught her own name contained within those pages.

Narrowing her eyes, Cailin carefully picked up her knife and fork and proceeded to dice up a link of sausage, a near impossible feat given the amount of food she'd added to her dish.

She was leaving London.

She knew as much. Ironically, it was what she'd been secretly longing for. But it hadn't been London-London that she'd wished to leave, but rather the London Season and Polite Society's scrutiny.

She'd not expected he'd meant they'd leave . . . less than a day later.

*What did you expect after nearly landing yourself in a compromising position with a duke?* Granted, her family assumed she'd been paying a visit to Lord Keir. That, however, was a small detail that was neither here nor there. The fact of it was, in her failure to adhere to the stifling rules of the *ton*, she'd almost ruined her reputation and brought about a scandal. And because of it, she'd lose the freedom to explore the corners of London she'd aspired to know.

Her silver fork scraped along the bottom of the plate, sending a tiny tuft of scrambled eggs over the side; the fluffy yellow rained down upon the previously stark white tablecloth, now marred by her mistake. She stared intently at the mess she'd made.

She'd spent almost twenty years making her own decisions and living her own life. Yes, an overprotective Rafe had always been there, but neither had he thought to make decisions for her. He'd known better. And she didn't intend to allow him, or this father she'd just recently learned of and his proper duchess, or her equally proper sister-in-law.

Resolve brought her spine slowly back, and setting her fork and knife down, she boldly looked up at her still-silenced family.

"Do not let me interrupt whatever it was you were talking about," she said, raising her napkin and patting at the corners of her lips. "You seemed singularly engrossed in your discourse." Cailin leveled a sharp glare at her brother.

He had the good grace to blush.

Only, Cailin wasn't done with them. "Or was it that you were discussing sudden travel plans of which I know nothing about?"

Her father winced. "Cailin—"

"We're *leaving today*?" she demanded of the room at large.

The duke gave a slow, reluctant nod.

Fighting for a semblance of calm she did not feel, Cailin,

with measured movements, picked up her fork and knife and sliced up a piece of ham.

*This* once more: the departure, coupled with this private familial meeting she'd been excluded from, pointed to her newfound lack of control. It was an altogether new, unwelcome, and infuriating state for she who'd once had control of her life, a household, and her dealings in Staffordshire.

"You don't have to take part in the London Season," Rafe ventured and, with a shrug of his shoulders, picked up his fork and resumed eating.

As though that settled . . . some matter that hadn't really been a matter.

"My being here was never"—she jammed a fingertip into the tabletop—"about being part of the London Season."

"It is for the best," the duchess said in soothing tones, ones Cailin would not have expected a powerful peeress to even be in possession of.

"And we will return," her father beseeched, turning a hand up. "This is just . . . temporary. We, however, did not properly consider . . ." He floundered, seeming to search his mind.

"We'll return when the London Season is over, so you don't get yourself tripped up any more than you already have here," Rafe said with his usual bluntness.

Edwina flinched and, leaning close to her husband, whispered, with every other word discernable. ". . . lack of control . . . certainly doesn't want you or . . . should be considerate of . . ."

Piecing together her sister-in-law's words indicated there was at least someone who was on Cailin's side.

Nodding tightly, Rafe returned his attention to Cailin. "We didn't consider just how dangerous it would be to you and your reputation not knowing the rules of Polite Society."

"Because I brought shame upon the household yesterday." Grateful for the cover provided by the table, Cailin clenched her hands on her lap and curled her toes sharply into the finest slippers she'd ever worn. Really, the first pair of slippers she'd ever worn.

"You did no such thing," the duke said quietly.

Her father's wife stretched a hand across the table and found Cailin's fingers. "In our eagerness to have you here, and in our desire to honor your wishes of visiting London while not being part of Polite Society, we failed to consider that the two could not be so divorced."

"So I shall go to one of your properties and be hidden away?" she asked, unable to keep the bitterness from creeping in.

If she was to return to any land outside of London, let it be Staffordshire. Let it be the familiarity of the quiet, sprawling lands that weren't some playground a nobleman had manufactured from the beauty of the English countryside.

"We aren't hiding you away at all, my dear," the duchess promised. She looked to her husband.

"Not at all," he said. "Just the opposite."

Her stomach sank. *No. Do not say it . . .*

"It will be a smaller, more intimate hunting party with friends."

"An opportunity for you to be more comfortable with the peerage," Edwina proffered.

This was . . . worse. She'd be scuttled off and trapped in a country house with strangers who'd scrutinize her just as closely as all the people here in London.

She clenched her teeth.

"Might I speak with His Grace alone?" she directed to the room at large, startling the family around her into silence once again.

Because her exchanges with her father had been short and few. From her observations in the village she'd called home, men didn't know how to be around children. They knew even less about how to be around their female kin.

His Grace inclined his head, and the servants immediately filed out . . . Edwina and the duchess quick to follow suit. Rafe, however, lingered.

God love her overprotective brother. "I said alone, Rafe," she drawled.

"Yes. Of course."

Still, he made no move to leave.

Cailin smirked. "As in *now.*"

This time he jumped and followed after his wife, who waited at the front of the room.

The moment they were gone and a servant had drawn the double doors shut, allowing them privacy, she looked to her father. One thing Cailin had learned from having overbearing brothers was how to assert herself and take command. Otherwise, a woman found herself voiceless and powerless. "I obviously don't wish to leave London."

"No. I understand that. And you needn't call me 'Your Grace.' If you feel so comfortable . . . 'Father.' If not now, then in time."

Briefly disconcerted, Cailin lost the words she'd prepared. He would so disarm her. So much about her recent time here was alien to her. Her relationship with the man who'd sired her, and whom she'd only recently learned of, proving among the most foreign.

"Cailin," the duke went on. "This going-away is, as your brother said, not forever—"

"You misunderstand the reason I've asked to speak with you," she interrupted, and her father's eyebrows came together.

Yes, she expected it wasn't every day a duke found himself both interrupted and gainsaid. With him now off-kilter, she pressed her advantage all the more. "In fact, I didn't ask to see you alone to debate the situation."

"Oh." He blinked slowly. "Well, that is reassur—"

"Rather, I wanted to tell you how it is to be."

"Oh," he repeated; this time, the single-syllable utterance was pained and worried.

"I'll go visit your country estate and take part in your house party."

He narrowed his eyes. "Go on."

"I want Lord Keir hired back as your man of affairs," she said flatly. This was something she had done, and she intended to rectify it.

"Absolutely not. That's not something I can do, Cailin."

God, if, with his obstinance, he wasn't cut of the same cloth as her brother Hunter. And Wesley. And Rafe.

Between a trio of stubborn brothers, all of whom were set in their minds and ways, however, Cailin had become quite adept at handling them. "You absolutely can, Father. As a duke, I trust you can do almost anything." She winged an eyebrow up. "And hiring back a man whom you previously employed, and then sacked, seems quite doable."

"The Balfours—"

"According to Lydia, you've helped the Duke of St. James and his brother through the years," she cut him off, refusing to cede a centimeter. "And you'd suddenly pull back supports for no reason, at all . . . other than your adhering to propriety." She released a sound of disgust and gave her father an up-and-down look. "That hardly seems reasonable or honorable."

He flinched.

For just like that, Cailin had hit him squarely in that place that she'd come to learn men of all stations cared so very much about—his honor.

Having managed to silence him, she pressed him further. "This is not negotiable. If you expect me to participate in your house party, then *I* expect Lord Keir is reinstated to his post."

The duke hesitated, and then sighed. "Very well," he said, tiredly.

And for the misery that was this day, the loss of what she'd dreamed of for herself in London, there was this notinsignificant triumph.

Her shoulders back and her chin held high, Cailin started for the doorway.

"Cailin," he called after her, and she stopped, glancing back.

"As your father, I'd be remiss if I did not . . . further inquire about your efforts on behalf of Lord Keir?"

She gave the only living parent she'd ever known a pointed look. "Unlike you and my brother, I'm not comfortable seeing a man lose his employment for crimes he didn't commit." With that, she let herself out . . . and nearly ran into her sister-in-law.

By the blush that filled Edwina's cheeks, it was clear she'd been listening in.

"There you are!"

"As in the breakfast room with my father, where you left me," Cailin drawled. "Yes."

Edwina turned several shades darker as she rushed to keep up. "No. No. I meant it more 'There you are!' as in a happy exclamation as we're able to make the trip to the bookshop."

Cailin cast her sister-in-law a sideways glance. "And you were not listening in."

Edwina pinkened. "I may have been listening . . . a bit." She brightened. "But I did dispense with your brother so he couldn't listen in, and I also managed to coordinate time for just you and I to be together."

And for that she should only be grateful. Because there was no doubt her brother, having witnessed what he'd referred to as the "almost-kiss" between her and the Duke of St. James, whom her brother had believed to be Lord Keir, would have heard her attempt to secure the gentleman's employment and made something more of her intervention.

They reached the enormous foyer, which didn't have an ounce of space to spare; it was filled by servants bearing trunks and valises and hatboxes.

Even with the furor of preparations, two maids were immediately there with light-weight muslin cloaks for her and Edwina.

Drowning. She was drowning. Suffocating.

She was a girl again, wading too far out into the river in her village and getting sucked down. The waters had closed over her head; filled her lungs and nostrils; robbed her of breath, stealing all hope of air until, miracle of miracles, a hand reached in and Wesley plucked her to freedom.

Wesley, who, even before his wish to fight Napoleon's forces, had always been a hero to *her*. Knowing her ten-

dency to wander off, he'd always stayed close to Cailin—
ofttimes protecting her from herself.

And clasping her cloak close, she followed her sister-
in-law.

The moment she was outside, Cailin breathed deep, letting the spring air fill her lungs.

But this time . . . managing to take in air after floundering was different from her near drowning.

There was no Wesley. There was no easing of the tight-
ness in her chest, and breathing did not come easy once
more.

Everything changed when Wesley had gone. With his
seeking their father out, and pursuing the dream he'd
wished for himself, he'd also set off a chain of events that
impacted every other Audley. And Cailin, not unlike the
youngest of her brothers, had been seduced by change, too.
What a fool she'd been.

Feeling her sister-in-law's eyes on her, Cailin looked
over and found the other woman at one of the duke's many
carriages—patiently waiting.

Forcing herself into movement, Cailin joined Edwina.

A short while later, a servant pushed the door shut and
the carriage sprang into motion. Seated on the bench of her
father's carriage, Cailin stared out at the passing London
landscape.

There was something equal parts refreshing and equal
parts . . . sad about the impending departure the duchess
oversaw that morning.

No, London was not what she'd thought it would be. But
only because she'd not allowed herself to think about what
would be required of her. The London she'd imagined had
welcomed her as an anonymous village woman from Staffordshire, free to explore and roam and discover a world
she'd previously only wondered about.

And with one rash visit to the Duke of St. James's household, Cailin had cost herself the opportunities she'd sought
in London.

And the rub of it was, Cailin knew the reason for it.

Because the fact remained, even with her sister-in-law's monotonous lessons doled out for weeks, she didn't know the rules of Polite Society. She'd spent twenty years in Staffordshire and just several months in Town.

She'd come here wanting to explore a world different from her own. Only to discover her smaller, less grand world had proven greater in ways. In ways she'd not properly appreciated, because she'd not known how the other half lived. And she wanted to go back to the familiar and welcome freedoms she'd enjoyed; to a time when she could converse with men and women alike without fear of having her words picked apart and judged or critiqued.

She'd wanted culture.

And instead . . . found a cage.

"Why do you enjoy this?" Cailin asked over the rhythmic *clip-clop* of the team's hooves; she directed that question to her own visage reflected in the carriage window.

Her sister-in-law didn't pretend to misunderstand. "I enjoy puzzles. I haven't even told Rafe that. I've always enjoyed them. My father would send me puzzles, and I would sit on the floor and just slide all the pieces this way and that, until they slid into place. Until I could make sense of them."

Cailin pulled her gaze reluctantly away and faced her sister-in-law.

"And Cailin . . . that is how I look at Polite Society. The women whom I used to be hired to instruct . . . they were women like me." And Cailin. "They were born to a different society, and yet they were just as capable of being part of this . . . one just needs to find how to shift the pieces in a way that makes sense." She smiled. "Until they fit in."

Until Cailin fit in.

She scowled. "One can hardly find one's way or place if one is being scuttled off." Like a dirty family secret.

Which was essentially what she'd spent her whole life being.

"Ah, but you are not being scuttled off," Edwina protested. "You are taking a journey to a different place, one you haven't been to before; and, why, one could say you're still seeing the world, just a different side of it."

Cailin managed her first smile that morning. "You are an eternal optimist."

"I am." Edwina smiled her usual beatific smile, which had managed to break through even Cailin's brother's brooding.

A somberness quickly fell over Edwina's features. "It is only for a short while," Edwina reassured from the opposite bench of the duke's carriage. "We will return, and you will be free to visit all the museums you wish."

Unable to meet the other woman's eyes, Cailin looked outside once more. "I know," she murmured, directing her response at the crystal pane that reflected back Edwina's visage.

Only . . . it wasn't just about that.

It was that she didn't know her way.

It was that . . . she didn't even really know if she *wanted* to know her way here.

She was thankful when Edwina chose to let the discussion end and instead popped her notebook open and proceeded to scribble away notes—no doubt notes that involved Cailin and the duke's intimate house party.

Her sister-in-law? She didn't understand. No one understood.

Rafe had suspected she'd feel stifled. He'd known she'd hate this world . . . and she hated that he'd been right. Because if society had been open for her to explore, and had not wasted her time with fittings and visits with the duke and duchess's equally regal friends and dinner parties, then London? It would be, if not the place she'd hoped it would be, better than what it was. She could not say as much to him, Rafe, who'd come to enjoy London and even found his way at society events.

She was, simply put, adrift . . . and feared she'd never find her way in either world.

# Chapter 12

G ood God, man, what happened to you?"
    That question, from Sandon Marsden, the Earl of
Seagrave, greeted Courtland later that afternoon as he
found his way to Forbidden Pleasures for a much-needed
drink . . . and escape.

From around the buxom red-headed beauty on his lap,
Seagrave, Courtland's oldest friend since Eton, eyed him up
and down.

Within the span of a day? "Too much to mention,"
Courtland muttered, availing himself of a seat. There'd
been Cailin's visit . . . and the sale of more items from his
household.

Another scantily clad woman with a tray in hand sidled
up to Courtland.

With a word of thanks, Courtland accepted the glass
offering and welcomed the filled snifter. Setting her tray
down, she proceeded to rub his shoulders, her long nails so
sharp they managed to penetrate the fabric of his jacket,
and then she reached around, shoving her searching palms
inside his jacket.

Alas, he was growing either old or tedious in his advancing years.

Or mayhap it was simply he'd been worn wary by the events of these past days.

"No, thank you," he said, dismissing the woman.

As she sauntered off, his friend must have sensed something in Courtland's mood, for he said something to his companion.

She pouted her rouged lips, then scrambled onto her feet.

Giving her an affectionate pat, and a coin, Seagrave sent her on her way.

"Well, out with it."

Courtland lowered his voice. "Keir lost his employment with the duke."

"Ahh, bloody unfortunate, that," Seagrave said quietly, with a sobriety that was uncharacteristic of his usual jovial self.

But it was also a sign of the other man's closeness to Courtland's family that he'd respond with such solemnity and sincerity.

"Yes."

"I always took Bentley as the fair sort." Seagrave swirled the contents of his snifter. "What in blazes could your brother have ever done to merit a sacking?"

"He didn't do anything." Except . . . that wasn't quite true. They'd both taken part in a ruse that saw him and Courtland in this mess.

The earl's brows dipped. "Well?"

Courtland closed his mouth. Too late. He'd already said too much.

The other man motioned with his spare fingers. "Out with it."

"My brother was tasked with collecting Bentley's missing children, and I may have attempted to . . ." That wasn't correct. He hadn't attempted to do anything. He'd done it.

Seagrave leaned in. "Yes?"

Courtland squirmed in his seat and muttered under his breath. "I may have had the idea to pass myself off as . . ."

His friend cupped a hand around his ear. "Come again. What was that?"

"I may have had the idea to pass myself off as my brother," he said, still quiet, but this time more clearly.

The earl stilled, and then, tossing his head back, he roared with laughter that managed to reach across the revelry of the club and bring everyone's focus square on them.

"I hardly see why this is grounds for such hilarity," Courtland grumbled.

"It is just . . . you and Keir are still up to your boyish antics, playing at being the other." He paused to wipe away the moisture from his eyes. "When no one could possibly believe, after spending a lengthy time with your brother and then you, that you are the same people."

"My father did."

"Your father was a fool."

Yes, Seagrave was correct on that score.

"We've fooled plenty of instructors and tutors and nurse-maids."

"Fair enough. But someone who really knows you, and who is as astute as Bentley, was always going to gather you'd pulled the wool over on him."

But it hadn't been the duke. Rather, it had been the clever, eminently kissable Miss Audley.

He opted to leave Seagrave with his erroneous assumption—that Courtland and Keir's brotherly deception had been found out . . . and not the kiss Courtland had shared with Cailin.

Passing his snifter back and forth between his palms, he studied the amber contents within.

"What?" Seagrave asked with an acuity only a best friend could possess.

"There is the loss of Keir's salary," which, though help-ful, still hadn't provided the manner of monies to put one sister, let alone three sisters, through a London Season. Or maintain the properties, or the lifestyle expected of them.

"Ah." The other man briefly sat back.

"Ellie had the idea . . . that I . . . Ellie suggested . . ." God help him, he couldn't even bring himself to utter the horrifying possibility.

The earl stared expectantly at him.

He'd make him finish the damned thought. "That I should wed an heiress." He hissed out that last vile word.

His friend gave no outward appearance of horror or shock. Instead, a calm passivity filled his features. A boredom.

"Marriages are based on convenience. What one party has to offer the other. In your case"—he pointed his glass in Courtland's direction—"you have a dukedom. Every lady wishes to be a duchess."

"How is it I've never realized how mercenary you are?" he muttered.

His friend lifted his shoulders. "I'm no more mercenary than any other member of the peerage." Catching the underside of his chair, he dragged his seat forward. "People wed for connections and wealth every day. It is what is expected. Just be fortunate you have a dukedom and not a mere baronetcy."

"And you'd have no problem with turning yourself into a fortune hunter?" Because the idea of it left Courtland physically ill.

"I wouldn't." Seagrave offered another shrug. His spine grew erect, he tipped his chin back, and he spoke in solemn tones. "I would step forward and do what so many English noblemen have done before me. Marry for a fortune." He dissolved into another fit of amusement. Perhaps it was the fact that he'd gotten himself into the rub he had.

"You'd proceed to just piss it all away," Courtland said.

Laughing once more, Seagrave toasted Courtland's prediction.

When his amusement had faded once more, Seagrave set his half-empty drink down. "The solution to your problem is so simple even your baby sister pointed it out. Find a bride, fill your coffers, and then live your life."

And then Courtland's transformation into his father . . . would be complete.

"Well, this is certainly a sight," Seagrave murmured to himself.

Absently glancing up to see what accounted for his friend's sudden interest, Courtland didn't move. Yes, it was certainly a sight, indeed. Stalking purposefully through the club, his features set in their usual seeming glare that deterred even the always-all-too-eager-to-please prostitutes, Keir headed for Courtland's table.

Courtland furrowed his brow. "What in hell . . . ?" he muttered.

"Or hell hath frozen over," Seagrave said, his voice filled with amusement. "Both work. Whatever is he doing here?"

"I . . . don't know," he said.

Keir reached the table, and without bothering with proper greetings, he slapped something down. "I received this a short while ago." Grabbing a chair, Courtland's twin seated himself.

Before Courtland could speak, the same young woman who'd attempted to solicit Courtland's company sidled up with another glass.

"A drink, my lord," the crimson-haired beauty purred, stroking her painted nails down the front of his chest. "I can also get you—"

Blushing, Keir avoided her clever hands. "No and no," he said crisply. "I don't want that." He motioned to the drink still held in her fingers, before turning his back to her dismissively.

The young woman stood there, wide-eyed, blinking slowly several times.

Catching her gaze, Seagrave mouthed an apology, and then tossed her another coin.

"My, my, you have quite the way with women, Little Courtland," Seagrave said the moment the young woman had gone, using that teasing nickname he'd fastened to Courtland's brother since they'd been children of eight.

And it was as though, with that, Keir seemed to recall the company Courtland kept . . . and the place they now met. His mouth flattening, Keir scowled and glanced about. "This place is terrible, you know." This place, with the crystal chandeliers and crimson carpeting and gold-painted wallpaper, was a visual feast in decadence for the wicked. With the raucous noise of ribald laughter and the clink of coins, Keir would always abhor such a place. "If the news weren't so good, I'd have felt a good deal worse for even coming here." Courtland's younger brother shuddered. "My God, why would you bother with this place?"

"Oh, I don't know," Seagrave said with another twist of humor in his drawl. "Perhaps it has something to do with the lovely women and the fine drinks and wagering." He ruffled the top of Keir's head, and Keir swatted the other man's hand away, his scowl deepening.

Courtland reached for the official-looking page Keir had slapped down. His gaze immediately registered the seal. "What is this?" Courtland asked, bringing them back 'round to the reason his brother had brought himself to this hell he'd never set foot within otherwise. Even as he put that question to his brother, Courtland was unfastening the already-broken seal.

He went motionless.

"He hired me back," Keir said in his usual flat tone, even with the miraculous information he'd come here with.

Courtland's heart stopped, and then it picked up a fast beat as he processed those words and then read and reread Bentley's note.

> I have had a change of heart. I am requesting your
> services once more and ask that you resume at your
> usual time on the morrow.
>
>                                              Bentley

Speechless, Courtland lowered the page.

"Well, this is decidedly good news, indeed," Seagrave announced, and stretching an arm out on either side of him, he patted Courtland and Keir on the back.

Keir winced and shrugged off the other man's touch.

"This . . . is good news," Courtland said, finding himself. "Unexpected news."

Grabbing up the bottle of brandy they'd largely made work of that afternoon, Seagrave set about filling their glasses and motioned over a nearby servant for a third for Keir. "A toast is in order," Seagrave said when a glass was placed before Keir.

"No toast is necessary," Keir declared, shoving himself to his feet. "You did manage to secure my place and . . . thank you." Courtland's twin dropped into a bow, and without another word, he left.

"Your brother is . . . one of a kind," Seagrave said the moment he and Courtland were alone.

He was.

Which was the reason Courtland had set out as a defender and protector of his younger brother through the years. The world knew precisely what to do with, and how to be with, charming, affable people. It was the souls who were rough about the edges whom society was at a loss of how to deal with.

"Well, I'd say that takes care of your worries." The other man paused to flash a grin. "That is, for now."

Courtland gave a crude gesture and looked at the note his brother had left behind. As much as he wished he'd been responsible for bringing about the sudden change in Keir's circumstances, the credit belonged to the duke. And likely Cailin, who'd offered to speak with Bentley. It appeared at some point the other man's anger had eased and he'd found his usual benevolence.

Now the funds would be there to see Hattie through the remainder of her third Season—which nearing the end as it was, it seemed increasingly unlikely she'd make a match.

And yet . . .

"You and your brother are not one for toasting this day?" Seagrave said with a sigh, and leaning over, he touched his glass against Courtland's forgotten one.

"I was not responsible for the duke's change of heart."

The other man rolled his eyes. "It does not matter who or what is . . . just that it's a good day, and Keir's work is cemented, and you are spared for now . . . from—"

"Doing what I'm supposed to," he said quietly.

His friend stared at him for a long while and then groaned. "You don't need to be the champion of—"

"My twin brother and sisters."

Seagrave flinched. "Very well. I'll allow that." He paused. "But you don't need to be Lord and Savior to the rescue for your brother and sisters all the time."

"I hardly think anyone is going to consider me a Lord and Savior in any regards."

And certainly not where his brother and sisters were concerned.

He was coming to see that he couldn't rely upon Keir's salary any longer. As the one responsible for his family, Courtland was wrong to have accepted it for as long as he had. Ellie's urgings slipped in, unwanted, and reaching through even the din of the raucous pleasure palace. A responsibility so obvious even a child had identified it.

"My God, man, you are still all stony-faced and brooding. You're really terrible company." Seagrave wagged a finger. "I was willing to overlook it given the reason for your moroseness, but I'll not be as benevolent when your circumstances have changed once more." Shooting an arm up, his friend motioned for the twice-rebuffed beauty.

The young woman appeared in an instant and immediately took up her place on Seagrave's lap.

"There, that is decidedly better," Courtland's friend said with a rakish half-grin as he drew the courtesan close.

Giving his head a shake, Courtland glanced past the tableau of the earl with the prostitute, his hand up her skirts, the pair of them laughing. It was a wicked pastime Courtland had taken part in any number of times through the years.

Somewhere along the way, however, he'd also begun to tire of it.

Perhaps that was the sobering effect of finding oneself on the cusp of debtor's prison.

Or mayhap . . . confronting his circumstances and the straits he'd been left in by the previous duke, he'd realized just how much he'd become like that old cur.

Or perhaps it was because of the interesting bluestocking who'd marched up his steps and commanded a meeting in broad daylight.

A wistful grin pulled at Courtland's lips, and he raised his glass—and froze. His gaze locked on the wide front windows and the ducal crest across the street from Forbidden Pleasures.

As if he'd conjured her, the lady was there: her features drawn, her mouth as tense as it had been the day he'd arrived in Staffordshire. Only . . . he knew this was no mere vision, as his dreams and memories of the lady and their embrace certainly didn't include him sitting at his tables in a wicked club while she visited . . . he stilled, taking in the signage above the lady's head—a bookshop.

Unlike the previous women he'd kept company with over the years, Miss Cailin Audley preferred . . . a bookshop. He sat up straighter. Courtland knew from even their brief meetings what she'd be searching for, too. She'd be looking for books on fossils and nature. Or . . . perhaps she wouldn't? Bluestocking as she was, there'd be any number of other topics to interest the lady. Intrigued, as he remained by the—

Just then, the lady looked up . . . and over.

Snapping to the moment, his heart racing, Courtland flung himself onto the floor.

Bloody hell.

"Christ, man!" his friend exclaimed. "Are you all right?"

From where he remained tucked under his table, Courtland downright lied to the other man. "I'm just fine."

"Of course you are." Seagrave paused. "It's just you hiding on the floor that's got me a tad bit baffled."

"I'm not hiding," he fibbed for a second time in almost the same breath. Not that he should care if she saw him here. Except . . . for some reason, he did care about her opinion. "I dropped my timepiece."

"Oh." There was another moment of silence. "And . . . do you need help . . . locating it? Or standing?"

"Here it is." Courtland shot an arm up, revealing the gold piece in question.

"Splendid. Then I expect it is safe for you to join me at the table . . . and not *under* it," his friend drawled.

Straightening slowly, Courtland adjusted his chair and settled himself across from Seagrave once more . . . and glanced to the window once more . . . when he found his friend's stare upon him.

Courtland immediately yanked his focus forward.

With a sigh, Seagrave whispered something to the young beauty still perched on his lap. She nodded and placed a kiss on his lobe, hopped up, and sauntered off again, leaving Courtland and Seagrave alone. Dropping an elbow on the tabletop, the earl leaned in. "Tell me, did your . . . uh . . . fall, really have something to do with that gold chain that's still affixed to your waist . . . or the young lady chatting outside that bookshop across the street?"

Courtland winced. Good God, the other man missed nothing. Though, in fairness, Courtland's attempts at discretion, a skill he'd mastered through the years, had all but failed him in this moment. They appeared to have failed whenever Cailin Audley was near.

"I'd rather not say," he mumbled.

Seagrave smirked. "Alas, ole chap, I fear no words are necessary. Your actions have spoken enough this day."

Tossing back his drink, Courtland stood. "If you'll excuse me, I have . . . other matters to attend." Only, he didn't. If he were being honest with himself, he needed to leave for the simple reason that he . . . didn't want to risk Cailin Audley seeing him in the den of sin that was Forbidden Pleasures. It was a foolish worry to have. The whole of Polite Society knew him to be a rogue. They knew him to be his father's son. So why did he care?

"Tired of the company . . . and perhaps seeking out someone else's," Courtland's friend called after him.

Lifting his finger once more in a crude gesture, Courtland made his way through Forbidden Pleasures, his friend's laughter trailing after him.

Accepting his hat and cloak from a servant at the front of the club, he donned both before making his way outside and over to the boy still holding the reins of his mount. Courtland stopped beside his mount . . . and then slowly came to a stop. His gaze crept across the street to the emporium the lady had disappeared within a short while ago.

*Do not think about it . . . do not think about it . . . take the reins and go . . .*

"Your Lordship?" the child asked quizzically.

Courtland briefly closed his eyes. "I'll be but a moment more," he murmured, and with that sprinted across the street, weaving and darting to avoid passersby, each of whom lifted a hand in annoyance . . . before registering his identity and converting that rude shake to a wave.

Making his apologies as he went, Courtland gave a distracted tip of his hat.

It was a familiar way to find himself . . . welcomed and respected for reasons that had nothing to do with who he was, and everything to do with the title affixed to the beginning of his name.

Slightly out of breath, Courtland reached the front of the shop. Doffing his hat, he beat the article against the side of his thigh, and with his spare hand, he attempted to put to rights his tousled hair.

He let himself in; even setting the tinny bell a-jingle as he did, no one rushed to greet him. No one fawned. In fact, the cavernous bookshop, filled with patrons absorbed in their perusing and purchases, offered . . . an anonymity he'd never before known. And it was . . . a refreshingly welcome change to being greeted and fawned over.

Jamming his hat on once more, Courtland scanned the establishment, skimming his gaze over lords and ladies, all of them unfamiliar; a different crowd than the company he usually kept. He strolled through the impressive emporium, taking in the circular counter wide enough for his carriage and team of horses to pass through.

He continued his search of the patrons perusing titles at the floor-to-ceiling shelving units.

Everything said: leave.

All good common sense indicated that he should go. After all, at every turn he'd landed himself in enough trouble where the young woman was concerned . . . and that peril had almost proven disastrous for Keir and their sisters.

So why did he march through the shop and make his way up the staircase?

Reaching the first landing—with four in all—Courtland did a survey of the lounging rooms. Men and women with books in their hands, surrounded by even more titles, read underneath galleries. No one paid him any attention, the material in their hands far more engrossing than his presence.

How had he failed to appreciate before now the wonder that was a bookshop? Courtland was more than half-certain he never wished to leave this land of anonymity, where the words on those pages mattered far more than his presence or title.

Making his way through each floor, Courtland at last reached the top level, sparse in terms of patrons, and with a frown he stopped.

It was as though . . . she'd disappeared.

Which was undoubtedly for the best.

*Care'll kill a cat and all* . . .

Still, Courtland did a sweep of each lounge . . . and then stopped.

*Everything* stopped. Why, the very earth ceased to spin on its axis.

Unlike the other patrons, who'd had just one book in the private reading quarters they'd commandeered in the Temple of the Muses, stacks upon stacks rested upon a small table beside her on a leather button sofa, leaving the lady completely and fully surrounded by a fortress of books.

Had hers been an intentional attempt at hiding from the world? Or rather, had her fascination with those titles compelled her to add to a vast collection so deep that it formed a wall around her?

Cailin drew her legs up and shifted the small book she read so it rested upon the makeshift table made by her knees. Raised as that little leather volume was, it allowed Courtland free rein with which to study her.

A number of curls had come free of her plait, and those curls hung about her shoulders; the loose, natural ringlets bounced as she turned the pages.

And his breath caught funnily in his chest, lodging in the strangest way; one that made drawing air into his lungs a challenge.

He'd had relationships and dealings with all manner of women through the years. Many of them actresses. Some opera singers and ballet dancers. Others, widows. They'd been sexually inventive and brazen.

None of that overt sexuality, however, could hold a proverbial candle to the seductive sight of a woman wholly enthralled by a book in her hands.

It was also every reason he should leave.

Being caught here alone only threatened to undo the good news with which his brother had come to him a short while ago.

And yet, God help him, Courtland found himself striding closer.

# Chapter 13

In her short time in London, Cailin had grown accustomed to people looking at her. Or watching her. It was all really the same.

From her father and his wife, to Edwina and Rafe, to the lords and ladies whom she met or passed, there was always a set of eyes upon her.

Whatever reasons compelled those gazes, be it concern on her family's part or bald curiosity from the peerage, she'd become adept at knowing when stares landed on her.

It was why she'd known the moment, nestled away in the top floor, last lounge of the Temple of the Muses, that someone was examining her.

Again.

Snapping her book shut, she picked her head up and glared. "Is there something I can help— *Oh.*" Recognition set in and erased the remainder of that cool response she'd already prepared in her head. "You," she blurted.

He quickly doffed his hat, revealing perfectly those tousled golden curls that no man had a right to. "Me."

"What are you doing here?"

His face went flush.

Belatedly, she swung her legs over the side of the chair and stood. "Not that you can't be here," she said in a rush, realizing how rude her response might sound. "And not that I expected you shouldn't be here. It is just . . ." He continued to stare back, allowing her to finish that thought. Looking entirely too amused. Cailin tipped her chin up and spoke truthfully. "Unexpected."

"I am often in these parts," he explained, his distracted response directed to the books she'd gathered. "This is . . . quite the selection," he murmured, and then with the command only a man of his rank could manage, he took up a spot on the sofa she'd abandoned.

She wanted to be annoyed.

She wanted to bristle with indignation at that impudence.

And yet, this didn't feel rude so much as . . . a casual act by a . . . friend.

She'd not had friends here in London. She'd not had people to speak with. She'd tried to befriend her father's servants here in London, those working-class men and women whom she'd felt far more comfortable with and around; but even as they'd been warm, they'd still maintained a formality befitting the treatment of a duke's daughter . . . a status to which she'd never grow accustomed.

Why, even her conversations with Rafe and Edwina had become centered on Cailin's place in Polite Society.

Of course, the duke wasn't a friend. Not really, and not in a reciprocal way. But he felt the closest thing to one . . . and in her case, she'd come to see him as one.

Suddenly, he looked up, and she felt her face go warm at having been caught watching him.

"Forgive me," he said. "May I?"

She stared blankly back, giving her head a confused shake.

Courtland held aloft a frayed leather copy she'd found earlier.

The book. He'd been referring to the title and not . . . joining her. "You may," she said, sliding into the seat she'd previously occupied.

With that permission, he returned to his study . . . not of her, as she'd earlier believed, and not the way other people did, but instead of the volumes she'd hastily gathered up and tucked herself away to read through.

He was no friend. Apart from a handful of exchanges—all of which had been tense in different ways—they did not know one another. Not truly. Even so, there was an ease to his being here and his casual examination of the titles she'd collected. He wasn't here to speak about whether she should or should not wish to be part of Polite Society. He wasn't here to lecture, and there was something . . . oddly, unexpectedly comforting in his company.

Picking up her book on fossils, she flipped through the pages, searching for the spot where she'd left off.

All the while, however, her gaze kept creeping up to Courtland: Courtland, who with his head down and his gaze locked on his pages, was riveted by whatever he read.

Tipping her head, she found herself no different than the voyeurs she'd accumulated in her time in London—studying him—the Duke of St. James.

The men of the Cheadle mines? They didn't read. Her brothers were included in those ranks. After all, the days were full, and by the time the miners returned, exhaustion robbed a person of the ability to find pleasure in anything and everything that wasn't a restful slumber. As such she found herself . . . entranced by a man so unlike any other she'd ever known. He was an oddity, but in a way that was only g—

He looked up.

She drew back, hating the telltale color warming up her neck and face once more. "Have you read that before?" she asked, because she needed to say something.

"I haven't." He perused the titles, lifting the occasional one with his spare hand. "I've read this one . . . *Systema Naturæ*."

Cailin's spine grew. "Have you?"

"My mother purchased it for me. I was perhaps eight or nine years old, and after I'd read it, proceeded to create my own edition." A wistful smile pulled at his lips. "As a child,

I was so very certain I would be a great scientist, discovering new species and answering questions about past ones."

It was an endearing image he painted; one in which she saw him not as this all-powerful duke before her, but rather as an inquisitive little boy, eagerly illustrating and writing his own comparable work. And if she'd had a part of her heart left to lose, if she hadn't known better than to guard it, she would have lost a bit of it to him with this telling.

"And as a man? Do you not still hold the same interest in those subjects?" she asked without inflection.

"Alas, my studies were cut short. Tutors only teach what their employers instruct, and as such, science and the arts aren't indulgences a duke's son had time for," he spoke in a rote way. "Nor is work." He added that latter part as though an afterthought to himself.

Did his response, however, come from his place as a duke? Or rather as the child he'd once been? She waited, wishing for him to elaborate so that she might know . . . more about him, and that which had stifled his interests.

When it became clear he didn't intend to say any more, Cailin swung her feet back and forth on the floor. "Then, I should think I would never wish to be a duke."

"That would make two of us," he said quietly.

She started.

"We are all a bit in a gilded cage, aren't we?" he rejoined, more a statement that didn't require an answer on her part, one that so closely mirrored what she felt about her own circumstances that she found herself unnerved.

Feeling another unexpected kindred connection to the man beside her, Cailin covered one of his hands with hers. "There is no shame in celebrating learning, and there's certainly no shame to be found in work, Courtland." She paused. "Do you have a problem with work?"

"Yes." When she narrowed her gaze upon him, he quickly added, "No." Her brow dipped; Courtland grimaced. "That is, I don't *personally* have a problem with it because dukes cannot work. Noblemen cannot," he clarified.

She stared at him a long while, and as he shifted his attention back to the book in his hands, it soon became clear he'd no intention of saying anything else on the matter. "Noblemen cannot work?" she echoed his admission. "And whyever not?"

"Why not *what*?" he asked confusedly.

Cailin rolled her eyes. "Where I'm from, the miners and everyone within the village's community are employed in some purposeful existence. Do you think you're somehow better?"

"Not at all," he sputtered. "It is not that."

"Then what is it?" she asked, exasperated, certain she'd never figure out how these people lived.

"It just . . . isn't done."

Her response exploded from her lips before the final syllable had even left his mouth. "Well, I think that is rubbish." Cailin came from a world where work was what people did; it shaped their lives and defined their existences. "A man or woman being employed isn't something to be scorned, Courtland, but something to be celebrated and admired. Earning something with your hands"—she lifted her palms—"is an accomplishment. Having it handed to you through the hard work of others is mere luck."

"I don't disagree with you," he said. Courtland closed the book he'd ceased reading. "It is simply the way of Polite Society."

More about "the way of Polite Society." God save her. "Goodness. If I don't ever have to hear those words again, it will be too soon."

"Yes, you and me both, Cailin. And yet, if I do take on investments or involve myself in trade, it would and will reflect upon my sisters and their futures and the matches they will . . . or, more likely, will not make. I may believe conducting work is honorable, but that does not change how the rest of society views it." That admission rang with frustration.

She'd believed there was nothing she had in common with Courtland, a duke, only to find his existence was as stifled and suffocating as her own and perhaps, in a way, even more. For Cailin had enjoyed freedoms in Staffordshire . . . until she'd arrived here. Courtland had only ever known a life where people dictated what he could and could not do.

"Do you want your sisters marrying such men, Courtland?" Cailin went on to clarify: "Ones who'd shun them for your doing something so honorable as *working*?"

Courtland opened his mouth and then closed it. He tried again. On his third attempt, he managed but one word, a single syllable. "I . . ." He shook his head, a lone curl toppled endearingly across his brow; the rays of sun gleaming through the windows highlighted the browns and blonds and golden hues of that single strand, and her breath hitched as she was filled with an overwhelming urge to brush it back.

Unable to stop herself, she reached up, surrendering to that temptation.

"No," he said softly.

Mortification held Cailin suspended in time, Courtland's rejection acute.

He slowly unfurled, his powerful back straightening, his gaze in the distance as though he'd ceased to see her . . . and then he whipped his eyes to hers. "I wouldn't."

It slammed into Cailin like the force of a fast-moving carriage. He'd not been rejecting her touch, but rather the ways of Polite Society.

"Not that I believe there's anyone good enough for my sisters, but I certainly don't wish for them to tie themselves forevermore to a man who'd be so pompous as to look at an honorable life working as somehow wrong."

His words grounded her back to the moment. She gave a pleased nod. *"Exactly."*

Suddenly, he grabbed her hands in his, startling a breathless gasp from her.

He drew first one wrist to his mouth, placing a kiss upon that sensitive skin, and then kissed the other. "Thank you."

Her pulse raced. Butterflies fluttered wildly in her belly. "F-For what?"

"For opening my eyes to . . ." He paused, moving his gaze over her face, and it was as though he were searching;

waiting, weighing his words. And then, Courtland quietly added: "So much, Cailin."

The moment he released her hands, there came a sense of loss at the separation.

As he returned to scanning the pages, Cailin sat back in her seat. They settled into a comfortable quiet.

"You've amassed quite the collection of books," he murmured after a while; his remark a surprisingly ordinary one following such an explosively intimate, powerful connection.

Coward that she was, Cailin welcomed the shift back to something less *personal*.

"Yes." She sighed. "I'm taking them with me." At his questioning look, she explained. "I am . . . headed to the country."

He scanned a piercing gaze over her person. "Because of me?"

"Well, not really," she said in a bid for lightness. "Because of my continued meeting with Lord *Keir*." Her attempt at jest fell on deaf ears. Instead regret filled his eyes. But not pity, and she was grateful for the absence of that unwanted emotion. She sighed. "Nor is it even because of you. Not really. I do not know the rules of Polite Society." She expected she should feel a greater sense of embarrassment at that admission. Perhaps . . . it was that she knew this man from Staffordshire, even if it had been just for that one visit, that made him a familiar face different than the other people here.

"And that matters so much?" he asked carefully.

"Not to me." Given she didn't see herself—and never would—as a member of Polite Society, it shouldn't. Except she did care. "I came to visit you yesterday and nearly ruined my reputation and yours." She paused. "Or your brother's." Cailin drew her knees up and brought them close to her chest. "Either way, it is the same." She dropped her chin atop the table made by her legs. "Foolishly, I believed I'd come and find anonymity and enjoy a more cultured life," she said softly, more to herself.

"And instead?" he asked quietly.

She bit at her lower lip. "And instead, I found that there

are museums and bookshops that exist here, but what is the good of having them if one doesn't have the freedom to visit?"

"And can you not?" he asked, and she felt him shift on the seat beside her.

Cailin angled herself, facing him, and it felt so very good to free herself in this way, speaking without worry. Somehow it was always . . . comfortable with him. There was something so easy about talking to him. "No. I cannot. Because my days now consist of lessons on propriety and rules, and there is no freedom here."

"And there was so much freedom in Staffordshire?"

"Sooo much so," she said, squeezing several syllables into that one word for emphasis. "In my village, the men are largely all employed at the Cheadle mines. But there are women who work there, too." And children, a practice she'd found singularly awful; that, out of their necessity to survive, people and families required small boys and girls to risk themselves with that grueling work. "And the women who do not work in the mines, we are responsible for the households and financial decisions. We have actual voices, and here, absolutely no one wants to hear anything from any woman." And certainly not a duke's bastard daughter— she gripped her book tightly—which is all she would be here. A person considered less because of her birthright; but just enough that she merited their gossip and interest.

"I do . . . that is, I want to hear you," he said quietly. "Every time you speak, it opens my eyes to how narrow-minded I've been in failing to see or know of the world you speak of."

"You cannot see something if you don't know it is there," she said simply. "There's a difference between ignorance and *willful* ignorance." Cailin leaned in. "It is what you do when you have your eyes opened, how you choose to live your life with newly acquired information, that matters."

She felt his eyes upon her like a physical touch.

Something crackled in the air, a charged energy that hissed to life.

His gaze fell to her mouth; and she knew.

Not because there'd been a handful of chaste, stolen kisses in Staffordshire from anyone in her life. Because there hadn't.

Not even because he'd kissed her before. Which he had.

She knew with an intuition born to Eve: the primitive instinct of a woman who sensed temptation all around and craved a taste of that sweet fruit.

He lowered his head, and she lifted hers, in silent encouragement.

Courtland hesitated a moment and then inched ever closer, as she inched up.

And then he touched his mouth to hers.

Where their kiss in Staffordshire had been explosive and raw, this was tender and sweet . . . one befitting this moment and their shared connection . . . and fleeting.

"Cailin?"

That quiet query from somewhere in the shop brought her and Courtland immediately apart.

"It is my sister-in-law," she whispered, her heart hammering at being discovered again with Courtland.

Edwina called a second time for her; this time her voice grew closer. "Cailin?"

Her own regret was reflected in the stormy gray pools of Courtland's eyes. "I should go."

"Yes."

Given her family was already suspicious of her relationship with Courtland's *brother*, nothing good could come to either of them from his being here.

Except as he slipped away, Cailin found herself missing his presence already and hating that this parting would now be forever.

# Chapter 14

Courtland couldn't remember a time he'd enjoyed himself more than that afternoon in a quiet lounge, at the top of a bookshop, with Cailin Audley.

He could have spent all day there, the two of them tucked away; himself closed off from the reality that was his life and circumstances and his station.

Alas, reality was a cruel, unkind bitch of a mistress.

There was nothing Courtland despised more than going through the morning notes that had arrived.

It was a grim task, looking at the debts being called in and having to sort through what was a priority to be paid and when.

Unlike his father, who'd had a completely hands-off approach to dealing with the familial finances, Courtland had immediately immersed himself into all the details of his properties and the wealth—or rather, the lack thereof—coming out of the estates.

For so long, Courtland had thought that was enough. Now he knew the flaw in that thinking. The idea that he was doing more than his father had, and doing the same as respectable gentlemen, was never going to solve the sea of problems he'd inherited.

"... *A man or woman being employed isn't something to be scorned, Courtland, but something to be celebrated and admired. Earning something with your hands ... is an accomplishment. Having it handed to you through the hard work of others is mere luck ...*"

He'd inherited everything. Every luxury he and his family enjoyed had been a product of nothing any of the men within the Balfour line had wrought, but rather came from the labors of others. Instead of appreciating that gift and nurturing it, and providing support and assistance to those who'd brought their wealth, not a single one of them had thought about the men and women doing that important work.

Work that Cailin had spoken of so effortlessly when discussing the people of her mining village.

His mind raced with the possibilities he'd never before considered.

Building something with his own hands. Making something from what he did have and growing it into something even more ... and greater.

Staring at the stack of notes delivered a short while ago by his butler, Courtland reached for the top one first, and as he did, after his meeting with Cailin, this was the first time in which he'd felt hope at his circumstances.

She'd *enlivened* him.

Furious footfalls pounded outside, bringing his focus up.

The door exploded open, with such force the panel bounced back, and nearly hit Keir in his face, which was a mask of fury. Entering Courtland's offices, he pushed the door shut and stalked over.

At his approach Courtland's stomach fell. Cailin. Someone had seen them. Bloody hell. That was the only thing to account for that rage from his twin. This was bad.

Mustering a smile that felt strained to his own facial muscles, Courtland spoke the moment his brother stopped before him. "Good morning, broth—"

"Do not," Keir seethed. He pointed at Courtland's chest. "Do *not* with morning pleasantries. How could—"

Courtland cut into that stinging lecture. "It was a brief kiss. Very brief." He held his fingers together to emphasize just how brief it had been.

And yet as brief as it had been, as tender as it had been, he'd wanted the moment to go on. He'd—

Keir's eyes bulged, and a crimson flush suffused his cheeks.

Courtland's stomach turned again. "Never mind," he said belatedly.

"What kiss?"

Oh, hell. Had Courtland ever been good at this roguish business? He coughed into his fist. "No one you need to worry about . . . this time." It was a lie. There were no two souls closer than him and his brother; that bond had always been strong. But as powerful as the friendship had been, all the emotions between them had been as volatile. They'd sparred as boys with the same ease with which they'd loved one another. But this? With the fire brimming in his brother's eyes, this was decidedly a moment Keir would have liked to beat him senseless.

And fortunately, Keir let the matter of Courtland's most recent embrace with Cailin Audley rest.

His brother dropped his palms on the table and leaned forward, arching across the damning stack of notes. "We are in dun territory."

Oh, hell.

He'd been wrong. There was something else that could account for his brother's outrage.

Courtland had let on enough the extent of the state they now found themselves in.

"Oh," he said, sitting back in his seat. "That."

"'Oh . . . that'?" Keir closed his eyes in uncharacteristic-for-him restraint.

"I'd shared . . . some of it with you."

"You didn't say we were on the cusp of debtor's prison!" Keir exclaimed.

No, he'd said just enough to secure his brother's help in finding a capable man of affairs, but not so much as to have Keir sacrifice his own wishes for the mess Courtland had inherited. "Well, in fairness, we're not." He managed a sheepish laugh. "*I* am."

Courtland should have expected that any levity in this moment—or for that matter, any moment—wouldn't be received by his twin.

Suddenly, Keir's entire body recoiled. "My work was given to me of pity," Courtland's brother whispered. His face went white. "He knows the full extent, doesn't he? It's why he offered me the post."

"No!" That disavowal exploded from Courtland. "I've been planning to tell you the whole of it, Keir," he said quietly. After he'd managed enough discreet sales to pay down some of the more ruthless creditors.

But then he'd lost his position as the duke's man of affairs. And Courtland had seemed intent on creating that mess he'd made for his brother.

And then, with his brother again employed by his duke, he'd anticipated Keir would be consumed with his work once more.

"When were you going to tell me *this*?" Keir hissed.

Wincing under the sting of fury and outrage, Courtland dragged a hand through his hair. "I was going to get around to it."

"Get around to it?" His brother's voice rose a notch. "Get around to it?"

"How did you—"

"It doesn't matter how I found out."

"Higgans?"

His brother went tight-lipped, too honorable to lie, but also too loyal to betray his friend. "You were having debt collectors come through."

It was the man of affairs. That had been Courtland's underestimation. He'd not, however, anticipated his man of affairs would have spoken about their state to Keir. Which he should have. The two, both spares of their late fathers, had been almost as close as Courtland and Keir.

"I've been discreet," he said tightly. "I've managed to keep the state of our affairs from our sisters." With the exception of Ellie. Courtland, however, opted to omit that particular detail. "Polite Society has not yet discovered the state of our finances." For had the *ton* known, there was no doubt it would have been mentioned on the front of every gossip page. And every father longing for the title of duchess for his daughter would have been darkening his doorstep.

*That is inevitable . . .* , a jeering voice taunted.

Keir grabbed one of the leather winged chairs, dragged it close to Courtland's desk, and seated himself. "You sold off the contents of the library?"

"They weren't titles the girls read." The gothic ones and romantic tales and military ones he'd hidden from their father he'd also since kept safe from the sales pile. For now.

"The portraits?"

"Mother and the familial portraits I've retained." And he would. "Only the frames holding father's likeness I've sold off," he said with a grin.

It went unreturned.

"You are planning to sell the jewels Mother managed to hide from him," his brother said bluntly.

A muscle rippled along Courtland's jaw. "Higgans has said too much."

"Answer the question," Keir shouted.

"I am," he confirmed.

His brother cursed.

Knowing Ellie's proclivity for lurking about, Courtland glanced in more than half-fear at the closed door panel. "Will you . . . lower your voice? As for the jewelry, Mother hated them," Courtland said, feeling the need to defend this decision. However, she'd retained them . . . for her children. Courtland now understood why. She'd been aware of precisely the state her husband would leave his children in.

Keir brought a fist down on the desk; and the notes that

had arrived jumped, the neat stack toppling, and the letters cascaded in every direction. "Her daughters deserve to have a piece of her."

Yes, they did.

Courtland knew that.

Hearing his brother speak aloud the words he'd already known caused a tightening in his chest.

"And do not blame Higgans. Higgans knew those pieces should be retained so the girls have a link to Mama."

Unlike him.

He flinched, that insinuation clear.

"I should also point out: Higgans is also working largely without a salary when, with his acumen, he could secure any post."

That much was true.

And here Courtland had believed it impossible to feel any more pathetic this day. Everything was falling apart; all coming undone. This increasing sense of powerlessness was suffocating.

Restless, his hands shaking, he set to work tidying the pile of notes his brother had knocked down.

Feeling his brother's gaze on that slight quake, Courtland made himself stop and lowered his palms to the sides of his chair.

"I know you didn't create this situation," Keir said quietly.

"Why, thank you." And yet, Courtland had had mistresses over the years. He'd also been lavish with his gifts. Because he too had trusted his family's finances were in order. When, a year and a half earlier, he'd inherited the mess he had and learned all, he'd dismissed his last mistress. But he'd continued with memberships to his clubs.

Maintaining a proper, respectable image had been at the forefront of his mind.

And he'd deluded himself, too. There had been that. He'd let his mind see, but also gloss over, the fact of the dire straits they'd been in.

"It wasn't yours to take on alone, Courtland." And there

was a trace of hurt there in the tones of his twin that cut like a blade.

He'd been wrong before. *This* was the worst. Not the disappointment. Not the disgust or fury. It was the hurt he'd caused his brother. Even as well-intentioned as he'd been.

And suddenly, all the pressure that had been weighting him, the frustration at circumstances he'd inherited and been unable to fix, and everything he'd carried alone, snapped his patience. "How is there making it right, Keir?" he demanded. "We need funds. And funds don't simply materialize, as you know. The lands are rubbish. I've reduced our staff." Keeping on the most loyal and the eldest who'd been with them. But even that couldn't continue forever in their current state. "I've insisted we switch from tallow candles to beeswax."

His brother's cheeks went ashen.

Good, he was furious with Courtland for having failed to share . . . let him have all the ugly truths Courtland had been protecting him from. "And you insist I didn't tell you. But you knew. You *kneww*," he repeated, adding an extra syllable to drive home his point.

Keir's face went several shades paler. "I didn't," he whispered.

"My God, man, do you think I'd take your damned salary to pay for Hattie's trousseau if I wasn't one foot from the Marshalsea?" Was his opinion of Courtland so low? But then, why shouldn't it be?

Courtland's brother sat motionless; his eyes ravaged; his features arranged in a wounded mask.

All Courtland's muscles seized. He'd not wanted to do this. Even when Keir had come today demanding answers, he'd wanted to paint an image that wasn't . . . so grim. And yet, there was no way around it.

And in that moment, he finally realized . . . *I do not have to solve all of this on my own.* Since he'd assumed the title, Courtland's pride had been blinding. He'd been so focused on hiding his situation from everyone, including his siblings, that he'd not seen that help had been there before him, always.

Courtland's gaze slid over to a fuming Keir. All along, his brother had been right there, a capable man with a head for numbers and investments. Certainly more capable than Courtland. "You are right to be upset."

That seemed to startle his brother, shock replacing the anger in his gaze.

"I should have confided in you," Courtland said solemnly. "And more, I should have sought your guidance. I'm doing that now. We can fix this." He held Keir's eyes. "Together."

Keir said nothing for a long moment. His mouth moved as if he were trying—and failing—to formulate a reply. And then he nodded.

"Do you have ideas?" Courtland asked.

"I may have some," his brother said slowly, and then leaning forward, he availed himself of a sheet of parchment on Courtland's desk. "May I?"

Courtland nodded, even as Keir was already helping himself to a quill and ink.

"I've been studying the Board of Agriculture reports for several years now, and they've put forward many new innovative farming methods, ones that, given my observation of our family's lands, not only stand to increase crop production and quality, but earnings. I believe our best course would be to pursue the Norfolk system." Courtland stared on as his brother proceeded to create a crude drawing. "It is a four-crop rotation that will increase fodder production. The fields will be sown with wheat in the first year, turnips in the second and . . ." Seeming to feel Courtland's stare, Keir paused and looked up.

"You disagree," he said, his quill stilling over the page.

"Not at all," Courtland rushed to assure him. "Just the opposite, Keir. It's . . . brilliant." He motioned for his twin to continue. "Please."

And as he resumed, Courtland listened on.

". . . will provide you with two cash crops and two animal crops," his brother said, directing his pronouncements at the notes he rapidly took.

Why had Courtland waited? Why had he not gone to the brother not only skilled in numbers but who, despite his birthright as ducal spare, had been proud and unafraid to work? And how frustrating it must have been for Keir to see their family's properties and have ideas as to how to improve them, while being made . . . powerless. First, by their father, and then worse, by Courtland himself.

*Because you didn't know Cailin. Because you were as small-minded and pompous as every other lord in London.*

When his brother had finished, Courtland rubbed the back of his neck muscles. "So the question is, until those ventures are established and profitable . . . what do we do?"

"We pay off what we can, when we can," Keir said simply, putting down his quill.

*We.*

Courtland found himself smiling.

To give his fingers something to do, he picked up a note, grabbed his knife, and slid the blade under the seal.

*Creditors.*

He set the request aside, laying it out.

And moved on to the next, stacking letter after letter.

All the while, Keir watched on.

That had been Keir's way; when Courtland was a boy, even as a twin, it had been unnerving as hell to have someone capable of saying nothing and watching with piercing eyes.

"We appeal to the creditors and debtors and take whatever generosity they're willing to extend because they're enamored of the damned title," Courtland said, setting aside another note.

He picked up the next . . . and stilled.

Sliding the blade under the ornate gold seal of the Duke of Bentley, Courtland dropped the knife and hesitated before reading the damning words written there.

He'd been found out after all. The brother was going to request a meeting at dawn. As Courtland deserved. Were his sisters so involved with a rogue like Courtland, he'd have happily ended the man. And yet, where would that leave any of his siblings? Keir would be out of work, once and for all; left to inherit the penniless dukedom. His sisters— His mind balked, and he refused to think what fate awaited three headstrong, unconventional misses. As it was, there'd not been a single suitor for his sister. When—

"Courtland?" Keir asked quizzically.

Taking in an even breath, Courtland unfolded the note . . . and stopped—this time for altogether different reasons.

He glanced over at his brother. "It is an invitation." And not to a duel. Giddy relief pulled that observation from him.

"Yes, I understand His and Her Grace have arranged for an intimate house party at their Leeds estates."

It wasn't a duel. It wasn't the latest, greatest stumble made by Courtland.

"They are retiring early for the Season, and the duke is assembling his annual house party so that Bentley's daughter might make a match."

All his muscles coiled, and a wave of something burning, something insidious and green, something that felt very much like jealousy, coursed through him.

On the heels of that came the sobering reality of his exchange with a despondent Cailin Audley. *"I am . . . headed to the country . . ."*

Did Cailin even know the fate they intended for her? She was aware they were rushing her off . . . but did she know there'd be a sea of suitors?

She'd mourned the fact that she'd be robbed of the opportunity to explore London, and if she knew about the intentions her family had for her, she'd rail for altogether different reasons. For . . . she wasn't going off alone with her family. There was an entire affair planned; one that included Courtland among the guests. With meticulous care meant to ground his thoughts, Courtland folded the note along its crease and smoothed the pad of his thumb over that line. "Is there any indication which gentleman the duke . . . might favor for the lady?" he asked, his voice surprisingly steady.

"I don't know," Keir said, once more defaulting to his loyalty to his employer. "However, the list is unconventional for Bentley."

His ears pricked up. "Unconventional?"

"There are a number of self-made men among the invited guests. People whom . . . the lady might feel more comfortable with."

Unlike the peers who'd been rot to her. Aye, the duke had been wise to encourage men who not only had similar roots as his daughter but also could offer her the life she deserved.

And another pressure weighted his chest that day.

An image slipped in of the lady surrounded by dashing gentlemen vying for her attention; and one of them, a worthy one, with gads of wealth that would see her libraries filled and allow her the freedom to travel in search of those fossils that so fascinated her. Something visceral and stinging wound through his veins; a vicious, fiery hot envy. His fingers curled sharply on the corners of the thick ivory vellum, and he wrinkled the invitation.

He didn't want to see that.

He didn't want to be anywhere near that.

"Courtland?"

He jerked his head up. "Hmm?"

"I trust you'll accept that invitation."

That was the safe expectation, given their families' connections to one another; and it was Keir's employer, Keir's employer who'd also generously forgiven Keir for Courtland's behaviors that day in Staffordshire.

The fact that Courtland had known the duke since Courtland was a babe likely accounted for his inclusion in the event. Because there could be no doubting, with Courtland's reputation and what the duke surely knew of his finances, Courtland would never find himself at even the bottom of the other man's list of potential husbands for Cailin.

That thought should relieve him.

It *should*.

But it didn't.

His brother leaned forward, and the leather groaned. "Courtland?"

"Hmm?" he asked, jolting back to the moment.

Keir looked back peculiarly. "I said, I trust you'll accept the invitation."

Courtland didn't want to go. Because he didn't trust himself around her. And more, he didn't want to witness better men than him vying for her hand. "There is much to be done here," he hedged. He despised the yearning for more . . . and the reminder of how little he had to offer one such as Cailin.

"But . . . but . . ." his brother stammered, rendered effectively speechless.

Of course, there were also so many reasons to go.

Seeing her should not rank among the top of those reasons; and yet, selfish, fixed on his own happiness as he'd so often been, Courtland couldn't shake that reason from his mind.

"But . . . he is the duke. And there are benefits to going," his brother said, and it took a moment to process that those were Keir's words and not a mere echo of his own thoughts. "He's invited the entire family, has he not?"

Courtland managed a nod.

"You can drink the duke's brandy"—is that really what his brother thought would motivate him?—"and the meals would be another expense that we needn't worry after." Courtland winced. How matter-of-fact Keir was with that enumeration. "The horses will of course be stabled and fed in the duke's barns. The household expenses here in London will be decreased significantly if you and the girls leave. And—"

"Enough," he said sharply, and his brother immediately stopped mid-sentence. "Just enough," Courtland repeated anyway.

"I'm sorry," Keir said quietly; and for a moment, Courtland saw before him not the capable, skilled man his brother had grown to be, but the downtrodden boy who'd been bullied by villagers and their father. And Courtland hated himself for turning into the duke once more.

"Forgive me," Courtland said, scrubbing a hand down his face. "I was short. None of this is your fault. Quite the opposite." Keir had worked, while Courtland had continued to live the lavish life they'd enjoyed before their father's passing. Why, back in Oxford, Courtland had been carousing while Keir was studying and applying himself to a future. "I . . . have to see to . . . matters here." Now that he'd resolved to begin working toward improving his estates, there was much to be done. "More good can come from being here."

"But you don't have to. Bentley has me remaining in London. I can see to both his affairs and ours while you join the duke."

Join the duke?

It wasn't Bentley he gave a fig about seeing.

Cailin . . .

The moment her visage slipped in, reality reared its head. He had nothing to offer her. Not at this moment. Unlike the other hardworking fellows whom her father had included among his guest list.

His brother stood, and Courtland looked up. "I believe it would be . . . a mistake for you to reject the duke's generosity, and I'd ask you to reconsider your decision."

Yes, it would be a mistake.

Keir made to go, but then stopped at the front of the room. Turning back, he faced Courtland. "In the future, I'd ask that you are transparent with me about circumstances affecting me and my sisters."

"Of course," he promised, coming to his feet. That was the least his brother deserved. "And . . . you have my assurance that I'll not sell Mother's jewelry until . . ." they absolutely had to.

Keir nodded, and with that, he let himself out.

The moment he was gone, Courtland sat down hard in his seat.

His brother wasn't wrong. Just as his brother did not

speak about turning Courtland into a fortune hunter: as his brother, and his twin, and his best friend, he knew that great fear Courtland had forever carried. And Courtland appreciated that he'd not urged him onto that path. Even as that was the only one staring down at him. Because he had no skills. Or land that yielded profits.

Not yet.

It would take time, and there would be a process.

It was also, in short, the reason he didn't wish to make the journey to Leeds and see Cailin be courted by a swell of men who were all better, more respectable sorts than himself.

A small figure stepped out from behind the curtains. "Well, that sounded even worse than usual."

With a shout, Courtland jumped to his feet so quick the chair went flying out from behind him, tumbling to the floor. His heart thundering, he took in with horror the sight of his youngest sibling skipping over, like she was out on a jaunt through the park and not as though she'd been listening in on the dire state he—they—now found themselves facing. "Ellie," he croaked. A pretend pistol in hand, she hopped into the seat previously vacated by Keir. "What are you doing?" he pleaded, as he righted his chair and seated himself.

Studying her toy weapon the way a military man might inspect his actual firearm, she pointed it past Courtland's shoulder and, squinting her left eye, she aimed the pistol at the wall behind him. "Listening in." As usual.

God, he really needed to start checking behind the curtains.

"I'd start with Mother's jewels."

He stared blankly at his sister. Surely she wasn't saying what he thought she was.

"If you're looking to pay off as much debt as possible, and spare yourself debtor's prison, Mama's jewels should be the first. She didn't really like her jewels." She'd only wanted her husband's affections, not some baubles he'd had his man of affairs purchase on an occasion. "That will buy you time." She lowered her toy weapon. "Some of it."

Yes, she was saying precisely what he'd thought she was. "Ellie, you cannot—"

"What?" she interrupted. "Listen in?"

"Yes. It is not polite," he said, the irony of him doling out lessons on propriety not lost on him.

Ellie snorted. "And here, society's leading rogue lecturing *me* on being . . . polite."

And apparently the irony hadn't been lost on his sister, either. Courtland winced, his mind balking at the idea of just what other information his sleuth of a sister was in possession of . . . about him. Determined to steer the course somewhere far safer than his wicked reputation, he brought them back to the matter of the morn. "Be that as it may, you cannot listen in on my business dealings," he spoke in the same tones his stern tutors and instructors had adopted with him.

"Why not?"

He blinked slowly.

"I mean, they are our dealings, too, are they not?" she pressed. "Furthermore, it is the only way a lady can find out what exactly is going on." She swung her legs over the side of the chair and let her feet fall to the floor. "You men would be content to keep us in the dark about our fates and futures, and your sisters will be the last to know that there is absolutely nothing."

"They're your sisters, too," he pointed out dryly.

She sighed. "This is true." Suddenly, she looked his way, with a maturity befitting a woman of twenty-four and not a girl of fourteen. "You know, it is not your fault."

No. He didn't. Because it was. "I know," he said anyway, for her benefit.

She pointed her pistol at his chest. "I don't like liars, Courtland, and also, you're deuced bad at it."

He sighed. "It matters not who brought us to this state, it is my responsibility to . . . fix it."

"And fix it you shall. What of that lady?"

Cailin flashed in his mind's eye once more, and Courtland tamped down a groan. Not this . . .

His sister leaned forward. "You are worried about being Father, I suspect, and marrying for a fortune."

He hesitated a moment, and yet, it was futile: the imp before him apparently saw and knew all. Why, she'd gathered the whole of their circumstances before all of his siblings. Courtland gave a reluctant nod.

"Court her, Courtland," she softly urged. "You like her, do you not?"

His cravat tightened several notches, and he immediately wrestled it loose. "I—"

"You cost Keir his employment because of her—"

"He got it—"

"Yes, yes. I'm not focusing on his having secured his post again. But rather your interest in the lady."

"I have nothing to offer her."

His sister laughed. "You are a duke. You have a dukedom. And she can be your duchess."

Their discussion at the Temple of the Muses replayed in his head. He couldn't imagine a woman who'd less interest in belonging to High Society than Cailin Audley. And wedding a duke? "She doesn't wish to be a duchess." He dropped his elbows onto the arms of his chair and slumped slightly in his seat.

Ellie's eyes formed enormous saucers, and she leaned forward so she arched slightly across the edge of his desk. "Indeed?"

"Indeed." Apparently, he'd found the sole woman in England who didn't aspire to that title.

Ellie clasped her hands to her chest and went soft-eyed. "Oh, then she is the perfect duchess for you."

He stared at her with a dawning horror. "I thought you were my only sister who wasn't romantic."

A blush stained her cheeks, and she pointed her pistol squarely at his chest. "Have a care, brother. I'm not romantic, but I'm also not one who'd see my brother as miserable as my mother was."

A pang struck his chest. Intuitive as she was now, and as she'd always been, she'd forever seen so much. Too much.

He'd just taken it for granted that she'd been too young to be aware of their mother's perpetual state of sorrow. Or mayhap it was simply that it had been easier to let himself believe she'd not known about their parents' cold, emotionless union. And somehow the topic of his inevitable marriage to some inevitable lady seemed eminently preferable a topic to talk on. Tapping his fingertips upon his opened ledger, he nudged his chin in his sister's direction. "I'm afraid I don't understand how a lady having absolutely no desire to be a duchess means she'd make a perfect duchess."

She pointed her eyes to the ceiling. "How could a man be notorious as a rogue and yet so hopelessly confused when it comes to matters of the heart." Resting her palms on her knees, Ellie leaned all the way forward once more. "She isn't a woman who wants to wed you because of your title, but because of who you are."

He wrinkled his brow. "She doesn't wish to marry me at all. Of course, we haven't discussed the matter of marriage. At all. Not because—" His sister stared back with rapt attention, and he instantly stopped that rambling flow. He cleared his throat. "You were saying?"

Ellie threw her hands up. "I am saying if you have to marry, you don't have to marry for the reason Father did. You can marry because you genuinely like a woman, Courtland. Because you respect her, and because you enjoy being with her, and because she feels similar sentiments for you."

Courtland reclined in his seat once more, and catching his chin in his hand, he contemplated his sister and her words. Ellie's was, simply put . . . a novel concept. At least, not one he'd considered: the prospect and possibility of forming a union with someone whom he actually admired and liked; forging a future that wasn't because of societal connections, and in his case, built solely on necessity.

Perhaps . . . his youngest sibling wasn't that far off the mark.

He and Cailin *did* enjoy one another's company.

And yes, she didn't necessarily wish to be a duchess,

but . . . surely that was just a small obstacle she could come 'round on.

He saw that he had little choice when it came to keeping out of debtor's prison and caring for his siblings.

Ellie's thin lips formed a terrifying grin. "Eh, once again, you see that I'm right, don't you, brother?"

"Run along, minx," he muttered, and with a little giggle his sister hopped down, gave a jaunty wave, and left.

Ellie had been correct . . . just not in the way she'd thought.

At last, Courtland had allowed himself to imagine what a marriage to Cailin could be.

It had been Cailin who'd opened his eyes to the fact that he needn't be passive in his finances. Courtland needn't turn himself into a fortune hunter. Granted, marriage to a wealthy heiress would be the immediate cure to his situation and, according to Polite Society, a more respectable way than his dealing in investments and trade.

But he intended to forge his own way . . . societal opinions be damned.

And although he might not be in a place to offer her security, with the help of Keir and Higgans, Courtland would eventually be able to offer Cailin a life she deserved.

Eventually.

That was if the lady's family didn't rush her into marriage with some other chap.

Cursing into the quiet, Courtland grabbed a quill and dashed off his acceptance.

# Chapter 15

Cailin arrived in her father's Leeds estate on Monday. By Wednesday, the duke and duchess's guests had begun to arrive.

At first, she'd only paid a passing attention to each arrival throughout the day. Losing herself exploring the mammoth stone-front home and property as vast as the village she'd spent her life in, she'd just stolen the chance glance at the front drive when carriages rolled up.

Except . . . somewhere around the fifth carriage she'd happened to spy, she'd also begun to glean—something was amiss.

Because descending from every single one of those carriages was, not one of the duke's usual, more mature, graying friends, or the duchess's friends, but rather . . . a young gentleman. Followed by a young gentleman. And a young gentleman after him. And another after him.

This was no coincidence.

Stalking through the halls, with servants pausing to dip curtsies as she passed, fury fueled her steps.

She tossed the door to his office open. "I'm here to— Oh,"

she blurted, and then swiftly moved her gaze to the ceiling. "Forgive me." Yes, well, this was why one knocked, then.

There came a gasp and a rustle of fabric.

Alas, the image would be burned indelibly in the worst way upon her mind: the sight of her father and his wife upon his lap, locked in a passionate embrace, the pair of them very much in-love newlyweds. Which, in fairness, was precisely what they were.

Gauging how long it would take to make oneself presentable, and tacking on an additional ten to her silent counting, Cailin forced herself to look at her father.

One would have never guessed anything had been amiss: both duke and duchess stood shoulder to shoulder, serene, and perfectly composed.

Such was the skill of those most powerful of peers. Well, she didn't want to bother with serene or composed; she was livid with rage. Fury wound its way through her all over again, and she recalled her purpose in being here. She folded her arms. "I would like to speak with you."

Her father and his wife exchanged a look. They spoke quietly to one another, and there was such an intimacy to that private discourse, the way each of their bodies arched naturally toward the other's. She bit the inside of her cheek. She'd wanted that. She'd longed for that special bond shared only by two lovers, and for a moment in time she'd believed she'd had it. But she'd not. Not truly. After Ian had been injured, he'd turned away from her; shutting her out, and she'd realized . . . love . . . it hurt more than it was worth. So what accounted for this stab of envy?

A recollection of Courtland slipped in: him beside her on that sofa, conversing with her so freely, about interests they shared.

Her chest shuddered, and her breath caught on a horrified inhale that brought two sets of stares over her way. What in blazes was she thinking?

Just then, the duchess patted the front of the duke's lapels. Cailin's father nodded once, and the duchess moved out from behind the desk.

She favored Cailin with a small, supportive smile before slipping out.

The moment she'd gone, Cailin found herself. She stalked over in a whir of skirts. "Do you have anything to say?" she demanded.

He paused.

She'd managed to unsettle him. Good, let him, the all-powerful duke, know what it felt like to have his world off-balance.

"Hello?" he asked sheepishly.

She rocked back on her heels. *Hello?*

The duke cleared his throat. "Ahem. If you would?" Her father gestured, and she followed that motion to the chairs across from him.

She'd be damned if she allowed him to speak from that throne-like seat. "I'm not sitting." *There.*

And it was as though, for all the ways in which he was clueless as to his dealings with her, he sensed the control she sought. He moved out from behind the desk and joined her on the other side. Perching his hip on the side of that broad piece of mahogany furniture, he positioned himself there, as more an equal in this discourse.

"This isn't an intimate dinner party," she said flatly.

There was another brief pause. "Perhaps it might seem as though it is less than intimate," he began slowly. "The word suggests it should be a small gathering." *My God, did he really believe I was seeking clarification on the difference between affairs among the peerage and the paupers?* "But by Polite Society's standards, it—"

"That isn't what I'm talking about," she interrupted. She narrowed her eyes. "And you know it."

He hesitated, and it was a damning moment of silence; one that confirmed what she'd gathered about the intent of the affair.

Or rather, what she'd gathered too late.

For had she known what this would be, what he intended? She'd never have come.

Because here, in the country, with a house party centered on her, there was even less escape than there'd been in London.

*Say it*, she silently screamed. Demanding he own up to what this hunt really was. And when he still wouldn't, the thin thread of her control broke. With a sound of disgust, she marched around him and took up the place he'd abandoned at his desk, commandeering it as her own.

"Where is it?" she demanded, yanking open the center drawer.

"Cailin?" he implored as she rummaged.

And if she hadn't been so incandescent with rage, she might have appreciated that another nobleman, any other father would have attempted to put a forcible stop to her search.

"Where is the guest list? I trust you'd have it here— something so very important." Except she had already located it. Yanking it free, she looked at the names compiled, skimming and scanning. She narrowed her eyes on the names written there, most of them unfamiliar. But in fairness, with the exception of her and her family, *all* of them were unfamiliar. She counted. Inventorying all these strangers.

Three quarters down the page, she stopped. Cailin might not have been born to this world, as everyone was so keen to remind her.

She may have made, and would continue to make, all manner of missteps where Polite Society was concerned. She might not even understand.

What she did not have to be born to this station to realize, however, was their plans for her.

Deflated, and feeling defeated, she sank onto his seat. "You are trying to marry me off." When only a damning silence answered her, she looked up blankly.

At some point, the duke had come around to join Cailin. He hovered beside her shoulder.

He looked as lost as she felt, in this new life . . . and in this new family.

"Aren't you?" She bade him to answer, when he neither confirmed nor denied that supposition.

Dropping to his haunches, he stretched out a hand. "Cailin," he said, his voice strained.

She slapped his fingers away, and he recoiled.

"Do not," she seethed, flying to her feet. Her heart racing, and fury and horror licking at her insides. "You've no right to lure me here on a lie of escape, when what you really intended to do was rid yourself of me."

He paled, his features contorting in a paroxysm of grief, and he straightened. "No," he whispered. "Never. That isn't what I—"

"You didn't throw together this hasty party to find me a husband?" she demanded, shaking the sheet at him.

"Yes." He dragged a hand through his hair. "No."

"Which is it? Because it can't be both," she jeered, giving the page another wag; this time under his nose.

"I want to see you settled," he said, his tone beseeching.

Funny that: she'd never believed a duke capable of begging, and yet her father now was. Had he not sought to betray her in this way, perhaps she would have even been moved by that evidence of his humanity.

With a sound of disgust, she threw the guest list down on the immaculate surface of his desk, a piece of furniture finer and more costly than all the pieces in her family's Staffordshire cottage combined.

"You do not even know me. You never knew me . . . and because I'm here, what, a few months, you think you get to tell me how I should live my life? And you'd presume to fill your household with gentlemen so that you can marry me off." Her voice fell to a whisper. "That way you can be free of your . . . responsibilities," she spat. "Free of your—" She waggled her hands. "Obligation, so that you can go back to living your life and feeling like you've atoned for your sins."

Her father sucked in a jagged breath.

One time, she had been attending a boxing match in the village when an ox-sized fellow squared off against a smaller, wirier fighter. The bigger boxer landed a blow to his opponent's midsection, felling him. In this moment, her father had the look of that downed fellow.

To give her hands a task, she rested them along the back of the leather winged chair he'd been expecting her to take.

"I love you," he finally said, his deep voice quavering slightly. "I would have only ever wanted you in my life, Cailin," and then the duke seemed to have found himself, his voice steady, unwavering in its strength. "But you have to understand. I do not have any heirs, and it is unlikely I ever will. No matter how unfair, that is the way of primogeniture. I will, of course, see you and your brothers cared for, but one day," he said, taking a step toward her, "when I pass, all of this"—he swept a hand over the room—"will go to another. The properties and the wealth that go with it. The baubles that fill the rooms. The portraits that hang on the walls. Everything," he added. "And I would know that you are cared for and looked after by a man who is honorable and good."

"I was in love with a man who was honorable," she said tersely. "I've no wish to do so again."

Surprise brought the duke's eyebrows up.

And the moment that revelation came out, she wished she'd remained silent. Because . . . speaking about Ian to her brother, or father, or anyone for that matter, left her uncomfortable. "I didn't know," he murmured.

"Why should you? You do not know anything about me."

At that assault, he brought his broad shoulders back. "If he'd been as honorable as you insist he is, he would have never left you," her father murmured.

She gasped.

"I'll apologize for not having discussed your opinion on the matter of marriage. I could try and tell you that here in Polite Society, the expectation is that a woman wed." That was the expectation everywhere. "And so I allowed myself to believe it wasn't a betrayal to throw together a hasty affair for . . ." His cheeks went red. "The intentions that I had. I now know, even as my intentions were good, my actions were wrong." And then, as though it were her private sanctuary he'd invaded and he sought to give her back full possession of it, he exited quietly, drawing the door closed with a soft click behind him.

Cailin remained in his offices; the echo of the words she'd hurled at her father with an intent to wound made for lonely company.

To hell with him. She'd not feel bad for having said what she had to him.

*Cailin* had been the one to convince Rafe to make the journey here. *Cailin* had been the one who urged him to allow their father entry into their lives. And how did that same father treat Cailin? By attempting to hide her away, and marry her off, while keeping his motives toward her furtive.

He'd betrayed her, and as such she'd nothing to feel guilty *for*.

That was what she told herself.

Except speaking to the duke as she'd done hadn't made her feel better; lashing out at him had only heightened this absolute sense of . . . isolation.

It was a state she'd been familiar with since she entered the world and the mother who'd given her life had perished. Her brothers had spent their days working from the moment the sun rose until the moment it slipped from the sky. And her time had been spent overseeing the cottage. Yes, there'd been visits with other villagers, and exchanges during the occasional fairs, but there'd not really ever been a shared connection between her . . . and anyone. Hers had been a largely lonely state. She'd not felt badly for it, either. How could she have, when it was the only way she'd known?

Or she'd *thought* herself unbothered by it. Perhaps . . . all the while she'd lied to herself.

Mayhap that was why she'd fallen so hard and so quickly for Ian. He'd represented her first real connection with *someone*. And that was, no doubt, why she'd been so fearful of letting anyone in *after* him.

She'd shared of herself and been burned with hurt and loss.

Cursing into the quiet, she let herself slide down into her father's seat.

Blast it all.

There came a slight heavy knock, one as confident as the duke's, and a moment later her brother entered.

She cautiously eyed her brother's approach.

He dropped his large frame into the seat she'd been unwilling to take during her exchange with the duke.

Not taking her gaze off Rafe, Cailin picked up the guest list and held it aloft. "You knew," she stated without preamble. "That this was all about marrying me off?"

"I didn't," and the wounded quality of that denial confirmed his sincerity. Not that Rafe was one for prevaricating. He told a person precisely what he thought and didn't dance around truths. "That is, not until we arrived," he muttered, dragging a hand through his hair. "But by that point, we were here and . . ."

"And there never seemed like the right time since we arrived?" she asked dryly.

"It's not that simple, Cailin," he began earnestly and immediately stopped, as Cailin strangled on the pained giggle climbing her throat.

"Nothing about this is simple, Rafe."

"But it is. You don't have to marry, Cailin." He shrugged his big shoulders; those same broad shoulders he'd use to carry her atop when she was a girl and he played at father. As had Wesley and Hunter.

Her heart spasmed. How she missed them. How she missed all of them being together.

Rafe gave her a look. "Do you truly believe I of all people would ever make *you* marry, Cailin?"

Her lips twitched. "No," she finally conceded.

"No, *of course* I wouldn't." He snorted. "I'd be happy if you remained unwed and lived with me and Edwina forever."

*Live with him forever.*

Her smile fell.

Because . . . what was the alternative for a woman who didn't marry? One was still reliant upon the generosity of one's family.

Hearing him speak those words, however, reminded her that he was still her devoted, loving older brother, that they were still of the same team. "The whole reason I wished to go to London was to explore the city and museums and now—"

"And now you have to balance doing the things you don't want . . . with those you do. You couldn't have one without the other, Cailin," he said sadly. Rafe took her left hand in his larger one, both of their palms rough and their nails short. They were the hands of the Audleys and not children of a duke.

But that was what they were now.

She bit down hard on her lower lip. "Why must you always be right?" she said, hating that she'd deluded herself into believing she could have it all. When life around her had proven that women couldn't have anything . . . and women born as a duke's by-blow had even less.

He gave one of her curls a tug, bringing her gaze up to his. "Because I'm your big brother."

She knocked her shoulder against his, and he returned the gesture in a gentler way.

"I let myself imagine what the experience would be," she whispered, staring emptily at the tops of her hands. "It wasn't, however, what things really could have ever been here." Not when she was the daughter of a duke—and a bastard daughter at that.

Rafe scrubbed a hand along his face. "Oh, Kay-Kay."

And in that moment, she nearly dissolved into a blubbering mess. Tears welled, and she blinked frantically and furiously to keep them from rolling down her cheeks in a torrent she knew could never be stopped.

For Kay-Kay was the moniker her brothers had used for her when she was a babe unable to speak her own name. Over the years, her big, powerful brothers used it less and less. Until not at all.

Until now.

Unable to meet her brother's gaze, and let him see those tears that would gut him, she glanced down at the lengthy list of names . . . when her gaze snagged on one near the bottom of the page.

She sat upright; her heart pounded a bit harder.

For not all the names included were those of strangers. There was one . . . plus a handful more that were familiar.

*Courtland.*

A rush of warmth and relief coursed through her at seeing his name among those who'd been included. Which was silly. She'd only met him but a handful of times . . . and yet, there existed within their every meeting . . . an intimacy; where she'd spoken about books she'd loved, and frustrations she'd carried regarding her circumstances, and he'd listened and shared in that exchange with her.

And then, there'd been their embrace. One that she secretly thought of still; an explosive moment of passion in Staffordshire that lingered in her dreams. The memory of his embrace had only been reinforced by that tender kiss shared between them at the Temple of the Muses. Different than the volatile sparks that had consumed her that long-ago day with Courtland, but no less . . . consuming for the memory of it. And him.

"Cailin?" her brother's voice brought her head snapping up.

Warmth rushed her cheeks, and she returned the list to where she'd found it. "What?" she asked tiredly.

"I meant what I said before . . . I'd be content if you never wed." Rafe paused. "But what I didn't say is, what you want matters more. Your happiness is most important, and even as I disagree with our father on"—he motioned to the place she'd put the sheet of names—"how he's handled this, I would be happy if you found love."

It was a significant admission from a brother who'd glowered at every village boy who'd even walked too close.

A little laugh escaped her, and her eyes slid shut; the irony not lost on her that her brooding, once-always-scowling brother had become . . . a romantic. He now spoke of love and romance . . . the same sentiments she secretly yearned for.

"Ian—"

She came quickly to her feet. "I'm not talking about Ian with you," she said on a rush, wanting to discuss her former sweetheart with Rafe even less than she had wished to speak of him with the duke.

He proved dogged in this as in everything. "I was as keen to never discuss his name again, but that was wrong. I know your heart is still broken, but it's important that you talk about it."

"My heart isn't broken," she said, and she found with no small amount of shock . . . that it wasn't.

"It isn't," she repeated when Rafe only stared at her with a gentle disbelief.

It had been.

But somewhere along the way, she'd thought of him and his betrayal less. Actually . . . not at all.

Since Courtland arrived in Staffordshire and turned her world upside down with the promise of more waiting for her.

"And what if he were to come here tomorrow?" There was an earnest quality to that question. "What if you had a second chance at a life with him?"

A little laugh escaped her. "Why do I think if I said I wanted that, you'd drag him here yourself like some kind of fairy godmother?"

"Do you?" he pressed, and Cailin sighed.

"None of this is about Ian." And leave it to the world in general to believe her current discontent stemmed from her past relationship.

In the end, Rafe relented. "Very well. Let me ask you this instead, Cailin: what *do* you even want from life?"

She stared at him, startled by the question; and worse, startled by her own lack of an immediate answer.

"I don't think you even know, Cailin," Rafe said when she failed to respond.

"Of course I do," she shot back . . . belatedly.

He ignored her protestation. "And I think it is time you start looking inside yourself and determine what it is that will bring you happiness . . . and seize it, Cailin."

With that, her brother gave her hand another gentle squeeze and then left.

She sat in her father's empty office, alone with her brother's words playing in her head.

How dare he. She knew what she wanted.

Didn't she?

Her brother spoke of Ian, but none of this was about Ian.

These past months since coming to London, she'd been so focused on everything she didn't want to do and bemoaned her lack of freedom. But what did she really want of life?

Purpose.

Happiness.

Freedom.

Three states that women struggled to find.

Restless, she wandered to the windows overlooking her father's vast properties, taking in the endless view of emerald pastures, trees, and rolling hills.

Suddenly, she stopped.

Her gaze snagged on the powerful figure striding below.

Courtland.

He was here.

Her discussion with Rafe immediately forgotten, Cailin took off running.

# Chapter 16

In the end, Courtland had decided to accept the Duke of Bentley's invitation.

Because of their families' long-standing connection to one another.

Because Bentley also happened to be Keir's employer.

Because he'd been far more generous to their family than they'd ever deserved.

But in that moment, as Courtland turned and found Cailin flying across the grounds toward him, he acknowledged the lie to himself.

His being here had nothing to do with all those reasons connected to responsibility and expectations . . . and everything to do with wanting to see her.

"Courtland!"

Some one hundred yards away, she flew with the speed of a sprite; her plait whipping back and forth, slapping at her shoulders as she ran.

His breath stuck in his chest, and in that moment, he rather thought he lost his heart to her.

She reached him, out of breath, perspiring at her brow,

and her cheeks flushed the most magnificent shade of red from her efforts. "You're here," she exclaimed.

He opened his mouth, but she continued speaking excitedly. "At my father's"—her lips firmed into a hard line—"*house* party." Cailin's distaste and disgust for the event her father had planned couldn't have been clearer had she spoken the words aloud. So she knew what this affair was really about, then, and the woman whom he'd come to know would only ever despise it.

And he wanted to say something about it. He wanted to rail with her.

Cailin tipped her neck back to better meet his gaze. "I was glad to see you here."

His heart knocked funnily in his chest. "You were?" he asked, his voice strange to his own ears.

She was happy that he'd been included among the list of potential—

"Of course." Her eyes and mouth went soft, and the whisper of a wind rustled the air around them, stirring a loose tendril that had escaped her plait. He reached up to brush that stray strand back into—"Now, I have a friend here."

His hand froze and then fell to his side.

*A friend.*

It was certainly the first time a lady who wasn't his sister had referred to him as a . . . friend.

Yes, women were generally glad to see his name included at social events, but only because they saw a prospective bridegroom, and a duke at that.

This was a singular first: his company desired not because of his rank, but because . . . of him.

It left him heady, this dizzying sensation.

Cailin cocked her head, and her features dipped slightly. "I've shocked you with my directness," she said stiffly.

"No!" he said quickly, shooting a hand out before realizing his boldness—and that he'd touched her; and he yanked his fingers back. "My apologies."

At every turn, he found himself off-kilter with Cailin

Audley. It was as though she had her smallest finger on the earth's axis and dipped it, knocking a steady ground out from under him. He forgot everything he thought he knew about women, and all the skill and ease that had come in charming them . . . for one simple fact—she was unlike any woman he'd ever known.

"Walk with me." Hers wasn't so much a question.

He hesitated a moment before falling into step beside her.

If anyone looked outside and saw him and Cailin alone together, without the benefit of a chaperone, they'd bring scandal down upon the house party . . . and themselves. And yet, he recalled her thirst for freedom, and selfishly, he wanted this moment between them to be uninterrupted by the oppressive rules of Polite Society.

On the heels of his own happiness at being here with her, he registered the details he'd failed to note.

The white lines of tension at the corner of her mouth.

They walked at a brisk clip. For someone of her smaller height, she moved at an impressive pace; her steps weren't the mincing ones lords and ladies had governesses ingrain into their daughters. Rather, there was a purpose to her movements that he found himself appreciating.

Just as much, he appreciated the easy silence between him and Cailin. He didn't feel a need to fill a void of quiet for the simple fact . . . there was no void.

"Your father's estate is among my favorite places to be," he said as they continued toward the expanse of woods on the perimeter of the duke's property.

Cailin cast him a sideways glance. "And you are familiar with the duke's estate."

"Our fathers were friendly." Two rogues. One who'd never remarried, and who'd managed to tame his wild ways, while the other had let his thirst for drink and women and wagering be the end of him . . . and his family. "Two once-young dukes, it was a natural friendship." One that had made little sense to Courtland as he'd come to know Bentley. Bentley, who'd been nothing like Courtland's wastrel father. Discreet when his father had flaunted his mistresses. Careful with his finances when Courtland's sire had all but burned the money that had come to him through his wife's dowry. They'd been opposite images of one another. "At some point, your father began hosting a summer house party and included the children of those guests in attendance."

They reached the end of the lawns; a manicured path that had been constructed extended out into the small forest.

They paused.

Tapping a hand against his thigh, he eyed the path they'd just traveled. Bentley's mammoth stone manor proved a mere speck on the horizon. Even on the chance guests happened to peer out the window, they'd struggle to spy anyone so far from the estate; and they'd certainly not be able to make out their identities.

He turned his gaze back to Cailin.

She eyed the manufactured forest, certain trees chosen for cover, a measured distance between the thin oaks, suggesting there'd been a careful selection of the trees that grew here. And then, lifting her skirts slightly, she ventured along the path, moving inside.

Courtland hesitated, warring with himself and the rules of propriety that bound them, but he was a moth and she was the flame, and he understood at last why those creatures were content to burn; he followed after her.

The coverage of leaves blotted out the light, layering the space in a deeper darkness.

As she went, Cailin eyed the grounds wistfully. Periodically, she paused to touch the trunk of a tree. "A gardener designed this. Did he not?" She tossed that question over her shoulder.

"Yes." That knowledge came from the team of workers who'd tended these grounds when he'd been a boy visiting.

Sadness wreathed her features. "It is so different from Staffordshire. There is something . . . artificial about all of this. It should be untamed, wild, and not manipulated so."

Somewhere along the way, they'd ceased speaking of the copse. In fact, did the lady even realize as much? Did she know at some point she'd begun speaking of herself and Polite Society, and its walls around her? Such a woman would never freely remain in Town. Even if he was the manner of a man with a fortune and security to offer her, instead of *her* being the one with fortune and security to offer *him*, she was destined for a place different from his world.

Except . . . "It isn't all terrible. There can be beauty found among it," he said quietly, and Cailin blinked slowly, as if she'd forgotten she wasn't alone and only just recalled she spoke to another—to him. "Come." And as though it were the most natural thing in the world, he took her glove-less hand lightly in his, hating the scrap of fabric that denied him the full feel of her palm.

"What is this?" she asked.

"You will see." He guided her on a different path, one that meandered. The stepping stones, once smooth and new, were now aged, ground into the earth and nearly concealed by moss and grass, revealing signs of being deliberately forgotten; articles once specifically placed, but at some point in time, the gardener had ceased to tend them.

They reached the end of the trail, which emptied out onto the shore of the river and stopped.

Cailin gasped, her fingers slipped from his, and he grieved over that lost connection; but that selfish regret proved short-lived.

"My goodness," she whispered, her gaze taking in the downed tree trunk that had been repurposed as a makeshift plank that extended across the river, linking the two shores.

Gathering up her hem once more, she slipped inside the playground. Cailin tipped her head back and studied the clever fort that had been built among the trees.

And he recalled the same wonderment he'd known as a boy at the nature's playground his duke had made of his properties.

Time had likely left the trees he and his siblings, and all

the other children who'd come, and danced happily across, aged and weathered.

Cailin headed for the lone swing, dangling from the wide limb, that the children who'd tired of playing pirates and swimming had fought over. She stopped briefly and caught both sides of the thick coils of rope, and then she gave the empty seat a slight push. "This is magnificent." She exhaled that adulation on a gentle sigh.

Courtland drank in the sight of her as she gripped the aged rope in her fingers.

"Yes," he murmured. Yes, she was. "My father wasn't one to bother with his own children," he said, distracted by the sight of her in her wonderment. "Bentley created this playground for when the children of his guests would come visit." As a boy, Courtland had secretly wished a man like Bentley had been his father . . . and not the heartless one who'd never had a use for Courtland and his siblings.

"What did he care about if not his children?"

He stared.

"Your father?" Cailin asked.

She didn't concentrate on what he'd revealed about *her* father. Rather, she focused on what he'd inadvertently shared about *his*.

"He cared solely about his own pleasures," he said, adding a finality to that statement. He didn't want his miserable sire to intrude on this moment with Cailin.

And seeming to sense that and honor it, Cailin returned her focus to the grounds.

"I am so very glad you had this place to play, and that my father provided you and other children with it," she murmured, and there was none of the anger, outrage, and hurt she should feel.

After all, she'd grown up in a mining village, without the comforts that should have been afforded her as a duke's daughter.

Cailin should have shared in the wonder of this place and been left with more than the ashes of children's joy and freedom, burned down by the passage of time. Why, had

Cailin even ever known the simple pleasure of riding upon a swing?

"I'm sorry you didn't," he said quietly. *She should have been here.*

And what would it have been to know her then?

"My father didn't know of my existence," she confided. "My mother kept us from him. She was afraid he would sever their relationship were he to know about us."

Sadness glimmered in her eyes, and he would have traded part of his soul to Satan to erase that look from her expression.

And then, she drew herself up onto the bench, her skirts riding slightly, revealing a pair of trim, delicate ankles and mud-stained white satin slippers. His mouth went dry. They were just ankles. Really, a mere extension of a foot and leg that converged to join a part of the human form . . . he'd never before considered. Or appreciated.

"They're ruined, aren't they?"

At her question, Courtland blinked and then promptly flushed, realizing she'd noted his scrutiny . . . and also thankfully mistaken the reason for it. "I daresay they are," he said, his voice thick to his ears, and for the first time in his life, he felt like a green-boy.

"And you're not horrified?"

He grinned. "It would take a good deal more to horrify me than stained slippers."

Cailin stuck her foot out straight before her, and the skirts drifted up, exposing a greater portion of her leg; a well-muscled calf, one that he had no place ogling, but God help him, he couldn't look away.

"They're finer than anything I've ever worn," she remarked, turning her toes back and forth as she studied her own feet.

She deserved to be attired in the finest, most exquisite fabric. Items he couldn't give her.

Cailin pumped her legs and set the little wooden slat into movement over the river.

And Courtland stopped in his tracks, drinking in the

sight of her, the setting sun casting its hues of burnt orange and crimson upon her.

At some point her hair had escaped its earlier arrangement and now hung as it was meant to upon this woman—about her shoulders and down to her waist, bouncing golden waves that danced under the slight breeze made by her efforts.

The air lodged in his chest, sticking there painfully, and he was certain he'd never get proper air flow into his lungs.

"He is trying to marry me off," her voice emerged, tinged with sadness.

It took a moment to register that abrupt shift.

Cailin tipped her head back, her gaze locking on his. "That is the reason my father is hosting this affair," she murmured.

Yes. The duke had assembled a list of gents who'd make her an exceptional match, and he despised them all. Jealousy, a foreign-for-him sentiment, one that was completely new to him, slipped like poison in his veins.

The lady dragged the tips of her boots along the earthen floor, jolting her ride and bringing it to a slow.

Coming forward, Courtland caught the ropes and helped her come to a complete stop. "Here," he murmured, and she hopped off.

She frowned back at him. "Did you hear me?"

There was a warning contained within her query; one that cautioned him against a lie. "I did," he said, weighing his words. Considering his response. A woman as proud as Cailin would only ever resent any interference in her life. How had her father failed to realize as much? "That is—"

"The way of Polite Society," she cut him off, and a sound of exasperation slipped out. "Do you realize how many times I've heard that?"

"I was going to say, 'disappointing to you, no doubt.'"

She stared back, wide-eyed. "You were?"

Discombobulated, and unable to make sense of the way she now gawked at him, he fiddled with his cravat. "I . . . was there something else I should have said?"

"No," she replied, with an adamancy that pulled that lone syllable from her lips. "Just the . . . opposite. I expected you were going to remind me of the ways of Polite Society."

He flashed another half-grin. "I'd be the last person to lecture anyone on the ways of Polite Society."

"Because you're 'impolite'?" she asked curiously.

"Yes. No." God, he was tongue-tied around her. "Because I find them as silly and ridiculous as you," he finally said.

She released a refreshed-sounding little sigh. "This is the reason I like your company, Courtland."

He felt a frisson of warmth settle into every corner of his chest, and he'd wager he grinned like a schoolboy.

"If it helps, prior to wedding your father, the duchess hosted house parties of her own, and was notorious for marrying off many ladies."

"How does that help?" she asked, staring at him like he'd sprouted another head.

And just like that, he'd fallen out of her good favor. "I . . . uh . . . I suppose it does not?"

"No, it doesn't," she muttered, and stalked over to the edge of the lake. With that, she scooped up a handful of stones, and sifting through them, tossed aside some and held on to the others. She skipped one. It hopped four times upon the serene surface before sinking under the depths.

Courtland joined her. "You do not want to marry a nobleman?" he asked just as she drew her arm back.

Her mouth tightened, and her stone sank without so much as a hop this time. "I do not want to marry *any* man."

And the vehemence hinted at a woman who thoroughly and completely knew her mind. Something that made her—a lady who didn't wish to wed, completely out of reach to him—someone who had to wed. And it was utter rubbish . . . he knew he'd nothing to offer her. He knew she'd be far better off with almost any gent other than his poor, duke-ish self; and yet, that did nothing to chase away the . . . disappointment.

Feeling her stare, he turned his gaze upon the rippling

waters. "That is quite a firm response." Did she truly hate this world, which he belonged to, so much as to be closed to the possibility of love from an honorable man? "There will come a time when you will . . . fall in love, Cailin," he said quietly, hating with every fiber of his being the man more worthy than him. "And there is no reason to say that the man you do come to care for isn't here."

Stunned eyes flew to him. "You're a romantic, Courtland?" she asked softly.

Was it surprise there? Or worse . . . pity?

His cheeks flushed. "No." Or he hadn't been. Before her. He tried again. "I've never considered myself a romantic. In fact . . . I understand what it is to want nothing to do with marriage," he murmured, sliding his gaze across the private sanctuary they'd found themselves in.

From the corner of his eye, he caught Cailin turn a reluctant gaze to him. "You do?"

"My parents were deuced miserable," he confessed, not knowing where that admission had come from. Never had he spoken about such matters with . . . anyone. He didn't talk about his parents. Not even with Keir, his twin and the other half of his soul. Not Seagrave. Until Ellie had raised their parents' sad marriage, not even his own siblings. And even then, he hadn't been able to talk about it with his youngest sister. Something about this woman, however . . . everything came . . . easier. "I heard my mother at one time had been . . . intrigued by the thought of my father. But he was a rogue, and happy to not be married."

"So why did she marry him?" she asked quietly, her voice the softest, faintest murmur, barely discernable.

Too much a coward to meet Cailin's probing stare or question head-on, he directed his gaze to a point beyond her shoulder. "Security."

Because his father had needed her fortune. *Not unlike how you need some other lady's . . .*

At this moment, however, pride kept him withholding that piece. Because she didn't really need to know. Not really.

"It is always about security, isn't it?" she murmured.

"There is something to be said, however, for security," he noted.

"As a duke, I expect you don't know anything *but* security."

She would be wrong. Standing on the precipice of debtor's prison, he appreciated that truth now more than ever. The discourse having moved entirely too close to circumstances he was too mortified to speak with her about, he shifted them back to talk of his parents' unhappy union. "For my father, there was of course the matter of the ducal line." That obsession with procreating and securing the St. James line had always baffled Courtland. For if the duke had truly cared about the title and the legacy, surely he would have dedicated himself, if even in just some small way, toward maintaining the prosperity of it and not pissing it away on mistresses and lovers.

"And is that important to you?" Cailin asked softly.

He shrugged.

He'd been a man with emotionless entanglements and hadn't thought of marriage, because he'd not wanted to think about the fact that he'd be transformed into his father. Only recently had he begun . . . thinking in a new way. It was his sisters who were to blame. For planting silly, romantic thoughts there; when those weren't options for people like him.

"My mother was in love with my father, and what did that get her, other than a broken heart? And I? I tried my hand at love, Courtland." She wandered over to the swing once more, her movements distracted as she settled on the wood slat. "I've no desire to travel that path again."

His jaw slipped a fraction, going slack, and he felt knocked off-balance. Of anything she could have said, that was decidedly not it.

She'd . . . been in love.

Prior, he'd hated the faceless stranger who might one day win her.

This? The reality proved worse than the imaginings of a

potential suitor whom her father had brought to his Leeds estate. This was . . . real. There'd been a man who'd earned her laughter and won her heart, and with every fiber of his being, Courtland despised him.

"You were in love," he repeated. Or worse . . . "Or . . . are in love?" he ventured, braver than he believed, for he asked a question he didn't want the answer to. Not really.

"No!" she exclaimed. "That is, not anymore. I *was* in love." And for reasons he didn't want to think about, the idea that there'd been one to win her heart left him . . . bereft.

*You know the reason . . .*

Courtland's insides knotted in so many vicious vises.

He'd come . . . to care about her.

Worse.

His mind balked, shied, and resisted the truth creeping in.

*I love her.*

God help him.

This was bad.

# Chapter 17

It was the second time that day mention of Ian had come up. First, by her brother, and she'd insisted she'd not wished to talk about him . . . because she hadn't.

Just as she'd taken care to avoid thinking about him, or discussing him, she never wished to speak of her former sweetheart.

Something, however, about this man before her made it . . . so much easier for her to confide the most intimate pieces of herself.

Nay, it wasn't some unexplainable or intangible reason. Not really. Her life had become one in which the people who loved her also happened to believe they knew what was best for her. Somewhere along the way, she'd found herself rendered powerless, and she hungered for a semblance of the control and freedom over herself she'd once enjoyed.

As such, being on the fringe of her father's estates, in this child's playground in the woods, with this man who wasn't attempting to control her or impose his opinion about what he thought she needed, Cailin found herself . . . buoyed with a welcome and healing lightness.

Courtland drifted closer, stopping so he faced her but remaining three paces away so she might freely swing. "Who was he?" Courtland asked quietly, and Cailin pumped her knees, setting the swing into a slight motion.

Who was he? "His name was Ian. He was a miner." Cailin stared past Courtland. Wiry where Ian had been brawny, charming where Ian had been brusque.

In fact, Ian had been altogether different than the man before her. Stubborn with his smiles, and gruff and rough around the edges, she'd found that hesitancy to him endearing.

"Rafe was the foreman, and Ian came from Scotland, looking for work in the mines." She smiled wistfully as she recalled her brother's lively discussions after work with Hunter and Wesley about the new miner. "Ian was new to Staffordshire, and when you live in a small village, where you grow up with the same people and their families, anything and anyone new is . . . fascinating. All the women were vying to meet him first."

"And you did?"

"Oh, no," she clarified. "I had no interest in competing with the other women for one of the new miners." Cailin gave her legs another kick. "At the May Pole fair, we were introduced for the first time."

She recalled that meeting.

"He charmed you, then?" There was a tight quality to that question, and she looked over at Courtland.

His features, however, were perfectly even.

"Just the opposite." He'd been nothing like Courtland. In fact, she'd never known anyone like the affable duke who did not take himself too seriously, as her brothers tended to. And he didn't rely on spirits and trips to the tavern to soften him as the men of the Cheadle mines did. "He was brooding and dark . . ." And she'd at last understood why the ladies had been intrigued by him. "He was a mystery." At the time, she'd wanted to solve it . . . and him. "One day, he challenged my brother, arguing that the conditions needed to be improved, and I knew I wished to marry him." Her lips pulled in a grimace. "Or I thought I did."

"What happened?" he asked gently.

What happened?

Her eyes slid shut, and she drew in a steadying breath; the hell of that day still fresh . . . as fresh as any and all of the accidents that had ever taken the men and women and children who'd been part of the mining community family. "There was a fire," she said, gripping the ropes, and the coiled twists bit into the flesh of her palm. "He'd been trapped. They managed to get him out, but he was badly burned on part of his body, and his leg damaged beyond repair." Feeling Courtland's eyes upon her, she gave her head a clearing shake. "Or that is what I was told of his injuries. He refused to see me afterwards. I visited him . . . after . . . and he shouted through the door. He blamed my brother. Blamed my family. He said he never wished to see me again. That every part of coming to Staffordshire had been a mistake. That I had been a mistake." The pain of that rejection; the gut-wrenching discovery that the bond she'd believed to be special and strong hadn't been so very special or strong, after all.

"At first, I didn't believe him," she said. "I was certain Ian was trying to turn me away . . . and then . . ." She pressed her lips into a flat line and shook her head slightly.

Courtland sank to his haunches so he and Cailin were nearly eye level. "And then?" he asked softly.

"He said the only reason he'd courted me was because I was the foreman's sister, and he figured it would get him greater advantages and wages . . . and that after nearly being killed as he was, he now saw there'd never been any benefit to courting me."

Courtland closed his eyes briefly, and when he opened them, fire blazed within. Fury: it burned hot, with a lifelike force. Because of her. For her. He cursed. "I—"

"You don't have to apologize."

"I was going to say I'd happily kill him."

"It is fine," she murmured. And oddly . . . this time . . . now . . . it was. Somewhere along the way, the agony of that betrayal had receded. It no longer struck like a knife. "I was young. I dreamed of love and let myself see it in a place it didn't exist." Her lips pulled in a grimace. "All the signs were there, you know. He never kissed me."

Courtland's eyebrows crept up.

Embarrassment brought her toes curling sharply into the soles of her slippers. "He insisted it was because he respected me, and was waiting . . ." Unable to meet Courtland's eyes, she looked at the earthen floor, over at the placid stream, the sky, overhead. Anywhere but at him. "Now I know it was because the only purpose I served for him was . . . the connections I had to his foreman."

She'd never told anyone about that greatest of rejections. Not her brothers. No one. She'd been too humiliated; eaten alive at embarrassment Ian had felt the way he had—or rather, the way he hadn't—about her. Mortified that she'd been so blind as to not see his true motives.

Warm knuckles brushed the curve of her cheek, gliding in a downward stroke along the line of her jaw, and Courtland gently guided her back so that she faced him.

"Along with being a monster, he was a fool," he murmured, and her heart danced under his quixotic caress . . . and the adamancy of his words.

"My first kiss was . . . you." She paused. "I'm still sorry about that, you know," she said softly.

He frowned.

"Not the kiss," she hurriedly explained. "About this." Cailin raised her fingertips, brushing aside his hand, and stroking that place he'd taken a jab. "I kissed you that day," she reminded him needlessly.

She still would never be able to say what accounted for that boldness that day, but that kiss had haunted her memories . . . and dreams.

The column of his throat worked. "Yes," he said hoarsely. He caught her wrist gently, his long fingers easily wrapping in a delicate embrace about it. "And you needn't regret any of that day. I'd happily have taken another blow from your brother to have known that kiss."

He leaned closer and then stopped, and then he erased

all the distance between them, wide enough for only the whisper of wind that drifted over the shore. "But make no mistake of it . . . your brother was right to pound me that day." His gaze locked with hers, the power of his stare sucking the air from her lungs. "I was going to kiss you again," he stated, his voice a shade deeper than a baritone, but so smooth as to roll over her like honey.

Cailin shivered, delicious little shivers. "I know." She slid her gaze over the harshly angular planes of his face; beautiful like those statues she'd admired in the museums, only more splendorous because he was living and breathing and warm. "And I wanted you to," she whispered.

His breath hitched noisily. "Cailin." Her name fell from his lips as a raspy entreaty, and he proved a master of re-straint; and that evidence of his self-control only deepened her appreciation for this man, and strengthened his pull over her. "I want to kiss you," he said hoarsely. "Which undoubtedly makes me a bounder." No . . . it didn't. For she should have been the one thinking of Ian, but at her telling, she'd not felt the sadness she expected she should. She was only aware of . . . Courtland. "Here you are, sharing the love you feel for another," he was saying. "And even with that, I find myself wanting to take you in—"

Catching the front of his wool jacket, Cailin drew him close and kissed him; that motion tipped her forward slightly, and she fell against his chest.

But his hands were immediately there, catching her, steadying her; drawing her from the swing, he lay back, braced on his elbows.

And then it was like that closeness melted the control he'd so perfectly exercised. His hands were immediately on her. All over her. Exploring.

He swept long, powerful hands along her waist, and con-tinuing his quest lower, he sank his fingers into her hips.

This was what it was to be desired, and it was heady and empowering.

She whimpered at the possessive grip he had upon her, and a sharp little ache formed at her center; that acute sensation that he'd roused in her months earlier, and one that had kept her awake many nights, tossing restlessly with an unfulfilled yearning.

He brought his mouth down over hers again and again, and with a sigh, she parted her lips, and he slipped in; he swept his tongue inside, tasting her, and she tasted him in return. Theirs was a passionate dance, and the pressure between her legs grew, and she moved her hips rhythmically in a bid to relieve that ache.

"Cailin," he rasped against her mouth, between kisses. That was it. Nothing more than her name, uttered in the husky, hungry tones of a man who yearned for her the same way she ached for him.

He edged her skirts up, exposing her lower limbs, and drew the garments higher.

Out of breath, like one who'd run a race, he edged away slightly and glanced down between them, raking in with his gaze the skin he'd exposed. And the hot desire in his eyes scorched her from the inside out.

Then he pressed a palm to that spot, and a shuddery gasp escaped her, her eyes sliding shut as he briefly assuaged an ache. That relief proved fleeting, as he pressed the heel of his hand to her thatch and eased. He continued caressing her in that way; and panting, she let her legs fall wider, urging him on with her body.

"You feel so good," he praised, and then he slid a finger inside her.

Another breathy gasp slipped out as she arched up into his delicious touch.

Then, he began to stroke that lean, long digit within her; her tight channel grew accustomed to that glide of his finger.

Cailin clung tightly to him, her hips moving in time to his touch. "Courtland," she whispered against his mouth.

He kissed her gently. "Let yourself just feel, love."

*Love.*

It was intoxicating; she'd never been anyone's "love." Not truly. And she wasn't so naïve as to believe Courtland loved her or that this was more, and yet in this moment, she could let herself believe . . .

There grew a frenzy to her thrusting as she pressed herself close to him.

"Come for me, sweet," he urged, a husky command, and she bit her lip hard.

Come where? Whatever place he spoke of . . . she wanted to go . . . with him. Then he added a second finger to her channel, and she moaned. Reflexively, she tightened her legs about his hand, urging Courtland on, urging herself on to this building pressure, so keen as to straddle a line between exquisite pleasure and the most acute pain; only it was a different kind of pain, the likes of which she'd never known. One where she'd happily turn herself over to it. And be destroyed by its power.

He deepened their kiss, thrusting his tongue inside once more, and it was as though he sought to devour her. He stroked his tongue in time to the slide of his fingers, and she arched, her body climbing and climbing.

Cailin froze, suspended in time a moment, and then she tumbled over the edge.

Crying out, the sounds of her desire lost to his kiss, she exploded into a thousand tiny shards of splendorous light, feeling, and sensation.

She arched, she twisted, and she pushed herself against Courtland. Coming. She was coming. This was what he'd been speaking of. And this? Was more wondrous a place than she could have ever imagined. More glorious sensation than she had ever known her body was capable of feeling.

All the while he continued to stroke her, that devastating caress wringing wave after wave of pleasure from her.

Arching her back, a sigh slipping out, Cailin collapsed atop Courtland, her body replete.

Her chest rising hard and fast, in time to the rhythm of his own, she lay there.

Never had she felt anything like this.

And it was because of this man . . . because of Courtland.

She turned her cheek, resting it upon the hard, broad wall of his chest, the high-quality wool of his jacket smooth against her skin, and she stared out at the river.

Lying here, on the edge of the shore, with his arms wrapped about her, she wished that she'd not closed herself off to the possibility of . . . more. Particularly when there was a man . . . like him. A man who . . . made her feel again. And think about things for herself that she'd vowed to never again want.

The haze of desire instantly lifted, and her eyes flew open.

A sickening sensation settled in her belly, replacing all the wondrous sensations that previously gripped her, as for the first time, she saw something she'd failed to see or recognize—Courtland Balfour, the Duke of St. James, was dangerous . . . because of her awareness of him, and for the yearnings he'd awakened inside her.

# Chapter 18

Following his exchange at the edge of the shore, Courtland knew but one thing: he wanted nothing more than a drink and his own self for company, so he could sit alone with his regrets—and also the memory of the feel of her in his arms.

He'd never had any problems pleasuring women, and he'd brought any number of them to that glorious peak, and yet . . . it should so happen that he'd found the one woman whom he wanted . . . and mutual passion wasn't enough for him, society's most notorious rogue.

In truth and fairness, it was precisely what he deserved.

She had absolutely zero interest in marrying him . . . or anyone.

To have been so detached emotionally, seeking nothing more than a physical connection with women, that he should now find himself hopelessly and helplessly captivated by the one woman who wanted absolutely nothing to do with him.

Beyond the physical, that was.

Or a friendship.

"A friendship," he mouthed as he eyed Bentley's red velvet billiards table. "A friend—" That second silent uttering went unfinished.

"Is something wrong with our friendship?" Seagrave asked from the opposite end of the table, consternation furrowing his brow.

Bloody hell. Courtland's shot went wide, and he scowled at the table. "Damn it, man."

"I'll take that as a 'yes.'" Seagrave smirked and moved into position; leaning over the side, he let his stick fly and set the target ball sailing effortlessly into a pocket.

"She has no interest in marrying."

The other man stared blankly back.

"And . . . that is why you are here?"

"Yes. No." He dragged a hand through his hair. "Yes." Or that had been the intention.

"So she isn't interested. Find another," Seagrave advised as he eyed his next shot. "There are, after all, any number of young women in attendance who would be more than happy to wed you and land herself as Duchess of St. James."

Courtland could rely on his emotionally deadened, even-more-of-a-rogue friend to take that position.

"That is rotten advice."

Cursing, Seagrave's shot went wide.

They looked over as Ellie slipped out from behind the duke's red velvet brocade curtains.

"Good God, man, you need to start checking behind the curtains."

"I had the same thought not so very long ago," Courtland muttered.

"That is fine." Ellie gave her head a toss. "I'll just find a new hiding place."

Courtland waved off the other man. "And worry not. She's already aware."

Preening, his sister joined them at the table. "And I'm the one who advised him to court Miss Audley."

"Of course you are," Seagrave drawled. "Taking marital advice from your fourteen-year-old sister?" His friend chuckled. "Yes, whatever could go wro— Ahhh," he let out a startled shout as Ellie brought a spare cue stick down over the top of his hand.

Cursing quietly, Seagrave shook out his injured digits and then drew them in, cradling them close.

"Yes, I'm certain you telling him to marry a cold, mean lady with a fortune who wants nothing to do with him is infinitely wiser," Ellie said, batting her lashes. She pointed the stick she'd pilfered at Courtland. "And that is just one more reason you shouldn't be taking marital advice from the likes of him, Courtland."

"The likes of me?" Seagrave mouthed.

The door opened, and his middle sister sailed in. "What are we discussing?"

Could this day get any worse? "Nothing," Courtland said swiftly.

"Your brother's marital options," Seagrave volunteered.

Lottie beamed. "Indeed?" she asked breathlessly, and raced over.

Over the top of her heavily curled head, he glared at his faithless friend.

"Traitor," he mouthed.

"What?" the earl asked with entirely more amusement than the moment merited. "I figured as the youngest knows, so too they all did."

"Well, they didn't," Courtland said tersely.

"Know what?" When no one rushed to answer Hattie, she looked between the men, and then over at her youngest sister. "Know *what*?"

"Who is courting who?"

Their quartet looked to the front of the room as Hattie, with a book in hand, sailed over. And of course, this should prove the one time his bookish sister should not have all her attention trained on her blasted pages.

"No one—"

"Courtland is courting a young lady." Lottie giggled. "How is it I failed to appreciate that Courtland even carries the word 'courtship' in his name."

"Because there's no one who's been more removed from courting anyone respectable," Hattie said matter-of-factly.

"Until now," Seagrave pointed out.

Oh, for Lord's sake.

Courtland glared sharply at the other man, who lifted his palms up. "What?"

"He did it." Ellie pointed at Seagrave. She gave him a look and shrugged. "No female friend would have so outed you."

"No, I believe you are correct on that score," he muttered.

"I am the last to know everything?" Hattie lamented, stamping her foot. "Who is she?"

Courtland reached for his brandy and took a long, healthy swallow. He could count on any number of loved ones present to—

The quartet answered in unison, their replies only slightly staggered: "Miss Audley."

Hattie clasped her hands to her chest. "Oh, I must spend more time with h—"

"Absolutely not," he said quickly, immediately killing her smile and earning himself a glare.

"And whyever not?"

"Because the point of it is for Courtland to court her," Ellie explained, patting her eldest sister's hand.

"I declare, when we return to London, we shall host a ball of our own and invite Miss Audley," Hattie exclaimed.

"A tea," Ellie suggested instead.

"A tea?" he asked, struggling to follow.

"Well, we cannot afford a ball," the girl said and then paled, slapping a palm over her mouth.

"Ellie," he gritted out.

"I'm sorry," her lips moved in a silent apology.

Otherwise, silence thundered around the billiards room, punctuated only by the slight creak of the parquet flooring as a discomfited Seagrave rocked on his heels.

"What?" Hattie whispered. "I don't . . . understand."

Oh, Christ. It had been inevitable. The secret he'd worked so hard to keep from his siblings. Alas, one more blasted thing from which he'd been singularly unable to protect them. "You needn't worry. I am . . . sorting it all out. The situation is not as dire as all that." Worse. It was worse.

"Worse."

All eyes swung to the matter-of-fact owner and deliverer of that sober admission.

Ellie drew herself up onto the edge of the billiards table, and turning it into a makeshift bench, she swung her legs back and forth. "It is worse."

"Worse?" Hattie's voice emerged high and reedy as she clutched at her throat.

Courtland glared his youngest sister into silence, and when she dropped her eyes to the floor, he returned his attention to Hattie. "It isn't *worse*. It is just a matter of working through the numbers."

Leaning around his shoulder, Ellie said in a loud whisper: "There is nothing to work through. Father left nothing, and we are on the cusp of ruin."

Was it him, or did she sound . . . gleeful about it? Courtland scraped another hand through his tousled hair.

Hattie cleared her throat. "Perhaps we might speak about this later." She aimed that admission in Seagrave's general direction.

"Oh, come," Ellie scoffed. "Seagrave is family, and he certainly knows our finances. Isn't that quite right, Sandon?"

"Ind—"

"Even heee knows?" Hattie bemoaned, cutting across the earl's confirmation.

"Does it really matter?" Ellie asked, tossing her arms up.

Hattie hesitated. "I suppose not."

No. No, it did not. Now, his sisters were aware of the state they found themselves in; the one Courtland had spent the past year and a half attempting to get them out of. They, however, were as deserving of the truth as Keir. In withholding such information from them, he'd proven no different than Bentley keeping secrets from Cailin. He'd not be that man. Not again. "It isn't so dire," he promised, and following his meeting with Keir, this time he could actually provide them that real assurance. "Keir and I have crafted a plan forward which will improve our circumstances tremendously."

It didn't help the mood of the room.

An unusual silence for this chatty lot descended over the

room once more. Even Seagrave, always charming and ready with a quip, had adopted a somber set.

"What happens if we cannot address our debts?" Hattie ventured.

"We will," Courtland said before the full question had even been asked by his eldest sister.

"But if we cannot?" she urged, the worry emanating from her brown eyes, hitting him like a kick to the gut; for those were the sentiments he'd attempted to protect her and Lottie and Ellie from.

"Then Courtland is in debtor's prison," Ellie answered to the room at large.

The explosive gasps brought his eyes briefly shut.

"Do they send dukes to debtor's prisons?" Hattie asked, looking to each member of their unhappy party for confirmation.

"Of course," Ellie scoffed. "Debt is a classless crime, after all. We are not the only noble family that has spent more than we could afford to keep up appearances."

"Is that what we've done?" Hattie whispered, scrabbling with her throat once more.

Courtland gave his head a firm shake. "N—"

"Yes," Ellie replied.

"I wonder what debtor's prison is like?" Lottie whispered.

"Well, most of the men work, and if you are able to pay something, they can even work outdoors," Ellie explained.

"How do *you* know so much about the Marshalsea?" he asked before he thought better of it; even as the question left him, however, he wanted to call it back.

His youngest sister gave him a funny look. "Never tell me, you're the one facing debtor's prison and you haven't done *research* on it?" With *those* tones, she would have put a disappointed tutor to shame.

"I . . ." As four sets of stares landed on him, Courtland shifted on his feet. When she presented it like that . . . his sister wasn't wrong.

Warming to her telling, Ellie motioned for her audience to return their attention her way. "Men, being the heads of households, are invariably the ones held to blame for financial matters, and as such, the Marshalsea is largely composed of male prisoners."

"Prisoners," Hattie whispered.

"Occupants, if you prefer."

"I do," Hattie said, her voice weak. "Much better."

"Can we please—"

"*Shhh,*" Courtland's sisters shushed him into silence.

"Now, as I was saying." As Ellie proceeded to regale her riveted audience, Courtland, muttering to himself, stalked over to the drink cart, grabbed the nearly empty decanter of brandy, and watched on. Why, even his best chap in the world wore a look of fascination, wholly absorbed in Ellie's telling.

Returning to the billiards table, Courtland refilled his glass.

He'd never been one for wishing that his sisters were obedient and well-behaved and compliant. Until now. Now, with his future a free subject of their casual discussion, he could in this moment see the appeal in those traits other heads of households managed.

". . . even though it is usually men," his sister explained. "Sometimes . . ." Ever the storyteller, she paused, ensuring all eyes were upon her. "Sometimes," she repeated in a more mysterious, hushed tone, "it is women."

Horrified gasps went up again.

Oh, for the love of all that was and was not holy. "Women do not go to the Marshalsea," he said, setting his glass down hard on the edge of the table, and finally, the quartet looked to him.

Ellie frowned. "How would *you* know?" she asked, without inflection. "By your own admission, you haven't done the research. I have."

*Fair enough.*

Ellie returned to her lecture on debtor's prison. "Sometimes, if there is no one to provide support, wives and children are *forced* to join their husbands and fathers in prison."

Hattie covered her face with her hands.

Yes, well, he understood how the eldest of his sisters felt in this moment.

"Sorry, old chap." Seagrave gave Courtland a commiserative glance.

There were any number of things for his best friend in the world to be sorry about. The state Courtland found himself in. The fact that Courtland's sisters were the handful they were. The list really could go on and on.

"What of sisters?" Lottie piped in hopefully.

Ellie shook her head. "I expect it is the same?" she ventured with a hesitation indicating this particular question fell outside the scope of her knowledge. She brightened. "It must be. After all, who would support us? No one."

"You needn't sound so cheerful about it," Lottie mumbled, collapsing onto the edge of the table beside Ellie.

It was hard to say which sister wore the glummest, grimmest expression.

"You have my promise I won't let you ladies head off to the Marshalsea," Seagrave offered, and each of Courtland's sisters looked to the earl with varying degrees of—

Courtland scowled, then immediately straightened. He recognized those looks.

"That is, I won't let you head off, as long as you aren't making my life a misery as you are your poor brother." With a wink, Seagrave gave the top of Ellie's curls a ruffle, and Courtland's youngest sister swatted at his fingers.

Ah, now this was familiar and welcome. The last thing Courtland required at this bungled time in his life was his sisters going goggle-eyed for a rogue like Seagrave. Some of the tension eased from Courtland's shoulders. Some of it.

"It isn't all terrible in a debtor's prison," Ellie went on. "If he is working outdoors." She paused, her little nose scrunching up. "Of course, some starve to de—"

"Ellie," he clipped out the two syllables of her name, and those sharp tones seemed to cut across her casualness. "I'm not . . . going to debtor's prison," he said when the group was silent once more. "And neither are any of you."

It was a false promise. One he had no place making; and one he didn't know if he could keep.

# Chapter 19

Following the moment of passion she'd known in Court-land's arms, Cailin had lost sleep, lying awake thinking about it; her body burning with the memory of what they'd shared.

In the light of a new day, after a restless slumber, she'd arisen, confronted with a new sentiment—dread about the awkwardness of when they came face to face again, alone, once more.

As it should so happen, she needn't have worried about either discomfort from being with him . . . or, for that matter, being alone with him.

Standing on the side of the grounds, the space trans-formed into a play area of sorts, Cailin took in the sight of Courtland mingling on the fields with three young ladies and a gentleman.

She cocked her head.

He'd not joined the other men for the hunt, as she would have expected . . . as all the other male guests had. Her father. Her brother. Almost all other gentleman in attendance.

Instead, he remained with three younger ladies, one

whom she recognized as his sister and two others, who, with their flaxen curls, bore a striking resemblance to one another. The group spoke, and there was such a frenzy to their voices, joined all as one, as if each lady present fought for supremacy of the discussion.

All the while, Courtland conversed with the handsome gentleman at his side. Slightly shorter, but broader in the shoulders, the chestnut-haired fellow would be considered handsome by any standards, and yet he did not possess the Viking-golden beauty of the man beside him. Dismissing him, her gaze slid of its own will over to the man who'd occupied all her thoughts.

Arms folded at his chest, Courtland was nodding at something the other man said. Whatever response he gave earned a boisterous laugh from that gentleman.

Just then, Courtland looked up and over, and his gaze locked with hers.

Cailin froze, feeling a kindred connection to those poor deer caught by a hunting party; and Cailin felt trapped, wanting to flee for having been found staring but unable to make her legs work, embarrassment suspending her movements.

In the end, the choice of running was stolen by Courtland's sister.

"Miss Audley!" Hattie cried excitedly, rushing over to meet Cailin. "I have been hoping to see you. You must join us."

"I couldn't," she murmured, resisting the urge to look at Courtland; Courtland, whose piercing stare she felt all the way to her soul. "I've never played." There'd never been time for games in Staffordshire, where the days of a miner and a village woman were long.

Hattie scoffed. "Oh, nonsense." Then, with all the confidence and command of a duke's daughter—a duke's legitimate daughter, that is—Hattie looped her arm through Cailin's and forced her to walk beside her. "And you must meet my sisters."

As she approached, the previously boisterous group had returned to their lively discussion. This time, the gentleman at Courtland's side debated some point or another with the youngest lady present. Courtland's family and friends did not stop to gawk as all of Polite Society had. They didn't treat her any differently, and as she stopped before them, the tension slid from her person.

"Miss Audley, allow me to introduce you to this motley lot," Hattie said and proceeded to make introductions between her and Courtland's sisters and best friend.

With the polite pleasantries aside, there was a brief break in the previously lively exchange. Cailin cleared her throat. "I should let you to your fun—"

"Do not," Courtland said swiftly, at the same time his eldest sister spoke.

"Nonsense!" Hattie exclaimed, linking her arm with Cailin's. "I daresay I never agree with Courtland, but on this, I shall make an exception. You must remain. We are just to begin lawn bowling, and we were debating what the teams should be."

"You see, Ellie"—Hattie gestured to the youngest, who raised her hand, waggling her fingers—"is by far the best among us."

"I resent that!" Lottie frowned at the eldest of Courtland's sisters.

"Well, it *is* true," Lady Ellie said, striking a pose; she proceeded to pick at her nails. "I do not bother with most games, Miss Audley," the young lady said. "But because lawn bowling is a game that requires both speed and tactical skills, I excel."

Lottie stuck her tongue out, with Ellie following suit, and then chaos descended as the pair of sisters launched into a vociferous argument.

As the quarreling commenced, Courtland joined Cailin, and leaning close, he whispered, "My youngest sibling fancies herself a military tactician."

"Does she?" Cailin asked.

"Oh, yes. She's studied every famous military commander through time, and I expect she'll be the first female to land herself the role leading the king's army." They shared a smile.

Her heart stumbled, in a dizzying little way. His charming grin proved a potent destroyer of a woman's ordered thoughts . . . as had the words he'd shared about his sister.

As he trained his attention on his bickering siblings, Cailin lingered her gaze on him. Shouldn't a duke have been horrified at or disapproving of the prospect of one's sister's fascination with military matters? Or that was what Cailin would have expected of any nobleman. Why, even her own father expected Cailin learn certain lessons and behave in a certain way. And as she took in the unconventional lot before her, people freer with their views and emotions and . . . *everything*, Cailin came to the staggering realization . . . that she'd unfairly made assumptions, not only about Courtland and his kin, but all people born to his station.

She'd erroneously believed that noble families weren't capable of the same warmth and love and regard as those born outside that lofty station.

Which had been narrow-minded of her to think: to think that families here could not and would not know the closeness enjoyed by families such as hers.

Only, this closeness . . . was different, the bond warmer in ways than that which she knew with her siblings; all largely brooding, taciturn men who didn't wear their emotions on their sleeves.

"Ladies," Seagrave was saying. "Ladies," the earl repeated. And muttering to himself, he placed two fingers in his mouth and whistled.

That shrill noise managed to penetrate the debate.

"Now," the gentleman went on when all attention was on him, "I believe it is fair to say, though it is debatable, which among you ladies proves most skilled."

"No, it isn't," Ellie muttered, and the middle Balfour sister stuck her tongue out once more, with the younger girl quick to follow suit.

Lord Seagrave carried on, loudly over the melee, as though he'd not been interrupted, and as though Courtland's youngest sisters weren't on the fringe of a physical altercation over who had the right to claim the status of "champion lawn bowler": "I believe we can all agree there is no debating who the absolute worst among us is."

That managed to silence the group. In unison, every set of eyes went to Courtland.

It took a moment to register the insinuation. She laughed. "Impossible," she said before she could call the words back. But the idea that Courtland, with his athlete's physique, would perform poorly . . . in any way was an incongruity that didn't fit with his form.

"Why, thank you," he said, inclining his head in acknowledgement of that confidence.

"He isn't deserving of your loyalty." Ellie paused, and then added, "At least not in terms of his game play."

"And thank *you*," Courtland muttered.

Ellie tilted her head. "You are welcome." Courtland's minx of a sister sidled closer, and cupping a hand around her mouth, spoke in a less-than-discreet whisper. "Courtland is so glad you are here," she said slyly.

Cailin felt herself blushing and gave thanks for the cover afforded by the bonnet that concealed her cheeks. "Is he?"

"Oh, yes. Because Seagrave is in fact correct . . . with you here, he is no longer the worst lawn bowler present."

A startled laugh escaped Cailin.

Courtland tugged one of his sister's ringlets. "Here now, you can hardly know Miss Audley isn't a better bowler than all of us. As such, a wise military general would know not to underestimate an unfamiliar opponent."

Over the top of Ellie's head, he caught Cailin's gaze again and winked.

And all her fears of what it would be like being with him after the copse disappeared. There was nothing uncomfortable about this. Or them.

"You really must play," Ellie said. "If for no other reason than to even us out. As long as you and Courtland are not both on my team, as I'm the best player, but I am only so good as to make up for two poor players."

Cailin's shoulders shook with mirth, and she forced a

solemnity to her lips. "That is, of course, an understandable concern you should not have to contend with."

"She is nothing if not ruthless," Courtland whispered.

"Honest. She is honest," Cailin corrected. And refreshingly so.

"Then, I shall take Courtland and Miss Audley for my team, because I am quite confident in my skills as 'best' player," Lottie volunteered.

And apparently, the prospect of being spared the worst players among the lot was enough to make the youngest girl allow the matter of "best" player rest.

"You've never played, Miss Audley?" Lottie asked, as they headed down the long field to the balls stationed there.

"I am afraid I've not embellished my incompetency as it comes to lawn bowling." There'd been no swings or children's playgrounds. There'd been no lawn bowling . . . or other games. And she'd not realized . . . there'd been anything missing, or anything to miss, until she witnessed the joyous exchange between Courtland and his sisters.

"Worry not. Courtland is a miserable player, but he is an adept instructor." Bending down, Lottie retrieved the oddly shapen sphere that wasn't quite a perfect circle. "Here." With that, she thrust the ball at Cailin. "I will steal us a few moments for you to practice. I cannot have you and Courtland embarrassing yourselves and my team this day."

Collecting it from Lottie, Cailin moved her hands up and down several times, getting accustomed to the weight.

"I do take lawn bowling very seriously. I hope you will as well."

Cailin smoothed her features into a mask of solemnity. "You have my assurance I will do everything to not let the team down."

Lottie beamed. "I knew I'd picked wisely!" Cupping her hands around her mouth, she sprinted off, dashing over to join the other team. "Courtland is going to provide Miss Audley with a brief lesson while we practice."

"I don't need practice," Ellie boasted, and proceeded to toss her missile toward a smaller yellow ball at the end of the field. The ball sailed in a wide right arch, before curving smoothly, until it brushed the edge of the other sphere.

Cailin's stomach sank. "Oh, dear."

"They are good," Courtland said, with a brotherly pride her own brothers had never been in short supply of where Cailin was concerned. In fact, in his devotion, Courtland was very much like Rafe, Hunter, and Wesley. It was one of the reasons she'd come to admire him. "Fear not, you cannot be worse than I."

"I've never played," she said dryly. "I daresay I cannot be better."

Courtland waggled his golden eyebrows. "Ah, yes, but I spent so much time perfecting playing poorly that *I* cannot be better."

They were supposed to be practicing, and yet—

"This I have to hear, Your Grace." And she did. At every turn, she found herself increasingly wanting to know everything there was to know about him. That reality should terrify her. And yet, strangely, it did not.

"Keir is younger by several minutes, and my sisters came at various points after us. We'd often sneak off and compete in very serious lawn bowling matches." His expression darkened, and it was as though the sun had been stolen. "The late duke . . . my father . . . our father, delighted in pointing out each of his children's many failings. That ruthless assessment extended to child's games, as well."

It was the second window he'd opened into his childhood, and she glimpsed through, her heart aching so much for the view within. "When we played, I would find ways for my shots to go wide . . . but it couldn't go too wide," he explained seriously, as if it were the most natural thing in the world to offer lessons on how to throw a match of lawn bowling. "Otherwise, my efforts would be entirely too obvious, and it would defeat the point of Keir and Hattie and Ellie and Lottie actually believing they were superior players."

And in that moment, she was sure her heart swelled three times its size from the warmth and tenderness that gave that organ's rhythm an extra beat. She glanced over at where his sisters now played and jested with Seagrave, and then back once more to Courtland. "You deliberately lost matches." He'd done it to inflate their confidence through game, when their father had been so determined to lay them low.

An endearing blush filled his cheeks. "Do not make more of it than it is." He bounced his ball back and forth from one palm to the next like a master juggler she'd witnessed come through during a village fair some years back. "I only started by deliberately losing matches. Now, I accomplish that feat naturally, all on my own."

Except . . . she wasn't making more of what he'd shared. She was making exactly as she should of it. When most men were too proud to concede anything, he'd graciously allowed himself to be a "loser" in matches so as to elevate his siblings.

Her chest tightened. How impossible must it have been for him and his siblings to be constantly found wanting. Cailin drifted closer.

"I'm sorry."

Genuine confusion creased his brow, as he brought his distracted movements with that ball to a stop.

"That your father . . . was the way he was," she said softly.

He waved off those regrets. "I had a loving mother, and equally loving siblings. I fared far better than most in terms of familial relationships."

And oddly, he spoke without so much as a trace of the resentment she and her brothers had harbored peppered in with his pronouncement. "They are very fortunate to have you as a brother," she murmured. How easily Courtland could have become the cold, brooding, resentful person her brothers had become after their father's failings. Only . . . he hadn't. He'd retained an ability to smile and laugh and be the charming man he was with his family and her.

The air grew thick between them; even outside, in the vast, open Leeds sky, it grew charged and heavy . . . and she remembered every kiss they'd shared. And the magic of yesterday's embrace in the copse. His gaze fell to her mouth.

And she knew. Even as an innocent, even without the

experience of the village widows or the wedded wives, she knew that he was recalling that moment they'd shared, and that the emotion tightening the harshly beautiful planes of his face was desire.

And—

"Will you stop gabbing and start practicing?" Lottie shouted from across the field, and they both jumped. "I can forgive having two poor lawn bowlers, but not if you do not take the game seriously."

Courtland grinned. "As I said. They are absolutely mercenary when it comes to games. Now, for lawn bowling . . ." He proceeded to explain the rules of the game, motioning across the field as he spoke and to the respective instruments used in game play. "The trick of it is, you do not aim straight," he said, pressing a ball into her palm. "You roll towards the ditch."

She laughed. "Now, I know you are funning me."

". . . and they are laughing . . . ?" Ellie spoke loud enough that her voice carried from the adjacent ring. "You've picked wrong this day, sister."

"I fear you may be right," Lottie wailed forlornly.

"Ignore them," Courtland mumbled. "And I do not jest at all. Certainly not about lawn bowling. Not when I know better with the crew on ahead facing me." He winked, that flutter of his golden lashes wreaking its usual havoc upon her heart; and then, he brought her arm back, guiding it through the proper motions, and with her back pressed against his chest as it was, and the heat of his frame spilling onto her person, she released the ball.

Or she thought she did.

She wasn't looking out at the field or at the missile she'd just launched with his assistance.

Rather, she remained, her neck angled back and her eyes locked upon him.

A solitary groan went up from one of the ladies somewhere downfield, and Lottie let out another beleaguered cry indicating Cailin's shot had missed the mark. She knew she should care that she'd just humiliated herself, and yet, as the players assembled, she couldn't bring herself to care or think about anything beyond Courtland.

Courtland couldn't remember a time when he'd enjoyed himself so.

Or, a time when he'd done so even while simultaneously making a complete and total arse of himself.

Granted, given he was on the cusp of having his financial state revealed to the whole of the world, embarrassment was a sentiment he should grow accustomed to.

For several hours on the duke's lawn bowling court, with Cailin, Seagrave, and his family, he found himself for the first time since he'd inherited the dukedom and all the pressing problems that went along with it . . . not focusing on those problems.

Instead, he remained fixed on . . . her.

Just then, Cailin launched another ball, letting it sail perfectly—in a straight line—which would have been a masterful feat had that been the correct way to toss the missile.

Alas, it landed, curved, and then rotated away.

As Lottie slapped a hand over her eyes, Cailin cast a glance Courtland's way and flashed a sheepish smile before looking to their sister once again.

The teams having since rotated, to account for Courtland and Cailin's equally poor game play, he stared on as Cailin's attention was called to her new playing partners. She conversed with Hattie and Seagrave, with Seagrave periodically eliciting one of Cailin's boisterous, unrestrained laughs.

Gnashing his teeth, Courtland alternately wished he'd not spent so many years throwing games, so he could have remained paired with Cailin, and wanting to pulverize Seagrave for being . . . well, Seagrave, which was, of course, unfair and wrong. And of course, the other man wouldn't dare do anything ungentle—

"Oomph."

Courtland grunted as Ellie let an elbow sail into his side.

"Our turn, big brother," she said.

"More specifically, your turn," Lottie muttered, and then, as Courtland tossed his bowl and it landed close to the mark— at least close enough not to make him look the complete fool—his middle sister brightened. "Though, I will say, for the first time in our family's entire history of lawn bowls, you do find yourself with more skill than someone on the field."

They looked as one over to Cailin.

"She is not so very bad," he said defensively when his sister had completed her throw.

"No," Ellie said, biting at her nail. She spit one of the remnants to the ground, in a display he knew he likely should have reprimanded and been horrified by; but his father had once castigated her for such behaviors, and Courtland would be damned if he was like that cur. Ellie eyed the field with the same intensity she did all pretend battlefields, squinting and peering intently. "In fact, her practice rounds improved some," she murmured and brought her arm arching back, testing the movement several times. "Only when we began actually playing could one appreciate that there was any person *worse* than Courtland."

Lottie sniggered.

"She's not worse than me," he said, again defensively.

"Oh, she's worse," Lottie said with an emphatic nod.

"She is," Ellie confirmed. "In fact, a person couldn't be more terrible unless they"—Ellie froze mid-motion, her arm curled back so quickly the ball slipped from her fingers—"tried . . ." she whispered, and her shot flew backward, to jubilant cheers from their opposing team, who, with that mishap, proved triumphant. Her words trailed off, even as Courtland went absolutely motionless. Ellie's eyes flared wide, and then she swung her gaze to Courtland, and then to Cailin, and then back again, and once more to Courtland. "Of course," she whispered, those two words a revelation bathed in discovery.

His focus, however, was already on Cailin; Cailin, with a misshapen sphere in hand releasing her bowl in celebration. Her arm moved in the perfect arc, and the missile sailed effortlessly and landed with a kiss against the jack.

At his side, Lottie celebrated, her jubilation a blur in his mind. And his heart did a funny little leap in his chest as the truth slammed into him.

She'd gone and thrown her efforts . . . for him—in the same way he'd done for his siblings.

He frowned. As soon as the warmth slipped in, that analogy killed the moment and made him cringe.

"You men and your bruised egos," Ellie said, tossing her arms up in the air. "You are the only one who'd dare frown at that discovery, brother."

Only . . . his sister, for all her entirely too-mature intuition, was off the mark on this one. After all, what chap, head over ears for a lady, wanted to find himself being compared to one's sisters and brother?

"What discovery?"

"Nothing," he and Ellie said simultaneously.

"I said, 'What'?" Lottie repeated, stomping her foot noiselessly on the lush lawn flooring.

"The fact that it is the first time you've defeated Hattie."

Lottie opened her mouth and closed it several times, and then cocked her head. "Indeed? I'm fairly certain I have—"

"You haven't," Ellie interrupted.

A wide smile formed on their middle sister's lips as she accepted that lie, and with a jubilant laugh, she skipped over to their eldest sister. As both women launched into a prompt debate, Cailin stepped between them. Whatever she'd said immediately ended the spat and brought all three women to laughter.

She was the manner of woman he'd not allowed himself to consider for himself.

First, because he'd been so deuced scared of marriage, and making a bungle out of it like his father; and when it had been too late, there'd come the discovery he was staring down the Marshalsea.

But if he *had* imagined a wife for himself . . . Cailin Audley would have been the very woman he'd have longed to have at his side. As a partner. One able to laugh and play games, and who'd champion even a miserable bounder like him over a mere game of lawn bowling.

Just then, she said something that caused Hattie to hug her younger sister, and the bickering ended in amicable sisterly affection.

"She is perfect, you know," Ellie said at his side.

"I know that," he responded automatically. Because it was true. Because he couldn't catch himself from denying it, even as it would have been the wiser, safer thing to say.

Especially to this young girl before him.

The most tenacious, most obstinate of his sisters widened her eyes. "Oh, this is bad," she whispered. "You've fallen hard."

Aye, he'd fallen completely head over ears and back again for the lady. "Let it go," he said tightly, and to give himself something to, absolutely anything to do as a distraction for him and a deterrent from this conversation, he stalked quickly across the field.

Ellie immediately fell into step alongside him. "Where do you think you're going?"

"Losing players tidy the field," he said tersely and lengthened his stride.

His youngest sibling instantly matched her smaller steps to his. "Why must you be so . . . grim about this?"

"I'm not grim." He clipped out each word. "I'm being realistic."

"That is entirely the same thing."

They reached the end of the field, a safer distance away from the subject of their discussion. "Actually, it isn't, Ellie," he said in quiet, solemn tones, striving for patience, dancing a delicate set between providing her realities while not crushing her innocence and dreams. His own disappointments and regrets . . . he would deal with and accept. But he'd not accept them for her or any of his other siblings. "One cannot simply . . . force a person to feel . . . things they do not feel. How well did that work out for our mother?" he asked as gently as possible. Bending down, he grabbed up one ball, a second, and a third.

"Yes, but father was a cur, and you are not." At his side, Ellie joined his efforts, filling her arms. "I saw you and Miss Audley speaking earlier—"

"She is a friend," he said, and his gut knotted. That was all. Even as he wished for it to be more.

"Friends don't flirt," his sister pointed out, undeterred. "Seagrave doesn't do it with me or Lottie or Hattie." She paused long enough to glance down the length of the field; her little brow creased. "Well, perhaps a bit he does . . ."

Scowling, Courtland whipped his gaze downfield.

"But how he is with Hattie and me and Lottie is entirely different than how you are with Miss—"

"The lady doesn't wish to marry, and I need to wed, and you know our circumstances." Now, all his siblings did.

And for that reason alone, it was more important than ever to step forward and do what was right and save them . . . now, from worrying.

With that, he started back toward the still-boisterous celebration at the other end of the lawn.

"I am disappointed in you, Courtland," his sister called after him.

"Well, that certainly makes two of us," he muttered. He cast a quelling look over his shoulder. Even as anyone overhearing that should, could, or would interpret that disapproval as a product of his poor game play, one could also never be certain what would come next from the scamp's mouth.

Alas, he really wished he'd spent time perfecting the ducal stare meant to silence a person. In moments such as these, it would come in decidedly handy.

Showing more restraint than he'd believed she was in possession of, Ellie raced over. "If you love her . . ." He blanched. Something in hearing it spoken aloud made it . . . real in ways he still denied. His sister paused. "You do love her, don't you?"

He felt his facial muscles strain under the agony of this exchange.

Ellie pointed her eyes to the sky. "You blasted rogues with your inability to speak plainly on matters of the heart."

He bristled. "I speak plain . . ." He paused, a frown pulling at his lips. "What do you know about rogues?" he demanded, his current misery briefly forgotten under the misery of a different sort. His youngest sister was growing up. All his sisters were—

Ellie laughed. "Courtland, *you* are a rogue. My father was a rake. Seagrave. That is plenty of exposure enough for a lady to learn something of that sort of gentleman."

"Fair enough," he said under his breath. And something in hearing himself lumped in with his father . . .

"Of course you're not like Father."

"I didn't say anything of it."

"You didn't need to. I'm not done," she said firmly. "Now, you are not like Father . . . if you follow your heart. But if you let her get away, Courtland, if you instead marry a dull, insipid English miss, just because she has a fortune and will save you and us from our circumstances"—Ellie's eyes locked with his—"then, you are very much the late duke." And with that dire pronouncement, she lifted her chin and sprinted off . . . to join his sisters and Seagrave and Cailin, her words lingering.

Ellie might be correct in that assessment . . . if he did what he'd ultimately have to do . . . then he would very much become his father—that is, if he hadn't made the full transformation before now.

What his sister failed to note, however, was . . . the duke? He hadn't loved anyone, because he hadn't been capable of the emotion.

And starting slowly onward toward the festive group, Courtland discovered, at last, something his cur of a sire may have been right about, after all: love was a peril that left a man weak, and given his feelings for Cailin Audley— and more, her lack of feelings for him—no good could ever come of it.

# Chapter 20

Cailin had anticipated the duke's house party would be hellish. With the number of guests, and lofty gentlemen in attendance out to court her, she'd expected she would want to be anywhere but at the sprawling Leeds estate.

Only to find . . . she'd been wrong.

So very wrong—and wrong about so very much.

The lively revelry unfolding in the noisy ballroom was more boisterous and exuberant than the more stilted affair thrown in London in her honor.

It was as though the countryside had a freeing quality, yet with the same men and women.

Children had been invited to mingle with the guests, the little sprites racing between the couples dancing the steps of a lively Scottish reel.

It was, in short, a jubilant affair she'd never have anticipated the duke or the duchess would attend, let alone host.

Just as she'd not imagined that Courtland, another powerful duke, should be . . . so unrestrained.

Her gaze went to that most powerful peer. Guiding his middle sister, Lottie, along the center of the line that had formed for each set of dancers to make their way down; the young woman laughed, periodically missing a step with Courtland righting her.

"My sister loves to dance," a voice said at her side; the noise of the room swallowed Cailin's gasp, and she looked over at the unexpected intrusion.

Courtland's youngest sister smiled and looked out at the pair of her siblings. "She's deuced bad at it. Probably because my father would visit her dance lessons and berate her for being clumsy and call out the instructor for not being able to fix her," the girl spoke matter-of-factly, as though it were the most natural thing in the world to speak about the cruelty of one's father.

Startled, Cailin looked out once again, finding Courtland and his sister.

Her chest ached from that meanness Ellie spoke of, coupled with the pieces he'd shared . . . about how his father had discouraged Courtland from reading the type of books that brought him joy. And here, she'd naïvely anticipated that people who lived comfortable lives had not known struggles, only to find how narrow-minded she'd been.

"Courtland has always been good on his feet," the young girl at her side said, slashing through those musings. "He would always partner with Lottie . . . he'd dance her into the breakfast room and dining room, as though a person should dance through life and not walk."

Cailin's heart swelled, and at that telling by Courtland's youngest sister, she rather thought she lost a part of her heart to him. "He is a good brother."

"He is the best brother," Ellie emphatically corrected.

"Is he?" she murmured, finding herself wanting . . . more stories about the duke upon the dance floor. There'd been a time when Cailin had been so very sure that there was no greater brother than her own, only to find there was a man such as Courtland, who encouraged his sisters to be who they wished to be . . . while also loving them with the same ferocity with which Rafe, Wesley, and Hunter loved her.

She braced for the young girl to say more. Only . . . no

further stories were forthcoming. And she wished desperately to have them . . . to know more about Courtland.

"I have three brothers of my own," she finally said.

The other girl looked back with interest. "Do you?"

"I do."

"Tell me about them," Ellie requested.

People in Town didn't seek out such . . . personal details. In her short time here, Cailin had come to appreciate that the nobility cared about the surface, and the gossip, but not the parts that were intimate. And it felt so very good to be with someone who spoke so freely.

"When I was a girl," Cailin began, selecting one of her favorite memories of her devoted brothers, "all I wanted in the world was a library, but there was no money for books. Some two months or so before my ninth birthday, every night Wesley, Hunter, and Rafe returned from the mines, they would only grab up a piece of bread before heading to their room for the night. You see, mining work is hard work. Exhausting." Courtland's sister listened on, enrapt, and Cailin warmed to the telling. "But those months prior to that particular birthday, my brothers seemed even more so." A wistful smile formed on Cailin's mouth as she recalled the nights when they'd come home. "Every night, I'd hear this atrocious snoring coming from their rooms. They sounded like big bears." She proceeded to impersonate that loud growling noise that had emanated from the room the three Audley boys had shared, earning a laugh from Ellie and stares from those nearby. "I didn't think anything of it . . . until the day of my birthday, when I learned the truth."

Ellie stopped laughing. Round-eyed, she leaned in. "The *truth*?"

"They'd managed to collect blank papers from the foreman, and every night would retire to their rooms. All the while they pretended to sleep, they were really busy writing . . . each writing books which they themselves bound together with thread, and then with some twenty original stories, created a library in my bedroom."

Ellie touched a hand to her chest, pressing a palm to her heart.

"Yes, that was much my response." Cailin's whole body hurt as she missed having all her brothers near.

"The best brothers protect their sisters' love of reading," Ellie said. "That is what Courtland did when Father tried to sell me and my sisters' favorite books."

And through the warmth of the happy memory from long ago came the young girl's words.

"Your father . . . sold your books?" she whispered.

The girl froze, putting Cailin in mind of the hare who made a habit of feasting on the carrots and lettuce. Then, she looked off into the crowd, and Cailin followed her stare over to Courtland. "Oh, dear. I'm afraid I have to leave."

Startled by that abrupt shift, Cailin frowned. "Must you?" Cailin said quickly, finding herself wishing to be regaled with more talk of Courtland and very much enjoying the company of another one of Courtland's sisters.

"I must. I was having such a good time with you, Miss Audley, I forgot I needed to enlist Courtland's help. There were some ladies giving Hattie a difficult time, and when that happens, I always like to drag Courtland about when people are being cruel. That tends to quiet them quickly." The girl turned to go, and Cailin shot out a hand, gently taking her by the arm.

Her earlier dizzying state was cleared by Ellie's revelation. "Who is being unkind to your sister?"

Ellie shrugged. "Several ladies. I overheard them teasing her outside the library."

Teasing Hattie. Bespectacled, book-loving Hattie, who was always ready with a smile and a story? Her jaw tensed, and Cailin forced herself to relax the muscles of her face. "You needn't interrupt Lottie's dance. I will . . . go in search of Hattie."

Ellie beamed. "Indeed? That is good of you."

Cailin turned to go when Ellie stopped her.

"Some think there are no hardships that come with be-

ing a duke's daughter . . . or now, sister. But there are," the
girl said, with more world wisdom than some of the old
miners Cailin had known in Cheadle.

With that insightful reminder issued by the girl, Cailin
quit the ballroom and headed in search of Courtland's
sister.

A quiet muttering reached her. Hattie's quiet muttering.

". . . where are you . . . ? Where are you . . . ?"

Hattie's softly spoken words came over and over in a
sing-song mantra.

Cailin went off in pursuit, and taking the corner, she
nearly stumbled over a figure on all fours crawling on the
ground. Cailin brought herself up quick to keep from toppling over the young lady. The woman with her head buried
almost in the carpet muttered to herself, giving no indication
that she had heard Cailin's arrival.

"Where are you?" the seemingly unsuspecting lady continued muttering to herself, and this time, her tone had dissolved, with tears threatening.

"May I help you?" she ventured, and the young woman
squealed, her palms slid out from under her, and her chin
hit the floor.

Wincing, Cailin rushed forward, dropping to her knees
beside the young woman. The familiar young woman with
ridiculously tight black ringlets, and plump cheeks . . . that
had once contained dimples but now, with her state of sadness, showed no trace of them. She sank back on her heels.
"You," she blurted.

The young woman—the duke's sister, Hattie—squinted
and peered deeply at Cailin. "Miss Audley, is that you?"

"It is," she assured. "And please, I believe we agreed to
refer to one another's names."

"Oh, it is so very good to see you, Cailin." And Cailin's
heart wrenched at the unkindness the young woman had
encountered, and here from guests invited by Cailin's father. Hattie's brow puckered. "If I could see, that is." The
duke's sister exhaled that last word on a sigh. "I fear I've
lost my spectacles."

Frowning, Cailin glanced about the silver carpeting. "Out . . . here? You're certain they are not in the ballroom."

"Oh, no. I had them when I left to find a spot to read." Cailin's gaze fell to the little leather volume in the lady's left hand. "But—"

Behind them, Cailin caught a flurry of giggles and whispers. She looked behind her.

A trio of ladies in white satin skirts watched on as though they were taking in a Covent Garden theater production.

Cailin glanced from Courtland's sister to the group of women, and then back to Hattie, and immediately identified the source behind the lady's woes.

Or rather, the three sources behind them.

"They took your spectacles, did they not?" she murmured as she stood, and then took Hattie's hand and assisted the half-blind young lady to her feet.

"They identified a smudge," Hattie said softly. "And then as they were passing them between one another to clean, one of the ladies dropped them . . ." Her voice trailed off. "Or that is what they said, anyway." Hattie added that last part under her breath, her cheeks pinkening with a tinge of humiliation.

Cailin pressed her lips together as fury licked at her insides. It was not, however, Lady Hattie who need be embarrassed. Sharpening her gaze upon that collection of mean misses, Cailin, with Hattie in hand, headed for the trio.

As they walked, Hattie supplied the identities of their visitors. "The lady in the middle is Lady Bridgett, the Season's Diamond. The Earl of Hanover's sister. She is sought after by all. The ladies on either side of her are sisters, Lady Beatrix and Lady Eugenie." Hattie continued in a whisper. "It is, however, Lady Bridgett whose favor is sought."

"Why would any gentleman seek her out?" she asked from the corner of her mouth.

Hattie's lips twitched. "Because she is worth one hundred thousand pounds, and she is . . . beautiful."

As they neared the women at the end of the corridor,

Cailin passed a gaze over the lady. Yes, with her trim waist, generous hips and bosom, and tall form, she was decidedly one who'd turn heads. "Ah, but what good is a pretty face if one has an empty heart?" Cailin asked.

"In Polite Society? People don't care about what's in one's heart, but rather what's in one's purses," Hattie finished on a hushed whisper as they stopped before the gathering. Courtland's sister turned her focus to Lady Bridgett. "Hullo!" Hattie piped in cheerfully. "I was—"

Cailin cut the young woman off. "I believe you have Lady Hattie's spectacles," Cailin said crisply, refusing to allow Courtland's sister to bow before this vile bully. She held a palm out. "I'll take those now."

The leader of the group, a lady blonder, paler, and taller than the pair of smaller, pudgier misses flanking her, looked down the bridge of her button nose at Cailin. "I don't know what you're—"

Cailin snapped her fingers. "The spectacles, please."

"Cailin," Hattie said, tugging her sleeve; worry wreathed her voice.

Lady Bridgett immediately went pinch-mouthed, and her features screwed in an annoyed mask, erasing any hint of the beauty she was so favored for. "Are you accusing me of taking the lady's spectacles?" There was a warning there.

At Cailin's side, Hattie dropped her focus to the floor.

"I am." Cailin released Hattie's hand and took a step forward. "Now, if you would."

Ladies Beatrix and Eugenie gasped.

The earl's daughter's eyes bulged, giving her the look of the trout Cailin had oft fished with Wesley and Hunter in the Staffordshire rivers. Then, the young woman seemed to find herself. Giving her head a shake, she smoothed her features into an even, emotionless mask. "I know you. You're the duke's *bastard*."

At the young woman's side, the ladies sniggered.

Hattie's fingers curled comfortingly within Cailin's. "Come," Hattie said softly. "I trust they do not have my spectacles any longer. That is, as they said, they dropped them."

The hell they had. And the hell Cailin would leave.

It would take a good deal more to offend her. Where she hailed from, people cared not about a person's birthright, but rather their character and sense of honor and decency and dignity; all of which the trio before her decidedly lacked.

"Am I supposed to be insulted?" she asked, adopting bored tones. Cailin feigned a yawn and patted her palm against her mouth. "The word 'bastard' did not always carry a stigma. In fact, William the Conqueror, of whom my father shares ancestry, is still referred to in state papers as William the Bastard."

Once more like one of those fish plucked from the waters, Lady Bridgett's mouth opened and closed, and Cailin would wager every book she'd since purchased in London it was the first time the beauty had found herself rendered speechless. Then, Lady Bridgett gave a little sideways toss of her head, motioning to the lady on the left of her.

Lady Eugenie jumped, and then, head bowed, she rushed over. Removing her hand from behind her back, she held over the spectacles.

Cailin snatched them from the lady's hands. "That will be all," she said coolly.

Giving a little clap, Lady Bridgett spun on her heel and marched off; her friends hastened after her, struggling to keep up.

"Here you are," Cailin said, holding out the pair of spectacles.

"That was rather magnificent," Hattie breathed, accepting the eyewear from Cailin. The young lady returned them to the bridge of her nose and sighed. "I just wish I could have seen it clearly so I might have watched their faces as you gave them that set-down."

Cailin held the young woman's gaze. "I should point out . . . I do not know whether the duke shares any blood relation to William the Conqueror, but it was a fun bit to add."

Both women looked at one another and broke out laughing.

"Oh, I am ever so grateful for your being here," Hattie said through her amusement, as she brushed the stray tears of mirth from the corners of her eyes. "For your rescue, but also for your company. Won't you join me? I was seeking out Her Ladyship's libraries." Cupping a hand around her mouth, she leaned in and whispered, "One can always rely upon a lord's library being empty." Her eyes twinkled. "All the better for me."

This time, Courtland's sister took Cailin's hand and tugged her down the hall, and stopping beside a doorway, she pressed the handle and motioned for Cailin to enter ahead of her.

The moment Cailin stepped through the threshold, her heart stopped, and she drew up quick. "Oh," she whispered. And here she'd believed there couldn't be a more splendorous library than the one in her father's London household . . . only to step into this paradise.

"It is lovely, is it not?" Hattie said conversationally as she drew the door shut behind them. "In my two Seasons sneaking off to read, I've become somewhat proficient at libraries, and your father's"—she gestured to the room at large—"is by far the most magnificent one I've ever seen."

Together, they ventured deeper into the Duke of Bentley's libraries and perused the shelves: spines revealing titles in foreign languages Cailin couldn't read or identify, and then works by authors whom she didn't know and couldn't place. "Yes," Cailin murmured. "It is . . . impressive."

"They have it all organized quite nicely," Hattie said while they walked, as though she were the curator of a museum providing information for a patron on tour. "The gothic novels and romantic tales . . ." She paused. "Of which I prefer, are over there." She pointed across the room. "They have books on mathematics there"—Cailin followed Hattie's gesture to a nearby shelf—"and then the scientific ones here." Cailin drew to a stop and sighed.

So many books.

So very many of them.

Cailin grazed her fingertips along the spine: *The Book of Healing.*

Papers on living and fossil elephant species: Georges Cuvier. Eagerly, she tugged free the title and smoothed her callused fingertip over the gold etching of one of those enormous creatures.

Hattie plopped herself onto the leather button sofa behind them, kicked her feet up, and popped her book open. "Our own is rather bare," the girl confessed. "My father was not a reader." She paused, her eyes going sad.

"And what of your brother?" Cailin asked before she could call the question back. Before she could even pause to wonder where that curiosity had come from. In a bid for nonchalance, Cailin cradled the book on elephant fossils in one arm and resumed her study of the titles.

"Which brother? Courtland?" From the corner of her eye, she caught Hattie cock her head. "He did not have much time for himself. Father was always forcing him to see to ducal affairs."

While Hattie returned to reading her book, Cailin continued a distracted stroll of her father's libraries.

*He did not have much time for himself. Father was always forcing him to see to ducal affairs . . .*

Sadness filled her breast. Hattie's words harkened back to the day she'd met Courtland at the Temple of the Muses and he'd just casually mentioned his being unable to read because of his responsibilities.

Prior to coming to London and getting to know Courtland, she'd expected a nobleman would be free to be who he wished to be. And yet, she recalled his words once more . . . that they were in some way confined to a cage.

Suddenly, the door opened, and she froze.

"I expected I'd find you here," that familiar voice sounded at the front of the room. A moment later, the door shut, and Courtland stalked over. "It took me an infernal amount of parlors before finding it," he muttered, loosening his stark white cravat as he walked. He dropped onto the seat beside his sister. "Your own?" he asked, tugging the volume free from his sister's fingers. "Or can I expect to be challenged by our distinguished host for you pilfering from his library?"

With a little laugh, Hattie scooted over a fraction, making room for her brother. "I daresay it would be the first duel fought over books."

Hanging in the shadows, Cailin took in the exchange between brother and sister.

The duke waggled his golden eyebrows. "Oh, duels are fought over all manner of offenses. I'm certain book-thieving would be included amongst them."

"Do you know"—he lowered the book a fraction and glanced over the top of that crimson leather volume—"if you are *truly* searching for love, I expect it would be easier to find it in the ballroom than on the pages of this boo— Oomph." Courtland winced and drew his leg back to rub his shins.

"I'm no more looking for real love than you are, big brother." Hattie softened that with a teasing smile.

Affection and familiar warmth and love and regard were commonplace in the small village from where Cailin came. Those same feelings, however, seemed in great shortage here in Town, where aside from her father and his wife, Cailin observed people of the peerage conducted themselves stiffly, with no outward display of warmth or affection.

"And do behave," Hattie said, and then, as if she'd just recalled Cailin's presence, she looked over. "We have company."

Courtland followed his sister's pointed stare . . . over to where Cailin stood.

The gentleman froze, and then Hattie's book slipped from his fingers and landed with a *thump* upon the hardwood floor.

Hattie gave him another kick in the ankle, and he grunted. "My goodness, you are fortunate I love you, because I'm fairly certain there's no more grievous affront than dropping a lady's book." Muttering to herself, the lady bent to retrieve her title.

Dampening her mouth, Cailin stepped out of the shadows. "Hullo, Your Grace. It appears we meet again."

Courtland's eyes went endearingly large, and then he jumped up. "Miss Audley," he greeted with a bow, and even as he straightened, he set to work righting the cravat he'd just loosened.

She found she preferred him . . . rumpled. It fit him as the approachable man whom she'd come to call friend. When they were together, she forgot he was an all-powerful duke and only saw a charming man whose company she had come to long for.

The younger woman looked to Cailin, and then took her hands in her own. "Thank you so very much for keeping me company."

Cailin gave a slight squeeze. "I should be the one thanking you for allowing me to join you," Cailin spoke in a whisper meant solely for Lady Hattie's ears. "And escape the tediousness."

They shared a commiserative smile.

Feeling Courtland's gaze, Cailin glanced over and found his eyes upon her; his thick, long golden lashes, however, concealed the sentiments within.

Unnerved by his scrutiny, she released his sister's hands, and as brother and sister took their leave, she found herself strangely regretful at that parting.

# Chapter 21

The whole of this night, Courtland had admired Cailin from across the dance floor, yearning for more than the two dances they'd shared; line ones that had seen them apart more than had seen them together.

Now, he thought of her. Draped in a vibrant violet satin gown that clung to her form, accentuating generous hips. Her décolletage, more daring than in any of the previous dresses she'd donned, had highlighted a glorious display of flesh that he really shouldn't have noted. Not with the dangerous history between them, that past exchange that had cost his brother his employment. But God help him, he'd earned his reputation as a rogue for a reason, and he'd be hard-pressed not to—

"Why did we have to go back?" his sister lamented, and with Courtland lost in thought, it took a moment for his sister's words to penetrate. "I was having a splendid time."

Having spent time alone with Cailin, he could certainly attest to similar feelings about the lady's company. Alas . . .

"Your presence was missed," he said, as they made the long walk to the ballroom.

Snorting, Hattie slid a glance upward. "By who?"

"Many people," he hedged.

Hattie dug her heels in, forcing them to stop. Dropping her hands atop her hips, she stared pointedly at him. "Well?"

"Lord Seagrave." Silently, Courtland gave thanks for the loyalty of that other man's friendship.

Hattie's eyes dipped. "He only requested the set because of you."

Yes, that was decidedly true. God help him for having not one, not two, but three clever sisters.

"Of course not," he said indignantly.

She eyed him suspiciously. "What if he does want a real match with me?"

Courtland's nostrils flared. "The hell he—" Bloody hell. He caught himself too late.

Hattie jabbed a finger hard at his chest, and he winced. "Ah-ha! I knew it." She let her arm fall. "Just as I know that every ball we attend, I can always count on you to dance a set and Lord Seagrave, who'll give"—she tossed up two digits—"two sets. Six dances apart." Hattie gave her eyes a mighty roll. "You men are nothing if not predictable."

"You enjoy dancing."

She sighed her exasperation. "Not with my brother."

It didn't escape his notice that she'd failed to mention Seagrave. He narrowed his eyes. "And what of—"

"Oh, for the love of Satan on Sunday." Hattie threw her arms up. "He's only a shade better than you, and only because he's *not* my brother."

He stared intently at his sister. Because mayhap he'd made a mistake in enlisting his friend's support throughout his sister's Seasons. "You're certain." Of course, the earl would never pursue one such as Hattie, but that didn't mean his sister was immune to Seagrave's charms.

"I am . . ." She froze. "I forgot *Pamela*."

At that abrupt shift, he looked quizzically at his sister and glanced about for the unknown-to-him lady in question.

*"Pamela,"* his sister explained, her tone affronted. *"Vir-*

*tue Rewarded."* When he continued to stare in what he suspected was abject confusion, she briefly closed her eyes. *"My book.* I forgot my book." With that she started back toward Lord and Lady Hanover's libraries.

And any of the very brief worrying he'd allowed himself, over the possibility his sister might be carrying romantic sentiments where Seagrave was concerned, was immediately put to rest.

*"Woah,"* he said, catching her lightly by the arm. "I shall fetch it. Your—"

"My set with Seagrave. I know. I know." She pointed at Courtland. "Get my book."

And there was a warning contained within his sister's tone. Bowing his head, he stared after his sister as she returned to the ballroom . . . and then reversing course, he set out in search of Hattie's book.

Muttering to himself as he went, Courtland returned to the library, and opening the door, he immediately found her, perusing the shelves as she'd been.

As he slowly began to push the door shut behind him, with Cailin's back to him, he took a moment to run his gaze appreciatively over the lady's form, the generous swells of her buttocks; and his fingers twitched with the yearning to sink his fingers into that flesh and draw her—

"Do you intend to stand there all evening with the door opened, risking discovery?" she drawled, her bored tones the perfect killer of a man's desire.

Coming to the moment, he stepped deeper inside the room and pushed the panel closed, shutting them in—alone.

It was a dangerous place for him to be with this woman. For them to be . . . together.

Cailin finally turned, shifting her focus from that all-important bookshelf that had commanded her notice to Courtland. Her brow dipped.

"My sister forgot her book," he explained, feeling like a green-boy, uneasy around those of the opposite sex. Crossing over to where his sister had been seated, he looked for . . . and immediately found that title she'd left behind.

Book in hand, he held it aloft, displaying it for Cailin as proof.

And now, he could leave.

Now, he should leave.

"I take it you are not enjoying yourself this evening?" he asked, as she slowly searched through an enormous black book in her arms.

"On the contrary, I'm enjoying myself very much." She paused. "At least, now I am."

Now. Because of him . . .

His heart soared.

She glanced up and gave him an odd look over the top of that title she cradled so lovingly in her arms. How singularly odd to find oneself . . . envious of an inanimate object.

Heat immediately climbed his neck. "Because of the book," he blurted.

"Yes."

Courtland should absolutely take that as his cue to see himself out; to leave the lady to her solitary company and the enjoyment she now found. Selfishly, however, he'd no will to leave. The women he'd kept company with through the years, the lovers he'd taken, had all been ones who'd relished not only attending social events but being at the front and center of them. They'd certainly never been women who'd snuck off to hide. At least, that is, not for any reasons that were respectable.

He stole a glance at the ormolu clock just past her shoulder. Seagrave was with Hattie. He trusted the other man with his life and knew when Hattie was in the earl's care, she was well.

As if she felt his stare, Cailin glanced over.

Courtland turned his sister's book over in his hands. "Hattie is forever sneaking off to read."

"Because she is being met with unkindness."

That gave him pause. "My sister?" Yes, she'd not had any suitors, but . . .

"I trust as a duke, you are unaccustomed to anything but adoration and respect. Alas, even being a relation to a duke does not necessarily spare a woman from society's unkindness. They are also staring and always whispering."

She spoke as one who knew.

"I . . . did not know." Guilt and remorse all ran together. As Hattie's brother, he'd had an obligation to know . . . and to make it better for her. "Thank you for making me aware." Of something he'd had a responsibility to have noted himself.

"You needn't thank me," she said, taking a seat on one of the button sofas. "I like your sister and enjoy her company."

What she'd shared, along with her presence here, gave him pause. "Is that why you are here, Cailin?" he asked, his gut clenching, for he didn't want to think of this bold, proud woman hiding away from people who were inferior to her in every way. At her questioning look, he clarified. "Are you avoiding those who would be unkind to you?" Because the idea of the lords and ladies present running her off made him want to storm the ballroom and destroy every last one of them.

Surprise lit her blue eyes. "Oh, no." She lifted her skirts a fraction, bringing his gaze downward to her trim ankles. His heart thumped at the innocent but still so very erotic reveal. "My feet are in misery."

She smiled, and he took that as an invitation to join her.

Cailin let her skirts fall, they slid back into place, and he forced his attention away from a temptation he'd never known existed: a lady's feet.

Just like that, however, the tension eased, and they were restored to a casual, comfortable place.

Courtland gathered up his sister's book, and then glanced at the copy Cailin held. "May I?"

Unlike the hesitancy of their first meeting in Staffordshire, back when she'd been mistrustful of him, she automatically handed her book over.

Skimming the title, Courtland opened the large leather volume and fanned the pages, taking in the engravings upon the pages.

Heads bent, they studied those renderings together, and in this closeness, there was an intimacy far greater than a sexual joining. He and Cailin were two people with shared interests and passions, united in their love for learning. Only . . . he'd forgotten his love for the subjects she explored so freely. He'd been shamed by his father into burying those parts of himself away, until Cailin had entered his life and made him recall all those better parts of himself.

"I forgot how much I enjoyed this manner of readings," he said wistfully.

"Your . . . father prevented you from reading them."

He glanced up.

"When we met at the Temple of the Muses, you mentioned that tutors only taught what their employers instructed."

She'd remembered that.

"Yes, he forbade me from *wasting my time* with scholarly pursuits that did not benefit the St. James line." His gaze locked on a black-and-white rendering upon the page. Courtland's periodicals and journals were some of the first items his father had sold to pay for his many mistresses' extravagant lifestyles. "He insisted my attentions were reserved for my ducal responsibilities." The irony was not lost on Courtland now that the same man who'd let the lands go to let, and the coffers go empty, had insisted that Courtland as a future duke should be so devoted to that title.

Cailin's hand covered his, and he looked over.

Sadness filled her eyes. "I am so sorry."

He shrugged a shoulder, not wanting that pitiable memory to steal the joy of this moment. "It is funny. I lived in London, near to all the museums and bookshops you yourself longed to explore, and yet, they existed beyond my reach, as they did yours." Except, even as he spoke, he realized how wrong it was to even dare compare their experiences. "Not that I am equating the two," he hurried to say. "Until my mother was forbidden from taking me to those places, I *did* get to experience them . . ."

Cailin linked her fingers with his, joining their hands, and lightly squeezed them. Raising his knuckles to her mouth, she brushed her lips over them in a tender kiss.

And with that, she freed him to speak without judgment about his interests and his life.

"When I was sent off to Eton and Oxford, I missed my siblings, and yet I reveled at the opportunity to study those works he'd kept from me. I remember the first time I read Nicolas Steno's papers," he murmured, recalling the joy of that discovery, the simultaneous splendor at the oppressive thumb being removed from his person and also guilt for having those freedoms when his siblings remained trapped under the duke's influence.

Cailin scooted closer. "I don't know of Steno."

Relinquishing the darker thoughts of his youth, Courtland warmed to his telling. "Oh, he was a clever fellow. He took a shark head and—" Remembering himself, Courtland stopped abruptly.

Giving a little nod, Cailin encouraged him on. *"Annd?"*

He grimaced. "It wouldn't be— Oomph." Courtland blinked slowly. "Did you just kick me?"

"More like a wee nudge," Cailin held two fingers up, a hairbreadth apart.

He'd had wee nudges before. This was decidedly a well-placed, impressively strong kick to the shins. He gave his head a befuddled shake. "I've never . . ."

"Been kicked?" she supplied.

"Yes." His lips quirked at the corner. "That is, by anyone other than my sisters," he added drolly. "I remain as unaware with them as I am with you as to what I did to earn your wrath."

"You were weighing your words," Cailin said. "You stopped yourself from saying whatever it was Steno did in his studies out of fear of offending me . . . because I am a woman. Is that not so?"

God, she would have made a master barrister. "I . . ." Courtland twisted at his cravat, before he realized what he was doing, and then stopped his distracted fiddling. He let his arm fall to his side. "You are correct. I was taking care with what I said, lest I potentially upset you."

"Because I'm a woman," she repeated for a second time.

He nodded. "Because you are a lady," he allowed. This time he was wise to draw his leg back a fraction, out of her reach.

Cailin arched a perfectly formed golden eyebrow. "I've cared for injured miners. I've helped babes be birthed and done the same with livestock. And even if I hadn't the experiences I do in life, I'd *still* not want to be coddled, Courtland. I've horrified you."

And it was hard not to fall a little bit in love with a woman so in command of herself, who desired unfiltered facts, and who spoke her mind so freely . . . and who'd also lived a life of meaning. "On the contrary," he murmured. He slid his gaze over the delicate heart-shaped planes of her face, taking in each tiny freckle left by the sun; the ones at the bridge of her nose that formed an endearing little pattern of Cassiopeia. With what she'd done in her some twenty years, she'd certainly proven she'd done more than Courtland ever had. Courtland, who couldn't properly look after his own damned siblings. It was a humbling discovery to make, and a humbling feeling to feel. "Steno dissected a shark head and removed the creature's teeth."

Instead of the horror he'd initially expected such a revelation would elicit, the lady's button nose scrunched up. "For what purpose?"

"He sought to compare a shark's teeth with the tongue stones." At her confused look, he clarified. "They're the petrified teeth embedded in rock. In doing so, he was able to confirm the fossils were in fact shark teeth."

Cailin sat upright on her knees. "Indeed?" she breathed.

It was, sadly, the one story he knew about this topic that she so loved. And with the adoration gleaming from her eyes, he found himself wishing he knew more about fossilized shark teeth. Because there was something so very magnificent about having a woman look at him the way this woman did now.

Not because of his title.

Not because of some dream she had of being a duchess.

But because of words he'd spoken.

This? It was heady stuff, indeed.

It conjured imaginings of Cailin as his duchess and more . . . imaginings of her in his bed. Under him.

Energy thrummed between them. Around them.

And she felt it, too.

Attuned to every slight nuance of her body, he noted the way her chest moved faster and the uneven cadence of her inhalation.

"You should leave, Cailin," he said hoarsely.

"Why?"

And instead of heeding his advice, she slid closer to him on the leather sofa. So close he felt the press of her thigh against his; so close the heat from her delicate frame burned like a physical caress.

He looked her square in the eyes. "Because I want you, and—" Cailin leaned over and kissed him gently.

"I want freedom of my life, Courtland," she said, between kisses. "A freedom to choose."

And her meaning couldn't be clearer: she'd chosen him.

She wanted a future with him.

And as she pressed herself against him, he at last understood that fall Adam had made—and the reason for it.

# Chapter 22

Cailin knew two things with absolute certainty: one, she'd no wish to return to the ballroom and the evening's festivities. Not because she'd had such a terrible time this night, but because she wished to be . . . with him.

Why had she resisted so long, opening her heart again?

Why had she feared when there was a man like Courtland? A man who could make her smile, and whom she could speak with about everything from how unfair the world was for women to fossils and books that wrote of those ancient stones.

And two: she knew, beyond the shadow of a doubt, with absolutely no equivocation . . . the only place she wished to be was here in Courtland's arms.

Parting her lips, she opened for his kiss, and he gave her precisely what she sought; what she'd hungered for.

Courtland took her by the hips and drew her astride so she straddled his body; her skirts rustled hedonistically about them; her skirts rucked up so her limbs were exposed to the night air . . . and his touch.

He caressed his hands up and down her leg, lightly

squeezing the muscles of her calf, her silken stockings a flimsy barrier between his touch; and the feel of his skin upon hers sent a sharp ache to her core.

Biting her lower lip, she moved her hips against him, recalling the pleasure she'd known in his arms that morning. Wanting to know it again. And more.

Wanting to explode and make love in every way with him. And then, he was.

Lowering the bodice of her dress, he freed her breasts to his gaze and his worship.

With a murmur of appreciation, he filled his palms with those mounds, and then slowly lifted one to his lips.

Her breath caught on a shuddery gasp, and her eyes slid shut as he closed his mouth around a swollen, sensitive peak. He sucked upon that flesh; the erotic pulling sounds as he did liquified her.

"Courtland," Cailin whispered, and she twined her fingers in his luxuriant golden curls, holding him close, never wanting him to stop, and he didn't. He continued to taste of her; circling that tip with his tongue, teasing it; alternately kissing and suckling. Until logic departed and she was reduced to simply feeling.

Courtland stopped . . . briefly, and she cried out, but he was merely turning his attention to the previously neglected peak. Lifting her breast, he lowered his head and took that tip deep. He laved the bud, and her eyes fluttered shut on a sigh; his kisses, that wet pulling sound so very erotic, fueled her hungering.

She moaned, and of their own volition, her hips began to move as she undulated against him, wanting to get closer to him, *needing* to.

He glided his fingers over her lower legs, caressing her calves and moving his searching caress higher to her thighs, and she held her breath, bracing, waiting for that touch; the one she'd craved since the copse. And then he obliged, touching her there, in that most intimate of places.

Her breath caught on a noisy intake against his lips as he palmed her damp curls. How was it possible another person might make her feel . . . like this? How was it possible her body was capable of this fire?

Courtland slipped a finger inside, and she lifted into him. "I have dreamed of touching you again," he rasped; his voice harsh like he'd been running a distance, and all because he gave her pleasure.

She felt the hard length of him; he also found pleasure in touching her. "I have dreamed of it, too," she confessed breathlessly, and then bit her lip hard as he increased the glide of his fingers. And just like before, with his touch he brought her closer and closer to that place of wonder and bliss; a place where pleasure bordered on pain and any and every thought fled, disintegrating into nothing for the sheer potency of this desire.

Cailin pressed her cheek against his, focused on climbing that precipice and reaching that peak . . . but she wanted all of him. More than just his touch.

She wanted to know what it was to be made love to, completely. "I want you to make love to me," she whispered against his ear, her admission near noiseless, so soft she wondered if she'd uttered it aloud, or whether that wish dwelled still in the chambers of her mind.

Only . . .

His chest heaving, Courtland stopped caressing that place between her legs.

He moved his gaze over her face; through the desire in those blue depths, indecision seeped forth. "Are you certain—"

She kissed him, silencing the remainder of his question. He and she together like this was all she was certain about anymore. With Courtland, there was only honesty—in their discussions, in their embrace.

Bringing up a shaking hand, he brought it around and proceeded to undo button. After button. One at a time. With each pearl cylinder that slipped free, he kissed her. Ten buttons in total. Ten kisses in total. Until the top of her dress sagged, and slipped, and he slowed, then stopped. Keeping that power in her hands.

Angling away slightly, Cailin shrugged free of the silk article until it slid down her shoulders.

Back when she'd imagined being in love, and when she was loved, she'd also thought what this moment would be like. She'd expected there'd be some degree of embarrassment at the intimacy that came with lovemaking. Only with Courtland, there was none. There was something so . . . comfortable . . . so right in being with him. In a short while, they'd forged a bond, and that closeness was why it was so very easy to come to her feet and let her pink-silver ball gown slip all the way down, past her waist . . . she helped it along her hips, and then kicked it aside.

Courtland took in a shaky breath; his chest rose and fell fast, and his lips moved, but he remained silent. Laying his arms back along the curved arm of the button sofa, he reclined in that seat; his fingers curled into the fabric of the leather as if restraint was a struggle, and yet he displayed it, anyway.

Then, locking her gaze with his, she shoved free the modest white undergarments until she was clad before him in only her stockings.

Courtland froze.

She stood before him, shivering slightly, feeling exposed and certain she should feel more shame for it. Some . . .

"Cailin," he said, his voice hoarsened, and then he reached out for her.

She went. Climbing into his embrace and shoving back his jacket, helping him free of it so that she might feel him, the same way he saw and felt her.

Reaching between them, Courtland undid the handful of jacket buttons and tossed aside his jacket. Next came his shirt.

Living in a mining town, and being the sister of three older brothers, Cailin had seen a man's bare chest before. Never like this. For she'd believed only a laborer possessed chiseled muscles and defined contours. Her mouth went dry. She'd been wrong. His skin, bronzed like his flesh had been permanently kissed by the sun, was sprigged lightly with a matting of fine golden curls. The flat of his belly rippled, revealing each of his abdominal muscles.

Next, he shoved his trousers down . . . until he stood gloriously naked before her.

Her heart knocked erratically as she dipped her eyes to that enormous length of flesh arching high and proud against his belly, and when she slowly looked up, she found his heated gaze on her.

Did he think she'd balk now that she'd seen him?

The sight of him only further fueled that pulsing between her legs; a yearning that ached to be assuaged. Stretching her hand close, she touched his chest, sliding her fingers through those spriggy curls.

He hissed between his teeth, his eyes sliding shut and his muscles spasming under her palm.

"I've hurt you." Cailin hesitated and made to draw back, but he delicately circled her wrist in his larger fingers.

"Please, don't," he begged, his voice quavering. "Stop. Unless you want to . . ." he said on a rush. "And then—"

Cailin kissed him into silence once more; and pressing her naked form against his, she ran her palms up and down his arms and shoulders, searching him as he'd searched her.

He stilled, and then cupping her buttocks, he drew her closer and deepened that kiss. Sliding his tongue inside, he touched that brand of flesh against hers, masterfully stroking, and her belly quickened.

Gently, reverently, he shifted, bringing her to rest under him, and he braced his arms on the other side of her, framing her between his broad, powerful body.

She ran her gaze over the taut planes of his face: glistening faintly with sweat, the muscles tensed; evidence of the restraint he showed. She'd been fighting for the freedom to make her own decisions the whole of her life; and with Courtland, there was no fight. He didn't seek to constrain her or control her, and she reveled in the power of this greatest choice for her as a woman—whom she would give her virtue to.

His tawny brows dipped. "What is it?" he asked with a boyishly endearing hesitancy. "You've changed—"

"Do I take you as a woman who doesn't know her own mind?"

"No," he replied instantly, the confidence of that assertion stirring all the most wonderful warmth in her breast.

Cailin stroked her fingers along the curve of his jaw, and the muscles eased. "I was thinking how I'd never thought to know this, and now I will." And now that she did, how could this one moment ever be enough?

She refused to let that unexpected—and worse, that dangerous—yearning for more intrude upon this moment.

Courtland's lashes dipped and his eyes darkened. He caught her wrist, dragged it close to his mouth, and placed a possessive kiss upon that place where her pulse pounded.

He settled between her thighs and, reaching down between them, he freed himself from his trousers. The length of him sprang hard and long.

Her breathing came in noisy little spurts, and she wrapped her arms about him.

Nudging her legs apart, he lay between them, positioning himself at her center. Only . . . he remained there, his shaft pulsing against her damp curls; and lowering his head, he resumed his worship of her breasts.

Sighing, Cailin let her head fall back.

As a young woman who'd known of her late mother's past as a nobleman's mistress, she hadn't been able to understand or begin to fathom how she, or any woman for that matter, would trade their honor for a man's embrace.

Now she knew. God help her, how she knew.

Closing her eyes, she surrendered to his ministrations, loving the feel of his mouth upon her, loving the sound of it.

"You are so beautiful," he whispered, moving a path of kisses along the curve of her cheek and up to her temple. "From the moment you stepped outside with that rifle trained on me, I was captivated."

Through the haze of desire, a smile tugged at the corners of her lips. "I could have killed you."

"I would have happily perished that day."

A soft laugh escaped her. "Happily?"

A wry grin formed on his mouth, setting butterflies dancing in her belly. "Almost happily. And certainly, more after your embrace and—"

Leaning up, she kissed him. How she loved that adorable way in which he let his words freely fall. Unlike the taciturn men she'd always known.

He cupped her breasts, raising each to his mouth, one at a time, for further worship; until all thought fled and she was reduced to a bundle of nerve endings. Incoherent moans spilled from her lips, throaty and desperate to her own ears as he stroked her with his fingers.

And then, his fingers were gone, and in their place was a velvety hardness as he pressed against her, sliding inside, slowly. So slowly. Slow enough so that she grew accustomed to his solidness moving within her, but also agonizing for the speed that only dragged on the moment as the pressure built and her body throbbed; and then he stopped, that barrier all that remained between her and the ultimate pleasure she craved . . . and the complete abandonment of her virtue.

Cailin wrapped her arms around his broad frame and held him. "Please," she begged.

He lowered his mouth, taking hers in a gentle kiss, and then thrust deep.

Cailin gasped, a shaky breath spilling from her lips and getting lost in his mouth as he filled her completely. She flinched at the feel of him inside, throbbing and enormous; the tight walls of her channel clenched around him.

Courtland touched a kiss to her brow. "I am so sorry," he whispered and slowly began to move, withdrawing and then sliding within her, once again in a delicious rhythm that chased away the remnants of pain so she was capable of only focusing on glorious sensation.

Cailin raised her hips experimentally at first, lifting up as he thrust within, and their bodies found a natural cadence. The leather groaned and the fireplace crackled, the embers within snapping and hissing; a noisy little symphony that played for them.

That pressure at her center grew and grew until she and Courtland arched against one another, striving for surrender and surcease, even as she wanted this to continue on. Even as she never wanted this exquisiteness to end.

"Come for me," he panted; tightening his fingers upon her hips, sinking into that flesh, he used her to leverage his thrusts.

And then, she did.

Cailin screamed, the piercing cry of her desire reaching to the rafters before he swiftly covered her mouth and swallowed the rest of that damning sound; the echoes of which, however, danced still in the air and lingered in her ears as she came in glorious rippling waves that went on forever. Gasping for breath, fighting to get air into her lungs, she found her complete surrender.

And then, Courtland stiffened.

With a low primal groan, he tensed, his shoulders tightening and his body arching forward; and then, withdrawing, he spilled himself onto her belly.

He collapsed onto his elbows, catching himself to keep from crushing her.

As they lay there, she brought her arms about him, running her palms over his perspiring back. For so long she'd resisted the possibility of opening her heart again. She'd been so very certain she didn't *want* to open her heart again. And that she couldn't.

Only to find, in the days and weeks in which she'd come to know Courtland, he'd slipped inside . . . and that realization no longer brought the terror that it once had.

Cailin smiled.

They'd made love.

It was an act as old as time. And one he'd carried out with any number of women before her. Never, however, had it been like *this* here with Cailin.

Like being smote by lightning . . . only to be reborn of the ashes.

Shaking—had he ever before shaken after making love?—Courtland sat up. Leaning over the sofa, he grabbed his jacket, fished out a handkerchief, and gently cleaned Cailin between her legs, and then he wiped the remnants of his seed from her person.

And this proved also the first time that he didn't know what to say after making love to a woman.

They dressed in silence. All the while he fiddled with his cravat, he searched for what to say now. "We will marry . . . of course," he vowed.

*We will marry.*

In the midst of straightening her stockings, the lady stilled.

Oddly, the thought . . . did not horrify him as it should. Just the opposite. Instead it conjured thoughts of more moments such as these . . . and the discussions they'd enjoyed. As for her, and her reaction to the possibility?

Digging for the courage to ask a question he feared the answer to, Courtland cleared his throat. "Is that idea so terrible—"

"Shh!" Her face paled.

So it was that terrible. "Forgive me," he said, a cinch squeezing his heart and mortification bathing his face in a heated flush. "I'm sorry. I—"

"Courtland," she said warningly, looking purposely toward the door.

And then he heard it.

From the corridor came a steady tread of differing-size footfalls. A quick stampede, portending disaster and discovery.

Oh, fuck. This was bad.

This was very bad, indeed.

The door burst open, and a small group of people all scrambled for placement in the doorway; the reactions of the duke and duchess and a handful of guests varying degrees of horror, shock, and disbelief.

Their stunned silence was broken by the tallest person present, a fellow with several inches on the other six. *"Cailin?"*

"Hunter," Cailin whispered, and Courtland followed her

stare to the enormous fellow in dusty garments glaring daggers at him.

Courtland's stomach slipped.

It was a name he recalled from the notes he'd studied on the Audleys several months earlier. Hunter. As in Hunter Audley . . . the duke's very big, very enraged—and by the way he looked at Courtland, like he intended to rip Courtland's head off—very violent son.

*Not that you don't deserve it . . .*

Just then, another figure, smaller than the rest, dipped her head in the slight gap between the duke's and duchess's arms, and he froze.

His sister.

Her eyes wide, his sister Ellie took in the scandal unfolding.

The youngest of the group, she went unnoticed by the quartet whose horror and horrified fascination were fixed on him . . . and beyond him, on Cailin.

Was there anything worse than having your greatest shame witnessed by your youngest sister?

"What is going on? Why has everyone stopped?" That question came from somewhere in the hallway.

He'd been wrong before. There *was* something worse. Having that shame, the evidence that his father's blood coursed in his veins, witnessed by all his sisters.

And just then, Ellie looked back toward their sisters, but before she turned her focus away, he saw it: her smile.

The lone grinning member of the group. Grinning the way a cat who'd swallowed the canary—and supped on a second for dessert—might.

His mind slowed, then stalled altogether.

No.

Impossible.

Ellie looked in once more, and that pleased smile remained.

*I am going to throw up.*

The duchess was the first to find her way in this stretch of misery that felt never-ending.

"Oh, God," she whispered.

It was the first time in his life he'd been anything but discreet. Caught in flagrante delicto.

Never before, however, had any of the women he'd bedded been virgins.

She'd wanted freedom.

Freedom to choose.

And it appeared that was the one thing she would not have.

# Chapter 23

A short while later, the crowd dispersed, and Cailin having been whisked away, a rumpled Courtland headed not for his rooms . . . but to another's.

Heart hammering, he raced through the duke's household until he reached a set of guest chambers; he didn't stop, but rather flung the door open.

His three sisters assembled on the bed, sitting cross-legged as they had when they were small girls, jumped.

He pushed the door shut hard behind him. "Did you do this?"

"I daresay you were the one guilty of your own ruin, brother," Hattie said with a frown. Coming to her feet, she hopped off the mattress and put herself between him and her younger sisters.

But not before he caught the same flash of nervousness—and worse—guilt.

His insides turned. "Please," he implored. "Say this isn't true. Tell me I'm wrong." He needed to be wrong. He wanted it more than he'd ever wanted anything, including salvation from his own financial ruin.

And yet . . .

Ellie's guilt-filled gaze fell to the floor. "I was helping."

Oh, God.

His muscles weak, Courtland sank to his haunches and struggled to breathe. Dropping his elbows on his knees, he buried his head into his hands, dragging and tugging at his hair. The memory of Cailin's pale cheeks as her family and some of the most notorious gossips converged upon them, following a moment that had been pure magic. All the beautiful intimacy they'd shared, stolen by a sea of interlopers set upon them by his own sister.

A tortured groan rumbled in his chest and filled his throat, remaining trapped there.

*No. No. No.*

"I don't understand," Lottie said, her tones frantic. "What has happened?"

Except . . . he couldn't bring himself to say it. For that would be the final element of confirmation. That query, however confused and desperate, confirmed there was only one guilty player in this.

Ellie.

Courtland forced his gaze up.

"Courtland loves her," Ellie whispered. "I know she loves him. And—"

"Leave us," he said, interrupting that confession and ordering Hattie and Lottie gone.

They hesitated, exchanging looks with one another.

"Now," he snapped, and in a flurry, they scurried to their feet and raced past him for the door, and then let themselves out, so he and Ellie were alone.

He straightened, and not trusting himself to not raise his voice in fury, he counted silently to ten; and when that didn't help, he ticked off another ten-count in his head.

Closing his eyes, he drew in a deep breath.

When he opened them, Ellie remained at the foot of the bed, her hands clasped before her almost painfully thin waist. That white-knuckled grip of her interlocked fingers left those digits as pale as her face. She'd the same look she had when she'd stood before the duke, for one volatile lecture or another, before Courtland came rushing in to pluck her from that ugliness.

How many times, however, had he not been there, when she'd been forced to confront the duke's rage at her unconventionality head-on?

And he despised the sight of it. Because she may have been wrong about so much, but she'd been right about one fact: he wasn't his father. He saw that now. Only . . . his father wouldn't have cared about Cailin's ruination. He'd have seen her dowry, and Courtland's desire for the lady, as being the only things that mattered.

What was worse . . . with her ruthless maneuverings, his sister had shown shades of their terrible sire. It meant Courtland had failed her in ways he'd tried desperately not to.

Still, this wasn't about what he'd done wrong where she was concerned. It wasn't about Ellie. All that mattered was what she had done to Cailin.

"Say something," Ellie finally said, the first to speak, when he still couldn't and didn't trust himself in what he'd say.

Courtland could manage just three words. "How could you?"

"Because I love you," she said simply. "And you love her. And I'm a master tactician."

"You are not a military field commander," he exploded, his patience snapping and his voice booming around the room. "You are not Nelson. You are not bound for the fields of Europe."

"I don't wish to fight in the fields. I wish to sail on—"

"You are never going to serve in the damned military, and you are *not* a master tactician," he barked, and his sister's entire body jerked like he'd run her through, and he wouldn't feel bad. He'd indulged her enough, and look what it had wrought this day. Still, he drew in several steady, slow breaths and regained his self-control. "I have allowed you to act as though the world is your battlefield, but it isn't,

Ellie," he said more quietly. "There is a difference between playing with pretend pistols and swords and playing with people's lives," he hissed.

Which was what she'd done. To the one person who'd deserved least to have her life manipulated so.

Ellie's lower lip quavered; recalling him to the first time he'd stepped into the nursery, when he'd looked down into her cradle and her lip had trembled so before she'd let forth a gusty wail. He'd scooped her up, and she'd instantly stopped.

However, in this moment, with her actions this day . . . he could not soothe away her upset. She was a young woman who'd made a dangerous decision that had even more dangerous consequences for another.

"You robbed Cailin of her choice. You destroyed her reputation and brought shame to her and her family."

"I may have been wrong in what I did, but I don't regret it, Courtland. You love her and she loves you."

"She doesn't love me," he said tiredly, and if there had been the hope of any such sentiments, they had no doubt died this day . . . in her father's well-stocked libraries.

"But she will come to love you in time. I will tell her it was me—"

"You'll do no such thing," he said, stealing a frantic glance at the door.

He'd broad enough shoulders to carry this . . . Were it revealed that Ellie was behind his being caught in a compromising position, all of Polite Society would automatically assume she'd acted in tandem with their elder sisters. *All* of their futures would be destroyed. And furious as he was with Ellie, neither could he see her ruined as she would be if the truth came to light.

He cursed blackly and roundly.

"I'm so sorry, Courtland," she whispered, her voice shaky. "I just wanted to help. I wanted to see you happy."

And he was reminded again that, despite her actions this day, she was still just a girl. A headstrong, obstinate girl who thought she was twenty-four and not fourteen, but who still played at pretend and who'd not properly understood the ramifications of all she'd done this day. "I know," he said, exhaustion setting in.

"You hate me like Father." She dropped her misty gaze to the floor. "I knew it was coming. He said I was an abomination, and I am. I hurt Miss Audley, and I hurt you . . ." And then her tears fell, silent except for her intermittent sniffle. "And now, Miss Audley will hate me. And I *do* so like her."

Courtland rubbed a hand over his eyes.

Everything this day had gone from splendorous to a splendid mess.

"I will speak to her," he said. That meeting was inevitable, and God help him as a coward, after this, if he didn't know how to face her. "You are not to speak about this to anyone, Ellie." He infused an adamancy into his tones. "You are to say nothing about what you've done. Not to anyone."

"I promise," she said, with a quavery nod. She made an X across her heart. "I'll do anything you ask me to do to make it right." Ellie rushed over and threw herself into his arms, and despite his fury, he folded her in an embrace.

Courtland set her aside and headed for the door.

"Where are you going?" she asked.

"To speak with Miss Audley," he said, and there'd never been a meeting he'd dreaded more than this one. Which, given the appointments he'd had with creditors, debt collectors, and—when his father was alive—the cruel duke who'd sired him, was saying a lot. None of those meetings, however, had mattered in the same way this impending one did, because he'd not loved and respected a single one of those individuals the way he did Cailin Audley.

His sister had spoken of "making it right."

And yet, as he quit the rooms and went in search of Cailin, he knew beyond a doubt, with an absolute certainty, just one thing: there was no making this right.

Ever.

# Chapter 24

Cailin had grown accustomed to people's stares.
Since her arrival in London, as the duke's long-lost
by-blow, any number of them had been trained upon her.

Fascinated looks.

Curious ones.

But none of those moments of scrutiny had been . . . like
*this*.

With her clothing rumpled and her hair loose about her
shoulders.

Not when she was caught in the most intimate of ways
with Courtland, their presence an intrusion into and viola-
tion of the beauty they'd shared.

And worst of all, included among those gawking at her
ruination had been her father . . . and two of her brothers.

Hunter, whom she'd been missing so very badly and
yearned to see again.

Just not like . . . this. With him witness to her public
shame.

Even the brief reprieve to change into new garments,
and have her hair tidied, hadn't helped. Standing in the

duke's office with an equally tense trio of men, who were in so very many ways the mirror image of one another, she discovered there was something even worse than the gawking, horrified looks those strangers and her family had heaped upon her tonight.

It was the absolute quiet of this room.

Nothing compared with the solitary silence left by her father and brothers. None of whom had spoken a word since a waiting servant had let her inside for her meeting.

A meeting was what Edwina had called it when she'd come to Cailin's room to summon her.

Edwina, whom she'd never recalled as subdued and grim.

Not even when Edwina herself had been ruined in a similar way by Rafe . . . caught in a compromising position in the midst of Rafe's entry into Polite Society.

Coward that she was, Cailin couldn't look at them. Instead, standing in the middle of the circular carpet, Cailin stared intently at her feet.

For the thing of it was, that moment with Courtland in the library had been the most magical, splendorous experience of her entire life. His touch had brought her body alive in ways she'd never known her body *could* come alive, and the intrusion of her family and his, and other random guests, had somehow twisted that moment into something so very ugly and wrong. Only it hadn't been. It had been beautiful and special and also what *she'd* wanted.

And it had been cheapened by an audience.

"It appears we are making something of a habit of this," she said, in an attempt at defusing the tension, hoping that reminder would have . . . some dulling impact upon her brother's rage and her father's grimness.

Alas, her attempt failed.

Incandescent with rage, Rafe narrowed his eyes upon her into such thin slits his irises disappeared. "Are you making light of this?" he demanded, his question abrupt. "Because I fail to see how anything about"—he slashed a hand in her direction—"this is amusing in any way."

"Rafe," their father said, quietly at his son's side, even as Hunter put a restraining hand on Rafe's shoulder.

Rafe shrugged it off, but Hunter said something, speaking quietly.

A muscle twitched in her eldest brother's jaw, and then he gave a slight, hard nod.

When Rafe returned his attention to her, disappointment spilled from his eyes in a way that was wholly foreign and unfamiliar. In fact, she couldn't recall a single time in the whole of her life when her eldest brother had looked upon her so. Yes, he'd been annoyed and short with her before. But this? This was so very different. It stirred a shame that brought her toes curling into the soles of her slippers. At what she and Courtland had done. And she hated it. Hated it for the reason that her first time making love had been so cheapened.

Shame had replaced splendor to become the sentiment of the evening.

And yet—

How dare Rafe or, for that matter, their father? "I'll have you know, I'm not making light," she said quietly, and when Rafe and Hunter and their father remained locked in their debate . . . a debate about her . . . she raised her voice. "I said, I was not making light." That managed to penetrate the discussion that had cut her out.

The men swung their attention back her way, and for the first time since she and Courtland had been discovered, she found herself; she found herself steadied. "I was pointing out that I am not the first to have been caught in a compromising position." She gave her brother a pointed look.

Color suffused his cheeks. "That is entirely different," he gritted out.

"Is it, big brother?" Hunter asked, a dry thread to his voice, startling Cailin with that unexpected show of support. When she'd only expected a like rage.

"Of course it is?"

Finding strength in Hunter's backing, Cailin struck a foot out. "Do tell?"

"Because it was Edwina, and I knew her—"

"I know the duke," she noted.

Her eldest brother's lecture immediately cut out. With him standing there, flummoxed, his lips moving and no words coming out, Cailin found a perverse sense of pleasure in not being the only one floundering this day.

And as a frown formed on Hunter's lips and even his support wavered, she suspected she'd said too much.

"What do you mean, you know the duke?" her father asked with a quiet calm, a sentiment that appeared to have skipped her brother.

Cailin, however, refused to back down.

"We have spent time in one another's company this week, and had several prior meetings," she said to her father.

Rafe found his voice. "Good God, Cailin. That isn't nearly the same. Edwina visited us at length in Staffordshire. We spent weeks in one another's company. We traveled from Staffordshire to London, and then even lived in the same bloody household when we arrived. You've had a handful of meetings with the cur—"

"He's not a cur," she snapped, rage filling her on behalf of Courtland. And also at her brother making her relationship with Courtland seem somehow less for the mere irrelevant factor of its shorter length than Rafe's. "I care for him. He is a good man, and a good brother, and—"

"He ruined you," Rafe said, cutting into her defense of Courtland.

She gnashed her teeth. "*He* didn't ruin me. I was as much a participant as Courtland this evening."

Her father flinched.

Hunter's cheeks flushed.

Something flashed in Rafe's eyes, however; worse than his disappointment . . . pity. And a frisson of unease found a path up her spine.

This time, when her brother spoke, he did so with a quiet calm. "No, Cailin." Rafe took a step closer. "He *ruined* you," he repeated, that slight added emphasis turning what had previously been a statement into a charge.

Cailin drew back. "I don't know what you are saying,"

she said tightly. Except . . . she did know what he was suggesting.

"St. James saw you both caught in a compromising position so that he might marry you." And then the fight seemed to go out of Rafe. His shoulders sagged, and his legs collapsed slightly as he sank onto the edge of the duke's desk. "Or that is what our father believes, anyway," he said with a weary resignation.

Cailin found herself incapable of words. Any of them.

Fortunately, Hunter lent his voice to the moment. "It raises the question, if your opinion of the fellow was so low, why was he invited here in the *first* place?"

It was a solid query. An unexpected one from her second-eldest brother. And just like that, she was reminded of the man she'd come to know Courtland to be: a devoted brother who deliberately lost at lawn bowling and who loved his siblings so deeply . . . he wasn't the cur Rafe would make him out to be.

Their father blushed. "Our families have been connected for years."

Hunter narrowed his eyes upon the duke. "You've been connected with a family you'd claim has no honor?"

"I d-didn't claim they didn't have honor," the duke sputtered, his face red.

So that was what was beyond Hunter's show of support—his loathing for the duke.

"Why the hell are you defending him?" Rafe demanded of Hunter. "Did you not see the same thing we all saw?" He slashed a hand around the room at all the people present who'd witnessed her ruin, and she felt her body go hot with embarrassment.

"Oh, I saw," Hunter snapped. "I just don't think blustering and bellowing at Cailin is going to undo what happened. Nor am I going to see her blamed when Bentley here"—he jerked his chin at the duke—"is the one who invited someone whom he had reservations about."

"I didn't . . . think he'd do . . . this," Bentley said weakly. And with that continued support—support that she might be receiving only because of Hunter's loathing for their father—she found her voice all the more. "What you are suggesting, Rafe, is preposterous. Courtland wouldn't do the things you and Father are accusing him of," she said, instinctively believing that all the way to her soul.

Rafe lifted an eyebrow. "A man who passed himself off as his brother? I rather believe he might."

She started. He'd known that?

"It did not take much to deduce, based on how you were found." With a menacing growl, Rafe slammed a fist onto the edge of the duke's desk, rattling the crystal inkwells.

Edwina put a resting hand on her husband's sleeve.

Cailin lifted her chin. "Courtland and I spoke of that, and it really isn't your business."

"Yes, it is. As is the fact that he ruined you in the middle of a damned soiree, Cailin."

"What reason would he have to do that, Rafe?" she demanded, then stalked over until her feet brushed the tips of his boots. "Hmm?" Dropping her hands on her hips, she leaned in. "Tell me why a nobleman with one of the most powerful titles, with wealth and fortune, would deliberately ruin a duke's by-blow?"

"He doesn't have everything, Cailin," the duchess said gently, speaking her first words since they'd assembled.

"He doesn't even have *anything*," Cailin's father added on the heel of his wife's pronouncement.

Those quiet pronouncements broke across her tense debate with Rafe and sucked the energy from her.

Flummoxed, she looked over. The duke's pained features, his face a whiter shade than pale, set off warning bells and worry low in her belly. "I don't understand."

Her father sighed and motioned again to the chair he was so determined that she take. Cailin ignored that attempt once more. "St. James's father and I were friends," he started.

"I know of your relationship," she cut him off, wanting him to get on with what he was saying.

Her father blinked in his surprise before continuing.

"The previous duke squandered everything. He was a terrible rake who never managed to reform himself. He married an heiress and wasted her fortune on wagering and drink and mistresses."

That description all fit with the terrible man whom Courtland had spoken of in the times he'd mentioned his father.

"When he died, he left nothing but debts." The duke released a beleaguered sigh. "It was one of the reasons I hired Lord Keir to work for me and paid him the salary I did."

Another discussion she'd had slipped in. This one with Courtland's sister.

*"That is what Courtland did when Father tried to sell me and my sisters' favorite books . . ."*

Courtland's brother had worked . . . because, based on what her father now shared, and what his sister had inadvertently revealed, there'd been a desperate need to.

"St. James . . . I have known him since he was a boy. I did not believe he was capable of it."

And his tone indicated her father had found Courtland guilty.

Cailin's teeth sank into the inside of her lower lip, biting the flesh, welcoming the pain and distraction. *She* didn't believe it.

*Or is it that you just don't want to . . .*

"Did you also believe him capable of bedding your daughter?" Rafe snapped.

"Rafe!" Edwina and the duchess exclaimed.

"Watch your damned mouth," Hunter warned, never one to fear going toe to toe with his big brother.

Heat exploded in Cailin's cheeks, and she balled her hands tightly, hating her brother in this instant, not for his crudeness but for the doubts he'd planted.

Restless, she whirled away and stalked over to the wide expanse of windows overlooking their father's sprawling estates.

The rub of it was, what Rafe suggested . . . what he

*said* . . . made sense. Except, at the same time, it didn't. Courtland, the gentleman who'd spoken with her about everything from fossils to freedom, would not betray her.

Would he? Alas, the seed of a niggling voice of doubt had been planted, took root in the fertile soil of her brother's charged accusations, and grew.

After all, as Rafe pointed out, when Courtland had arrived in Staffordshire all those months ago, he'd presented himself as Lord Keir, passing himself off as another. In that, Courtland had proven himself capable of deceiving her father and her and each of her brothers. He'd only done so because of his brother; he'd spoken of his love for his siblings, and it was a bond she could understand, where one would do anything one needed to for their sibling's happiness.

The doubts continued coming.

For if he'd himself stated he'd do anything for his siblings, could that not also mean he'd—

Her mind shied away from that possibility.

A pressure built at the back of her head, a dull throbbing that fanned out to her temples, and she pressed her fingertips there and rubbed to ease the sensation. And to help herself think. To try and make sense of what her father and brother were saying, and what they were suggesting, and compare that against what she knew about the man who played lawn bowling with his younger sisters and who'd perfected playing poorly at that game just to make his siblings more confident.

She let her arms fall and turned back to face the damning silent pair standing at that broad piece of mahogany furniture. "I do not believe it," she said quietly. "Just because he's . . . in financial straits, it does not mean our discovery tonight was orchestrated."

Her father and Rafe stared at her with such pity she gritted her teeth. "What?"

"Each party witness to your . . . to your . . ." Her father's mouth pulled in a grimace. "To what transpired," he substituted, "received a note, urging his or her haste in coming to the libraries."

Her heart stalled. Her mind lurched. And her stomach fell.

*I do not believe it . . .*

"I am afraid it is true, my girl," her father said, his voice aching, along with everything inside her.

And she blinked slowly, having failed to realize she'd uttered that denial aloud.

Reaching inside his jacket, her father brandished a page. He extended that folded vellum scrap, and, reflexively, Cailin brought up her palms to ward off the duke's attempt to make her see that which she didn't wish to see. Because if she didn't look at the page, then the allegations he made were just that: allegations. If she didn't see, then there wasn't tangible proof of ugly intent.

Rafe, however, would not allow her that cowardice. Fishing a similar scrap from his own jacket, he came forward and pressed the note into her hand.

Her fingers curled automatically around it, crushing the note; crumpling it.

"What is that?" Hunter demanded.

"You're not a coward, Cailin," Rafe said, ignoring Hunter, even as their father handed Hunter a copy of whatever damning page her eldest brother was so determined to have Cailin read. "And you certainly aren't stupid." He nudged his chin at the vellum, urging her to look.

Presenting them with her back once more, she forced herself to unfurl her fingers. Still unable to glance at the note she held, she took in several deep breaths, staring out instead at the lawn bowling field in the distance; that place where she and Courtland and his sisters and Seagrave had all played. Preferring the memories of those times together to what her family would force her to confront.

But, aye, Rafe had been correct in so much, and he was correct in what he'd said moments earlier: she was no coward, and so Cailin dropped her eyes to the page. And read.

Just a sentence long, the words written in bold, slashing strokes were a quick read.

And they were damning, too.

*. . . It would behoove you to gather in the library, and
see that which must be seen . . .*

Cailin's eyes slid shut, and of their own volition her fingers tightened, curling up once more into dagger-like claws,
and the page crinkled noisily under her grip.

"I do not believe it," she whispered, still unable to accept
or fathom that the discovery had been . . . deliberate.

"Kay-Kay," Hunter said gruffly, the first time he'd not
challenged Rafe and the duke, and it was because he now
believed . . . that which her mind still balked at.

Cailin whipped around. "I do not believe it," she cried,
fear and regret making her voice pitchy.

"I'll kill him before you marry one such as him." The
calm there lent a lethality to Rafe's pledge. "You needn't
worry about that."

And she shivered. For her brother was the manner of
stubborn, overprotective brother who would not be content
until he killed Courtland for this slight. "I don't want you
to kill him."

"I don't intend to let you marry him," he barked.

Marry Courtland?

A panicky laugh gurgled in her throat. How funny: just
moments ago she'd already brought herself around to the
idea of opening her heart and marrying. Or mayhap it was
a lifetime ago. Since the group of her father's guests had
barged in upon her and Courtland, time had become all
twisted and confused.

The duke held his palms up. "Nothing has to be decided
now. Certainly no one is killing anyone." He directed that
firm ducal command at Rafe, who tensed and then glanced
away. Cailin's father spoke in gentler tones when he returned his attention to her: "Now, it has been a long evening, Cailin. I advise you get some rest."

Get some rest?

Which implied she was capable of stilling her mind and
her frantically beating heart . . . and relaxing or slumbering.
Both were impossibilities. Even so, she was grateful for the

reprieve, and inclining her head, Cailin brought her shoulders back, and with all the pride a lady just ruined and—increasingly likely—duped might muster, she marched the length of her father's office, past the duke, past Rafe. She brought the door shut behind her, maintaining that smooth, measured pace, lest anyone was watching; because there was always someone watching.

As long as she remained part of this world, that sick fascination with her, the duke's by-blow—and now, likely a duke's wife—mired in scandal, would become indelibly part of her existence . . . forever.

Her breathing came shallow and labored, filling her ringing ears.

She quickened her step as she approached the library, wishing she'd taken another path to her rooms so she didn't have to see that door and think about the scandal that had found her there, one that had been arranged by—

A hand shot out, lightly entangling with her wrist, freezing her mid-flight, and she gasped.

"I am sorry," Courtland whispered, and then promptly released her. "I have been . . . looking for you. Hoping to speak with you before . . . I leave."

Before he was run off. She knew that was the inevitable outcome. That the hunting party was over, and among all the departing guests was certain to be Courtland and his siblings.

She studied him with wary eyes, trying to make out anything through his rugged features; but they were an unflawed mask that made his thoughts a secret.

"Will you speak with me?" he asked, and there was the faintest crack in his features, revealing an indecision.

Cailin bit the inside of her cheek, recalling all the ugliest revelations and aspirations cast forth by her father and brother. In her opposite hand, the note burned in her palm, as she entered the same room where she'd been ruined with a man whom she'd known to be cautious of from the start.

# Chapter 25

Oh, Christ.

The thought was a prayer inside his head . . . and a plea.

Since Cailin had been rushed from this very room, he'd had time to think about what he would say to her during this meeting.

He should have planned what he would say.

And in some parts, he had, before abandoning most of those words, hoping instead that, when he was alone with her, he'd find the right ones.

Only to find he'd been hoping in vain.

To give his hands a task, he turned the lock, and when he turned back to face Cailin, he found her watching him . . . with curious eyes. Her gaze alternately moving between the bronze door handle and him before ultimately settling all her focus upon Courtland. "It is funny you should lock the door now, when you didn't before," she murmured.

That was because the stolen moment with her here wasn't supposed to happen. Her meaning couldn't have been any clearer.

He flinched. "I didn't think . . . I hadn't anticipated . . ." That in returning to fetch his sister's book that he'd find Cailin still there. Or that he'd have taken her in his arms. And certainly . . . not anything of which had come after. "I am so sorry," he said hoarsely.

"About . . . what exactly?" she asked, a challenge in her eyes.

And God help him. He knew.

Courtland knew by the look in Cailin's eyes and the very question and statements she spoke now—doubts had come into her head.

"I'm sorry for . . . all of it," he said. And he was. He may not have set the stage for her ruination, but his sister had, and because of him, and because of what he'd shared in regard to his feelings for Cailin.

Cailin bit at her lower lip, troubling that same flesh that, not so very long ago, he'd had under his mouth; and still she didn't say anything. She, who, since he'd arrived at her doorstep and been confronted with a rifle, had always been so free with her words. And he wanted to go back to that moment. He wanted to go back to any time before this one, when there hadn't been this great ugliness hanging over them and their relationship. But regardless, they were stuck here, in this hell of his youngest sister's making.

Finally, she did speak. "My father said your father left you struggling financially."

Bentley had spoken to her about the state of his finances, which meant she knew the Marshalsea was staring him down. "Struggling financially" was too mild a term to explain his circumstances. "There is less than nothing," he explained. "My father was a wastrel. I inherited bankrupt properties and estates, and this title that I'd be as content without."

She appeared stricken. "That was why you thanked me . . . at the Temple of the Muses . . . for talking about work."

He gave a tight nod.

"Why didn't you tell me?"

"That I'm impoverished?" A pained chuckle shook his

chest. "Until just recently, with the exception of Ellie, my sisters didn't even know. It wasn't . . . isn't," he corrected, "something I have spoken of to anyone beyond my closest friend."

Her eyebrows dipped the tiniest fraction. "And we weren't really friends."

"Yes!" That affirmation exploded from him, and that little space between her brows puckered. "No!" he amended, blundering this as badly as he'd blundered everything with her from the start. "That is, we . . . were friends. Are friends?" he ventured, making that the question it was.

A question that she didn't answer.

Sadness filled her eyes, and he took a hasty step closer, toward her, but then stopped himself.

"I believe we are friends, Cailin. But I . . ." How could he explain in a way that she'd understand? In the end, he gave her what she deserved—the truth. Courtland tried again, willing her to understand. "Aside from Seagrave, I've never had friends. I had my siblings, and Seagrave, and beyond that, there was no one who had a use for me beside my title. The peerage doesn't discuss money." Perhaps if they did, he'd have found his way out of his situation long before that.

"That is silly."

His lips twisted up in a smile. "Yes, I know that now." He paused. Because of her. She'd opened his eyes to how ridiculous the *ton* was about so much: their views on the arts and sciences and work. All of it. "And then I met you," he said beseechingly, and then his words continued coming, rolling together, spilling onto each other in his haste to tell her everything that was in his heart. "I'd never met anyone who spoke so directly to me, and that was when you believed I was Keir, but then you met me, you knew I was not." Even though he was a like image of his brother, she'd been able to tell at almost an instant he'd been the one to visit her that day. "You saw me, and when you realized I was a duke, it didn't matter to you, Cailin, when it mattered to absolutely everyone." He forced himself to slow the flow of words spilling forth.

Through his ramblings, she remained motionless, her delicate features passive. It was her eyes, however. They were a window into her thoughts and soul, and even now, she moved that gaze searchingly over him. Did she seek the veracity of his claims?

He took in another steadying breath. "I didn't want to tell you," he began again. "Not because I didn't trust you, but because I didn't want you to know. It's everything I've been fearing and confronting since my father died." Emotion lodged in his throat and made it a chore to speak around it. He swallowed several times to move the words past that lump. "When I was with you, I didn't have to think about the fact that I'm in dun territory or worry about what would become of my family." He stepped closer, erasing all but a foot between them, and he took her hands in his. "I just enjoyed being with you, and I never knew it could be like how it was when we were together."

"I enjoy being with you, too," she whispered.

Enjoy.

Not "enjoyed." Those two little letters, which would have changed the tense and meaning, were omitted from the end, and from that absence, hope was born.

"I imagined a future with you. I came to . . ." Love. Her gaze sharpened on his face. And yet, to utter the depth of his feelings in this moment felt wrong, compelled when it wasn't. The scandal caused by his sister robbed that important admission of its believability. "Care about you," he said, substituting that weaker choice.

Did he imagine the glimmer of disappointment? Did he merely see that which he wished to see?

"And then you shared about the man you'd once loved." He stumbled over that last, hated word; the searing burn of jealousy leaving the taste of vinegar upon his tongue. "And that you didn't wish to marry. I know you don't want marriage, but after this evening . . ." There was no choice except for their union. Not one that wouldn't see her name forever ruined. "I do not have money, but I would do everything in my power to see that you are happy." Courtland's hands spasmed reflexively, tightening slightly upon hers, and her fingers locked briefly with his.

Her lips quivered and then parted; her eyes softened, her other features along with them, and hope filled his chest. Perhaps . . . she could believe in him, after all. And they could have a future.

"My brother and father believe our being discovered was deliberate."

And just like that, he went cold.

It'd been selfish and wrong and foolish to think and expect that he could have told her the words in his heart and omit tonight from the equation of their relationship.

Courtland stared dumbly down at their joined hands. For hers hadn't been a question. Which meant that it didn't merit an answer. Which meant he wasn't being asked to confirm that which he—

"Did you do this?" she asked tentatively, a sliver of fear whispered in those two words, and she pressed something into his palm. A note. A paper.

He stared blankly at the lone sentence, written by Ellie, confronted with the full extent of the efforts she'd gone to in order to ensure Cailin's ruin.

It had been inevitable that Cailin would ask about his involvement. Even essential to have it all said. And yet, to tell her would result in her resentments toward Ellie. He warred with himself.

"Courtland?" she pressed, an urgency in the uptilt of that query.

In the end, he settled for a vague truth. "I have done everything within my power to protect my siblings. It is my duty and responsibility to see they are cared for," his voice emerged flat.

"Oh, God," Cailin whispered, her palms going limp in his, and they slipped away, just as he felt *her* slipping away, and it was destroying him. Slowly and viciously and mercilessly, the agony of losing her eating him from within. "It was deliberate."

His arms hung uselessly at his sides, and he gripped and

ungripped his hands, making them into fists and relaxing them.

She gripped his coat and shook him slightly. "Answer me!" she cried, and the pain layered within the bell-like clear tones ripped a hole in his chest.

"It . . . was deliberate," he said. "Yes. That I cannot deny."

With a shuddery little gasp, she released him as if burned. As if disgusted.

How had he delivered those words so very steadily when they'd sounded the death knell for all he wanted in life—a future with her? Not just *any* future. He wanted them joined as partners, united in a loving union.

Cailin recoiled, and she fluttered a hand about her throat and chest before those shaking digits came to rest upon the place where her heart beat; and he was losing her.

*Nay, you've already lost her.*

For even if he thrust his sister forward as the guilty party in this greatest of sins, nothing changed for Cailin. She remained trapped in a scandal, partnered with him in it.

With a sound of disgust, she headed for the door.

"Cailin!" he called after her, even as he did not know what he would say, because the only words he wished to give her were ones that would make this better, and yet nothing could or would . . . ever.

She stopped, remaining with her back to him. The rapid up-and-down movement of her shoulders, and the noisy inhalations and exhalations filling the room, spoke to her frantic breathing.

"I never, ever wanted to hurt you. I only wished for your happiness, and"—he stretched a hand out before remembering that she couldn't see him—"if you'll marry me, I'll do everything within my power to see that you are."

At last, she angled her head, casting a glance over her shoulder. Such bitterness and resentment blazed from her eyes, sentiments that hadn't been there before, and he mourned the loss of her innocence. "My brother wants to face you on a dueling field, Courtland," she whispered.

"I deserve it," he said instantly. "I want to marry you." He rather thought he'd always wanted that. Courtland swallowed hard. "I want—"

"I don't really believe it matters what you want at this point, does it, Courtland?"

He jerked, thinking it would have been easier to be run through with the familial broadsword that hung, for now, upon his office mantel.

"I want you to leave," she said, her voice thick with tears, the sound of it twisting that pain within him all the more. "I'm aware you are responsible for your sisters. As such, in the morning, I want you to go before my brother calls you out." Cailin slipped away, leaving Courtland alone with the echo of silence and regrets.

The moment she'd gone, he sank to his haunches and remained there, simultaneously despising this library for what it now represented and foolishly clinging to the joyous moments that had existed here before everything got all turned up.

Lost in his own misery, he didn't register the approaching footfalls in the hall until the door opened.

Hope brought Courtland's head whipping up, his gaze colliding with a different set of rage-filled eyes. Of course, all of society should be privy to his disgrace. Why not Keir, who'd been scheduled to be in London? Dusty, and wearing several days' growth of beard, Keir bore little resemblance to his usual put-together, tidy self. "I thought you were set to remain in London?"

"I was," Keir seethed. "Bentley, however, had a change of plans and asked me instead to journey to Staffordshire and fetch Hunter Audley. What have you done?"

"I don't want to do this, Keir," he said tiredly, as his brother closed the door behind them.

"You don't want to do this?" Keir hissed. "I don't care what you want. You bloody well will. The Duke of Bentley is responsible for—"

"For what?" Courtland exploded to his feet. "Your employment? Is that what this is about?" he shot back, silencing his twin. He'd withheld the truth about their circumstances so Keir could have the work and future he wanted. Well, he was done. "It is always about someone else. Your work. Their Seasons. Well, I don't give a bloody damn about your assignment in this moment."

His brother rocked back on his heels.

And Courtland knew it was wrong to hurl the words he now did. He was their brother, and wouldn't have anyone else responsible for them, but in this moment, having lost Cailin and all hope of her affection or friendship, he was all out of energy for caring. But he couldn't stop. "She was ruined. Her reputation destroyed, and I cannot make this right," he whispered, mindful that guests still remained and servants were close, determined to maintain what secrecy that he could over Cailin's circumstances. Just as he couldn't make . . . anything right. And there was an agonizing frustration in his inability to make any circumstances right for those he loved. And yes, he was completely, madly, and desperately in love with Cailin.

The fight went out of him, and Courtland sat down hard on the floor and rested his back against the same sofa he and Cailin— He clenched his eyes shut tightly.

The floorboards creaked in a telltale sign that Keir had moved, and then his twin slid into the spot beside him, joining Courtland on the duke's library floor.

"People are saying it was deliberate," Keir murmured.

"It was." With a sigh, he forced his eyes open, held out the paper Cailin had pressed into his hand, and turned it over to his brother.

Keir read the sentence there. "You didn't do this."

At least his twin, for all the little faith he had in Courtland, knew that much. Courtland let his head fall back onto the edge of the sofa and stared at the ceiling overhead.

"You . . . love her." Wonderment filled his brother's tone.

Even as everything inside him hurt, Courtland managed to flash a wry grin. "Even being Father's image, I am capable of that sentiment, you know."

Keir frowned. "You aren't Father's image. You are nothing like him."

"Aren't I?" he rejoined. "I'm a rake like him."

"You were a rake. You haven't taken a mistress since you learned of our finances."

He started.

Keir looked at him squarely. "Yes, I know that. I've already examined the ledgers. Also that you surrendered your membership at White's and Brooke's and, more recently . . . Forbidden Pleasures."

Warily, he rested his forehead in his hands. "Making those small changes does not alter the fact that I'm like Father in the other ways that matter for our family. I have inherited the same empty coffers."

"You also never barred me from taking on employment," Keir said quietly, and Courtland slowly picked his head up. "You are working to improve your circumstances . . . and you care more about Miss Audley's circumstances in this moment than yours. Does any of that strike you as things our father would do?"

Through the noise of his own whirring thoughts came a voice, distinct and clear in his mind.

"*. . . There's a difference between ignorance and* willful *ignorance . . . It is what you do when you have your eyes opened, how you choose to live your life with newly acquired information, that matters . . .*"

Courtland stilled as the realization settled in his brain . . . and then grew. His heart knocked funnily within his chest. "I'm not him," he whispered, and it was as though, with the day's realization, he'd been . . . set free. All along he'd been fighting against having a future with Cailin because he'd feared being his father, but that restraint, the fact that her happiness mattered more than his own freedom, meant—

"No, you are not," Keir said.

Their father, who'd been complacent, doing nothing to grow the family's wealth and only spending it. Courtland may have made adjustments to how he lived, but he'd been passive. Yes, he'd made attempts to slow the ebb of their bleed-ing finances, but there had been no discussions as to how to grow them. How to change their wealth. Because it had been ingrained into him that dukes didn't toil. All the while having failed to realize that he and every other peer bene-fited from the labors of others.

On the heel of that realization, he came crashing back with an unwelcome plunge to the reality of that which he would not have.

Pain rippled across his heart.

With a twin's sense of knowing, Keir edged closer. "You have to tell her. You have to—"

"Let it go, Keir."

"But—"

"I said, 'Let it go,'" he repeated, at last managing to infuse that ducal tone his father had forced him to practice as a boy, which he'd desperately despised. "Making more of myself will be enough." It had to be.

Keir let the matter rest and left Courtland alone with his own thoughts, that exuberant rush that had briefly buoyed him burst . . . and the truth—he had lied to himself.

For even if and when he emerged triumphant on the other side of the dun pile he had one boot within, it would never be enough without Cailin there to share both the journey and the eventual triumphs with.

# Chapter 26

Not unlike the start of the duke's hunting party a week earlier, there'd been a flurry of activity within the duke's manor, with carriages arriving at the front of the graveled path that led to the main entrance. Only this time, those regal conveyances were loaded, as guests were rushed off in a hasty departure.

From where she'd stood surveying the grand black barouches, searching the better part of the morning for just one crest, she caught a glimpse of her brother's visage reflected in the windowpanes.

"You don't want to be caught staring, Cailin," Hunter said, and she welcomed that it was he in this moment and not Rafe, because if even for the wrong reasons, Hunter had been on her side in the library. "We're not the staring type."

Letting the curtain slip from her fingers, the filmy lace fluttered back into place.

She faced her brother. "I'm so glad it is you," she whispered, then Hunter threw his arms open and she rushed into them, welcoming the feel of being folded in his embrace, like when she'd been a girl suffering a small hurt.

Only . . . this was a big hurt. The worst she'd ever known. Worse than Ian's betrayal.

And not even her older brother's hugs could erase the great gaping hole in her heart.

"I've missed you," she said against the coarse fabric of his jacket. It was the quality of familiar wool, the manner of material they'd all adorned, and she welcomed the familiarity.

"I've missed you, too."

"And you've been enjoying your new role at the mines." Mines their father had purchased and given over to Hunter's care and control.

Her brother gave a sheepish grin.

"I don't want you to feel guilty. You've been happy, and I'd not begrudge you that." At least one of them had been.

Hunter moved a shrewd stare over her face. "You haven't been, though."

Except—she bit her lower lip, her gaze moving of its own will to the window—she had. Because of Courtland.

Her brother followed her stare. "Let's go for a walk, Cailin," he said.

She stiffened.

"No lecture," he promised, holding his arm out.

But then, with her brothers, everything was always on their terms. Ironically, her push to see them in London had been the one time she'd proven triumphant.

And . . . it was.

Despite the missteps she'd made, and the mess of these past twelve hours, it hadn't been . . . all bad.

There'd been moments of joy peppered in; moments when she'd not felt so very alone, and isolated, when she'd found a friend in Courtland and his family.

Courtland.

Cailin stole another glance back, for a final hint of Courtland's carriage, before joining Hunter. She didn't take his arm, but rather walked at a quick clip at his side. "I know what you are doing," she said from the corner of her mouth, as they made their way past a pair of maids rushing around with an urn overflowing with roses. "You're trying to keep me from the window."

"Only in some small part, yes. The staring thing."

If she could have managed a smile this day, that would have certainly merited an upturn of her lips.

"I really don't care who catches me looking, you know," she said. "I'd say, given last evening, me watching the carriages leave is hardly the scandal you make it out to be."

Her brother flinched.

And even as she finished speaking the words, Cailin realized the folly in them. The last thing she should do was remind any of her protective brothers about how she and Courtland had been discovered; lest he call him out. Her stomach muscles contracted. Unless Rafe already had?

Arriving at the pair of glass doorways leading outside, she reached past Hunter and let herself outside, then made for the same balustrade she'd sought sanctuary at earlier in the week, back when she'd wanted to escape this house party. Laying her arms upon the stone ledge, she rested her cheek upon the smooth cool stone and stared out. The early morning sun had barely begun its ascent; instead it hung on the edge of the horizon, as though that great orb itself was too weary to make its everyday climb.

In those grounds below, the grass slick with dew, she saw him striding across those grounds and herself flying after him. She saw them slipping off into those woods and meandering around the hidden playground, sheltered by a canopy of leaves and towering oaks.

And she wanted to go back to that moment. To the moment when she'd opened her eyes to the fact that everything about this world she'd found herself thrust into wasn't so very bad, after all. There'd been . . . him. Tears stung her lashes, and she furiously blinked them back, refusing to cry any more tears this day, and certainly not before her brother.

She felt her brother take up a place beside her, and she tensed.

Hunter positioned himself as she did, matching her

movements. His gaze moved over the grounds below, and he whistled slowly through his teeth. "Is this a castle or a house?"

"It is much, isn't it?"

"*Very* much."

They shared a commiserative smile, and it felt so very good to have him here . . . and to have this shared connection.

"Have you hated it?"

Had she hated it. She considered his question. "Some parts," she confessed. "I've missed the freedoms I had in Staffordshire." And yet . . . "Some parts I haven't." Every moment she'd shared with Courtland.

"The . . . duke fellow?"

Courtland. That was how Hunter referred to him. As the "duke fellow."

But Courtland . . . he was so much more than his title. He was the one who'd urged her to come to London and pursue the study of subjects that fascinated her. He made her smile and laugh and think.

She hesitated before nodding. Had Hunter been overbearing and out to lecture and verbally attack Courtland as Rafe had done, then it would be altogether different.

When he remained silent, Cailin looked over at her older brother.

He kept his stare trained out. "Bentley sent his man of affairs." Courtland's brother. "And I would've happily sent him on his way again, if Rafe hadn't been the one sending word, asking for me to come."

"He shouldn't have done that," she said automatically.

"*Of course* he should have." He scoffed. "I'm your brother."

"And you have people dependent upon you at the mines."

Hunter flashed another rueful half-grin. "Trust me, I know my responsibilities, little sister." His smile fell, and his lips formed a solemn line. "But you're *no* responsibility, Cailin. You're my sister, and more important than the Cheadle mines and anything."

Tears stung her eyes. Given Hunter's devotion to and love of Cheadle, and the speed with which he'd come, it was a testament of his love. Not that she'd ever doubted it—or any of her brothers'.

"I've missed you," she said, her voice catching, as she leaned her head against his shoulder.

"I've missed you, too, Cailin. The cottage is quiet."

And it would remain that way. Because their time in that place, she and Rafe and Hunter and Wesley all together, under the thatched roof and behind the stone walls, had ended.

"Do you know, I was so focused on leaving Staffordshire," she murmured, "that I never even had time to think about the fact that our time in that house had come and gone?"

"But there's new journeys for you, and Rafe and Wesley."

It didn't escape her notice that he'd not included himself among the Audleys who'd spread their wings and flown to lands away from the ones they'd always known.

"You could stay," she said, picking her head up.

"Me? Stay here?" He snorted. "I've been here less than a day, and I feel like I'm suffocating." Another rueful smile formed on his mouth. "Everyone's all trussed up. Bentley. Rafe." Hunter paused to teasingly flick her slightly puffed sleeve. "You."

She swatted his hand back playfully.

Then, he grew serious once more. "There's nothing for me here. I can't stay here . . . but you can come back."

Come back.

To Staffordshire.

To their cottage.

So that was why he'd come.

To bring her back.

"Rafe doesn't want to let you go," Hunter said, confirming the reason for his sudden appearance. "But he wants to see you happy more. And that's what I want, too, Cailin. Whatever that is. *Whoever* that is."

Together they watched as a monarch butterfly joined them.

All the while the magnificent orange-and-black winged creature fluttered along the edge of the balustrade, Cailin considered the prospect laid out by Hunter.

The butterfly lingered a moment near her hand before
taking flight. She followed its movements as it glided away.

"Do you want to talk about him?"

Courtland.

"There's nothing really *to* say. He's been a friend . . ."
Straightening, Hunter propped a hip on the stone railing,
and then folding his arms at his chest, he looked squarely
at Cailin.

"A friend?"

Her cheeks warmed. "I . . ." She dampened her mouth,
and because he'd been supportive since his return, and not
overbearing and judgmental, the words just came spilling
out. "I enjoy being with him." Since the moment he'd arrived in Staffordshire, a connection had been forged. "We
spoke about *everything*: books and life and London, and
what we disliked about it, and . . . and he listened to me."
When even Rafe and Edwina and her father and Lydia had
stopped or failed to hear her. Her heart seized. "I came to
care for him." That admission emerged as a whisper to her
own ears.

The question remained, however . . . what did he feel for
her? He'd insisted his feelings were true.

Hunter sighed, and then facing forward once more, he
looped an arm around her shoulder. "Was it because he was
the only option? Because . . . the one you really wanted
wasn't here?" he asked gently.

The one she really wanted? Who . . . ?

Confusedly, she stared up at her older brother.

He gave her a look. *"Ian?"*

She drew back. "My relationship"—her love for
Courtland—"with the duke existed because of him, and because I enjoyed being with him."

Hunter appeared as though he wished to say more about
it . . . before changing the topic once more.

"Did I ever tell you about the day you were born?"

At that unexpected shift, Cailin found herself brought up short. "No."

"Our mother, with the last words she spoke, asked Rafe to look after us. She asked him to be the parent you wouldn't have."

"It wasn't his responsibility," she said softly. "He was a child himself." Rafe would have been a boy—around the same age as Courtland's youngest sister.

"Someone had to step into that role. But at the time?" He looked at her squarely. "I wanted to hate you. All I knew was that Mama was gone . . . and you were here."

Cailin caught at her lower lip. She'd understood and appreciated that celebrating the birth of one's sister would have been an impossibility when one mourned the loss of one's mother on that same day. But something in hearing it spoken aloud . . .

Her brother caught her hands in his and brought them close, squeezing them slightly. "But then I held you. And all that anger? It just . . . left me. You were so slight in my arms. I'd never known a babe could be so tiny. In that moment, Cailin?" Emotion left his voice graveled. "I didn't think about responsibility. I didn't see you as some chore to take on. I just saw how very much I loved you."

A tear slipped down her cheek, and he brushed it away with his callused thumb.

"All I've ever wanted, from that day, was for you to be happy." He released her. "I don't presume to know just what that is anymore," he confessed, "and I'm not Rafe, who's always making assumptions at every turn, about all of us." A wry grin formed on his hard mouth. He leveled a gaze on her face, a piercing intensity glinting in his irises. "I want you to decide what or who you want in life. If anyone at all," he amended. His features tightened. "You don't have to marry St. James or . . . anyone, and certainly not because of any damned scandal."

Another tear fell, and she wiped it away. "Thank you."

He tugged one of her curls. "Don't thank me for that.

You are my sister. I love you. I just want what is best for you. That is why I came here. To give you . . . options."

Options. It was precisely what she'd been desperately longing for.

"Bentley asked to speak with you. Do you want to hear him out?"

His meaning couldn't be clearer. If she rejected that meeting, not even God himself could manage to get Bentley past Hunter.

She sighed and gave a reluctant nod.

Her brother hesitated. "You're sure you don't want to head back to Staffordshire? The two of us, left to do the baking and cooking—"

A laugh burst from her. "We'd starve." Notoriously, they were rubbish in the kitchens.

They shared a smile.

"Thank you, Hunter," she said softly, and going up on tiptoe, she kissed him on the cheek.

A short while later he returned with their father.

Sire and son: both men were tall, broadly powerful, and, in so many ways, the like image of one another. The duke said something to Hunter, who nodded, and then after a final look at Cailin, he stepped outside, leaving Cailin and the duke—alone.

Clasping his hands behind him, her father started over toward her. "I thought a good deal about what you said, Cailin . . . about how little I know you, and I realized how right you are. I don't know you. Not really. So much time was lost . . . for each of us." He let his arms fall, then held his gloved palms outstretched toward her. "And it is my hope that you will allow me to share these years with you. Like Rafe and Hunter, I, too, want to see you happy. That is my only concern."

Another well of tears rose in her throat. "I know it was not your fault," she said through that rising emotion. Her mother had kept the greatest secret from him. She'd known as much, but still had secretly resented him. "You were wronged, too." They'd all been. She saw that now.

His eyes glazed with a sheen, and he coughed into his fist. "Hunter was of the opinion that he knew what you were missing and came as soon as Rafe sent word. We shall focus on new beginnings, and it is my hope that this day may be one for you."

He appeared as though he wished to say more, but then headed back to the doorway.

The moment her father stepped out, another figure limped forward.

Cailin stilled, a dull humming in her ears.

It had been two years since she'd seen him, and then their last meeting had only been through the crack in his doorway as he hurled furious words at her, ordering her gone. Half of his face scarred, a patch upon his left eye, and a cane in his hand, he bore few similarities to the darkly handsome, flawless beauty who'd earned the sighs and whispers of all the young women in Staffordshire.

"Hello, Cailin," he murmured in his thick Scottish brogue.

*Ian.*


The Balfours were long overdue to depart the Duke of Bentley's estates.

Given the scandal they'd brought down, and the damage they'd done, they'd certainly overstayed their welcome by a good twelve hours and fourteen minutes.

And it appeared that they were determined to overstay their welcome all the more.

Standing outside Hattie's guest chambers, Courtland paced.

From where he stood, with his back resting against the wall and a foot raised behind him, Seagrave consulted his watch. "They do know you run the risk of pistols at dawn, I take it?" Seagrave drawled in hushed tones. Even as they were the last of the guests to depart that day, one could never be too certain who was lurking about.

And Courtland would wager his very life they now

spoke of that his loyal friend had remained out of concern that Courtland would need a second. "They likely know but are obviously a good deal less concerned than you or me with me escaping with my life," he muttered, checking his own timepiece. He'd sent the lady's maid that the girls shared between the three of them in to fetch his sisters, but she failed to return, and they failed to appear.

All Cailin had asked of him was that he leave first thing in the morning, and yet here he remained . . . with his mischievous sisters. "What is keeping them?" he said more to himself, that query earning a shrug from Seagrave.

Courtland rapped hard.

Silence.

And then . . . the door opened a moment later.

His sisters' maid greeted him with a sheepish expression. "Your Grace," she murmured and then, dropping a curtsy, rushed out.

Furrowing his brow, Courtland ducked his head inside the room, locating his sisters in a neat little row at the window. "What is—"

"Shh," they spoke in unison from where they stood with their noses pressed to the panes. Not a single sister glanced back.

He cast a desperate glance over to where Seagrave still lounged.

The other man lifted his palms and shook his head. "You're on your own with whatever this is."

"Will you both *hush*," Lottie said, scowling at them.

Alas, it was Ellie who took mercy on Courtland, filling him in on whatever spectacle below accounted for their refusal to take their proper leave of Bentley's. "There is a real-life pirate below, Courtland." She clasped her hands to her chest. "And I shall never forgive you if you prevent me from seeing him."

A pirate.

Behind him, he caught Seagrave's chuckle, and mumbling to himself, Courtland hurriedly let himself inside and walked over to the window, then abruptly stopped.

And promptly wished he hadn't joined them.

And that he hadn't looked down below, because his gaze wasn't on any pirate, but rather Cailin . . . and another man.

Dark and menacing . . . but also, dashing . . . and brooding. The fellow was the perfect brooding, gothic hero. Why, he even possessed a cane.

*"He was brooding and dark . . . He was a mystery . . ."*

Courtland immediately recoiled, his entire body arching away from the window, as though, in fleeing the scene, it somehow undid the sight below.

And yet, there was no undoing or unseeing.

He remained as frozen to the floor as his meddlesome sisters, but not out of a like fascination; rather, out of a sick kind.

Courtland stared with his gaze locked on the pair, her fair to the fellow's dark.

The two of them spoke, their lips moving at different times, each party unaware that every word shared, every moment they spent together, ripped off another piece of Courtland's heart. And another. And another. Until there was nothing more than a great big, hollow void in the place where that organ should beat.

The gentleman reached a hand up, as though to stroke Cailin's lightly freckled cheek, then stopped himself, and it was both a yearning and effortful restraint Courtland knew all too well. They were the actions and reactions of a man captivated.

Courtland forced his eyes away.

His sisters', however, remained with their stares trained out.

*". . . I trust as a duke, you are unaccustomed to anything but adoration and respect. Alas, even being a relation to a duke does not necessarily spare a woman from society's unkindness. They are also staring and always whispering . . ."*

Like a swarm of angry bees set free in his head, a buzzing filled his ears.

At every turn, Cailin had offered only kindness and support to his sisters, and this is how they'd repay that goodness? Voyeurs to this intimate moment between her and her former sweetheart. She deserved so much better. From so many.

He gnashed his teeth. Especially from the damned miner who'd been fool enough to let her get away. But he'd be goddamned if he allowed any member of his family to treat her thusly.

"Stop," he said quietly, directing that command at the back of their heads. "I said, 'Stop,'" he repeated, this time with such a force that each sister jumped.

Grabbing the curtains, he wrenched them shut. "Her life is not some bloody Drury Lane production," he barked, slashing a hand at the air. "And I'll be damned if I, or any member of this family, watches on like the worst sort of London gossips. Is that clear?"

Hangdog, his sisters nodded and dropped repentant stares to the floor.

His chest heaving, Courtland struggled to rein in the volatile emotion stirring in his breast. He closed his eyes for several long moments and concentrated on breathing.

"Who is he?" Ellie whispered, because it was too much to hope, ask, or expect that she'd simply let go the question of the gentleman's identity.

He was a man who didn't deserve Cailin Audley. Yet another one. Courtland forced his eyes open. "It isn't your business." *Our business. It isn't ours.*

"She is not in love with him . . . ?" Lottie looked between her siblings. "Is she?" she asked when no answer was forthcoming.

"I don't know," he gritted out. Did she still love him? He hoped to God not; a seething, fiery jealousy threatened to burn him alive within. She *shouldn't*. A man who'd failed to return her notes and shunned her so spectacularly deserved to rot in misery for all time.

"But who issss h—"

"I said that is enough, Ellie. Enough," he thundered, and then shut his eyes, but not before he caught the sheen of tears in her cornflower-blue gaze.

God rot his soul. And this day, and Cailin's damned sweetheart.

"I want each of you belowstairs in ten minutes' time. Is that clear?"

They offered shaky nods of acquiescence.

Desperate to quit this place, Courtland stalked from the room and headed belowstairs, and out to his carriage, so he could be free.

He might not deserve Cailin—no, rather, he did not deserve her.

But neither did that blighter below.

# Chapter 27

The day Cailin had gone to see an injured Ian, only to be jeered and mocked and ordered away, she'd thought about a time when she'd see him again.

In the earliest days following that harsh, unfeeling rejection, she'd imagined he'd come to her. That he'd say every vile word he'd spewed had been a lie, and that his love had been real.

As time slipped by, her heart had grown harder and bitterness had chased away all warmth. And in those days, she'd hoped they would meet again one day so she could tell him precisely what she thought of a cur such as him.

Somewhere along the way, however, that anger . . . had left her.

The bitterness that had consumed her faded, and she'd learned how to smile again—and laugh.

And it had been all because of Courtland.

Courtland, who'd hurt her in ways she didn't know if her heart or soul could ever recover from.

Odd . . . she stood here before her former sweetheart, so wholly detached from him, all the while thinking of another.

She'd always been the one to fill the endless voids of silence that had sprung from the laconic, surly Scot. She'd felt a responsibility to do so. Not this time.

Unlike with Courtland, who had never been short of words or laughter when they were together. He'd spoken freely, and chattered, and she'd loved that so very much about him. Because she'd not known men *could* be so free with their words, and smiles, and . . . *I wanted that. I wanted it so badly.*

"Yer brother fetched me."

"Did he?" Her nonsensical reply came from a place of knowing she had to say something but not knowing exactly what *to* say.

"He did."

They fell silent once more.

"I don't know why you're here, Ian," she confessed. "You said everything there was to say the last time we saw one another."

The unmarred portion of his rugged cheek paled a shade of white to match the puckered scars that remained from his accident in the mines.

"I 'ave returned to the mines. Hunter hired me to keep books."

She drew back. "Did he?"

"Aye." The column of Ian's throat jumped. "I 'ave purpose again, an' I have ah cottage now. 'Tis a wee one in Staffordshire. Nah far from yers."

How easily her ear had once made out each of those lyrical words; but time had passed and eventually she'd lost that effortless ability. Now, she picked through them carefully, deciphering the words he spoke about property and keeps and castles. "I am happy for your change of circumstances," she said softly, and strangely, she found she meant it. Nowhere did her admission come from a place of resentment. "I know how very much your work meant to you." She'd merely been a stepping stone for his aspirations in Cheadle.

A spasm rippled down the unscarred portion of his face.

"It did." He took a step toward her. The heavy emotion in his voice made his brogue all the thicker. "But I did waant a life wi' ye, tae. After th' accident, I believed ah didn't deserve ye. That I had hee haw tae offer ye. I wanted tae mak' myself a future I wasn't ashamed tae share wi' ye. N' I've done that, lass. I've work again, and a cottage fir ye."

Her ear sharpened on one word among all the ones he'd just spoken of the things he'd done.

He'd done it . . . for her.

Not them.

"*You've* done that," she murmured. The dark slashes of his eyebrows came together. "I—"

The doors exploded open.

"You don't deserve her."

That sharp, slightly raspy and out-of-breath exclamation from the end of the terrace brought her and Ian's heads whipping sideways.

Courtland.

He stood there, slightly bent, his hands resting on his knees. Fire brimmed in his eyes with so much rage directed at the man beside her.

Cailin's mouth slipped a fraction. Her heart hammered. What was he doing here?

"Wha th' h-hell urr ye?" Ian stammered, his cheeks going florid.

Courtland stormed over but then drew himself up, several paces away. "I . . . ah . . ." He tugged at his cravat. "You are . . . Ian? Are you not?"

Dumbstruck, Ian managed a nod, and Courtland seemed to find his footing.

His furious gaze slid away from Ian and briefly over to Cailin. Her heart fluttered in her chest. But then, he wrenched his stare back. "I'm . . . a friend, and as such, I'm here to say what should have been said, instead of your being escorted here by the lady's brothers."

He knew that?

"It did not take much to deduce," Courtland said for Cailin, so easy to read her very thoughts.

"This isnae yer business," Ian growled.

"No, it might not be." Courtland's nostrils flared, and he took a step closer. "However, I'll be damned if I go . . . not without . . . saying what should have been said to you. You didn't deserve her. Ever. A man who had the gift of her love, and who hurt her?" Courtland's voice climbed, growing strident. "You were a damned fool, man. And if you hurt her because you were hurt, well, then, that was never an excuse. She didn't deserve to bear the brunt of your anger and frustration with your circumstances." He looked to Cailin. "My God, man, she deserved to be treated as the queen she is."

Her heart hammered; it pounded and knocked against the walls of her chest.

She waited for him to say more. To speak the words she so wanted to hear from him.

And then suddenly, Courtland stilled. A ruddy flush suffused his cheeks. "Forgive me," he said stiffly to a flummoxed Ian. "I just . . . felt that needed to be said. If you'll excuse me?"

He slid his gaze her way, and she held her breath, wanting him to say more. But then . . .

"Cailin," he said solemnly, and with a bow . . . Courtland left.

Ian spoke first. "Yer in love wi' him," he said flatly. He brought his other hand to rest atop the head of his cane, both hands gripping that tool he now used to aid his walk, and he leaned over it.

She was. But she'd not have that admission spoken first to anyone . . . but Courtland.

"Ah see."

He couldn't really see anything about her, though. They were strangers to one another. Perhaps they'd always been.

"I don't want someone who'd reject me and take on building a life and future and fortune on his own, Ian," she explained. "I want someone who wants me to be part of everything . . ." Her eyes went to the place where Courtland had last stood before he'd marched off. "The good times, and the difficult ones. Goodbye, Ian," she said gently, and then, going up on tiptoe, she kissed his scarred cheek.

He winced, pulling away from that place she'd pressed her lips.

"I hope you find everything you were searching for."

"Ah did." His graveled voice was thick. His lips twisted with the bitterness she did not carry. "Bit it seems a've an' a' lost it, tae." And without so much as a goodbye, Ian marched off . . . and out of her life for a second time.

The moment he'd gone, she looked out over her father's lands.

What flaw did she possess that made the men who mattered to her believe she cared about *the material*? What made them think she wasn't one capable of taking on the hardest parts of life with them? What, when all she'd ever wanted was to be loved?

She reached the edge of the lawn bowling field . . . and stopped.

For that wasn't all she'd wanted.

She'd not just wanted that passionate romance. She'd wanted a partnership. She'd wanted someone who shared her interests, with whom she could while away hours just speaking about anything and everything. She'd wanted a friend.

She wanted Courtland.

Cailin hung along the side of the lawn bowling greens. The lush carpet of grass was slicked with early morning dew, and the early morn sunbathed the grounds in a vibrant crimson sunrise, burnishing the earth with it.

She'd hated everything about life among Polite Society, and only wanted to return to the familiar life at the Cheadle mines. There, she had friends. There, she had greater freedoms and greater control of her life. That was what she'd believed.

Or that was what she'd told herself.

It wasn't until this moment, with the hunting party called to an abrupt end, that she at last confronted the grandeur she'd made these past months in her mind of the life she'd left behind. Her life had been largely one of struggle. Even though there'd been connections with the mining wives and daughters and sisters, there'd not been truly deeper friendships.

It was also why she'd yearned so very much for companionship, why, in her relationship with Ian, she'd imagined more. So desperate for a human bond greater than the cursory relationships she'd known.

She saw that now.

Cailin meandered an uneven path, the echo of yesterday's laughter with Courtland and his sisters echoing here still.

She'd believed she couldn't fit into this world, because she'd been alone. She'd felt like a stranger in a stranger world, longing for her previous existence—the same existence that she'd longed to shed for as long as she could remember.

But it was only that that life had been what she'd known; and whereas she'd always wished to leave that safe world, once she'd been away from it, she'd learned that she had to discover life in a new place. It had been awkward and uncomfortable, with her making missteps, and because of the discomfort in adjusting to that newness, it had been easier to pine for the life she'd left behind.

"Ahem."

Gasping, Cailin spun.

"I'm sorry," Courtland's youngest sister said quietly. "I did not mean to sneak up on you."

"No. That is fine. Forgive me. I was distracted . . ."

The young girl chewed at her lower lip. "We are to leave shortly."

He was . . . still planning to leave? After coming out here as he had. But then, that was what *friends* did. Her heart wrenched. "Are you?" she asked, too much of a coward to acknowledge that she knew. She knew because she'd been the one to order Courtland and his siblings gone.

For everything that had passed here, she cared about him and didn't wish to see him hurt, and volatile as Rafe had been last night, she could not have trusted that he wouldn't call out Courtland. Courtland, who'd brought her so much joy in these past weeks, filling her heart. She l—

"My brother, he is the best of men," Ellie said, toying with the play pistol in her fingers. "My father would call me a freak because of my fascination with military pursuits."

Oh, God. A great pressure tightened about her lungs, squeezing them in a vise. "I am so sorry," she said softly, dropping to her haunches beside Courtland's sister. For everything she believed she'd been missing in her life, she had a devoted family who'd only ever supported her.

"No." The young lady waved off that apology. "It doesn't matter."

Cailin moved her eyes over the flaxen curls, the slight cleft within her chin an indentation the image of her brother's. The girl might say it did not matter, but . . . it did. A child should only ever know love and kind words.

"It used to hurt me," Ellie said, examining her pretend weapon, moving it back and forth between fingers caked with mud from playing. "It used to hurt me very much. Until Courtland took to calling me 'Captain' and insisted that I teach him the art of warfare. Then it became something special we shared."

And Cailin had been wrong. After she'd ordered him gone last night, she believed her heart incapable of anything but darkness, only to find in Ellie's telling the stirring of light. That was the manner of man Courtland was: a brother who loved his siblings deeply. From Lord Keir to the tales he'd told of deliberately failing at lawn bowling to Ellie's story now, everything he'd done demonstrated an overwhelming love for his family.

"I just wanted him to be happy." Ellie's whisper emerged faint and hesitant, calling Cailin back to the moment. "He cares about you *so* much."

Cailin's heart lifted and danced in her breast, before plummeting to the pit in her stomach that had formed last evening and remained with her through the sleepless night into now. "Oh, Ellie. It is complicated."

"It's not." Ellie shrugged. "Not really." Fire flashed in eyes that were a mirror of Courtland's. "He is the *best* brother, and the best of men. I just . . . wanted to tell you that." Her gaze locked with Cailin's, and there was a piercing intensity to that stare, as though she willed Cailin to see the truth of her assertions. "He would never do anything to hurt you or anyone. He is a protector."

Ellie's gaze moved past Cailin's shoulder, and she followed the young girl's stare over to where Cailin's father now approached.

"I have to go," Ellie whispered and then bolted, racing in the opposite direction.

Puckering her brow, Cailin attempted to call out, but the duke had already reached her.

"Your meeting . . . did it go well?" her father asked, awkwardly patting a hand against his leg.

She'd been outraged, seeing his involvement as an interference. Now, she saw . . . he was trying.

Her father had arranged this. For her.

He'd gone and sought out Ian and attempted to put to rights her relationship with her former sweetheart.

"It did," she said. "I had closure."

"Do you . . . ?"

"Love him?" She shook her head. Once upon a lifetime ago, she'd loved the thought of who they could be together. Those ideas, however, had been the illusions of a lonely young woman desperate for a true connection. "No." The man she loved was . . .

*He is a protector.*

Absolutely motionless, she stood there. Unable to breathe. Unable to move. Her heart knocked unevenly against her ribcage.

"She wasn't willing me to believe her assertions," she whispered. Ellie had been trying to tell her something altogether different.

"Cailin?" her father asked.

Ignoring her father, Cailin's mind remained locked on her exchange with Courtland's sister.

She'd been urging Cailin to look. Trying to get her to see that there'd been more.

Slowly at first, and then with a dizzying rapidity, her thoughts spun with remembrance after remembrance of her last meeting with Courtland.

"Cailin, what is it?" her father repeated, with a greater urgency; and she blocked it out, blocked him out, tunneling on the words of another.

Each one spoken in that heated exchange, pinging around the chambers of her mind, disjointed pieces that she now reassembled.

*". . . Until just recently, with the exception of Ellie . . . my sisters didn't even know."*

*"Did you do this?"* she'd asked him. Cailin pressed her fingertips at her temples, thinking. Thinking.

*"I have done everything within my power to protect my siblings. It is my duty and responsibility to see they are cared for."*

*". . . I just wanted him to be happy . . . He cares about you so much."*

The truth barreled into her, nearly knocking her back.

"It wasn't him," she breathed, her arms falling to her sides, those limbs as useless as every other part of her person, all of which remained frozen from the shock of the realization. "How could I have been so blind?" A joyous laugh blossomed in her breast as a buoyant lightness wound through her being. "It wasn't him, Father," she exclaimed. "It wasn't him," she repeated. Those three words played as a glorious litany within her head.

At his blank look, she stormed forward and gripped him by the shoulders. "It was not Courtland. He did not orchestrate last evening."

Her father gave her a pained look. "Cailin, I trust you are seeing that which—"

"I'm seeing the truth," she snapped, her smile fading fast as she released her father. "I love him." And she knew, from a place deep in her heart, that the man he was would never have carried out such an act.

His brow furrowed. "Who would—"

"It does not matter." Were it discovered what Ellie had done, the girl would be made a pariah and would find herself an outcast even before she made her Come Out. Cailin wouldn't consign a person to that fate, and certainly not a young girl, one who'd made a brash decision but who should also not pay for that sin for her adult life.

"I daresay it does—"

She held his gaze. "It does not."

He frowned, and then looked off in the direction Ellie had run. Understanding lit his eyes.

Oh, God, she'd doubted Courtland. Not from the start. But the reservations had been there, and he'd not even thought to defend himself. He'd taken the guilt and blame upon his shoulders to protect his sister. And he was—

"Leaving," she whispered.

Or he'd already left.

Gathering up her hems, Cailin went flying, taking off racing to the front foyer that, once bustling, was now empty but for a handful of servants. Panting from the pace she'd set, she skidded to a stop upon the smooth marble floor.

"Where is he?" she managed between gasping breaths.

The footman shook his head in confusion.

"His Grace," she gasped.

"I . . . believe he is in his offices, my lady."

"Not my father," she exclaimed, frustration and desperation making her impatient. Cursing quietly, Cailin rushed to the double doors, grabbed one of them, and let herself out.

Two carriages, fully loaded but empty of passengers, remained at the front of the drive.

He was still here.

"I believe he was seen wandering the grounds in search of his youngest sister," a servant volunteered.

Wandering the grounds in search of his youngest sister. Where would he be? Where . . . ?

Cailin stilled once more, and then she took off running.

* * *

Courtland found himself trapped.

Stuck at the Duke of Bentley's manor.

And all thanks to his sister. That was, his youngest sister. Again.

Cupping his hands around his mouth, Courtland bellowed her name for a fifth time. "Elllllllie?" Those stretched syllables echoed around the countryside . . . only to be met with silence.

Though, in fairness, Courtland didn't want to leave. Not like this. Not in *any* way.

Oh, he damn well *should* want to.

He'd two powerful men eager to have his blood on their hands—and rightfully so.

And one woman, who'd been shattered by him last evening, who wanted him gone.

But he was a selfish cur. He wanted to be with her still. He wanted to be with her always. And yet, there was not to be an always. There wasn't even to be a now. The moment he departed from this place, he and Cailin were . . . nothing. And the idea of an ending to these past weeks he'd shared with her left him desolate. But now? Now, it was so much worse. There was the return of her brooding, and damned dashing, miner fellow—the pair of them happily reunited for that happily-ever-after—

It was too much.

A spasm ripped across his chest.

Perhaps it was best to get out of this place, after all.

Courtland stopped, his gaze on the copse in the distance, and he stared at those trees that concealed the child's playground within, where happier memories of his own childhood dwelled and, now, also where the memory of Cailin lived.

He picked his way through the woods, heading for the trail he'd shown Cailin just days earlier. Had it really only been days since everything between them had fallen apart?

Then, he came to the clearing and stopped.

Why, even now she was likely shut away in a blissful reunion with her real love.

His ears picked up the crunch of brush and the snap of a twig.

Courtland spun around, just as Seagrave stepped into the clearing.

"Is she here?" Seagrave asked, scanning the grounds.

Courtland stared dumbly back.

Seagrave gave him a queer look. "Ellie?" The other man paused. "Your . . . sister," he clarified.

Courtland blinked several times to clear the fog in his head, remembering they still scoured the duke's properties in search of Courtland's eternally mischievous sister. He shook his head. "I . . . do not see her."

"I was certain she would be here," Seagrave said. "I'll check the garden maze."

"Thank you," Courtland replied automatically, grateful for the other man's friendship and loyalty.

Except . . . Seagrave remained.

Courtland pulled his gaze away from the placid waters and looked to his friend.

Doffing his hat, the other man beat it against his leg several times in that distracted way he'd done since they were at university, whenever a topic of some discomfort came up.

"What is it?" Courtland asked, another pit forming in his belly. "Did something else—"

"No. No. No other scandals." Seagrave's lips quirked in a wry grin. "At least, not yet."

Yes, with Ellie missing and the remainder of his sisters stuck here until she was located, any manner of trouble loomed.

"I saw one of the notes," Seagrave murmured.

"Oh." For really, what else was there to say?

"The funny thing about the 'I' . . . it was your father's 'I,'" Seagrave remarked.

"My father's . . . ?" Perhaps it was the complete absence of sleep last night, or mayhap it was just that he'd had his heart broken and in a spectacular way. But he couldn't make head or tail of what in hell his friend was rambling on about.

"The 'I.'" Seagrave lifted his left hand and made a motion of writing in the air. "The first letter must be bold and strong, with a distinctive slash for the 'I' different than a loop, which suggests weakness."

He puzzled his brow. "How do you—"

"Your sister," the other man cut him off. "Ellie. I came upon her when she was seven or eight, practicing the letter because hers were too soft, and the duke didn't approve of soft." The sneer on his lips, and the harshness in his tone, indicated his loathing for the late duke. "I suggested the softer 'I,' but Ellie insisted . . . and perfected it."

And Courtland stilled . . . the implications of what Seagrave spoke slamming into him. "I—"

"You don't need to say anything," the earl assured him. "We don't need to talk about it, and nothing shall ever leave my lips about any of your siblings. It isn't my place. It is, however, my opinion that Miss Audley deserves to know that you were in fact not the one to ruin her."

"It wouldn't matter," he said, his voice catching. He sank onto a nearby boulder and stared out at the waters once more. Scooping up a pile of rocks, Courtland hurled one at the river with such a force that it broke the surface and instantly sank. "The lady's former—" Yet, that wasn't the right word choice. Former suggested there was a current, and Courtland had never been Cailin's love. "The lady's former sweetheart," he offered instead, still unable to make himself mention the word "love," as it would tie her to another in a way Courtland had yearned so desperately for. "He's returned."

"And?"

Courtland hurled the remaining rocks in his hand at the water, and they rained down, plinking the surface like a flurry of teardrops. "And she's better off without me."

He felt Seagrave's stare on him and glanced over.

His friend continued staring at him, wordlessly, for a long while. "If you feel *that* way, and are unwilling to fight for her, then perhaps she is better off without you, after all," Seagrave said, and then gave his head a disgusted shake. "I'm going to search for Ellie so that we might take our leave."

As his friend marched off, Courtland looked after him, spoiling for a fight. Seagrave was right. The lady was better off without him.

Wasn't she?

Perching himself on the same boulder he'd earlier abandoned, Courtland slid his gaze over to the place where he and Cailin had talked and laughed together.

The world, his father, society all around him had only ever seen Courtland as his title, and somewhere along the way . . . he'd come to see himself inextricably tied to it himself; where everything he was, every decision he made, and every purpose he had ultimately connected to the dukedom. Upon inheriting it, and learning that there was nothing, there'd been a crisis in terms of his self-worth. If there was nothing left to the dukedom, what value did he have?

"I'm not my title," he whispered.

Cailin had helped him to see that.

He didn't have to be the boy he'd once been, shamed for his interests and denied that which fell outside the bounds of his ducal responsibilities, those moments and pleasures in life that brought him joy. He was not a title first. He was a man, one whose heart beat for Cailin Audley, and he may not have much to offer her of monetary value, but he had himself. If she wished for him to leave, he would, but not before he told her everything in his heart.

There came the crack of brush once more, and he turned to greet Seagrave.

Enlivened, he hopped up, greeting him in advance this time. "You were right. I'm going to f— Oh," he blurted, words failing. Cailin stood there, dressed in a pale yellow dress, the same shade she'd worn that first time they met, and he wanted to go back to that moment. "It's you." He wanted to start over, so that he could somehow get everything right this time.

"Hullo," she said softly.

"Hullo," he managed.

Had he really ever been smooth or charming with ladies? Those skills all failed him so spectacularly where this woman was concerned that he imagined he must have never been effortless around them.

Cailin darted her tongue out, and with his gaze, he followed that delectable tip of pink flesh and its path. "Were you going to fight someone?"

Fight someone? He tried to comprehend her questioning, when his mind was all a-jumble with her nearby. And then he recalled what he'd exclaimed as she'd walked into the clearing. "No!" he exclaimed. "I'm not fighting anyone." At least, as of now her brother had not called him out, and even then Courtland wouldn't fight the other man upon a field. Though he did wish to thrash her sweetheart. "Ellie, I fear, has gone missing," he hurried to explain. "We're turning up the household and the grounds. That is, I along with my sisters and Seagrave. Alas, Ellie's always been a master at hide-and-seek. She oft described it as a necessary military skill. One she read about regarding the—" Cailin's brows lifted slightly. "Americans," he added weakly. "It is a military skill of the Americans, she once said . . ." *Stop. Just stop.*

The whisper of a smile graced Cailin's lips as she glided over. "It was not you," she murmured.

He stared blankly at her.

Cailin stopped before him. "You did not ruin me. It was Ellie."

Courtland tensed. How did she . . . ?

"It didn't take much to gather." She took his palms in hers, gripping him lightly, and he enfolded them in his larger hands, wanting to hold on to her forever. "I should have realized . . . I am sorry."

He shook his head. "Please, don't—"

"I'm not finished." Courtland promptly fell silent. "However, you also should have confided in me."

"Ah, Cailin," he said, thickly. "I expected you would hate me anyway, and I'd rather spare my sister—"

"She is a child. I could never hate her. Nor would I blame you for the actions of a child, Courtland," she chided. "Nor, for that matter, are you responsible for the decisions of others."

Then she released him, and he went cold, his hands spasming at the loss, yearning to hold her close.

"I . . . it was not my place to interfere in your discussion . . . with Ian." Her brow dipped. "Not that I need to clarify, as I've only interrupted that meeting," he said. "It wasn't my place, and yet I'm glad I did, because he doesn't deserve you; but if you are happy, then I want you to be with him." *I'm a lying liar. I want to pulverize the chap and steal Cailin's love for my own.* Courtland slowed the flow of further words, exhaling through his teeth. "*Are* you happy?"

"I am." And she may as well have grabbed one of the downed tree limbs and shoved it through his heart. Selfishly he wanted her for himself, but he still loved her so much that he wanted her happiness, even if it wasn't with him. "My brothers arranged for Ian to come," she explained.

It had been easier when the fellow had simply been her "former sweetheart," which had marked their relationship in a past time and also left him more of a nebulous rival.

Ah, God, Courtland was a selfish cur, too, because he wanted her. He wanted her smile and her laughter, and—

"But that is not why I'm happy," she murmured, drifting closer, pulling him from his hellish lamentations. "He told me the only reason he'd turned away from me was because he didn't feel worthy of me."

Because he wasn't. No one was worthy of Cailin Audley.

"He's since resumed work at the mines and found a small cottage in Staffordshire."

"That is . . . wonderful," he said, managing to get the word out.

"Is it?" she murmured, smoothing her palms along the front of his lapels.

"I . . . isn't it?"

She shook her head. "I don't want someone to take care

of me, you know." She continued stroking her hands up and down along the fabric of his jacket. "I want a friend and love. I want someone who will be my partner and who wants to be my partner in return."

His throat swelled. "I want that, too." That admission exploded from his lungs. "I love you," he rasped, dropping his brow atop hers. "I do not have anything to offer you beyond my heart, and soul, and body, but Cailin, if you—"

"I want to marry you, Courtland."

He froze. "Did you . . . ?"

She smiled a cheeky little grin. "Ask you to marry me? I did."

His lips curved up, and he folded his arms around her, drawing her close. "Cailin Audley, you stole my proposal."

Cailin looped her arms around his neck, and going up on tiptoe, brought her lips close to his. "Is that a 'yes,' Your Grace?"

His smile widened. "That is a 'yes.'"

And then leaning down, he kissed her, and Cailin leaned up and into his embrace . . . and their future together.

# *Epilogue*

There were no doubt rules about arriving late to one's wedding.

After all, where Polite Society was concerned, there were rules for and about everything.

Cailin, however, had never been one for rules . . . particularly where the *ton* was concerned.

A breathless laugh bubbled up past her lips.

"Shh, love," Courtland whispered against her ear, his breath stirring her skin, and delicious shivers radiated out.

With the world dark around the satin blindfold that covered her eyes, she stretched her left hand out before her, all the while Courtland tugging her along by her right.

"Where are we going?" she asked for the third time since he'd spirited her out from her chambers, while she'd awaited Rafe and Hunter to accompany her to the gardens for her wedding to Courtland.

"I told you it's a surprise, love," he said, tweaking her nose. "Now, hush."

"Hush" because they were in the duke's sprawling country estate and the property swarmed with all the Duke and Duchess of Bentley's closest friends and Courtland's sisters.

It wasn't the wedding she'd feared they might expect of her . . . as the future duchess and the daughter of a duke. She'd assumed they'd wish for her and Courtland to have a grand affair in London at a cathedral filled to the brim with the most powerful lords and ladies, all of whom were strangers, none of whom cared in any way about her.

And yet, her father had not pushed.

When she'd explained she and Courtland had only wanted those people who were friends and family to them, he'd simply requested a list of guests for whom invitations might be sent and asked where she wished their nuptials to take place.

As such, it was surely inconsiderate of her and Courtland to sneak off at those same nuptials.

Suddenly, Courtland guided her to a stop.

The white satin cravat he'd looped around her head a short while ago remained firmly in place.

"Have we arrived?" Wherever it was he now took her, her intrigue redoubled.

"We have," he murmured, and then she felt a whisper of air caress her lips, a moment before he touched his mouth to hers.

Even under the cloth fold covering her eyes, they slid closed, and with a sigh, she leaned up and in to her almost-husband's kiss.

A kiss that proved all too short.

There was a faint rustle and another slight breeze.

And then the cloth that had been covering her eyes was gone.

Cailin blinked several times in a bid to adjust her eyes to the sudden change in lighting.

Bewildered, she glanced around the sun-drenched corridor, that hall with the gleaming silver knight's armoire serving as sentry.

"Curious, love?" he asked softly, pressing a tender kiss against her temple.

"I am fascinated by whatever it is that has you keeping us from our wedding." Cailin flicked the tip of his aquiline nose, similar to the way he'd touched her own moments ago. "I have begun to wonder whether you've had second thoughts about a formal wedding and wished to elope to Gretna Green."

His gaze wavered. "Is that what you would have preferred? Something . . . with just the two of us."

Going on tiptoe, Cailin looped her arms about Courtland's neck so that she might better meet his gaze. "We have just the two of us forever," she said, smoothing her palms over the front of his jacket lapels as she spoke. "I would have us celebrate this day with our family." His sisters and her brothers, all together.

On the heel of that came a rush of sadness. The first she'd known that day.

Courtland cupped her cheek in his large palm, and she turned her head into that touch. "Hey, now," he said softly. "Sadness is not allowed this day. Tell me what I can do to chase it away."

And knowing the man whom she'd fallen in love with, she'd absolutely no doubt that if she asked him to climb to the sky for a star, he'd gather a handful and grab up the moon for good measure. Yet, this was not any hurt he could drive back.

When she did not immediately reply, Courtland passed his gaze over her face. "You are sad not all your brothers are here."

How foolish to expect she could have kept a secret from him. She knew his soul as much as he knew hers. "I do believe you'd love Wesley," she said. "He has always been the most light-hearted of my brothers." A wistful smile pulled at her lips. "More optimistic about . . . everything. And far less suspicious of people's motives than Rafe or Hunter." Yes, when Wesley returned, they'd get on great.

"That has been my opinion, too," Courtland said. Reaching past her, he pressed the handle and motioned to the parlor.

With a quizzical look, she turned—and then gasped.

Trembling fingers came up to belatedly catch that shocked exhalation.

She was imagining him.

There was no other explanation.

And yet, no matter how many times she blinked, the sight remained.

Because how else to account for the tall soldier, clad in crimson with gleaming epaulets upon the front of his jacket.

Slightly broader across the shoulders and chest than when last she'd seen him, with a new scar at the right corner of his eye, he was different from the young man whom she'd spied sneaking away from her family's cottage in Staffordshire. "Wesley," she whispered, scarcely daring to believe it. Afraid if she so much as moved he'd vanish.

The youngest of her brothers lifted a hand in greeting. "Hullo, Kay-Kay."

And hearing his voice, hearing him speak in that low baritone made the moment real. Whipping her head back around, she faced Courtland and tried to form words . . . and failed. She tried again. "You did this."

"I knew how important it would be to you that all your brothers were present," he explained.

"You did this?" she repeated.

Courtland nodded.

So much love for this man swelled in her breast.

A sob exploded from her lips, and with tears blinding her vision, she tossed herself into Courtland's arms. He instantly folded her in his embrace, running his hands over her back in tender little circles. "Go see your other brother," he urged, whispering into her ear.

Cailin squeezed him tightly. "I love you," she rasped as he set her down on her feet.

"And I love you, dear heart." Courtland drew her hands to his mouth, one at a time, and placed a kiss upon her knuckles. "Now go see your brother. He's traveled a way to be here with us this day." With that, he released her hands and took a step back.

Spinning on her heel, Cailin flew across the room. Not breaking stride, she launched herself at her brother. He wrapped her in his arms. "I have missed you, Wesley," she sobbed, as he held her close.

"I've missed you, too, Cailin," he said in return.

Half-crying, and half-laughing, she held her brother tight; afraid if she let him go, he'd leave once more, for war, and miss this most joyous day in her life.

"Your soon-to-be husband put in quite the effort to make sure I was here," Wesley said when he set her back on her feet.

She rubbed her hands over her cheeks, brushing away those happy tears as she looked to her future husband. "Did he?"

An adorable blush lit Courtland's cheeks as he clasped his hands at his back and rocked on his heels. "He's making more of it than there is."

"No, I'm not," Wesley called over.

Courtland inclined his head. "I know better than to argue with my betrothed's older brother on my wedding day."

"Which, by the way . . . shouldn't it have already begun?" Wesley winked.

Yes, it should have. And this time, as she rejoined Courtland at the doorway, with Wesley staying close, she started for the audience that awaited them.

This day—her and Courtland's day—at last complete.

# ACKNOWLEDGMENTS

Whew, it takes a *village*. And these past couple of years I've been so very thankful to the people in mine. Raising a medically fragile child during a pandemic required me to lean on my supports, without whom, I would have never been able to get a word written.

Doug, my husband, my partner, and hero in real life, who has donned so many hats, from chef to teacher to webmaster to world's best dad and husband, and every other job in between so that I could continue to write with our children home round the clock.

My three brave, empathetic, and courageous children, who with their adorable antics never fail to provide me with an endless amount of source material.

My five o'clock accountability partner and dearest friend, the brilliant LaQuette, who provided a shoulder to lean upon, and so many much-needed laughs.

To Karen, my Obi-Wan, whose email many years earlier changed my life in every way. She is a beta-reader and a best friend, and she never fails to remind me to look after myself.

And to my fabulous editorial team at Berkley, Penguin Random House: Cindy Hwang and Sarah Blumenstock, who provided me with that dream I've always carried, of bringing my historical romance novels to print.